Only Once in a Century...

From humble beginnings on the raw frontier of an earlier America, the romantic legend of the mighty Kingston dynasty traces a glittering course through the history of a nation.

Here are the characters whose lives and struggles carved a vast railroad empire out of the virgin West: the imperious land-barons and industrial giants . . . the heroes and betrayers . . . the bohemians and lovers . . . the hard men who took what they wanted, and the passionate women who gave too much.

Resounding with the thunder of creation, lit with the fires of love and pain, THE KINGSTON FORTUNE re-creates for all time the triumph, toil, failure, and fury which form the legend of the fabulous Kingston dynasty!

THE KINGSTON FORTUNE

Other Avon Books by
Stephen Longstreet

BURNING MAN	09860	$1.25
THE DIVORCE	17244	$1.50
LION AT MORNING	08722	$1.25
THE PEDLOCKS	09084	$1.25

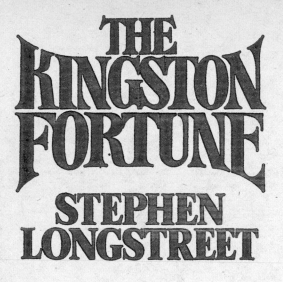

THE KINGSTON FORTUNE

STEPHEN LONGSTREET

There were giants in the earth in those days; and also after that, when the sons of God came in unto the daughters of men, and they bare children to them, the same became mighty men which were of old, men of renown.

Genesis 6:4

AVON
PUBLISHERS OF BARD, CAMELOT, DISCUS, EQUINOX AND FLARE BOOKS

THE KINGSTON FORTUNE is an original publication of
Avon Books. This work has never before appeared in any form.

AVON BOOKS
A division of
The Hearst Corporation
959 Eighth Avenue
New York, New York 10019

Copyright © 1975 by Stephen Longstreet
Published by arrangement with the author.

ISBN: 0-380-00366-X

All rights reserved, which includes the right
to reproduce this book or portions thereof in
any form whatsoever. For information address
Shirley Burke, Literary Agent,
370 East 76th Street, New York, New York 10021

First Avon Printing, October, 1975

AVON TRADEMARK REG. U.S. PAT. OFF. AND
FOREIGN COUNTRIES, REGISTERED TRADEMARK—
MARCA REGISTRADA, HECHO EN CHICAGO, U.S.A.

Printed in Canada

To
Irwin Blacker
University of Southern California,

Who insisted I use
The lecture halls and classrooms
of the college
To outline the
craft of the novel ...

Many Thanks

Going by rail I do not consider as
traveling at all . . . very little
different from becoming a parcel.

John Ruskin, 1856

While events in this novel do
duplicate history: the people and
their personal stories are fiction
and are not based on anyone living or
dead.

S.L.

Prologue

People who couldn't get into the Railroad and Ranchers Club of Southern California said it was so goddamn exlusive you had to be a sonofabitch and a millionaire and prove your grandfather had screwed Lillian Russell. The first qualification was sometimes true, the second always, the third never documented. The club had its own redstone three-story building within sight of City Hall, designed in 1900 by a follower of Stanford White. The entrance hall featured a stuffed grizzly bear, a Remington bronze of a horse wrangler on a bronc, a six-foot locomotive model of a Grant-built Class C-16-60 ten-wheeler of the Western, Great Plains & Gulf R.R., Engine 666 that pulled the first *Golden Eagle* in its record run, Los Angeles to New Orleans in 1889.

Those members of the Railroad and Ranchers Club who lived on the premises all seemed to have high complexions and the remains of white hair. They were hardly ever on their feet, usually sipped drinks, ruffling the *Wall Street Journal*, or merely waited for lunch or dinner. The card games of high-stake poker took place three nights a week with members who came from as far away as Santa Barbara or San Diego.

The club's unofficial historian, Waldo Gaylord, a retired corporation lawyer, was a paunchy, tall man with little remaining hair. He used to sit after lunch, a double bourbon in his hand (part of the right hand's index finger missing) and go into a monologue for the benefit of some unsuspecting stranger with a guest card or a reporter seeking filler for a two-pound Sunday newspaper. He'd appraise his victim with a wily legal eye and begin cheerfully, sipping his drink slowly.

1

"Interested in high iron and the Kingston family—eh—when steam—Matthias Baldwin's 4-8-2s—powered the biggest bastard of a rail system in the country? Oh, the trip with old Enoch Kingston or Rawly Kingston. We'd go east from the Pacific, no smog then, no Los Angeles's goddamn freeways' traffic. Ride past the Cucamonga Wilderness, and just before the Cajon Cut there's this ridge called Crestline, and six tracks of rails old Enoch built that lead to Kingston Junction. Yes—six full-gauge lines. There's a Kingston town—oh, already people talk of what it was *once.* . . . Let me ring for a refill—double bourbon?"

Waldo Gaylord hardly ever lost a trapped or willing listener. "The present-day Kingstons don't give a shit now about the great empty roundhouses, rusting repair sheds, the freight yards that once held a hundred thousand freight cars a year. Sun has faded the letters WESTERN GREAT PLAINS AND GULF RAILROAD—those that still can be read. And a door with: *Enoch Kingston*, PRIVATE. The yellow-brick division point is full of rats, moths and runaway dogs behind chain-link fences. The caretakers never lift their asses off chairs, just always snoozing. If Rawly Kingston were alive—well, he isn't. Some local freight lines are still sorted in an annex; timber from above Arrowhead, some desert dates from Twenty-Nine Palms, which the second Mrs. Enoch Kingston planted. There's still a few tank cars sucking up the last oil of wells fifty years old, near Twin Pines, when the Kingstons switched to diesels. Wells now hardly profitable to pump.

"Another? No? Well, I'll have just one more—to cut the morning slimes.

"Very few people remember when Kingston Junction was a main passenger point—before Amtrak took over. Open right-of-ways to Houston, New Orleans, Palm Beach, Caycee, Washington—a dozen great trains. Now it's all mile-long freights—more freight than any two roads in the nation, long track mileage routes through the Rockies, across the Panhandle, past Kingston Pass, up from the South through the cotton and tobacco and turpentine belts to the national capitol and Eastern Shore ports. Sheet, it's *all* business now—no drama.

"There was never anything, sir, like the Kingstons' great passenger record makers. The *Golden Eagle*—extra-fare

2

express that left daily from the old depot here in Los Angeles. Long before the Union Station was built, thirty heavy luxury cars—*varnish* in railroad talk—running on wide-gauge hard-ballasted tracks. All gold-colored cars, and a polished Class G 1-2-10-2 Big Six, a locomotive Rawly Kingston favored—with a boiler diameter of ten feet, and the biggest damn cylinders on any long-run train—a tractive power of eighty-five thousand pounds could race up the heaviest seven percent grades. Christ! rode the cab once myself—a grand roar behind its drawbars at seventy, eighty miles an hour. And food! Fancy Fred Harvey gourmet food. The Kingstons were heavy feeders. More darkies serving you than the Queen of Sheba. A roadbed smooth as shantung silk, and the wine in the parlor and club cars—Veuve Cliquot, Monopole."

He didn't seem sometimes to be talking to his trapped listener, but recalling his private visions.

"All the great trains Enoch Bancroft Kingston and myself traveled on, sometimes just the two of us. Sometimes, well, we were younger—with women. Not just the splendid W.G.P. and G. famous trains, the *Golden Eagle*, the *Kingston Special*, the *Great Rockies Express*. But the *Pullman Merchants Limited*, between Boston and New York; the *Frontenac*, the day train between Montreal and Quebec; the Pullman *Twentieth-Century Limited*, between New York and Chicago; the Pullman *Broadway Limited*; the *El Dorado*, between San Francisco and Sacramento (an excellent Napa Valley Wine); the *California Zephyr*, between Chicago and Oakland; the *Sunset Limited*, New Orleans to Los Angeles; the *Saratoga Special*—eight parlor cars and two dining cars. *All* gone, or a few debased impostors mocking the past . . ."

If the victim didn't rise and escape (or if Waldo had a grip on his coat sleeve) the monologue went on in that dulcet Southern-flavored voice.

"Nothing like the Rawly Kingston's *Eastern Shore Special*—all Pullmans. You could smell the soft-shell crabs and the terrapin stew boiling up in the train's dining kitchen. . . . You'd have a Havana cigar later, a mint julep in your hand, and come into Washington just as it got dark,

3

gossiping with senators and lobbyists, fat cats and assorted high-ranking crooks and pretty ladies—when women were bigger and had more curves. Sheet, it's all gone now. Western, Great Plains and Gulf carries only iron ore and dyed citrus and container cars, and cheap truck-and-notions for the Sears and the Monkey Ward stores. More track, more icers, reefers, more diesels with no more character than a pitcher of tap water.

"It was some different, I can tell you, when old Enoch Bancroft Kingston was running things, high and mighty, even when he was two years older than God and twice as mean. Fighting his own sons for control; and the time Howie Alvarez Kingston, his favorite grandson, got killed. Then that other time with what's-his-name—some said murder, some said accident. That was a sensation, you know. A big buster of a trial. Western Union set up its biggest wire board, reporters came all the way from London.

"The Kingstons were of two kinds—cunt-crazy, *or* pious and art collectors. They made one big mistake—they didn't stay in Kingston Junction. Now it's all this flying and jets. Once you couldn't get a better gin fizz even in Orleans. The Kingston boys always had women in their private cars—not just showgirls either—lapping up the bourbon, prime Kentucky sour mash served in shot glasses that held four fingers of the best. Remember that redhead who married the division chief at Turning Rock? Well, it's long ago. Ran off with a Kingston.

"Dukes or gamblers, society queens, Mrs. Potter Palmer, the great whores like Nell Kimball, Teddy Roosevelt, General Grant, Lillian Russell, they all rode the *Golden Eagle*, yep, or the *Royal Gorge*, the *Denver Night Mail*. And when the boys went off to war in Cuba, or got their asses shot off with Pershing in Mexico after Pancho Villa, it was W.G.P. and G. stock moved 'em, and later rolled the officers in their boots and spurs and Sam Browne belts to the Gulf ports to go over Over There with AEF. Sheet, by Pearl Harbor it was already diesels that brought the GIs and their brass to western embarkation ports for the Jap war. It wasn't even the *Golden Eagle* no more—just the *Western Gulf Special*. By then, the Baldwin 2-10-2s were rusting on sidings or cut up for scrap. No more main-

4

taining two hundred-twenty-pound steam pressure, and the thirty-by-thirty cylinders so rust-locked you couldn't get 'em to move unless you used that atom power that was coming in.

"I'm boring you—just a dirty old man wallowing in memory's shower bath. No? Never know why folk travel by plane in fancy buzzards all over the sky. Folk eating recooked garbage for food, and packed like wetbacks in busted trucks crossing the Rio Grande. No, the real Kingstons weren't here when they were needed."

If Waldo wasn't tired, he'd talk of Kingston parties in the big house in Kingston Junction, of when Old Enoch or his son Rawly gave a party in Kingston House up Laurel Leaf Canyon, just outside of town.

"A hundred barrels of oysters from Baltimore on ice, all the way by W.G.P. and G. *Sioux Fast Freight*. Buck deer, venison down from Wyoming, and wine corks popping like a battle at its height; all the men in their fine black hammer-tail coats, white ties, starched shirt fronts, and the women in silk and satins—diamonds you could use as headlights on the extra-fare trains on the high iron running fast. Fast-running women, too, some of them— but catchable—respectable often, smelling fine, all peach skin and blue or green eyes, hair done up, on display at parties out in the big gardens, the Kingston girls resenting being held in check. Horses, matched teams, stomping in the drive, dropping golden horse apples—nothing so beautiful as a good horse—and later the damn autocars, the Simplex chain-driven and Pierce Arrows. Wilma De Groat, married Rawly Kingston, she had a Rolls.

"You'd be smoking a good cigar in the gardens, roses and exotic plants by the big greenhouse, all glass, built to look like a railroad station, and below you'd see the Kingston's railroad shops, oh a mile away, the yards of the W.G.P. and G., all lit up, switching points all green and red dots, the rows of orange windows of some express rolling by. There were six or seven hundred, yes, mile-long freights, a day, and the two thousand station masters at their telegraph tap keys, keeping the icers and reefers moving along to feed the big cities . . ."

Of the younger brood, Waldo Gaylord approved only of Nick Kingston "the only grandson who really liked the railroads. When Nick was drunk, he'd get out of his banker's threads and he'd go inspect the junction point. He'd come back to the club looped. 'Hell,' he'd say, 'no emperor ever could dominate so much land, move so many people, feed so many faces. Iron,' he'd say, 'we do it with iron.' Nick was a fat little fellow; ran the branch bank for Drovers and Ranchers Bank in Frisco. Somebody would take him upstairs in the club to snooze it off. All gone now—the big mansion, the family, the fine trains, the posh passengers.

"All down the sheet-house now. Oh, you can hear the whistles, sure, it's the freight climbing up to Enoch's Pass—two linked diesels, hardly making a sound. It used to take double heads, snorting, smoke-throwing grand Baldwins, with old Cap MacHedrick at the throttle lever opening cylinder cocks, the piston rods working, the driving wheels connecting to the sliding side rods, all busy as fiddlers' elbows to get over the pass in the days before it was blasted to a lower grade. Computers now and efficiency charts, and stockholders getting their dividend checks twice a year. And maybe if some new merger goes through, the end of the W.G.P. and G. The town isn't alive anymore, no one has sat their rump in Kingston House for years. . . . Maurice, another double for the road—and me, I'm upstairs to bed."

The town isn't dead. The sixty thousand people who work in the Japanese export television tube factory and in the shops selling Frosty Floats and dreadful chemical hamburgers, or who run tourist motels and gas stations don't think so.

Some of the retired railroad workers on pensions and Social Security gather in the Caboose Bar on Railroad Avenue, or the Night Mail Grill by the annex. They drink beer and romanticize even more than Waldo Gaylord about Enoch and Rawly and Benjy Kingston, forgetting several murderous strikes, starvation layoffs, pay cuts, and back-breaking work. The other citizens of the town are mostly those who came for jobs in industry during past wars of the last two generations.

There is a ten-foot-high statue of Enoch Bancroft Kingston, of discolored bronze not patinaed, just soiled, set on a cracked stone base in Padre Square. If it were not for a plaque with the name of the subject and some dates, few would know the identity of the seated statue of a large man with a rich, curly beard and a top hat, holding in his hands a model of a diamond-stacked locomotive. No one in the town is sure when the statue was erected. The local newspaper files of the *Kingston Junction News* show it was put up in 1927 by the Railroad and Ranchers Club of Southern California. Waldo Gaylord—a young railroad lawyer then—made a dedicating speech, as did the governor of the state and a U.S. senator. The speeches were, as reported, high-flown and banal.

Winos sometimes sleep in the small plot of bush and grass around the statue. College students painted the head red during an antiwar rally in 1969. Most of the paint has now been removed.

One morning Waldo Gaylord got up as usual at nine-fifteen, put in his teeth, dressed in a light gray linen suit, and went down to the club dining room for his never-changing breakfast of two fried eggs on a small steak, hot biscuits, and two cups of strong coffee. Opening the *Wall Street Journal* (Western edition), he read the following item as he ate:

> The Securities & Exchange Commission filed charges of fraud against a dozen former officers of the troubled Western, Great Plains & Gulf railroad, a prestigious Wall Street investment house, and one of the nation's largest accounting firms.
>
> In a case that stems from the failure of the W. G.P. & G, the SEC said it uncovered an array of abuses, ranging from false profits to trading stock on the basis of insider information.
>
> Named in SEC suits filed in New York and Philadelphia were former W. G.P. & G. chairman Gillray Jones, former finance committee chief Martin Ott, and ten other executives.

Also cited for fraud were the Los Angeles and New York investment firm of Stoneman, Anspacher & Bowren, and the accounting firm of Wallabeck, Peel, Ballinger & Co.

Stoneman, Anspacher & Bowren was accused by the SEC of defrauding investors by not providing material facts about the purchasers of the railroad's commercial paper—a short-term IOU issued by corporations.

Without conceding or denying guilt, the firm agreed Thursday to an SEC consent order to halt such practices in the future.

SEC officials blamed the delay in filing their cases on the complex history of the largest railroad problem in corporate history, as well as a rapid turnover in members and chairmen of the SEC in recent years.

As he finished the article, chewing carefully with his splendid ceramic set of teeth, Waldo was happy that Enoch and Rawly Kingston would never read it.

1

The Battle

1

"I'll tell you this," said Uncle Floyd to his sixteen-year-old nephew—well, just shy one month of sixteen. "God may not help those who help themselves—but Enoch, you'll notice He don't stand in front of you with no flaming sword and say 'What you got *there*, boy?' "

"Who does the ole cotton belong to anyway?" asked his nephew. They were seated on railroad ties beside an army supply shed, eating a hot mess of broken-up hardtack and salt pork from a skillet set on some smoldering hickory embers. They were eating the slum, as the army squads called it, with large spoons they had pulled from their boot tops.

A short, overmuscled Negro was currying a tom-mule under a tree.

"How's the war today, Jasper?"

"Oh, it's just simmerin', Mistah Floyd."

In the hurly-burly spring of 1863, Grant was besieging Vicksburg, set there on a loop of the Mississippi. He and forty-thousand troops had been there since December the year before, and reports were the inhabitants of the city were down to rat filets and mule cutlets, while the Union regiments sat along bluffs, bayous, and plantations gone to rack and weed. An army with no lines of supply, not getting much food or comfort from riverboats herded by the ironclads firing back at the city. So it was foraging, down to rancid bacon, weevily hardtack, horse corn, the last of the coffee, and whatever chicken or bit of wild game the soldiers, sutlers, and camp followers could scrounge up.

The politicians, drinking hot toddies in the Willard Bar in Washington, were calling Vicksburg "the spinal column of America," and, as one senator in a stovepipe hat

11

figured it, "Break their back there and the damn rebels will die a quick death, cut off from their allies in the West."

But while Vicksburg refused to surrender, the rebs still held 250 miles of the flood-brown river down to Port Hudson's Louisana sandbars, snags and all, a wet-moving road, a transmission belt between their east and west. All around Vicksburg you could smell the dead and see the raw earth mounds thrown up by shelling and tunneled-out mines set off underground. The city held, starved, and its flags flew.

Now in April Grant was set to cut the New Orleans & Jackson R.R. and hoping to take the rail junction at Jackson, less than twenty miles from Vicksburg, where the N.O. & J. met the Vicksburg & Jackson R.R. If he succeeded, Vicksburg's rail supplies would then be cut off. Grant also was moving his muddy forces and bronze cannon south to take the city maybe from the water side.

Uncle Floyd and Enoch, his sister's boy, were at Hard Time Landing, assembling captured wagons in hopes that Admiral Porter's gunboats and the transports that had run the Vicksburg batteries down river would have a supply of iron T-rails and hook-spikes to keep what rail-lines the Union had operating in the just-captured territory. Privy gossip was that Grant was coming from all directions, tightening his stranglehold on the city. As the stumpy little general put it to Sherman as the soldiers moved down a country pike past burning barns, "We'll carry what rations of hard bread, coffee, and salt we can, and make the country furnish the balance."

And slim balance the army and Floyd Denton found it, though he was a skilled scrounger who had an eye for what could be eaten, drunk from a jug, slapped on the ass and told to shuck, or carried off for profit. Uncle Floyd was a large man in his middle twenties; he had already been a whisky maker, a mechanic about mill steam engines, had trapped for beaver with the last of the mountain men on the Gila, and had seen the inside of jails. He was a liar, an optimist, courageous under fire, and afraid at times of the wrath of God. Just over six feet, he seemed shorter because he was so broad. He had a thick head of brown hair with a big bald area in the center of it, a long delicate nose, a coarse, amusing face with washed-out greenish eyes, and irregular, over-sized teeth. Uncle Floyd didn't shave much, but he liked a good soak when water was handy and a popular camp-meeting preacher was around. He could deal cards very fast—too fast sometimes for the supply depot's sergeants. He slept badly, clutching at his nephew in the dark, awakening crying out, "Lord bless, Lord bless! Amen."

Uncle Floyd was a civilian mechanic in charge of three captured locomotives because he knew steam engines. He bossed the flatcars loaded with wooden ties, a few oak barrels of iron spikes, and some reheated and rehammered rails. Uncle and nephew were a little mad about locomotives and railroading. They kept the narrow-gauge tracks in working order with a work crew of some slaves from a plantation in nearby Vicksburg that belonged to Jefferson Davis. It amused Enoch, using rebel slaves to beat the South. Uncle Floyd had him made a sergeant in charge of a crew of the 20th New York, a mess of Irish soldiers, to carry and toss ballast and tamp it down with gandy tools. He'd harass the freed slaves into hustling the ties and rails without falling over themselves. The soldiers had their rifles stacked and ready; they were worried rebel horse raiders might come bushwacking out of Joe Johnson's forces to help their comrades hemmed up in Vicksburg. The Confederates coming from the east were trying to cut Grant's rail supply lines, hunting trains "like a suckling a shoat's tit." But Grant had no supply lines; Enoch knew that.

Union units by the score, like Uncle Floyd's, were out foraging (stealing was the right and proper word for it) and moving closer and closer to the rail junction at Jackson, east of Vicksburg. Cut that, Uncle Floyd said, and General Pemberton in Vicksburg was trapped.

On May 2 Union troops took Jackson and a lot of railroad tracks, and Uncle Floyd brought in "Old Sal," one of his trains, and told his nephew Enoch to "just pick up any iron plate, bolts, and tools in sight before the river gunboat boys get it."

Enoch, who dreamed of trains and girls—and sometimes preferred the first—was already a clumsy six-feet-two, and would grow another inch or so before he leveled off. He was so skinny that Jasper, the locomotive fireman, said, "Mr. Enoch, you one railroad man could hide yo'-self behind a spider web and no fly be able to see you." Enoch ate enough, more than enough, when he could get it. He had the splendid appetite of a gawky boy from a hardscrabble Illinois farm, could down two pounds of fried catfish, half a sweet potato pie, and a good section of corn bread sawed off with his genuine Kansas Bowie knife, when he could sit down at a table. Enoch had a trusting face, blue-green eyes, not enough fuzz worth a shave on his cheeks, and while he often forgot to brush his teeth much, they were white and even. His smile was beguiling and he was pretty ignorant. "Green as goose turds," Uncle Floyd put it. Before Ma died on the farm, he'd spent three years in a yellow plank school house in Massac County, Illinois. Followed by two years in a lawyer's office in Danville, finding the reading of law tomes and newspapers fun, moving his lips at first, for the big, joined-together words were at first hard to make out. But he was determined. (The now-long-dead father he didn't remember had been from Boston and had written a fine hand.) Enoch was bright and handy, too, when he took apart something like a Thompson clock or the draw bars of a train boiler. He couldn't resist a McCormick or a Manny reaper left rusting in a field; he had to try to get it working again. The two Winas built high-stack locomotives—"Old Sal" and "Bully Boy," which Uncle Floyd commanded, with their four pairs of driving wheels and cranky boiler connections Enoch could almost take apart and reassemble again in the dark.

Enoch owned three books: Bowditch's *New Practical Navigator,* a copy of *Robinson Crusoe* with wood engravings, and *Typee* by Melville. Someplace in the back of the boy's head, under the tawny uncut curly hair, he had the idea of getting to that Californy place the officers and men talked of. He had this vision of sailing to some island and getting hold of a dusky princess, maybe two; he was a randy kid for his age. For three months he had been banging Ginny, the high yalla cook's daughter, back there at the railroad base camp on Walnut Hill, flattening her into

14

the cornhusk pallet whenever he had time away from running the engines, which wasn't as often as he wanted or his skinny but wiry body desired.

By June Vicksburg was hemmed in solid. It was raining some, and Enoch sat under a wagon depot shed at Raymond, smoking a clay pipe and listening to Captain Eshbacher, who, huddled into his India rubber cape with his sword between his fat knees, was talking earnestly to Uncle Floyd, who was just back from a Baptist camp meeting, red-eyed from drinking sour mash with the brethren. The captain was a Jew, and Enoch had never been close to one of them. He had been warned against Jews and Catholics, but in the army they seemed just like anybody else.

Captain Eshbacher waved a gloved hand around. "Now, Denton, there's smuggling going on all along the roads from Crystal Spring north. You notice anything along the rail-lines?"

"Why, no, captain. I just haul salt pork, army bread, and hoss feed, and cut firewood for the engine boilers."

"It's cotton, Denton, bales of it. General Grant is hearing there's hundreds of bales being smuggled through the lines to sell to Northern speculators. The New England mill owners and the English looms are paying premium prices."

"Hungry for the stuff," said Uncle Floyd, stroking his pinfeathered face. "Hear that, Ennie?"

Enoch puffed on the rank burley in his pipe and nodded. He was not much of a talker as yet, just an observer.

Captain Eshbacher rose, adjusted his smelly India rubber cape, and looked out at the slanting lines of rain. "Damn country, half clay, half water. I've notified the provost marshals to keep their eyes open. I have a feeling some of our patrols are being paid not to see things."

"I'll be damned, captain." Uncle Floyd had a skull-cracker headache and needed to lie down.

The captain went splashing into wilder sweeping sheets of rain, a righteous Old Testament figure stomping through puddles towards where his horse was tied off under a pine tree, its hide giving off vapor. Uncle Floyd drew something in the damp earth with a short stick and hunched his shoulders as some rain drove in under the open shed.

"I need sleep—powerful preaching last night. Wake me at three this afternoon. I want one of the damn engines running smooth as buttermilk batter."

"You going to risk it, Uncle Floyd?"

"You bet your ass, Ennie, I'm going to risk it. I got three hundred bales promised and waiting from those high-and-mighty rebel gentlemen at Gallatin Station, and I got contacts with good solid New England peddlers with bags of twenty-dollar gold eagles not fifty miles from here, ready to buy it for the New England mills."

"It doesn't figure right to me, Uncle Floyd." Enoch was reading a primer on grammer, or at least twenty pages of one; the men had been using most of its pages to make spills to light their pipes with. He knew *don't* was wrong; *doesn't* was the way to say it.

"Now look here, boy. That's enemy cotton, your enemy's cotton. You want a blockade runner to come up river from New Orleans and snake it off to England? Or maybe some provost marshal sell the contraband himself and give us *what*? Nothin'. Besides, ain't you for the Union? You know our mills they need that cotton to win this war."

"Why doesn't the army grab hold of it?"

"Because why? Because it's fighting a hard war. Hasn't no time to go nancyin' round asking you got any enemy cotton. No siree, it's businessmen who have to get this done. Now this rain will let up before night and I'm mov-in' the train by late afternoon. Takin' two loads of pow-ally, just patted backs"), given fattening dinners, offered I'm taking along some of the Irish mackerel snappers I been keeping supplied in prime corn pressings. They can't read, can't write, and they don't care none what happens either, if they get fed and get likker. I'll run the train after we get the bales up towards Livingston and there'll be wagons and buyers working for Jim Fisk, *no* questions asked. Your share of three, four train trips will get you to Californy, unless you get killed, soldier boy. Don't you do that to my sister Kathy, your ma. Now I gotta sleep." Uncle Floyd always acted as if Enoch's ma were still alive.

The way Enoch saw it there wasn't much sense to the war the way it was being fought. It was such a mess of swamp all about and rivers with changing banks here and there. Camps were half sunk into the mire, and smelled of privies and horseshit, wood smoke, sweaty uniforms, and soldiers' feet. The food was getting worse, the weather went from sleet in December, to sky-cracking thunderstorms in April, to boiling the marrow out of you come summer. Everything was so smoked up by campfires whose wet wood burned so badly it made your eyes all red from cooking over the embers. Nothing but mud at the crossroads, and you scratching your armpits and feeling insects crawling every place. Only the love of railroading kept him from deserting. He loved "Old Sal" more than a hound dog he once owned.

Enoch got Uncle Floyd explaining the war to him and to Jasper, the fireman of "Old Sal." It's all a war to keep the Union in one big hunk, and not allow them goddamn blue-bellied, wall-eyed sonsofbitches in the South to have things their own way."

"Don't know for sure Yankees is any better," said Jasper, a very smart Georgia Negro.

"We are, you bastard. Don't say we ain't, or I'll kick you knock-kneed. Jasper, you and Ginny, it means you wouldn't get owned by anyone, would be free to come and go, just like any cane-carrying gentleman along the sidewalks of Richmond or New York."

Jasper said, "It also mean no one is going to hand me my cornbread and hog meat, or git me a linsey-woolsey shirt."

Uncle Floyd said, "Jasper, you're one mean-tusked burrhead. Don't know what's good for you. You go read Mr. Greeley in the *Tribune*."

Jasper said he couldn't read and didn't want to. Enoch got a tattered copy of a newspaper from a major's orderly who was wiping down a horse with it. Enoch read what Mr. Lincoln said about why they were fighting where they were:

> We may take all the northern ports of the Confederacy and they can still defy us from Vicksburg. It means hog and hominy, cotton without limit, fresh troops from all the States of the far South and a cot-

ton country where they can raise the staple without interference.

Enoch had read this to Ginny in their lean-to one morning after he had come back from delivering "Old Sal's" load of canvas tenting to the troops that were trying to take Haines Bluff north of Vicksburg. Ginny, still gummy with sleep, had greeted him with a frown: *"Huh, huh?"* They had been at each other like laughing and yowling mad cats, shaking up dust from the cornhusk pallet. Ginny was good and strong about pleasuring. He relished Ginny's young, gold-colored body and the pert upstanding tits so comforting to cup in both hands. Then, when it was all simmered down, they could lie close and she told him again she was mostly Shoshone, and her pappy was a white Indian trader and scout. She was so damn ignorant, and Enoch felt he was ignorant himself about a lot. So he read her Mr. Lincoln again. In the end, he slapped her for sassing him. Ginny said, *"Huh!* Just fer that I'm leavin'!" Stark naked, she banged open the door and went out of the lean-to. With a hard little heel, she dug a hole in the loose earth under the chinaberry tree and squatted down and peed into the hole, laughing as she did. He kicked the lean-to door shut with a bare foot.

Maybe, he figured, there were no serious women in the world. Before he died, maybe he'd try to find out. Before he died, he'd be offically the driver of a great railroad engine, and go to the locomotive drivers' fancy whorehouses in Caycee, and wear a diamond on his pinky.

2

If Enoch knew anything, he knew right and wrong. Ma
had explained honesty and dishonesty to him, and the
backwoods preachers had hollered it loud and often. What
Enoch had problems with was the boundary line, *when* did
right become wrong and dishonest become honest? It
wasn't in Bowditch's book, or in Defoe. Clearly, taking enemy cotton from rebels wasn't wrong. They were the enemy (killers, nigger-whippers, thinking they were God's
spit), who got so many country boys blown up with their
guts laid out on a rail fence after a battle. And the sonsofbitches were for busting up the Union. Clearly, too, the
New England men with the wagons and the gold eagles
were wary. If grown men weren't sure, what could a *boy*
know? They were just as much helping the Northern mills
as they were breaking the laws.

"Old Sal" pulled out with four freight cars at dusk, Jasper pitching flare-pine logs into the firebox.

Enoch figured it all over in his mind. *Bad* could be
good, like sinning with naked Ginny on the cornhusks, the
world just one happy pecker, Ginny violent and panting
under him, her tawny gourd-shaped breasts good enough
to eat. Every preacher said it was a sin of the God-cursed
flesh to fornicate and not marry. But one didn't marry a
nigger, even if Ginny claimed she was mostly Shoshone
Indian.

"Old Sal's" engine needed attention, the connecting rods
were a bit out of true and the worst of the repaired boiler
leaks might blow at any time. Enoch ran the string of cars
at twenty miles an hour down fair track while Jasper, the
Negro fireman, fed her fat pine chunks. The soldiers in the
covered freight cars were drinking and singing. Poor

19

bastards, a year or so off the Irish steerage ships, then dragged from the Bowery slums and into the army because they couldn't pay the three hundred dollars that kept a man out of the army. For Catholics with their beards and crucifixes, they were nearly as good as any white man he knew.

> O, who will shoe me bonny foot?
> O, who will glove me hand,
> Or will bind me middle
> With a broad lily band . . .

The rain didn't let up all the way south, and the moon was not out much when the rain finally did let up to a whimper. They unloaded the powder kegs to a sergeant and four men at a battery depot.

Uncle Floyd said it was a good night, not much moonlight. "I'd hate to have to shoot anyone now we're running south beyond our pickets. He was wearing a holster with a Smith and Wesson six-shooter. Uncle Floyd was good, Enoch knew, at knocking over the cans that had held the officers' oysters last Christmas. Enoch felt he'd be an even better shot, if he ever got over being rabbity, and didn't draw so ragged, too hot to get his shot off.

"Old Sal" ran on between crumbling washed-down bluffs and little streams that were all muddy and filled in places with washed-out deer-brush and shrub oak. Once the singing soldiers had to get down to remove a big hickory tree, its roots like twisted snakes.

> O, hand me down me bottle of corn
> I'll be drunk sure as ye're born . . .

Uncle Floyd kept looking at his German-silver railroad watch which he couldn't see until he held it near the coal oil lantern hung over the fire door. Enoch hadn't lit the wick of the big box headlight set up in front of "Old Sal" 's diamond smokestacks.

"Two short hoots, Ennie boy. Not long. *Short*."

Enoch pulled twice on the hooter and it echoed back among dripping trees and burnt-out timber patches. It *woohooed* from pastures with never a sight of a house light. He imagined rebel bushwackers waiting in the woodsy poison ivy pockets and among the rocky bluffs, big men, all hair, torn hats, and greasy pants, with rusty rifles and honed sabers, just waiting to ride out around the train, block the track, and let out rebel yells as they sabered them all. Enoch fingered the Colt navy revolver in his belt, felt his bowels and scrotum tighten. He'd get a couple of shots off before they hacked out his gizzard. So he'd die here, never see Californy, drive a big engine, or sail for a palm-lined tropical shore ... never spread out with the girls and women he hoped to top in a long lifetime of pleasuring—never smoke two-bit cigars and drink that officers' wine that bubbled ... or get as drunk as ole U.S. Grant ... A pity, he thought, I have such a natural way with living.

A red dot appeared down track like a glowworm's welcome; it swung back and forth.

"Brake, boy, *brake.*"

Enoch let sand out onto the worn rails, pulled on the throttle properly, set the brake. The train gear seemed to scream like a banshee, as the Irish soldiers put it. It skidded, and then "Old Sal" stopped, steam escaping from a petcock. The whole engine seemed to be panting like a tired long-distance runner.

Two men with big box lanterns, carrying what looked like Sharp buffalo guns, came up track, not hurrying, not hanging back either. Nothing Southern or romantic about them, Enoch thought, as Uncle Floyd turned up his lantern. No dainty plantation owners in white linen suits and elegant feet in pick-pointed shoes. Just two rough-looking men with short beards and palm straw hats.

Uncle Floyd got down off the engine cab and they talked, the three of them, while Jasper rolled his crystal-ball eyes and the Irish dropped down from the freight cars to pee in the wet leaves just beyond the gravel beside the track. Enoch heard Uncle Floyd laugh that fake horse-laugh of his, more like a mule's *heehaw.* Then there was some backslapping, and Uncle Floyd called out to the soldiers, "Come on, you gandy dancers. Help load them cars. A pint of prime bourbon rotgut a man if it's done under half an hour."

Enoch sat on the engine step and wished the moon wasn't up at all. From everywhere on both sides of the track, shapes appeared, rolling big bales or carrying them. Voices were talking loudly and someone was laughing. Enoch was surprised to see a woman, a blue cape over her head and men's boots on her feet. She was fingering some papers as she watched them from a bluff on the left side of the track. She had no expression on her face as she stared at Enoch, and he knew she hated him because he was a Yankee and to her he was just white Northern trash, and because she was desperate and had to deal with people like Uncle Floyd. He never knew who she was, never saw her again, but all his life he remembered her clearly—mostly in times of crisis.

When the cars were loaded and Uncle Floyd climbed back into the cab, smelling of whisky, and the soldiers were swigging and singing among the cotton bales, Enoch felt as if his stomach would cat up last week's meals.

Oh, I got drunk and landed in jail
Weren't not one sod to go me bail.

"Now, Ennie." Uncle Floyd gripped his shoulder too hard. "We don't back up. We go forward, a loop to the left goes 'round and gets us back on the track north. They throw the switch for the off loop. Jasper, toss that woodpile hard on the fire!"

"Yes, sar, Cap'in Floyd." Jasper was busting with amused excitement—nothing scared him.

Going back was even more nerve-tearing, for now they had contraband—four full cars of it. And the moon seemed gay. Uncle Floyd just waved at the patrols who waved back; were *they* getting a few gold eagles, too? Someplace ten miles below Jackson they heard rifle fire and mortars from the river gunboats. But they just kept going. Enoch was nearly asleep when they unloaded the bales in a grove of trees with little green fruit. He saw they were peaches. Would he live to see them turn fuzzy-ripe and come up here and fill his hat with them and bite into the sweet meat, letting the juice just run down his chin? From somewhere nearby, a dog barked and somebody kicked it, making it yelp.

The sun caught "Old Sal"'s brasswork as they came along running backward, not turning. The soldiers were all worn out, or drunk, or both. They were not singing. Even Jasper, who never tired, was rolling his head, all sweaty on his book-leather skin, as he tossed the wood chunks into the firebox with a grunt. Uncle Floyd seemed pooped. He sat up on the tender, his coat pockets bulging. And no matter how much whisky he had sucked up out of his bottle, he looked dead sober and wasn't smiling. He was sweated through like a horse that had been driven in too long a race.

"Greed, boy, greed. I'm as pockmarked with it as the next feller."

"The soldiers will talk."

"You gotta hundred dollars coming. They get bottles. The Irish are practical for all their mush. And we'll go out again." He pointed to Jasper; they had a witness. "T-U-E-S-D-A-Y," spelling it out.

At their depot, they all separated.

Funny, Enoch thought, how you get over the scareboo-ger fears, and how heavy the deerskin poke with the drawstring seems hanging inside from your belt. Right next to your cods, like an extra set of balls. Gold balls. He didn't even go and hide it; he just woke up Ginny in the lean-to and gave her the heel of a bottle to drink. He was so goddamn manly, thrashing out his release from tension on her, he just didn't let up. He was that horny after the fears of the night, so happy to be living and banging. He wasn't going out again, he'd tell Uncle Floyd. A hundred dollars gold would see him a good way to Californy.

Uncle Floyd and Enoch made the contraband run three times more.

On June 25 the Union engineers exploded a huge mine under a major rebel force and the whole siege became a tight, choking ring of attacks on Vicksburg. Yet the rebel flag could still be made out as it hung in the July air over the city's courthouse. Enoch had been called back for battle duty; he was with Sherman's XV Corps, out front, sweating and fearfully advancing through broken woods toward fortified bluffs, insects biting, the summer sun heavy overhead. Enoch had his gold eagles sewed up between two lengths of rawhide he was using as a belt.

"No place for a railroad man," he told the lanky soldier on his right, a farmer from New York State with little chin and a limp from a blistered heel. The farmer wiped dust off his nose as he sucked up water from his canteen. "Ain't fit for nuttin' this place for sure."

They were part of six hundred men moving straight ahead, the officers sweating in their heavy blue, shoulder straps unbrushed, and their whiskers all in disorder. The men could hear the ironclads' guns in the river, blasting away and bursting shells coming over Fort Hill, the one they were to take. The terrain was all busted up, overgrown with burrs, burdock, sumac. From the right, their own field guns were tearing up a lot of brush without doing much (they felt) to win the battle. Grant was going all out to bring down Vicksburg after "sniffing round like a dog at a fence post" since last December.

The officers were in a cluster looking at maps, and one fat major was trying to focus with his brass field glasses on the courthouse tower, but they were advancing in a section too far to the left of the city. A halt was called all along the line.

Captain Nash came over to Enoch's squad; his bowlegs in too large boots were always very comical, but the men no longer noticed them. "Boys, we're going up to take that bitch of a fort. I don't want no slacking off or straggling. The firing squads been always ready for any backtrackers, crawfishing or puking out, and other crimes." He cheerfully mopped his face with a red handkerchief. "It's going to be a great little fight. Sergeant Kingston."

"Yes, sir." The hell with the fight. To die here and never drive one of the big engines and then, money in plenty, go out to the islands. . . . It was more than a great little fight. It was cruel and mean.

3

The battle for the fort never made much sense to Enoch—figure it out any which way—because he couldn't fit the bits together into any whole picture of that day. All he knew was he was winded, poop-scared, and shaking when it was over. Part of the fort was burning. He went down to the river and just sat there on a log, his joints all stiff, his feet sore. He watched the water running by, and out twenty feet a snag was sticking up, with a body caught on it. Up river the gunboats were no longer firing. The sun going down in the west made red buttons on the water.

A horse sergeant came down limping, his boots in his hand. He pulled off his striped shirt and soaked it in the river. The sergeant had a brown torso and a long red scar over his left shoulder blade. His worn pants had the yellow stripe of the regular cavalry. He looked out at the body caught on the snag.

"Must be a reb."

"Why they not firing?" asked Enoch.

"Oh, hell, didn't you know? They give up."

"Give up?"

"Yep, Vicksburg. We just starved 'em out. They been smokin' sumac leaves for tobacco and eatin' bread made from pea flour."

Enoch rose and picked up some flat stones and began to skim them across the river surface. When he was a boy living with Ma on the hardscrabble farm among the tree stumps, he used to skim stones across the frozen pond and his toes would get cold and ache. Ma would fix him a broth with bread soaked in it, feed him with a big tin spoon. Well, Ma was dead of the lung misery that last winter on the farm, and it was no use thinking back.

The horse soldier flapped his wet shirt in the air. "It's Fourth of July. And my horse dead, blisters on my feet from walkin'. Fourth of July!"

"Could be."

"Where the hell's your rifle gear?"

Enoch shook his head. "Someplace. Went out on a water detail and couldn't find the company."

"Well, there's whisky and singin' out by the sutlers' carts—just up top of the ridge. It's rotgut, but it's whisky."

Enoch didn't feel much like celebrating. He had maybe killed or badly wounded two or three of the rebs just after they got past the first trench and were into the fort. It was mean. He had shoved in his bayonet at least twice. He could use a drink, a slug of corn pressings, rotgut or not.

Enoch found the sutlers' carts, a whole group of them selling meat pies and fruitcake and tobacco, and from under some canvas pouring out whisky from crocks into tin cups. He got some four bits from his pocket, pushed his way through, and soon stood against a tree trunk sipping raw crack-skull whisky, flavored, he suspected, with added pepper and chewing tobacco. Horse soldiers and gunner crews were leading their horses down to a stream. All around, the soldiers were beginning to feel like shouting and slapping backs, and talking of who was dead and who was wounded and who had soiled himself in the battle. After all, it was victory; it was the Fourth of July. U.S. Grant and the rebel General Pemberton had sat down together and said this part of the war was over.

Enoch was thinking of getting a second cup of the skull-cracker when Jasper tapped him on the shoulder. Jasper looked gray-green and worn down. He was carrying a bundle wrapped in horse cloth and tied off with artillery cord.

"Been lookin' for you, Mr. Enoch, half the day in a dozen places."

"Got steam up in 'Old Sal?' "

"Got a message for you from Mr. Floyd."

He handed over a folded bit of paper, an inch of the edge of a newspaper containing one word written in Uncle Floyd's hen-tracks handwriting.

SKIDADDLE

Enoch looked up. *Skidaddle*—Uncle Floyd's word for making a run for it. "What's this mean, Jasper?"

The Negro leaned closer, looked around him, and spoke into Enoch's ear. "They arrested Mr. Floyd—the provost fellas."

"They have?"

"Contraband they calls it." ·

"Cotton?"

Jasper smiled brightly. Except for no educating, he was smarter than most folks he called mister. "Cotton. Been arrestin' lots of people. Smugglin' they says, through the lines. Mr. Floyd he wrote that fo' you and give it to me to deliver. He said he had to get his hat and coat in a hurry and he said find you and you better—"

"Skidaddle?"

Jasper put down his bundle. "I got you some white folks' clothes and there's some cold meat and pones. I figure we better get 'cross river and find us somethang on railroad wheels goin' west."

"We . . . ?"

"This nigger ain't no fool. I fixed them train boilers. They know I knows how many trips we made, how many bales of cotton we brung out."

"Any steam trains going west?"

"Talk's 'bout movin' the army to take over whatever supplies the rebels has before they recover from this fight. They got a train over the river goin' to Fort Hudson. Maybe we can git on it. Maybe they need engine folk. They got holt of some captured Vicksburg and Jackson rollin' stock."

It was the biggest speech Enoch had ever heard Jasper make. Hell, he didn't know any more about niggers than he did of Jews or Catholics.

"That your whole name, Jasper?"

"Jasper August de Leon."

Enoch looked at the bit of paper with Uncle Floyd's message and then up at Jasper. "Mighty fancy name."

"Ole Cunnel August de Leon my grandpappy; he was a boar stud on the plantation. Mighty frisky white man he war among the beginner browns, gold skins."

"Reminds me, we have to get Ginny."

Jasper began to untie his bundle and he laughed good and loud and shook his head. "She went off with Colonel Eshbacher's hoss orderly, that there shavetail lieutenant. That's what she done."

"Well, just as well—no sense taking a girl with us," said Enoch, feeling betrayed. "Let's go find someplace for me to get out of these soldier duds. Damn Ginny, damn that glass-assed Lieutenant Rodgers."

"No place fer her with us when we got runnin' to do."

They made their way down the ravine, and Enoch looked over some tattered gray pants, a checked shirt a bit out at the elbows, and a short grease-spotted, tobacco-colored jacket.

"It's from a cook of the Michigan regiment. All I could grab. Give him my mouth organ fer it. Got you a hat, too."

Enoch looked at the shapeless wool beehive hat. "I'll keep the army boots and find a better hat someplace."

"How far you think we have to run to forget the army?"

"A long bit, Jasper."

"We both desertin', ain't we, Mr. Enoch?"

"You sign enlistment papers?"

"I made my mark."

There was a marvelous fight going on about them in the sutlers' section; even some dogs joined in, by the sound of it.

Jasper said, "Hate to miss a good dawg fight."

"How we cross the river?"

"Oh, lots of boats just fer the pickin'. Folk just run away and leave 'em when they see the Yanks was winnin'."

"Can you row?"

"I gotta know how to do *everythin'* or I don't get my vittles."

They buried the uniform under long-dead logs and leaves gone to mush. Enoch felt like scratching as soon as he got the shirt on and the yarn suspenders up, but he told himself it was just his imagination. He had transferred the three hundred dollars in gold under his belt, hoping Jasper hadn't noticed.

"You think they'll shoot Uncle Floyd?"

"He's the talkiest man, but he says they got their eye on him this time." Jasper made as if to aim a gun. "*Bango*

bango. Mr. Floyd he got a holt of a lot of them cotton bales. They even arrested 'Old Sal.' "

"Arrested a train?"

"Well, don't know what it's called, but they got her in the supply yard where the coat-marshal is sittin'."

Enoch figured it was time to get down to the river and find a boat with some oars. "Damn it," he said as he put a package of cold meat and cornpones wrapped in brown paper into his pocket. "You forgot my books."

Jasper just nodded and walked on. He led the way down the ravine and along a red clay path. All around on higher ground they could hear the celebrating of the soldiers, the whoops of the drunks, the clatter of horses and wheels on the run as the field guns were moved away from their forward position. There was shooting now, over near the captured forts; well, it was for the "Glorious Fourth," as Uncle Floyd always called it. Last year before he prayed as a godly man for the safety of the republic (and before he got into the bottle of hard cider), he called for three cheers for Country and Liberty. Too bad if they shot such a railroad-driving patriot, Enoch told Jasper.

They stayed low and whispering, avoiding parties of soldiers until dark. It was a creepy, frog-loud night when they stood by a small inlet with a snag lodged at the end of a short pier. Enoch stood looking at the whole Mississippi flow by. It didn't give a plugged dime about the victory, or the war, or the people who had been messing around for months on its banks. It was a serious river; it had to do its job, Enoch decided—carry water, eat away river banks, sink tree trunks to tear out steamboat bottoms, drown drunks, keelboat men, be the home of the big catfish with the whiskers that made such fine eating and were fools for a big hook baited with a skinned rabbit tempting them at the end of a trout line.

It was exile, the boy felt, and at sixteen—going away from that east shore. Going across was leaving the railroading mainland for him. The earth east of Big Muddy where he had been born, where he had been raised up more or less, had found knowledge of sorts, read, unbuttoned, gotten down on some growing girls in this business of what seemed natural, driven "Old Sal." Now all was behind him. Ma's grave in that rocky Illinois hillside, Uncle Floyd maybe already punched full of lead-made holes. But maybe not. Uncle Floyd was as wily as Bre'r Fox, and twice as crafty. Still, if he was gone, like the sad song had it—to the cold cold ground—it was one more ache—and time to move on.

The moon shone on the gray-silver surface of the wide river. A fish jumped into the air, as if from its own bad dream. Some large, clumsy night bird was flapping around up river, making lonely bird sounds. Sections of trimmed logs floated by; also some boxes flung overboard from the Union ironclads up river, most likely. It was lonely—lonely as a pious wet Sunday, and he wanted to stay. Yet he knew survival was all. So he walked over to where Jasper was bailing out a yellow-painted rowboat with a long-handled pan.

"It's a fur bit across, damn it, Mr. Enoch. So you get in if you're goin' with me."

Jasper was certainly lippy for a nigger, but then, as fellow deserters, they'd eat plenty of dirt together; better not rile him. The boat didn't leak too badly; it just smelled of dead fish. They sat side by side, one oar each, rowing slowly, the far banks hardly visible in the smoky night mist walking on the water. Enoch didn't mind losing the novel as much as the *New Practical Navigator*. He liked figuring out its mathematics, and it would have helped if he still intended someday, when rich, to reach those tropical islands.

So it came about that Sergeant Enoch Bancroft Kingston of the Quartermasters Railroad Supply Section before Vicksburg was for all time officially listed: *Missing in Action, Presumed Dead.*

2

The Work

4

Philip Phineas Canning used to tell Eastern investors it had been El Pueblo de Nuestra Señora la Reina de Los Angeles until the Yankees came with Fremont during the Mexican War. Then it became a stopover for the forty-niners, gold hunters going north. Beyond that there was little in the way of enterprise in El Pueblo Los Angeles except for the trade in beef, hides, and tallow. The Civil War boosted the village into a wider world, brought it alive from an adobe mud-wall Mexican town, not just with commerce, but with its street killings, gambling houses of the paisanos and Estodo Unidenses, with whorehouses and professional gamblers active in the *Calle de los Negros*—Nigger Alley—by the Plaza, that still had Spanish color in 1868. What made it different from most West Coast towns was the sticky black asphalt that was smeared on its roofs, a natural tar coming from a marshy and greasy pit on the La Brea Rancho where the bones of animals like saber-tooth tigers (that had never existed according to the local padres) were mixed in with the messy black mass.

After a session with Eastern investors at the Bella Union Hotel, the big man, Philip Phineas Canning, walked over to his corrals and stood under the big sliding gate with its sign:

CANNING FREIGHTING & COACH COMPANY

He was in his shirt sleeves, five-feet-nine, too-short pants held up by red suspenders, no collar, and no cravat. The hammer-claw jacket was discarded on the fence. He was inhaling deeply on a cheroot, pluming out smoke from angry nostrils. The bastards had drunk his whisky and nodded, not committing themselves. He was solidly impressive, as if his features were rough hewn by an ax and never finished. He was bearded, his nose overcolored; he had soot-colored hair. Behind him the mules in the corrals were kicking up a ruckus, and some Mexicans—who were *Agringodo*—fairly Americanized—were washing down a stagecoach and laughing more than they worked. At the north gate a freighting wagon pulled by a six-mule team was coming in from Wilmington on San Pedro harbor, heavy with crates of machinery, furniture, and bolts of fabric for Winters's General Store, unloaded from a schooner in the bay.

The big man smiled. Wilmington was his own port on the Pacific, created, erected by himself, twenty-one miles from Los Angeles. The wise bastards of the town had chortled when he set up a harbor next to the port of Pedro, which had hogged all the shipping trade at one time.

A clerk came out of the adobe and plank office building, pen behind one ear. He was clutching some papers he had been working with.

"General, it's Mrs. Canning sent a lad from Wilmington—if you're coming home for supper."

"I'll try, and send some of the peaches from the Tajanta Ranch to my house. And that crystal lamp that came in off the Cerro Gordo freighting wagon."

"You want to see the mule list?"

"Damn right. Have I got five hundred working mules or not?"

"As of two weeks ago, four hundred seventy-six."

"Close enough. Fort Tejon wagons—where the hell are they?" He took out a butter-gold watch and looked at its dial. "Late. Should have been in this morning."

"It's a far way, general."

"Hell! Rode a hundred miles in a day by myself. This is a freight wagon and mule job. Bad luck Chuck Kellow got killed last week. Nobody could drive wagons and mules like Chuck."

"Or drink panther-sweat whisky. I think the Tomlinson outfit had Chuck gunned down."

"No proof."

"John Tomlinson—he's a sick man, general."

"Not sick enough."

Philip Phineas Canning wasn't truly a regular army general. During the war, he had been appointed to the California Militia Fourth Brigade, which existed mostly on paper. He had been twenty when he came to California in 1851 from Delaware, eager, greedy, wise, and bad-tempered. In a few years he had hundreds of mules, forty wagons and fifteen stagecoaches earning their keep between the harbor and Los Angeles. He expanded to open a route to Salt Lake City, then over the devil's own desert to Fort Yuma in Arizona Territory. He was only in his late thirties now, the biggest freighter and stagecoacher in the Southwest. He liked wagons, he liked money, he relished entertaining the Union officers from Fort Drum barracks at his big house in Wilmington with a plenty of good food and drink. His wife was a good hostess—and, glory be, wine and cigars seemed to encourage the army supply officers to use the Canning lines.

What was chewing at him now? Why was he in such an uproar? He had his big home, his wagons and mules, had a pile of money—well, credit anyway. And a title. But he had a new itch—not just to beat John J. Tomlinson, his only real rival for freighter and stagelines into the Arizona and Tehachapi country, but something bigger—an elephant of a plan. The war had been over more than three years, and still his dream was just a lot of marked-up paper, and doubt in too many minds.

He had run and been elected state senator; he had worked hard—like a damn field hand, a *campesino*—on the Canning Bill. Had knocked heads, kissed ass ("not really, just patted backs"), given fattening dinners, offered money, and gotten The Canning Bill passed, authorizing a railroad from the harbor on the Pacific to Los Angeles. And the result of all his hard work? The damn taxpayers, under the thumb of Tomlinson and his goddamn freighting route had voted no to any county subsidy to get the twenty-one miles of track built. It was stale thinking out of a past of ox-drawn *carretas*.

He wasn't giving up; he was organizing to get another charter for a Los Angeles and San Pedro Railroad. John J. Tomlinson was ailing, and the farmers and ranchers were beginning to think of a fast rail-route to the harbor;

not just depending on dirt-road conditions, storms, and the diseases of mules to deliver the region's product to the rest of the world; to import what the outside had to offer and resell at higher profit. Canning had said, "Whisky and profit are the first signs you've got a civilization."

The sun was a bloodshot eye in the west, slanting over the pepper trees and the spire of the church in the plaza, when he turned to see the dust cloud down the road to the east, billowed up as if stirred by a big breeze. Time for the wagons from Fort Tejon. Bullion from the silver mines, Wells, Fargo boxes and military bundles. He paused after shouting for the corral hands to open the big gate, fanning himself with his derby in the dusty afternoon. He never could understand (in his old age) why people thought everyone in the West wore Stetsons and broad-brimmed hats. The Canning-favored hard derby was actually the most popular in the Los Angeles pueblo.

The mules were tired from pulling six wagons. They had come down the Cajon Pass in early morning and changed teams twice. It was a hard, dry run and the teams were not running—just moving at a good pace. Nothing tougher than a harness mule. The heavy freighting boxes swayed and jolted; the six wagons were not much given to springs. The lead wagon turned for the gate and the driver at the side of the relief driver (Canning had never heard of the term "shotgun"), his fists full of reins, just nodded to Canning as he guided the wagon into the freight yard with sound and manipulation of the reins. The other wagons followed, drivers dusty and raspy-voiced.

Canning slapped dust off his pants and walked into his office, checking his watch with the large face of the wall clock dial and its tick-tock pendulum. It wasn't much of an office. Whitewashed walls, a rack of shotguns and Henry rifles. A set of Texas longhorns hung over a fireplace made of petrified wood brought out from Arizona. A captain's chair and scarred rolltop oak desk, two coal-oil lamps with green shades hanging from iron brackets set in the piñon wood rafters of the ceiling. A letter press, a blackwood set of drawers, topped by a water pitcher, metal cups, glasses, and some bottles of popular whisky.

The driver ducked to keep his head from bashing against the low door frame as he came in. He was six-feet-two or -three, in his early twenties, broad but not fat. Reddish curly hair tending to dark brown, a moustache solid and long. His faded, overwashed yellow wool miner's shirt was dusty and the worn hat, of Union cavalry cut but without insignia, was layered with dust. He set his double-barrel twelve-gauge shotgun in a corner as he reached for a bottle and a glass.

"Afternoon, general."

"Afternoon. Pour me three fingers too."

When they each held a shot glass of amber whisky, they smiled at each other and knocked it back after a quick swish of the liquid around cheeks and gums.

"Second wagon broke a rear wheel at Pancake turnoff, had to put on one a mite smaller. The last hitch of mules aren't up to snuff."

"I'm firing the stationmaster at Three Arrows Crossing; he's stealing mule feed, deadheading passengers."

"Here's the bills of lading. I'm going to wash up and maybe play some poker at Buffum's Saloon."

Canning laughed and motioned for a refill all round. "Kingston, you're courting, you young bastard, the last *alcalde*'s niece. The whole town knows."

"Nosy bastards." Enoch didn't think it amusing. Canning always felt Enoch Kingston's worst fault was that he had no sense of humor. Witty sometimes, caustic and sarcastic in the saloons and gambling dives, maybe, but no easy, pants-slapping, belly-shaking humor. Can't laugh at himself. Got a wild hair up his tail.

"The Alvarez family's real good stock. Had one of the first Spanish land grants given 'em by the king himself."

"They're on the balls of their ass now. Living high on the hog on nothing."

"Sure, proud—keep up a front. The Rancho Alvarez will be worth money some day. It's in the right place—their mountain holdings, say—for rail going through to Outlaw Pass to Arizona. Texas, maybe to the Gulf."

"General, you've been listening to me while I was drunk and on the floor."

"Never knew you to be fall-down drunk, Kingston—just dreamy. I expect to start the railroad in September, from my wharf in the harbor into town. Working it out. Talked to harbor investors just today."

"Sure you did, general," said Enoch, feeling the dirt and stubble on his chin. The wily bastard didn't know a thing about railroads—wants to use me, exploit me. "And you want me to handle the track building?"

"This year. I mean it."

"And the locomotive is rounding the Horn in a Vanderbilt clipper?"

"Yes, damn you, yes!"

Enoch nodded. He didn't mind the blowhard's yelling. They had a standoff attitude towards each other, a respect. "I'm taking three days off. It's fiesta time. And I'm damn tired. You've got to find some more wagon bosses."

"Have to keep bringing the silver chests out of the Cerro Gordo mines. The Inyo trade is worth holding on to. It's the men who fail, not the mules."

"General, crossing the Mojave through Willow Springs and Little Lake you could burn the horns off Old Scratch himself."

"Belshaw's furnaces need charcoal and supplies."

"The hell with Belshaw. I'm not a wagon boss for three days."

Canning stood up and cracked his shoulder joints as he flexed his muscles. Temper, temper, he told himself. He was nearly as big as Enoch, and even in middle age still powerful. He put an edge to his voice, but placed an arm on Enoch's shoulder.

"Forget wagons for a while. I'm getting some gristle-heeled mule men down from Walker Pass. I want you to lay rail, say as a partner, on the L.A. and S.P. rails."

"What the hell is that?"

"The Los Angeles and San Pedro Railroad. You've heard me talk of it."

"Partner?" Enoch grinned, even though his kidney ached from the trip and he stank from his own and mule sweat. "Partner?"

"I've heard you talk about railroading, all about army supply trains and engines. You've laid track, you've repaired boilers, you know steam. Kingston, I'm going to make your goddamn fortune."

"I could have been lying."

Canning winked and pushed his derby to one side of his head. "Captain Nash told me a lot about you when he commanded your regiment. He's ranching now down San Diego way. I bought out his livery stables and coaches during the war. Spoke highly of you—not your character, but as a steam mechanic."

Enoch frowned and twisted the glass in his fingers. He wasn't too sure what the War Department had him listed under. Deserter? Missing in action? Buried in some mass grave of unidentified corpses? He carefully set down his glass on the desk top. "Good officer, Captain Nash. When I was a kid we took a fort together at some place on a big river."

"Vicksburg. Well?"

"Nope, general. I'll take a wagon train of freighters out to Buena Vista mines in three days."

Enoch walked out, drag-assed tired. It had been three days on the road from Yuma, a hundred miles of wheel tracks but no real roads. Steep passes, with him hanging onto the drag brakes. He was short-handed because of a knifing the night before, harnessing up at Los Travis dance hall. One driver dead and Xusus Martinez driving with a sewed-up gash on his stomach two inches long. No use bothering the general with such details; he liked to have a wagon boss solve his own problems.

As the office door shut, Canning decided against a third drink, *any* drink when he was alone in his office. He was meeting with the Los Angeles County politicians who were on his side. At the next election he wanted the county to authorize a vote for $225,000 in bonds of the company's $500,000 capital stock. The damn opposition was crying it didn't want to burden the taxpayer with this bond thing. Hell, it was the mule and horse dealers, the wagon builders and freighters who were screaming that a railroad would ruin their trade, that the barley and oats business would lose their profitable trade in mule and horse feed. And the farmers, those tobacco-chewing clod-kickers, were claiming that engine sparks would set the grain fields afire. He must ask Enoch Kingston about spark arresters he had read about in *Harper's Weekly*. Canning sat down at his desk and hung his hat on a set of deer horns.

Funny feller, Kingston. He had appeared in rags some

years ago, came across Death Valley with the Walker wagon train, his toes sticking out of his torn boots, with his wild hair and that hungry look of a coyote. I put him to shoveling horseshit in the corrals, and when the loads came in he earned his keep—beans and slab pork. Yes, and more, after the big flood, taking the wagons out in '66 with the roads two feet deep in water, bridges out, and fording streams to get the freight through to the San Joaquin Valley. Only a madman would have tried it—or gotten the others to follow him.

Canning prided himself on his judgment of men. But Kingston? Surly, secretive, a hard worker. Could read and write, borrowed books from Sol Winters's wife. After the first year, Kingston wanted to go sign on a whaler bound for the Japan Sea after sperm and blue-fin whales. He talked of a railroad being built in China. But he had broken an arm when a stagecoach overturned on La Merced Road. Damn fool, wanted to sail with a broken flipper. He was younger then, said he wanted to end up on some island and raise goats and drink coconut milk.

But Kingston had trimmed down his ideas, had turned into the top wagon boss since he had started sparking Maude Alvarez a year ago. He gave up going over to Madame Needle's cathouse Saturday nights with the drivers and horse and mule shoers. Not tomcatting anymore. He'd even cut down his drinking to civilized proportions. Kingston was going to get knived *or* have a shotgun wedding. The Alvarezes were a bit tight in the matter of deflowered virgins, or even attempts in that direction.

However on the partner idea, if Kingston said no, he meant no, the stiffnecked young bastard. There was something gravelly and hard about him—an odd bird, a harsh growing-up, maybe. On the surface, he was like every other drifter who had survived the war, the desert, hard times, the shots of road agents, and barroom bullies, missing the clap and the old rale in the frontier banging shops. Most likely he had been lucky as a cocksman or he wouldn't be courting in the Alvarez direction, not that it's going to make him happy in the end. Old Diaz Inigo Solviera de Avellaneda Hernandes Alvarez was a hard-nutted old snob, so damn proud of his Spanish blood lines he'd never let a Protestant Yankee—if he knew it—get his hand up the petticoats of his daughter. Or close enough either without bribing a duenna, or whatever they called the old battle-ax that guarded her.

5

Enoch roomed at Irish Agnes's boarding house just behind the *Aquila de Oro*—the Golden Eagle—gambling house, a fairly high-toned place featuring faro, stud poker, and an honest wheel. It was on the Calle de Los Negros—so called because so many of the people from below the border who lived there were dark, as people from Sonora in Mexico usually were. The Calle ran wild and loud, given to good times at a price, for the human mixture of Americans called Estado Unidenses, runaway Sidney Ducks (onetime Australian convicts), Mexicans, freed Negroes, and plenty of Chinese gamblers. It was a busy place after dark; lamps lit, its saloons and cafés open to outlaws run out of Montana and the Indian Territory, people who liked to gamble, to visit the whorehouses with the Los Angeles sports. The Calle de Los Negros was the liveliest street south of the Barbary Coast up in Frisco.

Enoch had enjoyed it in his own watchful casual way. He had gambled some, drank Blue Blazers at Buffum's fine saloon with its solid mahogany bar, its beveled expanse of mirrors, and genuine oil paintings of large women, mostly nude, reclining on scarlet sofas. In Buffum's private bar, deals were made in cattle, barley, and wool, for ranches being broken up, going cheaply or overpriced, for town plats being laid out.

Enoch stopped at Buffum's to pick up a small package tied with blue ribbons and exhanged small talk with Percy Johnson, a professional gambler nicknamed "Pistol," a man of middle age, dressed neatly but not too ornately to scare off marks and tinhorns. Pistol had wide Scotch-English cheekbones and very long-fingered hands, no rings. He sported a trimmed black beard with Chinese moustaches. As usual, his gray tall-crowned beaver hat rested on the back of his head. Pistol's ambition was to retire to a respectable life and give his wife a social position. He was watching the bartender mix a raw egg in some brown sauce.

"Still eating dust, Kingsy?"

"Still, Pistol."

Pistol Johnson took the mixture from the bartender, frowned and swallowed it quickly. He wiped his mouth with a silk handkerchief. "Big game last night at La Aquila. Missed you."

"Then I saved money."

"Kingsy, I won, from some fat man from Chi, a hundred lengths of steel—all he had left when he thought his kings could stand up to my aces. What good is it—the steel?"

"How big?"

"Wrote it out." Pistol took a folded paper from his waistcoat. "Thirty feet long, three inches wide on top, four on the bottom."

Enoch laughed and waved off the bartender who held up a bottle of Old Crow. "Those are train rails. Stolen from the Central Pacific, I bet."

"The fat man said he brought them out on the clipper *Sea Star* as ballast. I want to unload."

"Try Canning—he's talking again of building a railroad."

"Again, eh? Maybe I'll give him a bargain. They're in port at San Pedro. Playing poker tonight?"

Enoch shook his head. "Maybe tomorrow. Pistol, why don't you build a railroad? Everybody talks one."

"Wish I could." Pistol nodded. "All gamblers die broke, even in El Pueblo de Los Angeles. But it passes the time."

Enoch left and went down Sweet Rose Alley, which smelled anything but. The Chinese were smoking their first opium pipes of the night behind their shuttered windows. There was a tin tub kept down the hall from his room at the boardinghouse. He had the little boys from the *barrio* who did the rough work at Irish Agnes's fill the tub with hot water. He soaked and rested in the tub, smoking a stogie and letting the three days' journey from Fort Yuma wash out. Then he shaved his chin and cheeks with a long razor. He rather liked the dangling copper-toned moustache. *Muy bien*. It made him look older, and at twenty-two he felt he still looked *too* young. He didn't grow a beard like most; there was red hair enough on his head and upper lip. He wore it long behind and alongside his ears, rancho style, in low sideburns. He was filling out and he liked his face—maybe not pretty but service-able—and the teeth he scrubbed every morning with salt were all in place. His one vanity was his pleasure in their whiteness; that was why he didn't chew tobacco.

In his slope-ceilinged room—a mess, he admitted—there was a Spanish saddle with silver fittings in a corner, a buf-falo-hide trunk, a brace of Colt pistols hung in holsters on the wall, and a "brass boy" Winchester by a bed showing half of the chamber pot under it. There was a chair with a rawhide seat and a closet not crowded by his wardrobe. He grinned as he thought: all my worldly possessions ex-cept for some gold coins in Sol Winters's bank. Not much—heavy gambling had depleted his fund to get to the Sandwich Islands or to Hong Kong, any place Herman Melville had been. He would perhaps become the big man in building railroads in Asia. Buy himself an island.

Now he—lame-brained bastard, he said to his image in the mirror—was thinking of getting married. He moaned at the thought of the emotional muddle he was in as he got into his Mexican tailored pants, pulled on the too-tight polished boots, buckled on his star-roweled spurs, got into a good shirt starched stiff as a board, and hung a silk cra-vat around the bat-winged collar that sawed at his weathered neck. *What* had trapped him? Maude Alvarez had, love had, desire and a want to premanently possess her had trapped him. That marvelous girl's body he had held at the fandango dances, the stepping together in the *zorrita* and the *traganza* at the Alvarez Rancho. He had gone out there for the first time to repair the old Newcomen steam engine that ground the corn that fed Señor Alvarez, his prize horses, and also his *paisanos* and *campesinos*. Now visions of the islands with palm trees waving and blue crystal-clear lagoons seemed farther away then ever. Enoch planted a black low-crowned, wide-brimmed hat on his head, a proper town dude. He disliked the popular derby of the businessmen and the top hat of the sports and the sporting gentry. His was not a head for a derby or stovepipe, he felt.

He went out to the back of the boardinghouse where the stables were. As he had ordered, his horse Barnaby was saddled and ready. Chico, the cook's youngest, barefoot and in torn soiled white, stood grinning as he handed Enoch the reins.

"He have very good ride this mornin', Señor. It no *lluvia*."

"No, no rain." He handed over two bits in silver. "Go wash your face."

Chico had orders to exercise the big gelding every morning out by the Campo Santo, the old Spanish cemetery, for a good workout when Enoch was away freighting. He hoped the lazy little tad did his job. He had won the horse a year ago from Pistol Johnson in a two-day poker session. A better gambler's winning than those goddamn steel rail lengths Pistol had won. Steel! Everything was adobe, wood, and tar in the Pueblo, a town which was turning from a Mexican village into an American Los Estados Unidos city. Bricks, too. He road past the terracotta brick building with the big sign, gold on black—WINTERS FIRST NATIONAL BANK OF LOS ANGELES—the brick facade of the Bella Union Hotel with melodic band sounds that made the Calle Principal, as some still called Main Street, a lively place at night; music for the rustle of taffeta and satin and the frou frou of petticoats.

Soon Enoch had Barnaby trotting down the dirt road that led east towards Rancho Alvarez. The country was still wild in spots, still cactus and chaparral, mesquite growths, here and there vetch grass, and cattle stirring in the night. Now and again he passed a cluster of lamp-lit windows—settlers who had come to raise grapes, grain crops, some to piously start a nondrinking, non-meat-eating settlement of respectable fanatics. There were sheep pens and corrals with ponies for the *remuda* of ranch riders, hay barns, and more barking dogs. The land was changing. He inhaled the smell of it, the sun-tormented earth resting in the night. That very special new scent where someone had planted oranges and lemons, challenging the hard, wild nature of the canyons and the umber colored rainless hills. Citrus was shipped through Canning's harbor north to Frisco; there each orange was worth a jit—a dime. Some people ate them rind and all.

All this land needed was more water, more stage-coaches, and 'way in the future, maybe someday a railroad. As he galloped the gelding, he automatically picked spots where it would be natural to drive survey stakes for a rail right-of-way, something with not more than a five-degree grade; where there would have to be fill; where there would be a need to bridge with stone bases, timber trestle. It was all done by eye, hardly by a directed mind. He had no interest in American railroads—not after the fearful business of Vicksburg when he and Jasper had left in such a hurry. He supposed they had shot Uncle Floyd—all for one thousand bales of cotton. He had missed Uncle Floyd for some years. There were no relatives left to write and ask where his grave was, if anyone knew or cared. It was better not to ask the War Department. He might be still listed in some yellowed files as a deserter, or missing. Not that the department was very active about these things now that the Grand Army of the Republic—the ex-soldiers' organization—was important in politics and had the power to swing elections, make and give jobs. And U.S. Grant was President.

Odd, I never saw him in all those muddy, dirty months before Vicksburg gave up.

By pressing Barnaby, in half an hour, he was on Rancho Alvarez land, the hounds barking by outbuildings. El Palacio, the main house, was in sight. It was over a hundred fifty years old, built by Teniente Coronel Manuel Cortez Alvarez, heir to the land grant. The paper existed in a special chest at El Palacio and showed the king's own signature, including the great red seal of the royal line of Spanish monarchs.

Enoch found the pale yellow building impressive with its two towers, a great courtyard, exotic bushes and hedges, a grand porch with pitch-pole pine columns brought down from the hills, and tile roofs of clay baked on the rancho.

But only the facade was impressive, for there were taxes unpaid, the structure mortgaged to the Winters's

Bank, the horse herds pledged to San Diego moneylenders, and the cattle running wild in the cockleburr and cactus scrub, too lean to butcher for beef, their worth only as a source of hides when the lazy ranch hands drove them down for a roundup.

Still it *was* impressive and grand living; the long golden oak hall table, the remains of a silver service, a few gold goblets, and half a hundred servants running about, serving, cooking, washing clothes, stealing, laughing, fornicating, marching in processions, running to the parish church to confess under the image of Nuestra Señora de Guadalupe.

Enoch rode through the courtyard's big arch topped by the Alvarez family crest and motto:

INTEGRA HAURIRE FONTES

Maude, born Maruca Dolores Teresa, had told Enoch it translated as "To drink from pure fountains." He didn't think much of that, and she said, as she dropped her skirt and several multicolored petticoats, "You are an ignorant Yankee and have no poetry in you. It doesn't mean water; it means to grasp the best and highest of the truths of life."

He had said that he was about to make *sure* of that right then.

Once past the outer gate, he didn't go down the big, circling drive but reined the horse to the left, riding past rows of candelabra cactus and the horse-breaking grounds, into a grove of olive trees, the silver underside of the leaves spinning like coins in the night breeze. Here he tied off Barnaby to a low branch and moved across the orchard toward the side of the main house. A small hickory wood door was hidden by a tall growth of bottle brush plants. He tapped twice, lightly, on the door. It gave inward, and the fat face of Concepcion appeared, large, middle-aged, a bulky woman in a red skirt trailing the ground, and a shawl, her heavy-lipped mouth highlighted in the single candle she carried cupped by one hand to prevent its being blown out.

"Señor Estado Unidense."

He smiled at her, remembering her words: *"De los ene-migos los menos*—the fewer enemies the better."

He handed her the small package he had picked up at Buffum's Saloon. "The earrings I promised—enough silver in them to pull down your head to your hips."

"And the blue stones?"

"The blue stones."

He pushed past her vast stomach—it felt like a barrel of jelly—and went up the narrow staircase. There was a wider door at the top. He turned the bronze latch lever and was in Maude's bedroom, a round room in the west tower. It smelled of frangipani. Maude was seated on a low stool, looking into a hand mirror as she teased some black locks of glossy hair onto her high forehead. She was barefoot. She wore a dressing gown and he knew there was nothing else underneath.

She smiled without looking up, "Darling."

Maude had been educated in a St. Louis convent, fin-ished off at Miss Fondengel's Young Ladies' Academy in New Orleans for two years, and hardly ever used Spanish intimate terms. She was a bit short, but overendowed with curves and marvelous breasts. She would be fat someday, Enoch suspected, her skin would darken; but now as he took her in his arms she was all delight, beauty, and woman. (And a frisky girl of seventeen was a woman, as Madame Needle had expressed it to her sporting-house trade, "If a girl is big enough, she's old enough.") Maude had proved for the last six months she was, as the wagon drivers put it crudely, "mucho woman."

They kissed and caressed each other's bodies; the light from the lamp on a night table seemed to quiver with the ardor of their physical liking for each other. He undid the belt buckle of his pants, a buckle reading WELLS FARGO AND COMPANY SINCE 1851, with its image of a coach with passengers and a four-horse team.

Maude ran her fingers progressively over his burnt brown arms, neck, shoulders, in contrast to his white back and white buttocks as he shucked his clothes. There had been in her those foolish weeks of doubt. Was he for her? Did she love this man? Or was she a snob—one who had traveled, and who read French poets? Did she desire a stranger, an American, because of pride rather than the overpolite, ignorant dons with dry steer dung on their boots—they who still sat dreaming of the golden age of Spain in the New World, and wore their pants patched? She had resented the stagnant, outmoded society she had been born into. A fig for tradition she had told her father Don Alvarez when she was thirteen.

She thought of all this again as this rough, strong man rolled her onto the bed with the headboard carving of some female saint in holy ecstasy, surrounded by little short-nosed angels fluttering their wings. The bed had crisscrossed rawhide bands under the mattress for springs. They sank quickly into the center of the bed, right onto the handworked quilts that had taken months of sewing to finish. He could not wait, and she wanted to tease a bit and hold him off, to continue the caressing and the mouthing. She was touched with a perverse bit of contrariness which he hoped to knock out of her.

He laughed as she held him off, nuzzling her breasts with his head. "You bitch, you beautiful bitch. *Soy muy delicada.*"

"You monster, you Yankee monster." She laughed too, and she was pleased that the west tower was so far from the rest of the house. She never had liked El Palacio. She had seen bigger houses with magnificent ballrooms in New Orleans. Here the ballroom, the whole house, was provincial, in decay.

"The covers, the bedcovers," she cried, "They will rip. They are rare."

"Damn the covers." Yet he pulled them aside. Then they made love with the ardor, the cruel sweetness of the young, who feel this is the only moment and that it cannot be the same fury and glory for others. And so far it *had* been that exclusive private passion. . . . Night insects circled the lamp, a few gave up their short lives by sacrificing themselves on the heated ruby glass shade. The night wind in the olive trees was like a chorus of approval, lightly applauding. But they didn't hear it.

It was a good thing that the walls were thick adobe brick, that the main rooms of the family clustered around the other tower. For Maude was very vocal in orgasm; she took delight in her rising sounds of pleasure and satisfaction. Longer, louder certainly than Enoch, who was rather on the silent side while in high rut—only the expression on his face changed to something no one else except a few women had ever seen. A kind of drifting away from a reality he usually held onto, a slight opening of his mouth, the corners wet, and his eyes as Maude said, "bugged out on stems."

Then there was the rapid inhaling-exhaling sound of satisfaction in both as they tried to recover breath.

In a small room at the foot of the stairs Concepcion sat beside a lit oil wick, among riding gear, broken whips, and rusted horse bits and spurs. She held in her still delicate but age-spotted hands the two heavy silver earrings set with blue stones, trying them against her wrinkled ears under her gray hair. She was a distant aunt. No one was sure to which side of the family she belonged—the Alvarez? the de Espinosa? the distant Soriano-Fuertes? But no matter; in true Spanish hospitality, she was to be housed, fed, respected, and made to feel needed by acting as duenna for the motherless daughter of the house. The only daughter. The rest of the Alvarez brood were sons. Six of them: Juan, Felipe, Benito, Ramon, Diego, and Rafael. Concepcion had had a reckless past in Cuba, had buried three children and lost two fortunes. She was old, but she still relished the memory of many men. What did that selfish little fool Maude know what four active legs in bed could mean, when one once had been a roaring woman, black hair undone, spread on some strange pillow.

6

Philip Phineas Canning, for all his outbursts of temper which he usually kept under control, was a man without prejudices. He left that to his wife, who dominated the social scene—what there was of it—from their big mansion in Wilmington. Canning wanted to be liked and to have his own way. He was a champion of the Mexican-Americans—if they took off their hats to him—and he employed Chicanos not merely as corral hands and stable help, but often as drivers on his various lines. He was known as Don Cannito to many of the Spanish-speaking people from Soledad Canyon to Barrel Springs, from Lopez Station to San Jose. Unlike the Butterfield Stage Line, which did not use Mexican-American drivers, he insisted, "I hire anybody who will work. One man is as big a sonofabitch as the next."

Canning was one of the freighters who moved the silver and lead—rough-smelted bullion—the two hundred miles from the Cerro Gordo mines down from the workings to Los Angeles and to the docks for shipment to San Francisco, where it was refined into pure silver. Where wagons couldn't be used in the rough terrain, he used long strings of mule trains. He could not tolerate rivals and fought almost recklessly to grab most of the trade—often more than he could handle.

His railroad would give him exclusive control of the final miles of bullion transfer to the harbor shipping point—*his* harbor. But he needed money to begin preliminary operations of planning and surveying before the county would again vote on subsidy of the railroad bond issue.

He took Enoch, yawning from a sleepless night, to call on Solomon Winters, president of the county's first bank.

"Why do you want me along?" Enoch asked as they drove in the yellow surrey Canning favored.

"Because two are better than one in certain situations. Now Solly is honest, which may or may not be an asset to a banker. He's realistic. You could be starving on your farm, but unless he saw your collateral to cover the loan, he would not give you a dollar of the bank's money. You'll go under anyway he feels, so why prolong the agony? Of course, he'll feed a busted family—as he often does—and buy them pants, or a horse. But that he calls 'God's charity, not banking.' "

"You're out of luck, general. There are a hundred and ten mules still unpaid for, and we need a new mud wagon for the Fort Yuma run."

Canning had his own logic when he proposed something. "Damn it, Kingston, here you may be my rail construction boss, and you can't tell the difference between a clodhopper eating horse corn on two hundred dried-out acres, and a businessman who increases other people's money."

"What's the difference?"

"A businessman worth his powder should *never* be solvent or own everything outright. The more debts he runs up enterprising, the more it means he's not sitting on his ass."

Enoch nodded and pondered at what appeared a twisted logic. In the years to come, when he was millions of dollars in debt to banks, insurance firms and steel companies, building thousands of miles of rail-lines, he found that Philip Phineas Canning had been a pioneer in American business procedures dedicated to growth. As for now, Canning was hoping to be trading in railroad stock in his rail-line which existed only on paper—trading for what he wanted or needed *when* and *if* the bond issue won.

"It's up in a balloon for you, general, or it's sinking like an anchor."

"And if you're to be a partner with me, I'd better call you Enoch."

"Your wife calls you Phinny."

Canning pulled up the team in front of the bank, got

out, and attached a five-pound iron weight to the halter of the off horse. Sol Winters found a hitching post undignified, worthy only of a frontier saloon, so the bank did not provide one. Canning, impressed with his own outlining of his ideas of business, said with a smile, "You, Enoch, can go on calling me general."

The facade (and even the other three walls) of the WINTERS FIRST NATIONAL BANK—as the big gold and black sign read—was of solid red brick, baked in a local brickyard on which the establishment had a hefty mortgage. Brick was a luxury, and its use promoted confidence. There were two plate glass windows and double iron-grilled doors painted to look like bronze.

Inside there were four tellers' cages, a counter for minor business, a door marked *S. Winters.* To the right was the six-foot-high gold and apple-green bank vault door with impressive levers and dials, and on it a painting by an untalented artist; a picture of an Indian village with riders on calico ponies against a smoke-capped mountain peak lit by an orange sun set in a bed of cotton (which Enoch figured might be clouds).

Tellers and clerks wore green eyeshades; in this hot weather they showed sleeve suspenders; the more sedate officers, ornate waistcoats. Mr. Malcolm MacIntosh, the bank treasurer, always wore a gray beaver top hat indoors and seemed continually to be sharpening pencils with a small pocket knife.

As the two men entered his office, Sol Winters shook Canning's hand and took Enoch's and pumped it. Sol Winters was thin and short, but looked tall because of his slimness. He wore a black spade beard touched with gray; his spreading baldness was covered with hair worn long on one side and combed across a delicately formed skull. He was well tailored in heavy dark gray—his clothes came from New York, where his tailor had his measurements and sent him swatches of cloth as samples.

He offered a rosewood cigar box, and as they all lit up, the banker cocked his head to one side and said to Canning, "Phinny, why talk of rolling stock and locomotives when you don't know how the voters will decide?"

"Because, damn it, I've got gear and an engine coming around from the Horn; they will dock any day when the rails are ready. But not a rail comes ashore unless I have credit."

Enoch sat forward and rolled his cigar between his fingers. "Pistol Johnson, I figure, already has some of your rails."

"Christ, don't I know it! That crooked ship's captain claims I had no paid-up sales contract. He took them in lieu of cargo costs, and then the thief gambled them away. I'll have him in jail in a day or so."

Sol Winters shook his head. "Why make lawyers rich? As Abe Lincoln said when he saw a gravestone marked, *Here Lies a Lawyer and an Honest Man,* 'Since when are they burying two men in one grave?' No, Phinny, don't stir up trouble before the election."

"Those are *my* rails. An advance shipment for testing and for teaching a crew how to lay a roadbed. I'll pay out everything I have to teach that captain they can't cheat me."

Enoch said, "Legally or not, Pistol Johnson has control of the rails."

Sol Winters added, "Percy Johnson has killed men who put pressure on him."

"That low-down, whoremongering gambling man, I'll—"

Enoch touched Canning's arm. "Why not make Pistol Johnson vice president? Give him stock for his rails. He's a kind of local legend, isn't he? And we could get his guns on our side."

"Vice president!"

Sol looked from Enoch to Canning. He almost disappeared behind his desk as he leaned back in his chair and studied the smoke rings he blew toward the ceiling. "Percy Johnson is a popular man, a gentleman even if a gambler, who has a reputation with a six-shooter. Phinny, just think of all the important people he plays high-stake poker with, is friendly with, knows intimately. He goes to their homes and ranches for weeks as a guest. An impressive dresser, good talker. Investors from the East would feel right at home talking with him."

Canning neither understood nor respected subtlety. "I'll be damned if I'll be hornswoggled by a three-card monte shark who carries silver-plated pistols in his pockets like a lady!"

Enoch shook ash from his cigar into an abalone shell on the banker's desk. "He's no tinhorn. Had an education someplace which most of us didn't, leaving out Mr. Winters."

"University of Berlin, but during the student riots of forty-eight I had to leave in a hurry . . . however——" Winters waved off his past. "Also, though I hate to say this, perhaps you'll need guns if the Central Pacific puts track down from San Francisco and goes after all the silver mine business, grain transport, fruit."

"I'll be there first."

Enoch said, "Why not think of beating them, lay track beyond Los Angeles if you do build a line?"

Canning shrugged. "First things first. But we'll get the rail-hauling business from here to the port. Right now, freighting lines bring down from the mines fifty thousand dollars' worth of silver and lead bullion a day. Four hundred tons a year come through here—I figure in two, three years, seven hundred tons a year. Why, there isn't a torn-pants propector who doesn't get drunk in town and talk of fabulous sites and ledges, their pockets so full of rock samples they haven't got room for money to pay for their drinks." Canning laughed. He was wound up. "We haven't started yet, Solly, in touching the resources the good Lord set down here among us. And you doubt we'll be able to build a piddling little railroad!"

"Railroads aren't mules and wagons." The banker turned to Enoch. "The general tells me you know railroads. How is the terrain for extending rail-lines up and down the coast—east to the cattle markets?"

"Crazy. Steep grades, solid rock ridges, gorges and ravines. But somebody will do it some day."

Canning said, "Truth is if a country needs something, no matter how hard it is to produce, if there is a green-back to be made in it, it will come. But look—all I want right now is twenty-one miles of rail."

Enoch looked up at the ticking wall clock. He did not yet own a gold watch and didn't like to pull out the silver one connected to the impressive gilt chain laced across his buckskin waistcoat. "I have to go to meet someone. I figure you're right, general. There's money made getting things done. Those bastards up north do it—Huntington, Hopkins, Crocker, Stanford; maybe we wouldn't trust a female dog with any of them, but they began like you're trying too."

"They're talking of expanding rails south," said the banker as he put out his cigar by lightly rolling and grinding it in the ash tray. "*Just* talking?"

Canning said, "We all know they have plans for it, and we could benefit. Connect us with the outer world."

"I think Los Angeles will find their terms hard," said Winters.

"They'll not swallow me. I'm prickly as cholla cactus," said Canning. "Enoch, you mosey over and soft-soap Pistol Johnson. Tell him we'll take the rails off his hands for railroad stock and no questions asked. Satisfied, Sol?"

"Better wait until after the election. He'll not take stock in what isn't yet in existence. And if you lose the bond issue, what good will the rails do you?"

After Enoch had gone off to his appointment (which was a cherished afternoon with Maude Alvarez), Sol Winters said, "This Kingston, he's a new type to me. I sense some moods, even abilities. And yet he doesn't seem to care to be serious."

"It's a girl. Somebody could stick some Spanish steel into him because of her. That's serious enough."

The banker pursed his lips. "Ah, a girl." He seemed to muse over something that seemed very personal, then leaned forward and laced the fingers of his big hands, somewhat surprising in so thin and almost dainty a man—fingers with which he skillfully played a spinet and cello at home.

"My dear friend Philip, I'm going to give you credits, funds, so if the major shipment of the rails and your engine arrive, they can be unloaded on your dock."

"You're a white Jew, Solly."

The banker didn't wince. He knew native-born Americans did not mean anything bigoted by such remarks. In fact, it was a kind of approval and acceptance, even if his wife Hannah didn't accept it or think it much of an honor.

He said, "You understand, of course, the lien on the

shipments will be assigned to the bank until such time as, and if, the county votes the subsidy bill for your railroad."

"I know goddamn well, Solly, you're not going to do anything to finagle the supplies away from me."

"You forget, when you say 'Solly,' you mean the bank and its major stockholders, and you are among them."

Canning sighed out loud—a big sigh, a very vocal one. He never could understand why, when you wanted to help a community to grow, they always felt you were picking their pockets. Hell, all he'd take would be his fair share and maybe the governorship, or U.S. senator's seat.

The banker looked at the big man with admiration. He was still surprised at the sight of these native Americans grown so large, and how skillful certain types were in exploiting their land and its resources. Canning was a man of some abilities, a fine business man, but his vision was limited to horses, mules, the freight routes. His short rail-line project was a bit of a show-off item with added hope it would make money. The banker wondered if Enoch Kingston was a different kind of man. Just now he had so simply suggested solving the Percy Johnson problem. Kingston was an odd one, no doubt, and could face hard facts, while Philip dreamed a lot and didn't separate fantasy from facts. Canning's methods had worked so far. But when the size of projects, the territory to cover in this vast and almost frightening land would come into play, Kingston might be able to move without Canning's hunches, rages, and often mistakes.

After Canning left to check the day's freight runs, the bank closed for the day. The ledgers and the bags of gold and silver, the various paper monies were locked away in the huge ornate safe. Standing outside on the sidewalk, Winters saw to MacIntosh's locking the front door, making sure the oil lamp was pulled lower to illuminate the safe. Then he walked slowly home to his house on Olive Street, greeting people he knew with a nod. He was not a gregarious or expansive person and regretted the fact.

The family name in Bavaria had been Winterhalter, a gathering of uncles and cousins that dealt in grains and leather in Bamberg, Neumarkt, Schwabach. Aron Winterhalter, he who had done business with the Rothschilds,

Sassoons, and with silver dealers in India, had not been lucky in raising a family. Two sons had been lost to him: one at sea, another by a sudden mysterious fever in Hamburg; healthy one day, dead of a plague the next. In 1848, Solomon, the surviving son, a student involved in some sort of revolutionary upsurge for liberty, the betterment of mankind—some such rash romantic notions—had made himself a fugitive. Old Aron did not believe in revolution; in the end, the revolution always ate its children, and a new set of thieves and rogues took over. He believed only in the Torah and that God was to be feared, a vengeful force. He would find you no matter if you hid behind a thousand walls.

Old Aron didn't like the policies of Bismarck—*Furor Teutonicus*—the rising and always present hatred of the Jews by the *gemütlich* Germans. The family business in hides and grain fell away to nothing as discrimination rose against Jews, a periodic event among the as-yet unfederated German states. He decided to send his surviving son, Solomon, who was hiding in Oldenburg, to America with whatever cash he could raise on some warehouses.

Solly Winters, with his father's advice *"Glaube dem Leben*—have faith in life," ended up in San Francisco in 1850 (after some unpleasant adventures in various places, which he recalled only rarely, and not with any nostalgia) with all his inheritance—a bundle of blue tent cloth.

He sold the cloth to a man named Levi, who was doing very well making miners' trousers out of heavy canvas, riveting on the pockets with copper fittings for hard use.

Solly Winters went on to Hangtown in the wild country, where he found that the meager mining of gold by pan washing was hardly ever productive. He used the money from his sale of the canvas to go into partnership with a man named Studebaker who made picks and shovels, always in great demand in a mining area. Studebaker went back to Pennsylvania with $5,000 in gold strapped around his hips, there to go to building wagons with his brothers. Solly Winters went south to follow an eccentric, beautiful girl, Hannah Silverthorn. She was the daughter of an intellectual, former Hasidic student, who ate pork, read Hegel and Kant, and sneered at the Torah and the Talmud as the creed of a minor desert tribe of shepherds. Hannah's father had died in a shipwreck off Seal Rock in the Golden Gate. His daughter Hannah was overeducated for a woman, so most agreed; she read novels in three languages, spoke of artists named Turner, Blake, and Rembrandt. People said she most likely couldn't cook. An orphan with no inheritance, she went down to Los Angeles and became a governess to one of the Beshaw family, who were mining silver out in the wilderness past the Mojave. She read the Brontës and George Sand and sighed that Solly Winters was no Heathcliff.

They were married three months after Solly came to Los Angeles. There were thirty Jewish families in the county, and there was talk of bringing in a rabbi and building a larger *shul*. One Jew who married an Indian woman was considered an outcast, but on his death he was buried among his kind in the Ohab Sholom cemetery.

Neither Solly nor Hannah were Orthodox Jews; however, when the Winters store was doing well, they gave to the charities of the more pious and didn't like to hear Jews grouped with the "greasers" and "micks" and the drunken Indians who lay around in alleys sleeping it off or begging for a snort of forty-rod whisky. There was no general tolerance, but among individuals there were many good people.

WINTERS BARGAIN BAZAAR handled everything from horse collars to patent medicine for female disorders, most of them at least sixty-proof alcohol. He imported china and printed cloth and exported hides and timbers. The town lacked bank facilities, and after the Civil War Winters got together two dozen of the most prominent citizens and established Los Angeles's first bank. There were now two other banks, but neither of them would have been interested or daring enough to do business with Philip Canning's crackbrained railroad schemes. As for Solomon Winters, the town respected him under the very wrong impression that he was a silent partner of the Rothschilds and had knowledge of their dealings.

7

Canning put the situation to Enoch two weeks before the citizens voted on the bonds for the L.A. & S.P. R.R. They were sitting in the freighting office, Canning looking over a stack of posters. "If the county voters had any horse sense, they'd see the railroad will fatten their bellies and make us a city."

Enoch held up a poster.

VOTE! VOTE!
FOR YOUR SOUTHERN CALIFORNIA'S GROWTH
VOTE! VOTE!
FOR THE LOS ANGELES & SAN PEDRO BONDS
VOTE! VOTE! FOR YOUR BEST INTERESTS!
AND YOUR COMMUNIY
                    Committee of the HARBOR TO
                    LOS ANGELES RAILROAD

"Of course, general, you don't tell them it's coming from Wilmington. The sidewheel *Orizaba* from Frisco docks in San Pedro."

"Wilmington is also on San Pedro Harbor, isn't it? Next door to San Pedro. Why, I'd welcome their use of my dock with open arms."

"What if they don't vote the two hundred twenty-five thousand-dollar bond-issue subsidy?"

Canning grimaced and shook his head. "Enoch, I'd be up shit creek and no paddle. I've got twenty-five miles of steel rails coming round the Horn. Shipped a month ago from the Pennsylvania foundries. Be here pronto. And a locomotive, in parts for you to put together, is on the clipper *Ocean Spray*."

"General, when you go spurring for trouble, you ride hard."

"Never mind. Have you got the surveying crew's work finished?"

"Got the survey stakes down on the full route. And you'll find you need sixteen bridges—oh, little ones over gullies. The grade is four percent in just two spots. I hope your damn engine can take a grade. What's its boiler content? And is it four- or six-wheel drive?"

"Don't bother me with details. You're the engineer." Canning looked up from a survey map Enoch had prepared. "We can save at least three hundred feet of track if we don't follow the stream bed at Stallion Crossing."

"Going to the east of it may look straighter to you— and is—but your scraper teams and levers would run into granite and boulders. That means blasting powder, delays. Besides, I have an option for a year to buy the land along Stallion Crossing just beyond our survey. Trading stock for it, really. Want half?"

"You wily sonofabitch!" Canning rose laughing and slapped Enoch on the back. "You believe in the railroad!"

"Not yet. But it's not costing me anything, and if we go through, it's just some of my shares. The road becomes a success, that land could be a good place for warehouses, factory sort of sites."

Canning puckered his lips and held the survey up to a better light. "Who owns it?"

"Enoch said, poker-faced, "My future father-in-law, Don Alvarez."

"Enoch, as my old mother used to say, 'Well, I swan!' So he's going to be your father-in-law?"

"Doesn't know it yet. Sweeten the pot before you ask a favor. *My* mother used to say that."

"Come on, let's get these broadsides stuck up. We'll swing it. Old Tomlinson died last week. That's in our favor. He hated progress."

"You buying him out, his stagecoach and freight business? His widow can't run a line."

Canning lifted his derby off the deer antlers and tapped himself twice on the head with its brim before he set it in place as he had seen a Negro minstrel actor do once.

"You're no damn fool. I'm out to *kill* wagon freighting. No, I'm not buying. It's rails all the way from now on in."

Los Angeles County was divided on the railroad bond issue. Canning and Enoch posted the saloons, shops on Calle Loma (now High Street) attached their broadsides to walls along the Zanja—the canal that brought water and often little fish to the town—some folk held picnics there. The night before the election, there was a parade with torches and a kind of marching band with oilcloth signs, right through Sonoratown, as the Mexican section was called. Then up to the fancy places where Don Vicente, Abe Stearns, and the quality lived.

VOTE LOS ANGELES COUNTY INTO THE
UNITED STATES!
VOTE THE RAILROAD BONDS

The pre-election evening got a bit out of hand at Fourth and Main when a Chinese gambler, Sin Fat, fired a pistol in the alley at a whore named Conejo—the Rabbit—but *not* over the bond issue. Free whisky was offered in several saloons that showed signs reading:

RAILROAD EDUCATIONAL BRANCH OF THE
LEAGUE FOR L.A. & S.P. R.R.
COME IN FOR INFORMATION
AND REFRESHMENTS

The information came in the form of a leaflet and several shot glasses of whisky, a free lunch counter of ham, cheese, game, and sea bass paid for by Citizens for the L.A. & S.P. R.R. Committee.

At Madame Needle's sporting house down by the dry bed of the Los Angeles River, Joy de Kooning, a popular whore in the establishment knifed a man. The rumor got out that tired of election talk she had told a drunken Canning driver who took a swing at her, "Fuck the railroad, but not you." The town had a hard and wild night of it around the Plaza; the rest of the county didn't appear much riled up except for some *vaqueros* and other *muchachos* on the Puente Rancho, who shot up a hay barn.

On the morning of election day, Enoch dressed in a black swallow-tailed coat and a white ruffled shirt. He went to meet Maude and Concepcion at the Pico House, which had a ladies' entrance on the side street. Canning had his wife Becky and his three children up from Wilmington staying at the Bella Union Hotel. Several of his freighters and corral hands with heavy canes were set to watching the polling places. "Don't let nobody do anything we can't do."

At noon Sol Winters invited a group for dinner at his two-story house just off the Plaza. The noonday meal was called *dinner* then; the evening meal, *supper*. Mrs. Canning, a striking, large woman, a strawberry blonde as the term was, approved of putting the children, including the two young Winterses, out in the garden to eat under the grape arbor. She and Maude (so damn exotic, Enoch thought, in violet silk and fingering a pale lavender sunshade swung like a weapon), Concepcion in bile-green, and Hannah Winter, the hostess, wearing her dark hair in a chignon and displaying no jewelry except a Roman gold coin made into a brooch; all were cheerfully delighted to be able to dress up. Hannah kept the three servants running back to the kitchen for the watermelon-rind pickle, a bigger gravy ladle, and the *good* salt shakers.

"It's the servant problem everywhere," Mrs. Canning said as she watched the mountain trout platter being brought in. "They have become *so* uppity."

Hannah Winters said it was all in how one trained them. She was the town's intellectual; she imported Stendhal and had Dickens in monthly parts shipped to her from England. She painted small and very skillful watercolors of too-romantic Mexican ranchers, wild bulls, horsemen, and did detailed versions of the foothills and the coastline.

Solomon Winters, her husband, was too serious to enjoy California landscapes she used to say, when she had a few glasses of Don Sepulveda Rancho wine at some whist party. Always serious, Solly, always figuring bank and money matters on bits of paper, and when he was free of business matters he was practicing Mozart, Haydn, or Mendelssohn on his cello. He had confessed he had little time for his children, and that once his sole youthful ambition had been to become a professional musician.

Canning, for once properly dressed in a hard collar and blue cravat, could not eat much lunch. Enoch was hungry. After the trout there was a well-done roast of beef, the potatoes tucked in under. Rare meat was not popular. Mrs. Canning mentioned butter for the hot breads, but Sol Winters said there was no butter.

"Hannah's grandfather was the chief rabbi of London, and so *no* butter."

Hannah said, "It amused me, and it's healthier . . . Conchita, get the butter for Mrs. Canning."

"Oh, no. I don't want to be a bother. Is it sweet butter?"

Her husband was making little dough balls of the soft interior of some biscuits, modeling with thumb and forefinger and rolling the result across the tablecloth. "How do you think the vote is going, Solly?"

Sol Winters pulled down his waistcoat, wiped his mouth with care, smoothed his spade-cut short beard with both hands. He was a very well-groomed man. "My clerks tell me the people are coming into town; it's about a third bigger turnout than usual. The town may go against you, support the livery stable people, the other freighting and coach lines. But the county people—farmers, ranchers, crop growers—want a deep-water connecting rail-line."

Enoch winked at Maude and pressed his leg against her leg, pinched her thigh. "I hear the barflies and the Chicanos are voting in pretty good numbers—being escorted to the ballot boxes."

Becky Canning shook her head and reached with a spoon for the cut-glass bowl of spiced peaches. "I don't know if it's proper, giving the vote to just everybody out here. Isn't that diluting, you know, the Anglo-Saxon foundation set up by our Founding Fathers?"

"Holy Jesu," said Maude suddenly, as Enoch pinched her thigh. "*What* is this Anglo-Saxon *merde*? I'm Spanish, Concepcion is part Indian, the Winterses are Jews, and *you*, General Canning?"

Canning took up a toothpick from a silver cup. "Danes and Swenskies I guess, 'way back. Hell, Becky, your grandfather was a Polack ship's captain, and your Ma came from Dublin with a brogue thick as peat."

"Phinny, don't show your temper in public."

Enoch felt for his leather case of long thin cigars. "I guess it's me, the only Anglo here. Scotch-English on both sides."

A servant brought in a huge quince-and-pear pie, and Hannah Winters decided even Thackeray could not have improved on the banality of the conversation. Only Mr. Kingston sitting there didn't give it a thought—*he* had a girl on his mind.

By two o'clock the streets around the Plaza were active, the noise increasing, and a horse pulling a buckboard panicked, reared and ran away. People yelled "Runaway! Runaway!" Runaway horses were a daily traffic problem, and an excitement that drew people to windows and out of bars and shops to watch wild-eyed teams create damage to gear and to people, to themselves. The voting seemed brisk in some places, too slow in others.

Canning had hired a suite in the Bella Union and on a slate board was marking down reports—guesses, actually—from agents and county employees whom he "sugared," as he put it, with gold coins. The women and children retired at ten. At midnight he was beginning to worry; collar off, he turned to Enoch and Sol Winters who were sipping Pico punch. "It's going to be too goddamn close."

"Yes" said Enoch. Maude had gone back to the rancho with Concepcion at nine. There had been no time or a safe place for lovemaking. It had left him uncomfortable and sardonic. He felt mean, drawn taut by physical repression. The railroad *could* be a way to his marrying Maude. If the bond funds were voted, he could turn over some stock to Don Alvarez for the land along the Stallion Crossing right-of-way, use it as a lever to get consent to carry off Maude. If the vote went against Canning, the option dropped, it didn't look to be too good unless he carried her off into the mountains and lived among the bandits. Then an outlaw like Joaquin Murietta, he'd be hunted down by the *vaqueros* of Don Alvarez.

"So what if we lose?" he said, tormenting himself as if his tongue were probing a sore tooth.

Sol Winters was pressing his fingertips together. "We can't think that way, Enoch. The bank has guaranteed those steel rail shipments. They should reach port in a week or two—depends on the winds. For the locomotive there had to be full payment, or it didn't leave the dock back East. The bank paid for it."

Canning's face was damp and too rosy. "I've been cutting ties in the Inyo County forests. Thousands of them also behind Cerro Gordo. All I'm waiting for are the goddamn wheels, axles, and carriages."

Enoch stood up, put down his glass and dusted imaginary cigar ash from his sleeves. "Too bad we couldn't vote the Chinese. See you in the morning."

When Enoch was gone, Sol Winters said, "He's young; he can start all over again. We're past that hope. Phinny, we may be up—what's the name of that creek?"

"Why didn't *I* think of the Chinks?"

"Nonsense—it would have voided the entire election."

It was close. The $225,000 bond issue as a subsidy to the L.A. & S.P. R.R. Company's $500,000 capital stock issue won by only thirty-nine votes. But it was a victory. Canning bought champagne for everybody in the Bella Union barroom. His wife and children rode around the Plaza in an open carriage pulled by two matched bays, and people cheered, mostly at the splendor of the rig and the beauty of the horses.

Late that day Sol Winters came home from the bank and found Hannah in the back parlor sorting out some sheet music that had come that day from Vienna via Hamburg, London, and the Panama land crossing.

Hannah looked up and shook her head. "Solly, Solly, how could you have risked so much on that Canning gamble?"

He kissed her cheek and patted her arm; he was not usually a demonstrative man. "How could I not? It will never be for us here fully *our* America. But for our children that were born here . . ." He did not go on—just nodded his head, approving of something.

"The Mozart scores came, *liebchen*. You don't look good."

"We'll go up to San Francisco in the fall. You're right, Hannah, I risked too much. I permitted myself to become emotionally involved." He began to read the top score and hum to himself. Hannah felt sad for her husband. Only the music brought out his humanity and vulnerability. Even the children he claimed to work for, and herself, were only a small part of his life.

As for Enoch, he was riding to Rancho Alvarez and Barnaby was responding to the spur by acting up frisky and threatened to throw him. Enoch was never to become a very skilled rider. As he firmed his grip on the check reins he thought it would be a hell of a note to be thrown off a horse and killed *now*, when everything seems to be going to work out just fine.

8

Enoch's prospective father-in-law, Don Carlos Benito Vlad Valdas Camprodon Zorilla Alvarez, claimed to be descended from one of Cortez's captains, Bernal Diaz del Castillo. As he grew older Don Carlos was given to fat, but he still was magnificent on horseback, taking proper pride in poise, grace, and firmness of his horsemanship. When he appeared on fiesta days in his Old California costume, saddle, palomino horse, and himself hung with silver ornaments, Hannah Winters said he was like a figure out of Cervantes.

As Don Alvarez could hardly read and write—"one once kept monks for that"—he was not impressed when this was reported to him. He had a proper hidalgo's scorn—not actually dislike—of Jews, Protestants and Yankees based merely, he'd explain, "on tradition." For Don Alvarez was a kindly man, a widower long past any interest in women, modest in his wine drinking, and too much the gentleman to bother with the vulgar details of running the rancho as a business, or worrying over the bank's bookkeeping. "It will last my time, Don Solly. They will perhaps bury a beggar, but Jesus waits for me and He loves the poor."

His passion was hunting, and he had killed the last bear within ten miles of El Pueblo, had decimated most of the foxes, went into the mountain for wolf, and had a relish that ruined his figure for wild ducks, geese, venison, eel pies, and roast wild pigs. As for his sons, he demanded only respect and honor. Ramon had run off to sea and was never heard of again, and Diaz—with a desire for seeking profits—had become a serious grape-planter and had set up a winery at Arcadia that in two generations was to produce

68

one of the most popular and poorest of cheap wines, drunk by Skid Row winos and guzzling sots with no taste in bouquets.

Don Alvarez dressed in an already outmoded sober black, with a tight red-and-gold waistcoat, bolo string tie, a Laredo hat and silk shirts (rather worn) with lace cuffs. He bred his own pack of yapping hounds and was still a passable dancer. He went to confession at Father Calidus's church, and gave graciously to the poor what he could not really spare: cornmeal, olives, a sheep now and then that had broken its leg. On his saint's day he had a whole ox roasted in the courtyard. He was not at all the caricature the Yankees saw. "I accept the world, without, as they do, trying to seize it by the ears."

Yet he expected bandits someday, like Tiburcio Vasquez, to rise up in the mountains, produce arms, and drive the Yankees from Southern California. The land would go back to grazing, and the thirty-five thousand acres of good grassland the Yankees had planted would become briar and bush. He had no concept of present history or the growth of the republic and its "Manifest Destiny."

The main hall of the rancho was timbered and had plaster walls. Dominating the hall was a great stone fireplace with the family crest and its motto in tiles, said to have been brought over by the Spanish conquistadors who founded the New World branch.

A fire blazed; two wolfhounds slept near its warmth. In the candlelight Don Alvarez sat at the huge table, Enoch seated across from him. Don Alvarez's expression was serious and a bit lopsided, though he had many of his most vital teeth. He had also had a big supper and drunk an extra two glasses of wine. He wanted to sleep. This damn gringo stud who had been sniffing around his daughter was pointing to a map he had pulled from a saddlebag that now rested on a chair.

"So you see, Don Alvarez, you have a good chance of paying your back taxes, the mortgages the bank holds, the liens on your horse herd. The bonds I offer for the land will increase in value."

"*A mi que?* One of my sons takes care of such details."

"In a few years, as the railroad prospers, the bonds I

will give you for the Stallion Crossing acres will keep your rancho from ruin. If you refuse, soon some American will pick it up for back taxes."

"*Ah Dios, Dios, nada.*"

"It all depends on the railroad's going by that crossing. But if it goes directly through the ridge, your land will have little value. Now as *I* draw the final survey line, I do you a favor."

"You are most direct. To the point, as you say."

"You are right. I want a favor only you can give. Direct enough?"

Don Alvarez pulled on his small, pointed beard, twisted up one end of his fishhook mustache. "Ah, the *true* American touch."

Enoch said earnestly, heavily, "I would like the honor of being one of your family."

Enoch sat back waiting for the explosion. So far things hadn't gone as expected. But now ... the explosion didn't come. Enoch felt his fingernails cut into the palms of his closed fists. What was with the old fart? Was he gone daffy with age? Don Alvarez seemed half-asleep; one hand tapped the table top slowly, lightly.

"You are a foolish young man about some things, Señor Kingston. The hot blood of romance blinds you to the fact that I have known all about you and my daughter's meeting in town."

Enoch felt his skin flush, his brow become hot. Just in town? Christ, they still fight duels, don't they? The wily old bastard might know more. But the half-hooded dark eyes set in their rims of wrinkles gave no hint of all Don Alvarez knew.

"I love Maude, and, well, I know the honor it would be for me to marry into the Alvarez family."

There was a thin smile, not sardonic, just some private reaction on the old man's face. "You are not as much of a fool as I thought. You flatter well. You are also the true Yankee. Frank, honest and—pardon me—crude, hard in your intent."

"I didn't—"

Don Alvarez held up a hand. "And, of course, direct. If you come into the family, the railroad comes by my land at the Crossing. Now, as a descendant of four—not two or three, *four* noble lines and a great family, what shall I do?"

Enoch decided to go whole hog. "A sensible man thinks of his holdings, his heirs, his family's continual existence in the future. Besides—look around about you—I will make a son-in-law better than most available hereabouts."

"*Caramba!* these walls have never heard the like."

Enoch was sweating. Nothing was happening as he had expected. No Latin rage, no long speeches, even after putting the pressure on the prickly old bastard. He was just sitting on his ass, staring with that sleepy expression at Enoch, and his voice was very much under control, even polite, and if not polite, at least correct, calm.

"There was once, Señor Kingston, a Protestant king who was offered the throne of France—Henri IV, I think—on the condition he would join the True Faith."

Enoch said, "I didn't know that."

"And Henri said, 'Why not? Paris is worth a mass.' A practical man thinking, as you put it, of the future.... Yes." The old man seemed to doze off. A log fell away to cherry embers in the fireplace, there was a shower of sparks. A dog—the bitch—lifted her head and thumped her tail on the brown tile floor.

"What is your full name?"

"Enoch. Enoch Bancroft Kingston."

"Yes. So, Enoch, all I ask is that you marry in a church, a Catholic church."

"Of course." He silently let his breath escape his chest.

"You may have to . . . I'm sure—"

"It's all the same to me. I'll go through the rites."

"Yes, Father Calidus will see to that. Now, no more business. I leave it too you—the land matters—as one of the family-to-be." Don Alvarez rose, offered his hand for the first time. "One must move with dignity *but* with the times. All I hope is that my daughter is not deflowered."

Enoch thought, You damn old wily fox.

The wedding was set for August. Twice a week Enoch took lessons, between supervising the lifting of the rails from the holds of sea-beaten ships weathered from their trip around the Horn. He also directed the piling up of ties cut in the mountains, squared off and hauled to special places where the railroad would pass. Between such tasks Enoch, as a would-be convert, went into the cold interior of a country church where a lean old priest who knew no English, *"Lumen Christi,"* and a monk who smelled like rotting clams helped with the translation of the Holy Communion, Sacrament of Penance, and Acts of Contrition Latin texts. Enoch was instructed in knowledge of the Trinity, states of grace, confession, and the power of God's Vicar on earth, who, he learned, was Italian. He was accepted in the Faith one windy, rainy morning. After being dampened and the sign of the cross made over him, in the mixture of candle smoke and Latin, he was a Catholic, and at the following mass the priest intoned, *"Te Igitus Clementissime Pater"* and the monk packed away the ciborium, chalice, and pyx.

Enoch had to admit it all seemed splendid and impressive—the color, the drone of the high-sounding Latin. He felt rather elated at being a follower of Maude's faith and looked more kindly, at least for a time, on mankind and its strange ways.

But Enoch was hardly a man who believed much in the miracles or the spiritual content of his new creed. God, he felt, was for men; priests, dogma, theology, and churches were for women. What he had felt as a convert seeped away with the years, and while he had a personal belief in some grand supreme spirit, mysterious and powerful at times of trial and crisis, he did not follow any organized creed for the rest of his life.

On the festive day of the wedding, El Palacio was done up in colorful hangings. It had been cleaned, painted, and made worthy in some sense of the importance Don Alvarez gave to the wedding. For weeks there had been baking and the collecting of flowers and plants in pots. The courtyard was washed down with casks of water brought from the stream. The carriages, for some years deserted and used as homes by brood hens, were cleaned for the trip to the church; they were revarnished until they shone. The teams were reshod, their hoofs blackened, their tails braided.

Great iron caldrons were brought out; brass was polished. From the huge kitchen the odors of peppers and spices drifted through the house as hens and turkeys died under the ax in a glorious massacre. Cakes were decorated with jams and marzipan and frosting. Concepcion supervised the opening of chests from which damask tablecloths were brought. Silverware was burnished and what was short (for the Alvarezes had been pawning and selling off their plate for a generation) was borrowed from other old families. Three hundred guests were expected, even fifty Yankees—damned Protestants and a few Jews.

The morning of his wedding Enoch had been up at five putting kegs of railroad hook-spikes into locked storage sheds, spikes which would be hammered into the ties to hold the rails in place. He had been recruiting men to swing the five-pound sledges, the mauls that would hammer the spikes into the ties. He was also teaching Mexicans how to work the gantry, the long tool that tamped the ballast—in this case hillside gravel—that, wedged around and under the ties, would make a decent roadbed.

It was Pistol Johnson, now a stockholder and an official in the construction company Enoch was forming, who rousted Enoch away from a newly built supply shed at Twin Wells and got him to the Bella Union for a bath, a close shave by the Negro barber, and some rubbing of an unguent, smelling, as Pistol Johnson said, "like a whore's skirt," into the bridegroom's red hair. Finally he was dressed; the last festive touches were a choke-wing collar, a blue cravat, and a pearl stickpin that Canning had given him.

Enoch was driven to the church wedged in on one side by Pistol Johnson and on the other by Canning. The big man was uncomfortable in the restraint of collar, deerskin waistcoat, buttoned-up Prince Albert coat, striped trousers, and a pair of gray gloves, which he held in one huge hand.

"Jesus, Enoch, I wouldn't dress again like this even if I was being taken out to be hanged. Becky insisted on these duds."

"Now, general," said Pistol Johnson, who took great pride in his dress and wore pale yellow trousers, needle-nosed button shoes and very large ruby cufflinks. "A hanging is more fun, I'd say."

"Shut up, both of you," said Enoch. "No wonder they lost California, these Spaniards and Mexicans. Too much ceremony and dressing up. No time left to work. Hate to dress up."

"You'll do plenty of undressing on your honeymoon," said Pistol Johnson.

Canning moved a hand around his girth, pulled on a gold chain, looked at his watch. "I'm breaking ground, laying the first rail, driving the first spike—a solid silver one from Cerro Gordo mine—on September eighth. So don't go too far away."

Enoch unconsciously wiped his face with his own pair of gray gloves. He felt the actual fantasy of marriage was blotting out his island now; never to drink coconut milk under tall palms, feel the trade winds blow. He'd never see the tropics. All that was the nonsense of a farm boy's visions. He was fulfilling the work ethic of his nation, of its people. The surge and drive that made them cross from the eastern shore and take over a continent. "The Puritan ethic," Hannah Winters had called it. Even as a new-made Catholic, Enoch felt 'a man had to be what he was meant to be,' as his father had written in a letter Enoch once read.

They drove up to the church; the crowd was there, guests and watchers. Enoch's mind somehow came around to the kegs of spikes at Twin Wells; there had been nine kegs listed as deposited there. He had counted only eight.

He felt elbows jammed into each side of his rib cage and hard Philip Phineas Canning's growl, "Come awake, there."

The whole day was a foggy ordeal. He felt it was certainly nothing ever to face again *if* he could help it. The people he knew and didn't know, dressed to the nines, were all smiling. Hannah and Sol Winters, also the hay supplier, three of the town's biggest merchants, a ship builder, two undertakers, the head blacksmith and horse shoer of the Canning lines, the manager of the Bella Union, and Buffum himself of Buffum's Saloon. The better-dressed gamblers, the biggest land agents, and the still solvent, or nearly so, ranch owners and holders of now dubious land grants. Also many of Maude's relatives, near relatives, people important among the old Spanish and Mexican families of California; some even from Chihuahua, Coahuel Nuevo, Tamalpais.

The organ was playing and the priest and his assistants waited before the high altar. Enoch found himself standing, attended by Canning. In a glory of silver and black, Don Alvarez entered with Maude on his arm, and Concepcion, wearing her silver earrings with the blue stones, was close behind arranging the train of Maude's yellow lace gown. Enoch nearly laughed as Maude kicked out to drive Concepcion off as one would a too-friendly dog.

Maude was by his side, her face half-covered by a veil, her mouth very firm with just a touch of amusement. She pinched him with a gloved hand, and he heard her repress a giggle, that hard, amused sound she saved for moments when she had to control herself, as she put it, "so I don't wet myself."

The ceremony seemed to rush past Enoch, but it still set him damp inside his clothes. He made some responses when Canning nudged him. Wine was held up to sip, a hand was lifted and traced a symbol in the air. *"Deus, Pater, et Filius et Spiritus Sanctus."* The organ sounds swelled up and Enoch could hear the murmur of people in approval of the thing done in full view. Maude's veil was lifted and they leaned together to kiss; for just a moment she darted a bit of her tongue into a corner of his mouth, her expression poker-faced. Ceremony wasn't changing Maude. Through music and well-wishers, they walked out to a carriage. Some children crowded around, and the coachman swung his whip at their naked legs.

Then it was a ride out to El Palacio where the whole rancho of workers and horsemen and other guests all joined in greetings and good wishes. *"Salud, Ingles!"* while the band and their stringed instruments went into cheerful music, the horn players blaring out loud enough to worry the horses. The courtyard was filled with flowers and festive tables, the hall held more tables, and the ballroom shone, having been waxed by shaving candles and walking over the floor in woolen slippers for two days. Here was another band. Trays of *entremeses variados* appeared, and there was the roasting smell of sheep and steers basting over piñon charcoal logs in pits dug near the olive trees.

Enoch wanted to tear off his collar, unbutton his clothes. But the dancing had begun, and it was all part of the ritual, tradition. Maude's brothers, already brandied, were pressing their dark faces and thin moustaches at the bride. They were handsome in their red belly-bands, trousers split at the ankles and stitched with silver and gold.

The drinking was heavy—wine and brandies. Canning had sent over ten cases of champagne for those who felt superior to mere booze. Enoch drank. He danced with his bride, who nibbled at his ears and kept spinning him around and saying, "Poor Enoch, poor Enoch, was it *that* bad?" He kept twisting her around while the band pounded heels into the floor as they played.

He said, "You just wait until I get you alone."

Maude rolled her head, and the great coral comb in her hair shook the black lace over it as she answered, "Yankee bragging."

When it was dark and the more affected of the drinkers had been hauled off to beds or to their carriages, and the gluttons had lifted their faces from great pies, and cuts of beef with the rib bones still attached—from the *carne asado* and *sesos de ternera*, Don Alvarez stood with his sons and first cousins by the grand staircase. And he looked, Canning admitted "every inch the noble, the real stuff" among the peasants, the *gitanos* and the bowing gentry. Don Alvarez lifted a fluted glass of amber wine over his head, and two rings redeemed from a pawnshop just that morning gleamed on his fingers. His voice was calm and just a bit husky. It hushed the people still munching marzipan and *manzanas en dulce*.

"This is a new time, and we in this land are now people of two parts becoming one. A toast to all here, and may happiness be the glory of my daughter and her husband and her brood to come. Thank you, my guests. *Le agradezco mucho*."

Pistol Johnson suggested a toast "To our friend and historical figure, Don Alvarez."

Canning held up a glass. "To progress and the greatness of the nineteenth century."

One of the uncles of the bride toasted the true faith, beauty and the family loyalty.

Sol Winters said in his firm but thin voice, "To all those here that we do love and hold dear—and to the two fine, happy people."

Don Alvarez, who had been toasting steadily and returning toasts since the trip back from the church, waved an arm gracefully and took up a filled glass. "To one who rules the nation. Señors and Señoritas, I offer and drink a toast to the President of the United States, under whose kindly gaze we shall all prosper in this world." (A few close relatives winked at each other—the old bastard is getting sardonic.) Don Alvarez was helped away. The band went into wilder tunes.

Enoch and Maude had slipped away a half hour before Don Alvarez's final toast, outwitting the youths on horseback who were waiting with pans and horns to shivaree the newlywed couple on their way. A buggy with two buckskins harnessed to it was down by the pear trees, and a trusted house servant held the horses nervously moving about under an attack of biting flies.

Maude had changed into a blue velvet traveling outfit with a pert little hat. Enoch had on a white linen duster and a planter's wide-brimmed hat. He got the reins firmly in his hands, shouted to the servant to let go the horses— pronto! The buggy seemed to float down the trail that led south. They were going to a rancho outside the town of Laguna that belonged to a merchant and importer, Jules Silverthorn, Hannah Winters's distant cousin.

That ranch had a guest house on the shore bluff. It was cool that night, and the window drapes fluttered as the couple moved into each other's arms, as ardent, the bride hoped, as they had been all the months before the wedding. Enoch said it would be grand if they could conceive their first child right there. Maude smiled and bit his shoulder lightly and said that couldn't be possible as she was *already* two months pregnant.

For a moment Enoch looked down on his wife's head,

her hair spread fanlike across the pillow, her eyes studying his reaction, the mouth amused. He felt, what-the-hell, life was one damn thing after another, and proceeded with the business of being a husband.

9

At high noon the September day burned brightly over San Pedro Harbor and seemed particularly luminous on a group gathered around a flag-draped section of the Canning wharf of Wilmington. Almost everyone within miles who was not bedridden and could get away was packed along the shore to watch events. For the Los Angeles & San Pedro Railroad was about to begin construction right there by the wharf. Ties of smooth redwood had been laid out, and now a crew of ten men was hoisting a length of rail in place, the men grunting and smiling, shaved and in clean clothes—for this was an almost sacred ceremony.

Enoch pushed past to the main platform of the dignitaries. Some had came from as far away as San Diego, one even from San Francisco. Enoch shoved his way to where Philip Phineas Canning stood, large and uncomfortable in a tight bottle-green jacket with gold buttons and a tall dark brown hat. In his hands was a long-headed sledgehammer. A second rail was brought up to the ties.

"Damn it, general, you promised to inquire—what *gauge* is your locomotive going to be?"

"What's that to do with it now?" Canning bowed to the mayor, to his own wife Becky, Mrs. Kingston, the Winterses, and to several other well-dressed people who were there to see him drive the first spike into a hole already drilled in the redwood tie at his feet. "Why in damnation bother me with that now, Enoch?"

"Because, goddamn it, I can't delay the spacing of the track any longer. Is it narrow gauge or wide gauge?"

"What difference does it make? Track is track."

"I've explained a dozen times. It means we have to separate the rails at a proper regular distance so that the wheels will run on the rails, not *off* them. Narrow usually is a foot narrower—closer together. Standard gauge is four feet, eight and a half inches—that is standard mostly in the East."

"It's a locomotive of the type used by the Natchez and Hawsberry Railroad."

Enoch cursed a good bit—and he knew how to from working with mules. He decided he would measure off as if the expected locomotive was on narrow gauge, and he'd have to check to see what measured-off span was being used on the four coaches and freight carriers Canning was building. Natchez, as he remembered, wasn't much of a town, or worthy of wide gauge. He marked off a measuring stick and got the waiting men to lay rail for narrow gauge.

Meanwhile two bands were playing and children were underfoot. It was a warm day growing warmer, and out in the harbor two sailboats were tacking; the waves were cresting a bit but seemed too lazy to exert themselves. Gulls drifted by, red winged hawks circled low, and on the Canning wharf sheds buzzards in residence sat unmoving.

Enoch wiped his hands clean and went over to Maude, who was seated with Don Alvarez and Spanish-named pioneer families. Enoch hadn't yet quite been able to feel she was really his wife, but now, standing with Don Alvarez, a bondholder of the L.A. & S.P. R.R., Maude's brothers, and Spanish-Mexican rancho owners, he felt he belonged to this society—all of it: the town bankers, cattlemen, merchants, shopkeepers, land dividers, speculators, madams, saloon owners—even farmers gathered outside the platform. Pistol Johnson waved to him, lifting a square derby imported from England, a new style, the rage among the sporting gentry.

Enoch asked Maude if she was comfortable on the chairs set out by Drood and Paulkenstone, the popular Fourth Street undertakers.

Maude said, "Open my sunshade. You've gotten grease on your shirt cuffs."

He kissed one of Maude's ears, and as he did, Concepcion slapped his back. "In public, *amigo*?"

Don Alvarez leaned grandly on a slim cane with a silver hound's head handle. "The general should *delegate* the driving of the first spike. That's what servants are for, one does not do such a thing oneself. But I suppose it's the way things will be. We shall be doing manual tasks ourselves soon."

"That's right, Don Alvarez. Make a sport of it," Enoch nodded. His father-in-law was a windbag, he had decided, and a nod and a word would keep him satisfied. The sardonic old bastard was seeing himself as being important again in the community now that he could casually say, "Yes, I have bonds in the new railroad. What can one do? *Lo dicho dicho* . . . it is called the progress."

A team of horses, frightened by some dropped iron, ran away, the crowd scattering before their mad rush—skirts and petticoats seeming to fall from the shaken-open carriage. But it was only two ladies, and they were not hurt. Some boys caught the horses, but the carriage had lost two wheels and lay lopsided on the road.

The two bands had exhausted their limited catalog of newly learned music, and one was playing a marching song while the other played *"The Battle Hymn of the Republic."* Some teamsters were firing pistols over the stacked railroad ties where a keg of whisky and a tin dipper were cached for the work crew that had now placed the second rail on the lines Enoch had drawn for them in chalk on the ties. A sawmill to the south of the pier that Canning owned began to sound its steam siren at a given signal.

Canning stood with the spike maul in his hands waiting for the solid silver spike he would drive in—an act that would officially open the construction of the first rail-line. People heard him yell, "Where the devil is the goddamn silver spike?"

Enoch went down to find that the spike had indeed disappeared. What one of the construction gang was holding up was an ordinary iron spike covered with tinfoil from the lining of a tea chest.

Canning whispered to Enoch, "Some no good sonofabitch stole the solid silver spike. What kind of a railroad are we building?"

"It's all right, general. It was only silver-plated anyway. Go ahead." Enoch placed the foil-wrapped spike in the hole already half-drilled in the tie.

Canning lifted the sledge, found his coat binding, took it off, and waved cheerfully at the cheering crowd. "Folks, I like comfort, and I like what we're doing here. We're starting to place Southern California into railroad history. Los Angeles and San Pedro Railroad, you are *now* in business!"

In his shirt sleeves, pink arm-garters above the elbows, legs apart, he swung and the spike sank a bit. Two more blows and it was in. The crowd cheered and some horses reared but didn't bolt, for men and boys were hanging onto their bridles. Hand clapping continued. The work crew began to drive in more spikes. People gathered in knots to inspect the steel rails and the redwood ties; others opened their food hampers.

Canning wiped his face, handed Enoch the maul. "Hot work."

"Twenty-one miles to go," Enoch said, "if we get the rails."

Canning got back into his long-tailed jacket. "A mile and a half a week, eh?" He spoke cheerfully, buttoning up his coat.

"It depends, general, on how much rail and kegs of spikes the ships bring in."

"Hell, we'll forge the spikes *here* if we have to. And I'm cutting timber for the ties faster than it grows in the mountains. Now let's gather up the families and all go to the Bella Union for a little demon rum."

Enoch said he couldn't stay long. It was some sort of saint's day at the Alvarez Rancho; "Celebrating with roast suckling pig and the baptizing of some newborn babies."

"Damn it, Enoch, you'll be kissing monks' knuckles soon ... I see Mrs. Kingston is carrying. Nice and high. Means a boy for sure."

Maude was certainly carrying. High or not, the belly grew in the little house on Olive Street they rented for fifteen dollars a month. They were served by a Mexican-Indian maid, Caro, and a Chinese cook, Chow Lei. The rafters of the little house creaked, and at night Maude would wake him in the warm darkness to asked earnestly, "Am I getting ugly? Am I clumsy?"

"No, no, you're just like always."

"This weight is dragging me down. I can't ride. I get the early morning sickness. Oh, the marriage has ruined me."

"Maude, face up. Millions of women have babies. And anyway, this one was begun before we were married."

"Don't sleep, Enoch. Don't you *dare* sleep. I want to talk."

"I've got a hard day ahead—a construction company to set up. We'll talk at breakfast."

"You're gone when I get up for breakfast."

He loved her very much, and they made love, she more ardent and demanding than ever. And sad, too; she had been spoiled by everyone all her life, and thought of herself as special. But she was intelligent enough to sense that as Enoch's wife she was now in a situation different from what her life had been, and would never be again. It was at such times she felt that her body had betrayed her. Weeping, she would wake Enoch to hear him reassure her he still would love her no matter how ugly and heavy she got, and that their love for each other would never change. Even when he swore to the truth of all this, she would still nudge him. "Say it as if you *mean* it. Wake up fully. Open your eyes. Say it all with *conviction.*"

"I'm saying it. With conviction, damn it!"

"Darling, I'm frightened of what's happening to my body. Love, me, love me."

So Enoch would love her and in the morning awaken still sleepy. Not until Chow Lei had handed him the big pint bowl of very black coffee—Java beans fresh ground —did he shake the night of sleeping and waking and promising to love and love. Then he'd hurry out to the buckboard and gray horse and go out to stir up the work crews.

He was beginning to get again what he called "railroad fever." All that seemed to matter was getting scrapers to level off stretches of roadway, ties to be put down, rails carried and placed, then checking with a measuring stick to be sure the gauge was right. He was more than a bondholder. He was also a contractor. Enoch had talked it over with Sol Winters, and Sol had explained it seemed best to operate in the way Huntington and his partners did with the Central Pacific. They had made themselves outside companies as contractors and suppliers. The L.A. &

S.P. R.R. would give the job of building the line to a contractor, in this case Enoch Bancroft Kingston, who had formed the KINGSTON CONSTRUCTION COMPANY and gotten the contract. He was to set rail supplied by the WILMINGTON SUPPLY COMPANY, jointly owned by the Canning Freighting & Stage Lines and Winters's bank. The president was Percy (Pistol) Johnson, the vice president Enoch Kingston. Their lawyer (and also a bond holder) was Charles Auden (Chalky) White, who fortified Enoch's ideas by explaining the legal advantages of having three companies independent of each other, and yet interlocking as to mutual interests and controls.

Chalky drank, having, it was rumored, left a wife and gambling debts in London. Chalky's office was in the bank building. It contained pictures of Queen Victoria, Virginia Woodhull, *and* Thomas Jefferson. The law books were bound in now-decaying calf, attacked by certain California insects called silverfish. Chalky looked a great deal like William Shakespeare, only thinner.

In his office, as he sat smoking a bent-stemmed pipe, he told Enoch, "Legally, Enoch, each company is a unit, and any debts, lawsuits, injunctions, and other turmoils involving one or the other, no one can get a case or judgment against all three blokes. . . . Now, about shares and bonds, and voting and nonvoting stocks. But that's Solly's worry. You have a copy."

Enoch was careful to try and understand the various complications Chalky White had written out in the flowing script of a clerk he had brought down from Winnipeg in Canada. There were copies made on an ancient letterpress. Enoch wanted every point set down and fully explained. Canning trusted by a handshake. Enoch didn't.

Once he had a sign painted—KINGSTON CONST. CO.—Enoch had two hundred men divided into three gangs, and the work went on from the Avalon section of Wilmington on the port—this would be the southern end of the line. The work moved north, digging, grading, setting out the ties. The baulks were still that fine salmon-pink color redwood has before it weathers. Then the rails moved in over the ties, carried first on men's shoulders until Enoch had great grappling hooks made like large ice tongs, so the men could carry rails quicker and not have to lift the steel too high. Even so, there were two hernias; the men were made watchmen. The major delay was the irregular arrival of the sailing ships bringing rails around the Horn. Storm, shipwreck, and seamen failure could be expected. The Bessemer converters at the Nashua, New Hampshire rail-forging plant had to get the rails down to a New England port. The sailing ships were buffeted about by wind and water, and never could know how many icy, blizzardy tries they had to make to get through the Straits of Magellan, and what Pacific hurricane might not merely delay them, but sink them off Chile or Panama.

The construction car pulled by mules followed the work of spiked-down rails. Enoch found all turned to him for decisions and solutions. By December it was clear to anyone visiting the work gangs that things were going too slowly. Iron came from too far away in the shapes they needed, and Canning, while loud and excitable, was not a railroad man. Rails were not mules, and ridges to be leveled were not coaches.

New Year's Eve, Canning gave a great dinner in his Wilmington mansion. Midnight came as expected and all greeted the new year. Canning's temper was short. He smiled too much and forced drinks too often on his guests. Toasts were made, promises outlined, and singing took over. Later in the library (few books), Canning spoke to the men sipping brandy.

"Eighteen sixty-nine," he said, as the grandfather clock in the hallway donged out one o'clock in the morning. From the dining room, women's voices could be heard saying it was getting late. "It's going to be a fine year," Canning announced. "Soon we'll be riding in luxury coaches. Teak, Turkish walnut, red plush. Riding the entire final length of the L.A. and S.P. Railroad."

"How soon?" asked Pistol Johnson.

"It'd better be soon." Sol Winters inspected an unlit cigar in his hand. "Everything going out, nothing coming in. Crops, steers, fruit, silver bullion waiting to be shipped. Eh? What's the delay?"

Enoch was drawing fishtail rail-joints in the wine spills on the table. He could have these joints forged by local blacksmiths for those places where the rails needed snugger fastenings and rigidity over filled land. He looked up to find the people at the table staring at him. He remembered Maude was not present. She felt a holy terror at sight of herself, she said, *so* bloated. Her time was near, and she was looking "like I'm one of those captive balloons at the farmers fair in Riverside." At times Enoch felt it was a damn poor system for reproducing the race. God was no practical engineer; that was for sure.

"What?" Enoch asked, back again at New Year's Eve at Canning's.

"We want to know just how much track is actually down," said Pistol Johnson. Like most gamblers, he was not as calm as he looked.

"Oh." Enoch looked at Canning. "General, you have my figures."

Canning refused the hot potato. "Enoch, as contractor for our construction projects, what's the mileage laid down, as of *now*?"

"We're closing in on four miles of laid trackage."

Pistol Johnson shook his head sadly. "I drove out in a buggy this morning. I'd guess you're only three miles north of Wilmington at the end of rails."

Enoch knew that as well as Pistol Johnson did.

"The right-of-way is finished; the ties are down for miles. We're just waiting for the rails to arrive in port on the *Jenny Almont*. It's ten spikes to a rail, and four hundred rails to a mile—remember that!"

"Three miles," said Sol Winters, "in nearly four months. That means a year or more at this rate before we reach Los Angeles. We'll all be ruined by then."

"No, no," said Enoch. "It's only the shortages, *not* work problems. I've eighty men grading. I've got horse and mule scrapers and plows smoothing down grades, I've good spikers and bolters. We've got a raised roadway ready for rails eleven miles from Los Angeles right now. I've got twenty six thousand railroad ties in place, but I'm short about six thousand rails."

Sol Winters decided not to smoke the cigar. "I read in the *San Diego Union*—my cousin Silverthorn sent it along to me—what they write about us is this: 'Canning and Kingston haven't got a real harbor. They still have to build a real one at San Pedro and clear the bar to the general's goose pond at Wilmington. It would be much cheaper for all of Southern California to build a railroad line to San Diego where there is a real honest-to-God harbor.' "

Canning waved off the newspaper clipping held out to him. "The hell with these pipsqueaks. They want to connect with the Central Pacific some day coming south and have the C.P. bypass us, so San Diego can become the major southern port."

There was a whispering at the doors to the library. Enoch saw it was the Mexican maid, Caro. She was pouring out Spanish sounds at a great rate and pointing at Enoch, while the Canning houseman (only Becky Canning dared call him the butler) was trying to hold the maid back.

"Señor! Señor! You cum!"

Enoch rose. "My wife must be in labor."

"Señor, first baby cummin'."

Enoch said, "Pardon me," and put down his cigar on the mahogany surface of the table and rushed out. Pistol Johnson picked up the smoldering cigar and placed it in a bronze tray. It had, however, already charred the surface of the highly polished table. . . .

Enoch's son Ralston (after Enoch's long-dead father) Alvarez (after his wife's family), Kingston, was born at 2:34 in the morning on New Year's Day, January 1, 1869. It was not a hard birth. "Not for the man," Concepcion added, when told that by the midwife. "Never is for the man."

When Enoch went in to his wife, Maude seemed drawn and very tired. He kissed her damp brow. She pressed his hand hard, closed her eyes, whispered, "A boy. We made a boy."

Enoch saw him in the light of two oil lamps that lit up the bedroom. The walls appeared to be all bloody, for the flowered pattern of intertwining roses seemed to leap indecently from the walls to mix with the smell which he thought of as *sickly, womanly.*

Concepcion held up a twitching lump of red meat—a little like the muskrats he used to skin as a boy. It rested, brick-red on a folded sheepskin. "Eh? *eh*? Look at the parts. Already is *mucho* a man."

10

Hannah Winters writes to her sister in St. Louis:

May 15, 1869
Dear Netta:

You ask details of a typical evening to show you
why I lament so often in my letters. While we here
are still without a railroad, there have been suppers
celebrating the fact that the Pacific coast now is tied
to the East by rails. When the Central Pacific hurrying westward met the Union Pacific, it was at some
godforsaken place called Promontory Point on the
10th—but I'm sure you've all heard of it. Here it was
like the end of a great war. The news was brought
down to us from San Francisco as if it were Jeho-
vah's tablets from Zion, and the Huntington, Crocker,
Stanford, Hopkins cabal were to some guests we
had—as Sol put it, like "a new Moses carrying down
holy writ." So San Francisco is connected by rail to
the East; it's an achievement. But in Los Angeles we
still use ships—a dreadful paddle wheeler, as I recall
our last three-day trip to San Francisco—or the even
worse ride on the stagecoach, inns dominated by bed-
bugs, reeking of rancid fried pork; and as for the
habits of the traveling frontier yahoos, they spit and
belch and break wind, and put food in their mouths
with their knives, so you wonder they still have ears
and noses. End of a journey, *ich bin ganz ab.*

One of our guests was the Mr. Canning who is
building our niggardly little railroad—from the harbor two dozen or so miles away from our town, or as
Canning calls it, *our* city. It has a lot to learn yet—
beyond its prurient promiscuity—to be a city, believe

me. Dogs in the hundreds roam the streets at night, howling and mating, so like the tough rapacious crowd drunk on *aguardiente*—a grape brandy—that congregates nightly in the bordellos, grog shops and gambling hells in the Calle de los Negros district. I sometimes wish Sol had decided on London or Paris to set himself up as a merchant and banker. But he had great faith in this wild and usually too dry landscape. I used to despair in our early days here. He saw it as a garden spot, someday, with railroads coming from a dozen directions, making it a city with a great civilizing and merchandising junction.

Canning just smiles or raises his voice. He is a simple man, direct, has a mindless determination, but he gets things done with a peasant cunning. Not what *I* would call a deep thinker, but with a lively curiosity. He said at supper the Central Pacific will have to come to us. He swears a great deal, but tones it down in front of women. His wife is a dreadful snob, a face like a blancmange, *claims* descent from every important event in American history except the stoning to death of witches in Salem. Canning said, "If others can build a thousand miles of railroads across a continent, we can certainly get a move on and finish *our* railroad. The Union Pacific moved west g–d–fast, and the Central Pacific met them, and even if they had to go up into mountains eight thousand feet high. Why, they roofed fifty miles of roadbed in the snow with timbers, and *they* had trestles to build. Why are *we* so slow, Enoch?"

This to Enoch Kingston, who has the contract to build the road. He is the most interesting of the men involved with Sol in this project. He has a shy, silent quality usually—a held-back sagacity—until he speaks up. He is handsome in a solid, simple way. In his early twenties, I suppose. Big and *rather* clumsy among delicate furniture. I gather he is self-educated, or not educated at all. But he reads and borrows some of my books. There is a side to him of some ambiguity and irony that seems to take to literature. So rare here that at first I doubted him when he claimed to have read *Vanity Fair, Rodrick Random,* and some of Balzac. I had no idea Balzac was in translation. He *doesn't* share my enthusiasm for Walt Whitman; he thinks Whitman "half a white minstrel nigger show-off and half horse–s–." He blushed after he realized what he had said.

Anyway, when this Canning continued to pontificate—a man liking his own voice—he turned a claret color as his skin flushes when he gets angry—he said, "Why are we so slow?" Enoch Kingston pointed out that up north they had some big Chinese work gangs "that really hustle and keep going all day, with no drunkards or loafers among 'em. They laid nearly four hundred miles of track without a hitch, keeping their graders working fifty miles ahead. I have to watch our s–o–b–s so they don't take a nap or start a card game."

(You see the kind of society I am *forced* to entertain if this is what I write about—our *Junkerschaft*.)

Canning got to pounding the table, upsetting a wineglass on Tante Selma's gift, our best tablecloth. "They were laying rail two and three-quarter miles a day, even stringing telegraph wire. You know what the record day was?"

Poor Sol, trying to change the conversation, said, "Yes, yes. Don't get a heart attack, Phil." But nothing can stop Canning. His wife just sits, expressionless. "In Salt Lake Valley they laid *ten* miles of track in *one* day. Two hundred forty feet of rail in one minute, fifteen seconds. And how many men placed rail for that one day's record? No thousands of Chinks. Just eight *white* men."

Enoch Kingston just smiled a bit. He knows by now Canning is a man who lets steam escape—as Sol puts it—through his mouth.

"We'll celebrate, too, when our final ties are laid completing the line. Got one just like the one they used at Promontory Point, Utah. This here tie I'm saving is California laurel wood, six feet and a half long, six inches square. And I'm having a new solid silver spike made."

Sol whispers, "Silver-plated," and we all go into the drawing room. I call it a drawing room; they say *par-*

lor here. Sol plays some Mozart on his cello, his bank manager MacIntosh assists him on a silver flute, aided by Enoch Kingston's wife on the spinet. Yes, my fellow literary browser is married. Mrs. Kingston is a dark beauty, rather pert, spoiled by her background in a social stratum of a Spanish land-grant family that takes pride in Iberian blood lines. But I suspect a bit of Indian in the woodpile. Such, dear sister, is one of our gala nights brought to an end by coffee and mandel cakes at ten o'clock, when Sol puts out the lamps on an evening of life and gossip in El Pueblo de Los Angeles, and I go to bed after plucking out my first gray hair (one).

Sol works *too* hard on this railroad project. His color is bad, and I suggest we go to Europe next year and try Marienbad to drink the waters. But he says, "Look, Hannah, my *sheyneh*, the next few years are the vital ones. Americans stay at home to develop their own country; they don't gallivant around at spas or go looking at old churches." I could scream when he talks like these local *holzkopfs*, but I don't. The children are fine. David rides well, but *why* a boy of ten should be trusted on a half-tamed horse I don't know, but Sol insists. Trudy is losing her last baby teeth, and I cry like any sentimental mother and save them in a little silver box. I'm getting old at *too* early an age, I feel. I shall wither and dry out here in some vague indescribable malaise in what they call the Santa Ana blows, a hot, debilitating wind from the deserts. Some day I'll wake up and *discover* I'm seventy years old. Netta, is St. Louis *so* repellent, *so* boring? As far as I am from the beautiful, the artistic things of this world? Forgive your sister's self-pitying mood, this *Klagelied.*

Han.

PS. Now that there are steam cars running to the Pacific coast and carrying cargo, *please* send along any new Dickens and translations of Victor Hugo. Enoch Kingston had never read him, so I can share this with him. There isn't a copy of *Madame Bovary* in town. Send books by the new rails to San Francisco, marked *To be delivered by the Butterfield Coach Line* that comes down the coast to us. This will save the time of their coming around the Horn, or getting burned by red savages, or lost by some freight wagon turning turtle crossing a river.

Hannah Winters was not the only one who saw the feuding attitudes that began to dominate the relationship of Canning and Enoch. It was no open break. In fact, as Sol Winters pointed out to his wife, this badgering by Canning and needling back by Enoch seemed to speed the work on the rail-line. The completion of the transcontinental tracks up north—after seven years of effort—had been a goad, an inspiration to the Kingston work crews, hearing of the speed and skill of the Chinese and Irish work brigades of the Central Pacific and Union Pacific. It increased their own rate of work. But, as Enoch observed, "only for a few days." Still, as he mapped the progress of graders, tie-layers and rail-placers, there was progress towards Los Angeles. The problem as he saw it was to balance the slow supply of rails and ties with the movement of the work forward. Too often they sat among wild plum and hardwood brush and waited for some ship to unload needed rails brought by the passage over two oceans. So work crews loafed, sat smoking, engaged in fist fights, lied about fornications and their epic drunks.

11

The June day began cloudy, but by noon the sun had dissipated the white curtain that hid the progress, or lack of it,
of the rail-line from the sea into Los Angeles. Two tran-
quil tramps walking along that part of the roadbed on
which wooden ties had been laid had stopped under some
live oak trees to light up the remains of some cigars they
had picked up in their passage through the town. They
were travel worn, known locally as gristle-heels. The white
man was in a particularly tattered state of ruin. Boots broken, toes showing, the long-tailed greasy coat rather comical, the collarless blue shirt sweat-stained and showing
rents. He had not shaved for some time, and already a
scratchy beard was forming. The Negro tramp was
neater—at least he had used needle and soap. He carried
in a sling across one shoulder a bindle, which was a blanket tied up with heavy cord. He was wearing a straw hat
with a cut-down brim, boots once of sporting nature in
two tones of brown, but with cuts and slits made in the
sides to ease the feet larger than the boots.

They sat casually, listlessly, in the manner of homeless
men, sat under the trees on some piled-up ties, smoking
with the ease of drifters who had to make themselves
comfortable wherever they were, their posture and condition suggesting that they didn't expect more and didn't
care to make much effort to change things. They watched
some quail strutting about and a white-tailed deer leap a
fallen tree.

The Negro pointed up track where a large man carrying a surveying standard and an armful of stakes was
moving slowly along enjoying the day, followed by a boy
carrying survey chains and a roll of maps.

"Maybe we can mooch a handout."

The white man reamed one of his ears with a long-nailed finger. "Construction crews are mean bastards."

The surveyor looked over as he drew near them and tried to pass by without any greeting.

The Negro smiled, rose. "You care to stake us to some dinner vittles? Just two sojers going home."

"Bullshit," said the man. "War has been over a long, long, spell."

"You ever were a soldier, Mac?" asked the white man tossing his cigar fragment down.

"More than you were by the looks of you. And put the butt out. Those wooden sleepers cost money."

"Don't mean no harm," said the Negro, adjusting the bindle over his shoulder. "No harm at *tall*."

The surveyor seemed to change his mind. "You 'boes want some breakfast, go down track about a mile. The work crews been bunking there. Sam the cook can always use some dishwashers and weed-choppers."

"Mighty white of you for the tip," said the Negro, and he laughed at what he had said. He and his comrade went walking down track, moving slowly along the laid-out ties. At a place where the ground dipped a bit too much, they came to a work crew unloading broken rock from carts, and a half mile further on they came to the rail-layers. Two dozen men were lifting rail from a flatcar hitched to mules. Beyond were some unpainted shacks and lean-tos, the kind that could be dismantled and moved on as rails were laid.

A pine board on a shack read:

CONSTRUCTION COMPANY PROPERTY KEEP OFF
OFFICE

"Might as well ask for work," said the white man.

They went past a rough board door into an office where a young man with a very extended set of dark mutton-chop whiskers was rolling up three-foot-long survey maps marked with blue pencil and red ink.

"No jobs," he said. "No jobs at all."

"I know engines," said the white man, "Right down to fire-brick."

"Got no engine. Expect one any day."

"We'll stick around till she comes."

The Negro added, "Don't want no one to spoil your engine what don't know engines."

The young man fluffed up his whiskers and sniffed the air as if the two tramps smelled bad. They did, his nose told him. "Better move on before the mean-tusked sheriff gets here and—"

The back door to the office opened. A large man wearing a waterproof cape and a railroad cap came in. His muddy canvas pants were stuffed into riding boots a bit too elegant for a work camp.

"Mister," said the white tramp, trying to hide a smile. "Kin I talk to you?"

"Go see Sam in the cook tent. He'll fix you up some grub. We're not hiring. Better move on."

The white man said, "Where to? We were maybe in the war together, you, me, *him*." He pointed to the Negro. "Vicksburg, thereabouts?"

Enoch turned to get a better look at the tramps. He handed the young man with the whiskers a folder of papers. "Take these right away to Mr. Johnson, back at the lumber depot."

"Yes, sir, Mr. Kingston. Right away, sir." The young man went out.

The white man was laughing, his open mouth showing where a few teeth were missing. "Yes, *sir*, Mr. Kingston."

"Right away, *sir*, Mr. Kingston," said the Negro, taking off his straw hat, making a mock shuffle on the rough dirt floor.

Enoch smiled and shook his head in disbelief. "Uncle Floyd! Jasper! I'll be a sawed-off pump handle if I ever expected to hear from either of you again. I thought you were shot, Uncle Floyd. Or hanged."

"They tried, sure tried that court-martial. All officers in gold braid and polished swords with tassels. Oh, all proper Articles of War, they said."

"They said shoot 'im by some Act of War," said Jasper, moving around the table and the maps pinned on the walls. "They said get up a firing squad and put 'im against a wall. Give 'im time to pray—then *bang!*"

Floyd nodded. "But there was this here colonel and major among the military judges sittin' on my case. I sort of whispered to them between sessions before they were voting."

Jasper said, "Mr. Floyd, he had been payin' cotton money into their banks, you see, and to their wives and relatives, too; they got a share of those contraband bales."

"So, not to stretch the facts out," Floyd spread his dirty hands palms up. "I got ten years, and it was arranged by the colonel I was to escape from the train taking me to prison. You understand?"

"I think I do. Now, you're hungry?" asked Enoch. "Bet you are." He took a flat pint of whisky from a saddlebag hung on a peg. "Wet your whistles first. Goddamn it, it's good to see you both. It was a mean time for all of us. And after. Was for me for a while."

"Hell, Ennie, we ain't wearin' diamonds ourselves." Uncle Floyd's Adam's apple bobbed up and down as he took a long swallow of whisky, sighed, and wiped his mouth with the back of his hand before passing the pint on to Jasper. "It was nip and tuck for me for some time. Some fool of a Pinkerton man felt I was a real fugitive; I had to kill the feller with a ball-peen hammer. And out in Kansas I come across this black boy, standing at a country fair with his head stuck through a hole in some canvas, and people were throwing baseballs at him, trying to dash his brains out."

"It was a mean livin'," said Jasper, drinking. "Ah, that's prime corn pressin's. We teamed up, me and Mr. Floyd, tried for jobs on the Caycee and Ohio, but the Pinkertons were too nosy about some killin', so we just worked in the fields, barley-buckin', lumber-scowin'. And we figures this place got no winter out here, so we come along with a buffalo hide crew. We musta skinned a million buffalo just for the hide."

Enoch was rummaging in a closet and tossing out a pair of overalls, a jacket of blue canvas, a leather waistcoat. "Here, I'll get you both more gear. Now let's go find the cook and get his nose out of a law book. He wants to be a lawyer. Spoil a damn fine cook."

"You're doin' fine, Ennie, doin' fine, I can see that," said his uncle taking back the flask. "Filled out a lot. Where did that skinny farm kid go to? And building a railroad? I'll be a ring-tailed sonofabitch if I ever expected that from the scarebooger rube, all bones and no meat on him. Remember, Jasper?"

"I don't forget much, Mr. Floyd."

"I'm married. You'll meet Maude. Have a son, too, a regular buster."

"Don't want to be no bother," said Jasper, looking at Floyd finishing off the bottle. "I learned blacksmithin' and things like cogs and gears."

"We're getting some kind of a teakettle of a locomotive by ship. I have a half-assed riverboat engineer of steam engines, but no real locomotive man. Floyd, you and Jasper can maybe be crew."

Uncle Floyd pretended he didn't notice the dropping of the word *uncle* by Enoch. "Be right glad to help out, Ennie. Wouldn't we, Jasper?"

"Don't need no begging us."

Later, as Enoch watched the two men eat, he thought, *it can't be the same world. There is, of course, a connection someplace, but it isn't very real. Uncle Floyd—in his mind if not speech, he was still an uncle—he isn't at all the great big wild and wonderful cock on the manure pile I thought he was. Just a Weary Willie tramp, down on his luck. Conniving and stealing back there in the war. Just for a few hundred bales of cotton. No Jay Gould or Jim Fisk; those were the big thieves. Uncle Floyd was just picking up shavings from the big logs.*

Jasper seemed improved. He spoke better; he carried himself even in his lousy rags as if he knew the worth of himself. But then, Jasper always had a good head on him.

In the mess hall the cook put down a platter of fried porkchops and a stack of wheats, and pushed the jug of honey closer to the two men as Enoch encouraged them to eat. The cook said, Clap yourselves around these. I'll heat up some stew if you don't mind it being a day old."

"We don't mind," said Floyd. "Notice, Ennie, you got a narrow-gauge rail on them sleepers. Everything is wide gauge along the Mississippi."

"Will be here, too, as we expand. Central Pacific is coming down soon, and I've an idea of going over the mountains some day. Maybe run rail to Texas, New Orleans, Kansas. Just ideas, of course."

"Just ideas. You been over that land? Me and Jasper walked over near all of it."

"Feet never be the same."

Enoch said he had to go see to the rail-laying crew. Sam would fix them up with a place to sleep, and they were on the payroll.

After Enoch left, Floyd laid aside a pork bone and rubbed his fingers on his grass-stained jecket. "Raised that boy. Saw to his education in steam and machines. Taught him—well, not right from wrong, but how to face up to the world. He's changed a lot—in near six years—but happy to see us, notice *that*? But on his level. No coming down to ours. I mean he's high and mighty, he's hadda go hard. He's the management and we're—well, we're the hired hands. Was my dead sister Kate's only son. He's got something driving him, and he's going after it like a hound a shoat in the turnip patch. Used to be just a quiet boy listenin', learnin'. Am I tellin' the truth, Jasper? Ain't he different?"

Jasper poured them two fresh tin mugs of coffee. "You letting that whisky talk, Mr. Floyd. He's right kind and he's put us to work."

"Now don't you go playin' a yessuh nigger to him. You're no fieldhand cotton-choppin'-burrhead no more."

"Never was a cotton field-hand. I can read and write now." He turned to the cook slicing bacon." You, Sam, I heard you're reading law."

Sam, black, shiny, a space between his front teeth, nodded. "You bet your bottom dollar I am. Going to be the best black lawyer this California ever is going to see. More grub?"

"No, thank you," said Jasper. "Going to be a machine shop owner man myself. Boilers, windmills, threshers, and line plows. That kind of truck. It's all goin' to be machines from now on."

"Jasper," said Uncle Floyd. "You're just a fireman on a twenty-mile railroad that got no engine. Ha-har-ahar-ha." Uncle Floyd was pleasantly drunk and fed.

The cook took to stirring a pot of bubbling beans. "Oh, Mr. Kingston, he'll get an engine somehow off a boat and put her together, too. Why, this line woulda died long ago if he hadn't kept the men working. He yelled, he hit 'em, got 'em drunk, but he's got six miles of track down. Now, Mr. Canning, he's a wagon man, and railroading don't really fit. I was with the Central Pacific and General Dodge. He was *real* railroad, like Mr. Kingston. Mr. Canning, he has this love of horses, and this road is just a toy for him. But not for Mr. Kingston. He wants to go over Outlaw Pass, cross them mountains. Of course that's when he's had a few snorts after work hours."

"So he says, so he says." Floyd took out a pocket knife and sliced off a sliver of wood from the table edge and began to pick his teeth with it. "Now this here teeny line ain't goin' to mean nothin'. They got these big Baldwin engines now, mile-long freights, heavy rails, signal towers. You believe trains goin' fifty, sixty miles an hour? Work crews by the thousands. Me and Jasper saw Irish paddies and Chinks leveling and blasting. A mile of rail laid a day. Trestles a hundred fifty feet high crossing gorges and rivers. . . . Yes . . . that's real railroads. Still, it'd be nice, Jasper, to feel a locomotive cab under us, firebox full, steam up, my hand steady on the throttle, while blowing for a crossin' . . . *wha-hoo!*"

Jasper sipped his coffee slowly. "Knew, Mr. Floyd, you'd come around cheerful once you got some vittles and some whisky into you. You've got everything when you've got food and likker."

Floyd inspected his toothpick. "No, I'd like me a sweet-smellin' woman with a beautiful ass. That's how you know a woman is right—by the shape of the ass. Like a horse by the teeth. And I'd set out under a tree with her on some sheepskins for a summer, just her in reaching distance, and talking sweet to me, and me drinking prime Tennessee sour mash, the night warm and the weather all good sky. And a moon low enough to bite. Gotta, gotta . . ."

Floyd rose unsteadily and went out. Jasper gathered the plates and mugs together and set them down by a barrel of dishwater. "How they like us dark folk 'round here, Sam?"

The cook scratched his close-cropped head and added salt and chili powder to the pot of simmering beans.

"Well, it's like this. What's your name?"

"Jasper. Jasper August de Leon."

"Jasper, we're lucky—you see the nigger isn't low man around here. Lowest is the Indians. They are drunks, will sell you their squaw for a bottle, lots of 'em. Their squaws they spread their cossie for a pipe of tobacco or a snort of rotgut. Then there are the Mex—they call 'em greasers here. White folk treat 'em like dirt, cheat 'em, kick 'em off the sidewalk. Some of 'em once owned everything around here. Lots of land and cattle, had slaves, too. But now we Negroes are the lucky ones—we fit between the greasers and the white people. You don't give 'em no lip, but you don't have to tip your hat either when they come toward you. We haven't got any doctors yet, no politicians." Sam giggled and rolled his head as he stirred the beans. "But they're goin' to get a lawyer and a politician in Sam Pomeroy here. Mr. Kingston, he's encouragin' me. That Floyd, he's white trash you're runnin' with. He isn't like Mr. Kingston."

Jasper decided not to reveal the relationship of uncle and nephew.

12

"Damn it, I want the line open by November first."

"Sure you do, but where's your locomotive?"

"It will be here. It's July, and you're still only nine miles from Los Angeles."

They were seated in Enoch's buckboard in a grove of willows and cottonwoods, in sight of men laying rail. The weather had turned humid, and both men in the buckboard had their nerves rubbed raw. Heat rash was flaring on Canning's thick neck. He had pushed a handkerchief under his hard collar.

Canning's temper was on a hair trigger. Enoch had developed resentment of the big, blustery man who was not making the transition from wagons and horses to railroads with any ease. What was more dangerous in their relationship for Enoch was his suspicion that Canning was beginning to think he, Canning, had bitten off more than he could chew.

Enoch wondered if Philip Phineas Canning was going to try to ease him out. Enoch held only about two percent of the bonds. He was solving a dozen daily problems, meeting crises in transportation, faulty rails, and drunken work gangs who reported Monday for work in deplorable condition. Yet Canning could blame him if the road never got completed, or for costly delays in finishing the track.

"Enoch, there is going to be a big year in grain, a goddamn big harvest, and I want to haul it before the country thinks they've bought a cat in a burlap bag."

"Don't you go thinking I'm going to be that cat. It's *your* railroad, and you're not providing enough supplies."

Enoch's strong point had been his construction company. Canning, Sol Winters, and Pistol Johnson had a one-third share in it, but because of Chalky White's paper work, Enoch controlled the major interest. He also owned the scrapers, the horses and mules, the tools—or rather he had given notes for these to Canning interests to buy them. He was aware that if Canning was going to blow up and howl for the impossible, and if, as he suspected, Canning was thinking of using him as a scapegoat—even with the line so nearly completed—he would end up a very minor bondholder, or not at all, *if* the notes were presented for collection. Canning would get the credit for the whole project, and he would blame Enoch for all the delays. Enoch was beginning to grasp the beauty of high finance, for some.

Maude found Enoch a brooding husband that night as she was nursing the baby, his son Rawly. But at least, she thought, he's at home, which was not often now as the line slowed down. She offered him the slurping, milk-gorged baby.

"He's your child, too. Amuse him. Enjoy him."

"I do." It was growing, this child, *their* child, it was alive. Its dark eyes studied its father's face and pouted, then broke into a howl.

"Come home more often, stay longer, and he'd not cry." She took the child from him and rocked it in her arms.

Maude was in her most charming domestic period. With a healthy baby, well-filled breasts to feed him, she was enjoying her life free of the Alvarez rancho, and she liked being her own ruler in her small house. As for her lover turned husband and father, she tried to understand an Enoch new to her. The romantic courtship, the mutual seduction of each other, all were now past impressions of memory; memory perhaps too well remembered. But Enoch—the Enoch of that so recent past, the fiery lover—was changed into a driving man much devoted to his work. Maude was possessive. She resented any loss of him. Their life together was still as full of fire and passion, but to her it seemed rationed, curtailed. Just when she wanted his attentions most, he was lost by his building of a damn rail-line where no one had built one before, and where no one else was as expert in the field. Damn, damn. Sometimes when he stole a night away from one of his construction camps and he came to their bed, it healed her resentment. But later, after lovemaking, she would find his mind had gone off to some brooding solitude as he lay by her side. He was *there* and yet *not* there. He was back with the damn rail-line.

"I've lost part of you," she said.

"Like the devil you have."

She cuddled close, wound naked arms around him. "I want all of you. I'm hungry, I'm a devouring tiger," she added, hardly in a bantering tone.

Enoch belonged to an age of submissive women, and he ignored the rebellion he was facing.

Maude was sitting up naked in bed, disheveled, flushed from their lovemaking, and gesturing in the lamplight; she insisted on having a lamp lit when intimate. ("I'm not a God-sniveling New England brood mare who thinks it's a sin to see and touch and play.") She had been storing up her protest, her resentment. Enoch was trying to get some sleep. He had been up at five in the morning to get the work gangs on their toes.

"Not now, Maude, we'll talk some other time."

"We'll talk now, darling."

"What the devil about?"

"I want to live in the work camps with you."

"The baby, Rawly, he needs you."

"Concepcion has found a wet nurse. A good healthy woman—a regular cow."

He sighed. "Be grand having you in camp with me. But—"

"No buts—"

"It's rough, it's mean. No comforts. The men are brutes, drunks, some even rapists."

"How nice. I'll pack." She leaped from the bed as she was—jay-naked.

"You're not going, Maude. You don't know the—"

"I'll find out."

She was tossing clothes around, kicking shoes out of the way; stopped to hold up a feather-topped riding hat. "I'll take the pony, Ginger. I'll wear pants for riding."

(He no longer wondered why Uncle Floyd had said,

"What we want, there's lots of it. Too bad it's part of a woman.")

He spoke up. "No." But he knew by morning he'd say yes.

He was very much in love, very much given to taking great pleasure with her. Enoch knew little about women, would never learn very much more. He had no subtle instincts about relationships. He made his needs, his admiration, known directly to a woman. There was never any mystic quality in his emotional partnership with them. He had matured too quickly as a thinker. Clever, efficient, and even brilliant as he would become in his field of endeavor, he would remain emotionally a farm boy, dreaming of some enchanting island where life was casual, sensual, and in no way related to the existence he had led and would lead.

Lucita Jimenez, the wet nurse, turned out to be a very large and very dark Mexican woman, and the boy Rawly took to her huge nipples with a gurgle and lust as if he wanted to drain the big body of all its fluids at once.

Maude's trunk was in the back of the buckboard at ten; the early 4 A.M. departure had been abandoned. Maude wore a cocky little green velvet hat and a yellow traveling jacket trimmed with black braid. She sat on the seat beside him, amused at Enoch's dour look as he touched up the rumps of the team with his whip. The horses dashed away down Olive Street and kept moving west toward Twin Wells, which the track layers were approaching.

Enoch cracked the whip above the horses' ears. "I'll be a laughingstock at camp."

"Do you care?" Maude asked as they crossed a part of the street that was a rough-laid plank road, and she—jolted—held on hoping she didn't bite her tongue off.

"No, I don't. Only"—he chuckled—"I never would have thought of this."

"I'll do the thinking for this side of our life."

Enoch said no more—he put one hand on her thigh. He felt inflated with a kind of joy he couldn't explain. It was not just that Maude was at his side, and the good color and pattern of the maturing grain in the fields they passed gave a pretty picture of nature. It was in part a sense he was going to have to lock horns with Canning, and he was going to enjoy the combat. It was another paramount trait in Enoch Kingston that people were to learn about. It was his enjoyment of battle, more and more as he matured, but always with the cold-blooded directness of his awareness of the objective achieved that would result from his battles. He rarely wasted his energies on a fight that did not serve his purposes. In this he differed from Canning, who would charge anything that seemed to him a red flag of challenge—anything touching him in his dignity, mocking his social standing; or, when he was whisky-inspired to seek issue, to argue and dominate by sound and intimidation.

Maude was the sensation she had expected in the Twin Wells work camp. But Uncle Floyd remarked to Jasper, "It's not the Enoch Kingston we knowed at Vicksburg. That gawky scarebooger, he's growed up fast."

Then one day the news was tapped out to all the camps on the telegraph line Enoch had erected that at last the locomotive had arrived in Wilmington harbor. Uncle Floyd brought the news to the cabin where the Kingstons had set up housekeeping under the fragrant pines.

"She's a shiny wonder, Enoch. I hear come in several parts. So me and Jasper better get into work clothes. How do, Missus Kingston, looking pert this morning."

Uncle Floyd was wary of Maude; he said he didn't understand how any galoot worth his feed could be marrying up with just one woman, giving up the whole field of foolish females. And also, in Uncle Floyd's range of reference, she was a "Mex." He had been raised up to believe all races were (as he put it when drunk) "inferior to a freeborn, well-hung, honest, Fourth-of-July, rootin', hollerin' American."

But he remained polite to Maude.

"Enoch," Maude said. "Now at least there may be a railroad."

"Better be," said Uncle Floyd. "We been breakin' our ass—our backs—gettin' the rails ready."

Enoch tried to remain calm, but did a little jig as he got into his jacket. "I hope we built the right gauge road."

There was a great rush to the harbor on horseback, in surrey and buggy, even in heavy work wagons.

There it was, below, sure enough, Jasper reported, coming up from the hold of a big schooner a bit battered by the Horn storms. And soon the boiler and the four driving wheels were there on the dock. And all alone, like some primitive god, the tall smokestack and its diamond-shaped spark arrester. Jasper set to shining a three-foot-tall oil lamp with paneled glass sides—the locomotive's headlight. A pretty young gold-skinned girl of about ten or eleven was handing him clean rags as he polished the brass frame of the light.

"Fifty candles at least," Enoch said as he examined the lamp.

"Oil," said the girl. "No candles at all."

"Of course. I meant like fifty candles burning bright." Enoch patted her head of straight dark brown hair, worn cut short and brushed back. "Oil, of course."

Jasper rubbed away. "She's smart, Brook is. She reads, writes, ciphers like a banker."

"Good as any. Seven times seven is forty-two," said Brook boldly. Jasper stood up and examined his rubbing cloth. "This is my daughter Brook. And she's forward, but not disrespecting to no one. She's ten."

"Going on eleven."

"Didn't know you had a family, Jasper."

"Got me this wife Rosy-Mae, laundry girl at the Cannings. This child, Brook, is what they call hereabouts my stepdaughter."

"Good luck on becoming a family man. Now we'll put the locomotive all together and get it on the rails. Lots of brass. Lots of good black paint. But will she steam? And what's her valve gear like?" He walked to the cab section, read the red and gold letters: THE ROMAN.

"Seems a good name." It was a period when all locomotives had a name beside a number, and Enoch would have considered a nameless engine a discarded orphan.

Canning came up from the hold of the schooner, followed by Pistol Johnson; they carried a heavy bronze bell between them.

"Enoch! Look! Rings like a big church bell Christmas

106

night. Now how long before you get her all whacked together?"

"Don't know. Not even sure all the parts have come along. Don't see any link-and-pin coupling for attaching to the cars."

Piston Johnson held up a sheaf of papers. "Inventories, Enoch. Lists everything. There are also six diagrams. Just follow the numbered parts as in the directions."

"Thanks, Pistol."

Uncle Floyd was kicking at the burlap wrapping on some slide rods. Canning yelled, "Get your damn tramp's feet away from those parts!"

Floyd turned, thumbs hooked under his wide belt. "Mr. Canning, you better be polite to me as a hog on ice. Likewise a touch of respect or your fuckin' steam train ain't never goin' to run." And Uncle Floyd spit amber tobacco juice between Canning's polished boots.

"Why you sonofa—"

Enoch stepped between them. "Phil, you want that locomotive to get up a head of steam, don't be calling names."

Uncle Floyd had been taking a nip every hour or so since sunup and now he waved a finger under Canning's red, puffed-up face. He ignored the cane in the big man's hand, a cane held like a hammer, ready to rain down blows on someone's head.

"You see, *Mister* Canning, they sent this here engine in too many parts. I know more about locomotives than any hombre you ever met. I learned Ennie there everything he knows. He knows a lot. But I know *more*. There are allus a mess of links and parts that don't fit, and nuts and bolts misplaced or missing. I can save you weeks of time. Now this is a 4-6-2 type; can haul ten coaches up a grade of twenty-six feet per mile, *if* she runs at all."

Enoch was laughing and slapping his knee. God, the expression on that big pan of a face on Canning. "It's true all right. Floyd back in sixty-two, sixty-three kept the Union supply trains running all along the river; did it on spit and baling wire."

Floyd had had more than just nips. He was feeling in his prime again, and sassy. He spit loudly into the palm of his hand and held it out to Canning. "So let's shake on it,

Mister Railroad, and we'll get goin' to makin' *The Roman* walk about with two-hundred-fifty degrees of steam."

Canning looked about him on the pier. Everyone was watching as if a dog fight or a barroom rough-and-tumble were about to take place. He turned to Enoch without returning the offer of a handshake.

"All right ... you're in charge, Enoch. Use whoever you want. Just get it ticking and onto the track."

Enoch motioned to Jasper and Floyd, "Get blocks and cables. We'll erect a hoist out of spare ship's spars to lift the big parts into position. There's a crate of wrenches and levers and other tools in the hold. Put a guard on everything. Lots of copper tubing may give some folks ideas of making a whisky-distilling coil. And break out the kegs of machinery grease."

"How long all this take?" asked Canning, thumping the wharf's surface with his cane.

Enoch squatted down to inspect a steam gauge. "In plenty of time to put out the flags, set up the drinks, and *you* to make a speech for the first run."

It was this remark that some people accepted as the beginning of the disagreement between the two men.

Brook, Jasper's stepdaughter, pulled on Enoch's jacket. "Enoch, can I ride with my pappy the first time?"

Enoch said he didn't see why not, and he'd talk to Jasper to get the kid some shoes. But he forgot, because in the next two weeks they put *The Roman* together twice, once incorrectly.

13

The Roman, painted red and black, with its brass shined up, turned out to be a handsome locomotive, and when rails were laid to connect it with the track already laid, Canning immediately put it into service hauling freight and passengers from his harbor to the end of the track, just outside of Twin Wells. But wagons and stages still had to come out from Los Angeles to make connections. The townspeople in their homes could hear the train whistle like a great screech owl, but that was all.

The stumbling block—Uncle Floyd called it "a blocked signal" was the town of Twin Wells, crouched low in the dust four miles from the city. It wasn't much of a place, the horse droppings hardly ever removed from its two main streets, the termites busy as usual digesting its underpinnings, so that the wooden sidewalks tilted and the false fronts of Murph's General Store, Chin Lee's Laundry and the Full Moon Saloon tilted a bit. But it rested like a lazy, unmoving dog directly in the path of the L.A. & S.P. R.R.

There had been rumblings of resentment from the local mayor and some of the village officials. Also from the town blacksmith, who was the town constable, and his carpenter son-in-law, who was building a city hall. What alerted Enoch to trouble was an injunction by the village of Twin Wells objecting to the rails coming up through Sunset Street and the railroad thus "becoming a public nuisance."

Enoch took the legal paper to the bank, and Sol Winters read it slowly, peering over silver-rimmed eyeglasses from time to time.

"Canning has an injunction served on him, too. Yours is against laying rails through the town, and his to show

109

cause why the project should not be halted on the town's western limits. Can you put tracks *around* the place?"

"No, damn it, it would add three miles of unneeded track and we haven't the spare rails, haven't the ties cut and—"

"And three miles more of track will cost a lot of money the road hasn't got and can't get?"

"That's the situation."

Enoch refused a cigar and walked about on the turkey-red rug, then stared out of the banker's office window. He was looking out to the street where a mule train of freight wagons was coming down from the mines with the silver bullion. A Butterworth stage was loading in front of the Bella Union Hotel.

"Mr. Winters, I've been chewing the fat—just talking easy to Gus Mitulla, the mayor, he is also the local butcher. He wasn't shy—it's a holdup for a little loot to be spread among some of the better citizens."

"You mean a bribe?"

Enoch didn't turn around, just remained at the window looking down on the street and the general store display where some dogs were being chased away from pissing on a sidewalk box of sea crackers by a shopkeeper with a broom. "Forget labels. I think we will buy some supplies from the good citizens. Get our work crew's meat supply from Gus, timbers from Ralph Appel. He's the Grand Sun Lumberyard."

"It's still bribing."

"And we could have our emergency ironwork, tool repairs, done at Willie Denver's blacksmith shop. . . . Mr. Huntington of the Central Pacific spent five hundred thousand dollars a year paying off senators and congressmen in Washington. He told Phil that 'bribing for the good of the country—*then* you pay bribes.' "

"Well—yes."

"That's it—what will it add to the cost of the road?"

"These are small-town boodle-grabbers, and—"

The office door opened and Canning came in followed by Chalky White, the lawyer. Canning was cheerful, jingling silver dollars with his hand deep in a pants pocket.

"Enoch, I want the train, steam up, to enter Los Angeles, September sixth. We can get an armed work crew to move into Twin Wells at midnight and lay track through that horseshit stretch before dawn. Easy as pie."

For all his battering by adversity, Chalky had still retained that British look of aloofness and pawky humor. It was early in the day, and he had not yet had his full quota of whisky. "I would say easy, lads, to that idea. By morning every citizen of Twin Wells able to carry a pistol and lift a rifle will be out hunting down railroad men and blockading the bloody street. No."

Sol Winters was figuring on a small pad on his desk. "Enoch says it's merely a matter of dealing with certain merchants in the town."

"Does he?" Canning, as if amused, shook a finger at Enoch. "It's railroad money, and I'm saying not one penny goes to the grafters, the snake-oil merchants. You hear me?"

"You have witnesses I heard you." Enoch turned and started for the door. "The Kingston Construction Company is the railroad's contractor and you have no word in the running of its affairs as long as it lays rails."

"Look, Kingston," shouted Canning, now permitting his temper free rein. "You were just a shaggy wagon driver and I took you off the seat and made something of you. Don't go telling me I've got no word! You're getting too goddamn big for your pants, and—"

Chalky White felt it was time to divert attention from the slanging match. He took out some legal papers. "I have here certain injunctions of our own against seven Twin Wells town officials, *and* the village of Twin Wells. We can serve them and get delayed for months in the blazing buggering courts. But we'd win. So take your choice, Mr. Canning. I gather you've already discarded any idea of backing up and going around the village?"

"Got no extra rails for it."

Sol Winters got up from his desk and walked towards the door. "I want to check some end-of-month figures."

Canning shouted after him, "Tender ears, Solly? You don't want to hear what we decide?"

The banker didn't answer; he just closed the door behind him.

"Canning," said Enoch, calm enough but ready to repel a blow. "I don't give a tinker's tit what you call me at this stage of the job. Maybe I'll knock you down later. But unless we do as I think we have to, you can take your whole railroad and shove it up your hairy ass. And if you have to, add a mule or two and a freight wagon! Only you'll be bankrupt by then."

Chalky White put the papers back into his jacket. "That's a Mexican standoff, Mr. Canning. You fail to finish the line very soon, the project will become bankrupt. Los Angeles County will sue to take over the line built so far. So? Outside blighters and their interests—maybe the Central, the Southern Pacific—will finish it and own it."

Canning was waving his arms. "This sonofabitch Kingston, he told me to shove it up—"

Chalky White was unimpressed; he needed his late-morning second pick-me-up. "Forget personalities, general. Save the blinking road."

Canning waved one arm in Enoch's direction. "Go ahead, but don't tell me about it." He turned and walked out, stiff-kneed.

The lawyer said, "He's beyond his depth. On edge over the biggest project of his life. He's a mule and wagon man. Strike and crash through. Let's go down to the Bella Union and have a Ramon gin fizz."

"Just one." Enoch felt no sense of victory. He did what had to be done. Too bad Canning got so tight in the crotch. He knew it was the road to the final break with Canning. From now on they would be enemies, even if wary and uneasy partners in finishing the railroad. He had been prepared to accept that crack in their relationship for some time. Now it had actually happened. He knew Canning had great drive, courage, but he was set in the prejudice of an already disappearing era, too much wrapped up in what he thought of himself as the all-knowing pioneer. Rigid. That was what made him a man already outdated. The age of the pioneer with mule, ox, ax, and rifle was gone. A time to kill red hostiles, plow up the grass, face the blizzards and the dry season; those hard virtues were passing from the picture. One had to study new ways, revalue each situation as to it's relationship to the present, face new inventions, machines, accept the game of the money market, and the national speculators and manipulators. It was all becoming too big to play by

112

horse sense and bookkeeping numbers kept in one's head and under a hat.

Chalky explained names like Morgan, Carnegie, Rockefeller, men who directed attention to the new shape of things; "the bigger the grab, the more piled-up rewards."

After two gin fizzes with Chalky, Enoch promised they'd talk sometime about the growing transporation opportunities just waiting to be taken. He went home to find his son Rawly chewing the colors off a painted toy. Maude was washing her hair in a wide china basin out in their small garden, while Miguel, a part-time groom and gardener, picked caterpillers off the tomato plants.

The weeks in the work camps had given Maude a tanned skin, added some weight; for the camp fare was hearty, filling, and starchy. She was now eating potatoes boiled in vinegar. Hannah Winters had told her Lord Byron kept his weight down by feeding on that dish.

She lifted her head from the basin. "You look as if a cougar had clawed you."

"*Porque si.*" He added he'd had a run-in with Canning. She wrapped a towel around her head, told him she'd expected it. "He's big and loud, but he's mule-headed. Like one of his critters. Get into a boiled shirt. The Winters are giving a fancy dinner and a dance. Some Eastern bankers, come out to see the savages."

"Can't go. Have to get to Twin Wells and talk some people into letting rail through the village." He explained he had to be laying track through the town by morning. Canning had built the depot in Los Angeles at Alameda and Commercial streets; he had also announced that *The Roman*, with four cars attached, would steam into the station on the morning of September sixth.

"I can't go to the Winterses alone."

"Sure you can. I'll have Chalky White keep an eye on you."

"Revolting drunkard. He doesn't like women."

"You don't think I'd trust you otherwise?" He grabbed her and upset the basin of water, the tray of soap, and the lotions. He kissed her and the towels fell away from her shoulders and her head.

She struggled in his grip and laughed and nuzzled against him. "I'm glad *you* like women."

The baby stared at them and continued to gum his toy. Enoch felt horny and loving. He wished he could stay. They had been working with the idea of making another baby. But, as Uncle Floyd had said, "That Ennie boy, he changed, become duty's child." And so he had. He was building a railroad, and even Canning couldn't destroy the joy of it.

He left with an alligator hide bag containing gold coins, eagles, and double eagles—a fund he kept for just these times when a few coins slipped into some eager hand for a cow killed on the tracks, or the right to take down a section of fence, or resettling a privy would take care of things. He'd pass out samples from the bag at Twin Wells, and have the crews work from sundown until dawn, laying rail past that greedy place. He had Chalky's legal papers for the town officials to sign, releasing the railroad and the construction company from the injunctions. Chalky had insisted on that. "If they sign with an X, any of those damn sods, be sure you get witnesses."

The next day rail continued to be laid—and Los Angeles was ready with a greeting.

On the morning of September sixth, the last spike was to be driven into the last tie laid at the end of the road—at the depot. Already bunting had been strung up, a bandstand erected; vendors were lighting charcoal fires for snacks they would peddle, peanuts roasted, and fruit polished. *The Roman* stood steam up, two miles from town, puffing like a bull pawing the ground. Loaded with citizens from Wilmington, washed and combed, some even shaved, passengers and town officials from places along the twenty-one miles of the run from the harbor.

Philip Canning was up early and out from his room at the Bella Union Hotel; his wife and children were aboard the train. He was in a splendid mood. He stood at the depot, pompous but impressive, bulky in dark blue jacket, plaid trousers; his square derby, well brushed, rested on the back of his head, two rows of heavy gold watch chains crisscrossed his scarlet waistcoat. He handed out cigars to the reporters of the county's three newspapers. A photographer with his wet-plate three-legged camera stood ready. A tuba player was testing his *oompahs*. People were gathering, horses reared as someone set off Chinese firecrackers. Soon the depot and streets were crowded; even the fresh laid tracks were invaded, walked on, inspected. Some kids were trying to pull up a few spikes.

Enoch had a work crew still grading and tamping the ballast on a slight slope into the depot. A section of the platform had been set aside for "the town's best people," as the *Los Angeles Item* wrote it up. Behind wide red ribbons sat Maude and the Winterses, Hannah in a perky little blue hat. Pistol Johnson sat in the back, sporting a new set of side-whiskers he kept touching as if wondering were they still there. Chalky White stood blinking in the sunlight, a bit crumpled—he had slept in his clothes—the pockets of his jacket full of legal papers in case some last-minute problems arose, such as liens from unpaid suppliers or claims for damages, even legal games by the two wagon freighters who could be put out of business by the train. His best effort was a printed release form in case the locomotive blew up, maimed, or killed the people now cheering.

"Thar she blows," some old whaler shouted. Far down the line a train whistle was heard, then the clang of *The Roman*'s bell. A man in a red shirt riding a lathered horse came galloping by, waving his hat, then slapping his legs with it. "It's a comin', a comin' hell-fer-leather!"

It certainly was, and men held their horses on a short rein. Canning stepped forward to the edge of the platform. In rolled *The Roman*, all black polish, red paint, and shiny brass. Madame Needle and a bevy of her whores in holiday attire cheered loudly as the four cars entered the depot.

Uncle Floyd in a blue cap with a patent leather peak, sat at the locomotive controls in the cab, and Jasper was standing by the tender of fat pitch-pine chunks with which he had fed the boiler. Brook, his stepdaughter was by his side, waving a green railroad signaling flag. The band blared out "Yankee Doodle."

The train slowed, roared; sand fell from its sandbox onto the rails, the wheels slowed and seemed to skid; Un-

cle Floyd brought it to a halt just in time to prevent its
hitting the heavy X-stop of crossed logs. Then—Uncle
Floyd had planned it, or he saw his moment and used it—
he sent out a blast of steam past the driving rods from the
piston chamber, and Canning leaped aside just in time to
escape a scalding.

People laughed, people cheered. The locomotive seemed
to Hannah Winters to be breathing proudly, like a winner
in a race. There it stood at rest as if waiting for a wel-
coming reward.

Canning lifted both arms high, looked behind him to see
if he were out of steam range. His wife and children were
at the windows of the first car, cheering with the rest of
the four car train load. He waved for silence. The drums
beat a *rat-a-tat-tat*.

"Here we are, folks. From the harbor to our city by
steam cars. A mighty link of shiny rails, a marvel of our
industrial age, the noblest Roman of them all (cheers). Tomorrow at nine, the first passengers and freight can em-
bark for the harbor, at nine o'clock on the dot. The train
will make two full runs daily. Two and a half dollars is
the passenger ticket from here to there, or back to here (a
few groans). Freight five dollars a ton. Yes, it's done, as
the man said as he kicked the dog away from the post
(some boos). This rail-line was not of our doing alone.
No, siree. But it's our dream come true (cheers and "You
tell 'em, general!"). You, Los Angeles, city and county,
have ponied up bonds for every mile we built, our prominent banker and community leader, Solomon Winters, has
kept the books in good order, and—" Canning made a
slight grimace, "the work of the contractors, among them
Enoch Bancroft Kingston, is sure not to be overlooked"
(cheers).

The citizens of Los Angeles and Twin Wells (the tainted
officials happy and handshaking) mixed with folk from
Alameda, El Segundo, Redondo, San Pedro, Wilmington;
all who had come along for the ride and now were trying
to get as close to the locomotive as they could. Brook,
Jasper's stepdaughter, was showing Enoch and Hannah
Winters she had shoes for the event—white kid with
mother-of-pearl buttons. Hannah said they were very styl-

ish and, in an aside to Enoch, "We must get her a new frock."

Uncle Floyd was standing by the driving wheels, a wad of tobacco in one cheek, pulling off his gloves and talking to a gullible reporter. "Ain't nothing compared to the night run me and Mr. Kingston there, we drove General U.S. Grant himself through shot and shell, rebel horse soldiers galloping all around us. They had their field guns on the bluffs above us, trying to cut the rails, wreck the bridge, put holes through the smokestack. I knew we had to get 'Ole Sal' across the White Water bridge before the rebel bastards burned her down. Mr. Kingston—he's a dead shot—was picking off the horse soldiers. I was driving 'Ole Sal'—our engine—at sixty miles an hour when—"

Jasper was putting on a shirt and promising Brook some Mexican food that was being peddled from trays. Enoch shook the fireman's hand. "Firebrick standing up?"

"Mr. Kingston, it's a good boiler on wheels, but she's a woodeater."

Maude had come up. She smiled at Brook. "What a beautiful child, Jasper."

"Wild, but she reads, she plays the piano, ma'am, when she can find one."

Hannah came back from a peddler with two tacos for Brook. Maude said, "We must have her over to try our piano." Brook, biting into a taco said, "Somebody has spelled a word wrong."

It was true, on the locomotive cab a Wilmington sign painter had lettered LOS ANGELOS AND SAN PEDRO R.R.

Brook swallowed a lump of food. "It should be A-N-G-E-L-E-S. Not O-S."

Enoch took the ladies, one on each arm. He said, "There is a punch bowl inside." The two women "with lacy and embroidered posteriors," as Chalky White described it, were led by Enoch to the punch.

14

With the completing of the Los Angeles and San Pedro line, Philip Canning showed no desire to expand beyond El Pueblo de Los Angeles. He did lay some track beyond the depot, but only halfheartedly, and gave it up. He was satisfied to be pointed out and cheered as the man who had brought a railroad to Southern California. Enoch neither got nor wanted much credit for the actual construction. The new line prospered, and real estate value rose around the station. Train time saw it invaded by hotel hacks, produce wagons, and passengers with hand luggage, awaiting the departure of the daily runs from the Commercial Street depot.

It was a most busy scene on "Steamer Day," with one or more ships set to depart from the harbor, when many people rushed products to be carried to the sea. Passengers fought to get their bags and luggage in order, or found. Criminals, deadbeats, absconding bookkeepers, seducers, also could be suspected of seeking passage.

In December of 1869, Enoch drove in his buckboard to the depot to meet Chalky White, the lawyer. The two men had become more than friends. They had found in each other kindred attitudes, had become confidential with each other. Chalky saw in Enoch one of those mutations, driven men; perhaps who change things, move a nation's progress onward in some way that they were not aware of; did not know themselves. Enoch, the lawyer sensed, was not aware of just what his full talents, his almost blind drives, could lead to. Not as yet. Chalky was a well-educated, well-read man, one who had resigned from much of what the world consisted of. He didn't express to Enoch all he felt or saw in the young man who had brought through a rail-line under great odds, in face of much carping and attention grabbing by a man like Canning. As for Enoch, he felt that only in the lawyer and in Hannah Winters was he in contact with minds and attitudes raised above the average of the region.

Enoch, hitching up the buckboard team at the depot, found Chalky with his usual morning pallor; the Englishman avoided the sun. He was leaning on a post of the depot platform watching the loading of the train for its journey to the harbor. It was a busy scene, and the English expatriate thought of it as a living Hogarth print, or an over-active watercolor by Rowlandson. Boys and old men were peddling peanuts, tacos, apricots, and oranges. In the freight yard section just past the platform, there were ten-mule teams bringing up wagons of harvest crops and products. The hotel hacks were unloading passengers, and there were farewells and kissing and promises to write, while somewhere the *jong jong* sound of struck iron echoed. Enoch came up to and stood by Chalky White's side; they nodded greetings to each other.

"You'd think, Chalky, they were crossing the Red Sea, not going twenty-one miles."

"A journey, old chap, begins with taking just the first step."

Enoch looked to where Uncle Floyd in neat blue, already grease-soiled, was climbing into the locomotive cab. Jasper stood in the tender, passing down chunks of wood to an apprentice fireman.

"I wonder, Chalky, how long Floyd will keep to the speed we set, and see that the safety valve's in use."

"People love dangerous rides. You've made up your mind to sell out?"

"Yes, going to let Canning and Winters have my holdings in the line. I want to break off clean."

"You have plans? Or just going to sit on your arse in the sun?"

Enoch watched fat Max Jeffers of the Jeffers Inn, and Manders Welton, a too-thin fellow with a goat-tuft chin whisker, who ran the Bucket of Gore Saloon, searching faces, both moving down a row of passengers waiting to entrain.

"Watch Max and Manders bulldogging to see if any tin-horn debtors are making a run for it."

"Happens every day. Usually they pull somebody off the train, or the police do it for them. Gamblers in hock, running out on card losses, busted whores and their pimps doing the bilk, snake-oil salesmen escaping hotel bills. Big crowd today. Must be *two* steamers in harbor."

Several men with lettered brass plates attached to their top hats by buckskin thongs were pushing about, holding onto some passengers by their elbows and talking quickly.

"Ships' agents of rival lines. Maybe you'd like to buy shares in a Frisco paddle-wheeler, the *Arizona*?"

"No. Maybe I'll put what I get for my shares into land on Broadway, Olive Street. Anything near the Plaza is jumping in value. You said you might find some options for me."

"Land, lots, street frontages? Well, come boom time and bust time, come land lawyers, and who knows who makes the money? If you're going to hold onto it for a long time, land is right. But Enoch, what of your talk of railroad lines over the mountains, into the Southwest, to the Gulf?"

"Has to come, and damn soon. They're driving cattle now hundreds of miles, wearing them thin, to reach the rail-lines in Kansas. But somebody is going to build lines in the Southwest so the cattle can ride right through to Chicago. That's from where they feed the East, hungry for meat. I'd like to build a few hundred miles of rail for whoever is going to do it. But—" Enoch made a gesture of "who knows?"

Uncle Floyd in the cab was pulling the whistle cord in short blasts, the noise of departure increased. The last late passenger, collar undone, flung himself at the open rear observation platform of the last car—trying for the hand-rail and hung on, feet in the air. Someone dropped a round-top trunk, which burst open. A team of mules acted up, kicking their heels. Two policemen led away an angry young woman with brass-colored hair and a protesting man.

The train in motion gave off great jets of steam, the diamond smokestack pouring a good thick black smoke into the air. The bronze bell was set to ringing by Jasper as the whistle gave its last toot. The train moved slowly, gathered momentum in its *jug-jug* sound. Some people waved from open windows and folks on the platform were waving back. The boys and old men with their trays of quick eatables for sale drifted away or sat down on the platform to count coins under the long sign: LOS ANGELES & SAN PEDRO R.R. *Philip P. Canning, Pres.*

Those people who had come to see the train departure moved towards their waiting horses and wheels. The smell of spilled oats, fresh horse dung, engine grease, and wood smoke hung in the heated air. The *jude jude, jude* of the laboring locomotive grew fainter.

Empty wagons were moving off under the oaths and snapping whips of drivers. Down the line the train whistle could be heard giving two hoots as it crossed the creek bed of an arroyo. Smoke still hung in the air like pencil smudges. Birds came down to inspect the peanut shells on the platform.

Chalky White said, "Lots of money, and even better than money, credits for building railroads, all along the Gulf. Yes, to build a road up through Outlaw Pass to connect San Diego with everything between here and the East. And another to the South—well, why not even a line to New Orleans?"

Enoch laughed, "You Limey sonofabitch, you know I've been approached by some people who think that way."

"I asked them to approach you. Baring Brothers of London—private bankers dealing for clients in grain, gold, native products. They handle bonds, stock sales of the projects."

"My conditions are country-boy simple. I build it—I run it."

"Not a chance of you running it. Very complex, this matter of floating issues of bonds, stocks, by private banks like Baring, the Rothschilds."

"Let's see about a few local street-corner lots right here."

A flustered old woman in an India shawl, carrying a near-bursting suitcase and a parrot cage with an angry bird in it, came up to the platform of the depot and looked about her.

"Is the steam car in the deepoo yet?"

Chalky White took of his hat, shook his head. "Left about ten minutes ago, madam."

"Oh, blast, blast, blast it. My daughter is on the steamer *Atlas,* and I was to join her."

"There will be another train at four o'clock. The ship will wait for it."

She didn't trust anyone and showed it by her expression. "What makes you so sure the blasted teakettle on wheels will be on time?"

"I can guarantee it," said Enoch, "*If* the boiler holds up."

The old lady gave him a worried look, searching the wooden floor with a glance as if afraid it would explode. She lifted her head and walked off toward the waiting room, the parrot biting at the metal bars of its cage, muttering something in a language neither man could make out.

Chalky White took out his watch and looked at it as if fascinated by the minute hand racing along as it erased time. "What does Maude think of you selling your stock in L.A. and S.P. Railroad and buying land?"

"Swore she'd go back to her father's ranch if I did. But she'll calm down. They usually do, women."

"Do they? I hope so, for your sake. Never could live with anyone that left female gear chucked about. You know, be it wife, mistress, weekend friend, or boarder. I'm a solitary I suppose. Rather not pleasure with someone at night when I'd rather—" He acted a quick motion of taking a drink. Chalky made no secret that he drank himself to sleep every night. "We better not keep Canning waiting any longer. Feisty chap."

"How late are we?"

"Half an hour."

"Maybe ten minutes more delay? No, he'll have steam coming out of his ears."

Canning's office at the depot had two walnut doors and the gold letters:

PHILIP P. CANNING
PRESIDENT
L.A. & S.P. R.R.

Behind the doors was a small outer waiting room with a plump clerk—a relative, Enoch suspected—among some stacks of ledgers. A single walnut door was marked with the lettering:

PRESIDENT
PRIVATE

Canning had done up his office himself. A grizzly bear-skin on the floor, a steel engraving of *The Stag at Eve* over a stone fireplace that was not lit, several photographs of *The Roman, The Driving of the Last Spike*. Canning in several versions: at the throttle of the locomotive, Uncle Floyd scowling in the background, and Jasper holding a log of wood as if it were a corpse in his arms.

As the two men entered, Canning was examining a large-scale model of a locomotive resting on a table on a set of miniature tracks. He looked up at a station clock ticking on one green-painted wall, then went on pushing the locomotive back and forth on its short length of track.

"Baldwin is making these. What do you think of the model?"

Enoch walked around the table, peered at the drive wheels, touched a finger to the driving rods, stroking the cowcatcher. "It's too big for the line. Wood consuming cost could bust you. To make it pay off, you'd need fifty cars a day in two trips. . . . Well, you and Solly buying me out?"

"Jaysus, Enoch, be sociable—don't rush me. It's not a hogshead of sugar we're talking of, is it, Chalky? You take twenty thousand dollars?"

"Thirty," said Chalky. "That amount was mentioned. Drawn on gold in any bank we approve of."

"*We*, what's this *we* horseshit? And we *talked* thirty, sure—but we didn't clinch it." Canning was staring at the two men as if they were going through his pockets.

Chalky placed a hand on the model train engine and moved it back and forth a few inches each way.

"There are rumors of new companies to lay rails through Outlaw pass, cross the mountains. Also to the southeast."

"Craziest thing I ever heard. Gave up the idea myself.

That is, Solly did, seeing Los Angeles is going to be served by the Southern Pacific soon. They'd leave any rival line bare-assed with no tail feathers."

Enoch looked over the six-inch length of T-rail used as a paperweight. "S.P. says they're *not* coming through Los Angeles. The new line would be to San Diego."

"They're bluffing. Sure there's talk, some want a rail-line up from Texas to San Diego. But they've got no survey line laid out. It's all Texas talk, wind-and-whisky talk, that's all it is."

Enoch helped himself to a cigar from a rosewood box, sniffed the tobacco, rotated the cigar between thumb and forefinger, held it up to his ear. He put it back in the box. "Too dry. Me and Chalky have been talking about a rail-line, maybe to set up a corporation and to float stock. Want any when we do?"

Chalky looked down at the grizzly bear pelt and gently toed the teeth set in red plaster. He winked down at the yellow glass eyes.

Canning looked amused. "Dreamland railroad stock? Hell, no. I've got all the rails I want in the L.A. and S.P."

Enoch said, "The Huntington Pacific crowd in 'Frisco will gobble you up like trout a grasshopper on a stream. Thirty thousand for my stock holdings in L.A. and S.P.? Let's walk over to Solly's bank and make it legal."

Canning took his hat off a wall hook. "It's worth it just to get rid of you. But you ever need work like driving the mud wagon to Fort Yuma, there's always a job waiting." He turned to Chalky White. "Best goddamn wagon hand I ever had."

Enoch just smiled. He was developing a philosophy, a policy that if no advantage could be gained from a situation, silence was best. Not that he thought much of serious philosophers. Hannah Winters had asked him to try Plato and Kant, but it was hogwash—fancy, but still hogwash.

When Enoch got home from the bank with a receipt of thirty thousand dollars in gold bagged for him in the bank badly but as loudly as the delicate instrument could sound. vault, he found Maude banging away at the spinet, playing A Strauss tune. She turned around to face him, looked up at him, that trouble-predicting quiver in her jawline he knew so well—her lips wet, mouth half-open. "I can tell; you sold out."

"When you're mad, you sound like Phil Canning, but look prettier."

"You'll toss it away in land deals with your crazy idea of holding on to corner lots."

"May, may not."

"Promise me, no land. My family was nearly ruined by its idea that land was all. Promise you'll keep the money in the bank."

"No promises."

The scene that followed was not pretty. Maude yelling, the baby Rawly waking to cry in the next room. Enoch, too calm, too cool—only inciting his wife to try near hysterics. Maude at such times was not, he felt, merely unreasonable; there was in her an uncontrollable movement to moods, from almost a dark melancholia to an overextended elation. These often wore her out to shaking like an attack of Saint Vitus's dance. The medical knowledge of the time—and what little there was of it in Los Angeles—put it down to "having the female vapors."

Her tensions and rages would increase with the years. Enoch often told her, "Your father should have taken a dog whip to you as a child." Enoch never understood the nuances of a woman's emotional life, or the balances and counterbalances of her nervous system, so much different than his. Very few men did, or cared. Enoch cared, but was helpless to find any remedy but to "let things run out."

Maude's hair had fallen away from its pins and she pointed a dramatic finger at him. "You remove the money from the bank, get into a land scheme, and I will take Rawly and leave you."

"And you'll come back."

Later he sensed he should have taken his wife in his arms, kissed her, soothed her, taken her to bed. It was what he had wanted to do, for he loved her, and even at other times could relish, be amused at her unreasonable outbursts. He could usually calm and tame these by handling her, demonstrating his admiration, and admittedly his domination of her—when he could. But this day he was

125

still keyed up by settling up with Canning; his nerve ends had taken a battering to keep a cool exterior. He now merely turned away from Maude and walked out into the garden, petted the spotted coach dog puppy the Winterses had sent over for Rawly as a gift.

15

The day the Los Angeles *Star* printed an item that Enoch Kingston, in partnership with Charles Auden White, had taken an option to buy a 400 x 180 foot lot just off the Plaza, after a morning spent removing his personal effects, sketches and records from the Wilmington office on the Canning wharf, Enoch came home to an empty house, to find Maude, the baby Rawly and his nurse gone, even the coach dog, Sam. Miguel, the old man who gave the impression he took care of the three horses and the garden, said his, Enoch's family, had left that morning in a carriage sent out from the Alvarez Rancho; left, señor, *si*, with trunks and bundles. No, they had left no message, but "the señora, she said you, Señor, would know why she leave." To himself he muttered, *"Es de vidrio la mujer."*

The logical thing would have been for Enoch to go out to the rancho and bring back his family, just as the community social pattern expected in such domestic situations. Two things kept him from carrying out the project. He was very tired; the final break with Canning had rasped his nerves raw—so that he had wanted to shout, kick something, *anything* bigger than a cat. For days he had nursed an anger, a state he always tried to avoid. But there it was: he was angry at Canning, and now he was being outraged at Maude's fleeing. He had not made her any promises he wouldn't buy land. But also he had forgotten that he and Chalky had sometime earlier entered into an option offer with old Mrs. Guiragh Pico that they had not expected to get. She had that Spanish idea one must *never* sell the land, and she had sounded like one who meant to keep her vow. But she had changed her mind. So Chalky White, unaware of Maude's deep-seated threats, had arranged the option papers as a partnership the two men had agreed upon weeks before.

Enoch also knew he would say the wrong things to Maude if he went out to the rancho in his present heated state of mind. Better cool off—let the both of us, man and wife, get the spleen out of our rages, come together in a few days with less of the grue on us. That is marriage; always jockeying for position, ready in a little time to take up where we had left off.

A few days on her own with her Spanish relatives would serve Maude right. There was too much hot chili in the emotional makeup of all the Alvarezes. Enoch, as a man of his period, was unaware of any of his prejudices; he just felt that he came from an ethnic group much more stable, controlled, than that of the Latins. That this was mostly a myth didn't hamper its being widely accepted and acted upon. Enoch certainly accepted it, even if he was developing into a thinking man.

He ate a light meal of cold cornbread, sliced venison pie, made a miserable pot of coffee. He slept well, but in a tumbling about sleep—aware in the night that several times he reached out for someone who wasn't there. He came awake early, hearing Miguel's rooster in the garden shack anticipate the dawn. Irrational, stiff, irritated, he loaded a shotgun with birdshot and fired at the fowl, merely removing some of its tail feathers.

He ate breakfast with Chalky White in a saloon run by an Irish sailor named Kevin, who had jumped ship and lost an arm in a San Felipe mine accident. Enoch didn't care too much for the kippers, braised kidneys, or shirred eggs Kevin provided. Chalky insisted it was the only civilized food in town. "Only time I feel there is something in London I miss."

Enoch wanted to talk of Maude's rebellion, but didn't. Chalky finished off a good breakfast; unlike most habitual drinkers, he always began the day with a hearty meal. Then he sipped the whisky Kevin set before him.

"I've heard from Baring Brothers, the London bankers—their man in New York that is. The telegraph is a great bit of invention, isn't it? Barings are interested in forming a company with the Texas people for floating a rail issue. Cheer up—why the glum expression?"

"That option on the lot by the Plaza. Maude trouble."

"Bit of a diddle at home? Didn't mean to involve you in any domestic dust up. Still, there's a saddle company wants to build on that plot. I'll sell him our option at a fair profit, and you'll sleep double again."

"Maude is unreasonable. Went off to her damn family."

"Hard cheese, that," Chalky said. "Mrs. K. really putting the spur to you. . . . Well, now to this Baring Brothers' backing a railroad issue of bonds. Have done it in the Argentine, you know—solid, with the Bank of England patting them on the head. They are prepared to sell the bonds for a rail-line from the Texas cattle country north, and another line from San Diego across the mountains through Outlaw Pass. I need some figures on how many steers could be carried by such lines to Kansas City and Chicago."

"Damn uninformed, aren't they?" Enoch pushed aside the dish of kidneys untasted, and took a small notebook bound in elk skin from an inner pocket, turning some pages that seemed spider webs of smudged pencil markings.

"Ever hear of J. C. McCoy? No? Few folk have who are not in the big beef business. He started the big cattle drives north to Abilene, along the Jesse Chisholm trail, by offering to buy all steers end of rail-line there. Built a corral for three thousand head of cattle. Longhorn skinny carcasses mostly, but he took 'em—went on in 1867 to ship thirty-five thousand steers. Christ, Chicago is on its knees begging for more steers. The packers they just go out to meet the trains fifty, sixty miles outside of Chicago to get a chance to bid early for the beef, the hogs."

"Good! Now that's the stuff to give the troops, Enoch, to impress the bankers."

"Next year, three hundred thousand longhorns were shipped out of Kansas after the long walk from Texas. This year, Solly tells me, packers' figures show so far McCoy has shipped three-quarters of a million steers from the railhead."

"Give me that in writing, all those poor bossies walking from Texas. Now, how many cattle can a rail-line built from the herds' homes carry to replace these slow cattle drives?"

"According to how big a line is built, and what spur lines you feed it with. Millions of steers, if they want them. And some day they'll be able to butcher and dress beef, ice it and ship it in cars."

"Of course, but now, Enoch, stick to cattle cars."

"No dream—there is a refrigerator car a William Davis invented. But the beef lays right on the ice and turns a rotten purple color. But there is a feller, a man named Tiffany whose written me he's taking out a patent on a refrigerator car with bunkers for the dressed beef and tanks for the ice, solid vault doors to keep out the heat. Don't know if it's practical. So we'll just transport live cattle if they back a rail-line."

Chalky finished his drink and was so interested in the conversation, he was unaware of Kevin's pouring him a fresh one.

"I'd want Pistol Johnson with us. I know law, but money—hard cash, credit takes a hard-nutted chap. Now, how to begin? I mean, what will we ask for?"

"Survey crews for us to work with—checking, mapping, to see if rails, locomotives can be delivered. Then work crews to be hired. I want to use Chinese. Those monkeys are great with blasting powder, as they showed for the Central Pacific. Marvelous rock men. And it *all* has to come together at the right time."

"That's up to them and me. To set up an outside new construction corporation and how we three divide it. You work out in detail where we'd build the main castle, the rallying point."

"Division point? Not in Los Angeles. About sixty miles from here there's a place levels off at three thousand feet, fifty thousand acres. Outlaw Pass up above it, forty miles away, where we can cross the mountains, and another from this point for a route from a San Diego line east and south. Buy up that level land; it's worthless. Build a town, machine shops, work trains, set up a foundry."

"Rein in. Your father-in-law doesn't own this? No? Good. Easy does it. Just get the prospects of a road, two roads, down on paper, not the cost. On that we become overoptimistic."

Enoch wanted to talk of his share of the stock and bond issues. How he was to be paid beyond wages. He wasn't going to repeat the Canning business of just getting a small slice of the pie and little control of his endeavors. Canning was happy enough with his little *chug-chug* railroad. But he and Chalky and Pistol Johnson would be dreaming big and, *if* only dreaming, then let it all be so goddamn big it would be worth dreaming about.

Enoch left after promising to get figures, rough maps of routes all down on paper. He went back to his house hoping Maude, repentant and reasonable, would be there. She was not there. He saddled a horse and in a kind of compulsive urge—his head floating in railroad thoughts— rode halfway to the Alvarez Rancho, then turned back and spent the rest of the day laying out an ideal, but reasonable railroad system.

The idea of building a rail-line was a fantasy he only as yet half believed. But the maps he drew were real enough. A rail-line out of San Diego up to the division junction of all those acres he hoped to have, then south to Fort Yuma, Tombstone, La Mesilla and El Paso, Fort Davis, Uvalde, and end of the line in San Antonio. Looking over this route he decided why not go on and draw tracks into New Orleans? Go whole hog—it's only a game, anyway. Chalky was talking through his whisky head. Still, the important item would be moving steers north. He laid out a rail-line from Fort Chadbourne to Colbers Ferry (meant a bridge there) in Indian territory, to Tipton, into Kansas City, *or* St. Louis? On paper, anything was possible. He was too het up, as if he already had the project going.

He needed to cool off—so he left it at that, and saddled a horse and went riding. He couldn't shake the images of rail-lines. Perhaps it would be better to move track from San Antonio to El Paso and drive the cattle-carrying line north through Albuquerque, Santa Fe, Topeka, and so get into Caycee, Kansas City. He hadn't yet made up his mind when he was riding along an arroyo that led into the foothills and to an open space enclosed by splendid trees. Here he could look out across the valley toward the higher hills, umber and gold and untouched. He came for privacy to this clearing, which he had discovered. No one had yet built any houses or tried to raise crops. He had found the green heart of it a year before, and at times when he rode out to it to think out some problem, he'd wonder if this was not in some way his desert island, a tropical paradise that as a callow sixteen-year-old he had once hoped to find.

Today he was amazed to find he was not alone. A woman was seated on an unfolded camp stool, and on a board on her knees she was painting a watercolor sketch of the view below. It was Hannah Winters. He dismounted from his horse and tied it off to a sapling. He walked down to the painter and said hello.

Hannah Winters turned her head in his direction. She had a rat-tail brush held between her teeth, and a fat set of sable-hair ones in her hand. She mumbled something he took for a returned greeting. Hannah wore a field worker's wide straw hat to keep the sun from her eyes, and a kind of white linen traveling coat called a duster. She was wearing a riding skirt and boots under it.

He saw a chestnut horse cropping grass to the left, an English sidesaddle on its back.

Hannah took the brush from her mouth. He noticed that one of her teeth slightly overlapped another. In all their meetings, he hadn't really noticed. "You've found my secret glen."

"Found it myself couple years ago," he said. "Staked my claim, but I'll share."

"I've been painting her a week. I'm doing a series of local scenes for my sister Netta."

He looked at the large square of paper tacked to the board. "The color on the butte over there is good, but I don't see any pine bough stuck up front."

"That's a foreground formula to make the background sink back in space."

He looked at the sidesaddle on her horse. "You find it hard to ride sidesaddle?"

"No, I rather like astride—but Solly thinks it not lady-like."

"Don't ever try sidesaddle on an Indian pony."

They felt very comfortable with each other. The sun came through the trees behind the clearing, the horses cropped grass with a tearing sound of their teeth. Hannah had a basket of food, a rug laid out on the ground and a bottle of wine.

"I was just about to picnic. Sit down."

"You carry all this with you like an army?"

She set the board and the brushes aside. "Everything folds away and becomes some other shape, behind the saddle straps."

There was cold fried chicken, some kind of bread he had never eaten before, which she called *challah*, olives pickled with just a hint of dill and chili, pale yellow cheddar cheese and crackers. The wine was clear and ruby-colored. They took turns drinking from a silver traveling cup.

Hannah had at first seemed a bit shy at being discovered at work. She had a high regard of her skill as a watercolor painter, but she usually called it "just blotting" when someone praised it or was critical. They ate and made small talk; gossip, town items, the growing town and its problems.

Enoch felt the need of female company. He was still outraged at Maude's deserting him. There was in his nature a need for contact with women. When he had done his work, he had a desire to talk to someone—differently than the usual male conversation. It was to shyly communicate, but he would have been surprised if told so. It was one of the sides to his nature that he never truly fully understood. He was like that; he could accept certain aspects of his nature without wanting to take them apart and analyze them. With men, as he grew older, he was usually a facade—only with women did he reveal other sides of his nature.

He and Hannah spent the next two hours after picnicking talking about books they had read. He confessed he felt he was past novel reading. He talked of finding ideas, emotions in himself he couldn't understand. She told him she ached at the beautiful country and how dreadfully spoiled it was getting by the kind of building and settlements the land developers were opening up. Enoch explained Americans. They saw land as something to be conquered, tamed, be made submissive, and how one could not really get to the core of any problem with most of the men who had really taken over the land. Opinionated, driving men. Good men and maybe strong, but, like Canning, wanting their own way, even if it wasn't efficient or practical. The afternoon progressed. They had talked together very often, but never so intimately or in such an isolated setting. Hannah talked of her family, of her dead father, the former Hasidic student and follower of the texts of Spinoza, of her sister Netta, married to a St. Louis beer brewer. From there the talk wandered a bit. Neither mentioned wife or husband or children. Hannah was fearful of being critical of Solly. She admired and loved the man, she thought as she packed up her painting gear, but emotionally she lived in novels or rather saw herself as *not* living the lives of women who dared to sacrifice all for love in Russian and French worlds. Of course, only in the *best* Russian and French novels. The prose and the passion had to have certain grace, she had written her sister. "Do I dare say '*je suis prête*?' " She was not a foolish woman, but she had no outlet for her intellect, no one to share an interest in wider ideas and reactions. What she felt she needed never could exist in this new and raw land. Perhaps this big man had some qualities of grace—but he was drifting into the world of *doing*, "getting on with it."

At first she had seen him as a disciple, one who shared with her many of her emotional reactions to the arts. She had been wrong. He had read books she had loaned him, had been helped by her, directed by her ideas on manners, on attitudes. She had encouraged in him the thought that he was in some way unique, gifted, not just guided to produce material things. But she now knew his version of himself was not her picture of him. His uniqueness was toward material achievement—the solid, the real, the promotion of what was called *progress*, a word she disliked.

As they talked, their voices seemed to grow lower in tone and they sat closer together. Enoch became aware of her as a warm, ready woman. Older than himself by perhaps a good twelve, fifteen years which, he figured, made her safe from him. But she was well set up, firmly filled out, as was apparent now with her duster off, riding jacket set aside, close to him in shirtwaist and the full riding skirt. She took on for him, right then and there, a sensual quality that he had had hints of in the past, but now was strong as scent.

Just as he enjoyed female company, Enoch was also very simple in his reaction to women that pleased him. He was a natural womanizer. All his life he was much given to the need to possess women. It was another powerful drive, a trait in himself he never tried to analyze or explain. He derived great pleasure in copulation, a word he had looked up in a tattered Johnson dictionary. He admired grace in women, handling their bodies, listening to their voices. He was to possess many of them—some for a longer time, some for just casual once or twice meetings.

He was yet unaware of his full commitment to his dependence on sex when he turned from his work to some pleasure not connected with his projects. This afternoon, talking about the dogs that roamed the streets at night, and Mr. Ruskin's writing on art, he casually flicked a crawling ant from Hannah's right boot, firmly felt her ankle slim as a deer's fetlock under the fine leather. His hand was under the wide riding skirt, past the stocking gartered at the knee. She was aware he was caressing her naked skin below her drawers. She said nothing, having stopped talking at his touch. She just looked at him, no expression of outrage or surprise. But her breathing was taking on a low but audible sound that merged with the cropping of grass by the horses and the *bzzzz* of some wasps high up on a limb, floating around their brown paper hive.

The hand moved and was on her inner thigh, fingers fluttered, patted, grasped. What followed next was from no novel. No writer that she had read, from Sand and Eliot to Balzac and Tolstoy, had described the handling of a woman's pubic area, the probing delight, the shiver-producing invasion of that secret corner. His arms came from someplace to move her down on the rug on the earth. The man so close, the man who removed her drawers with no fumbling, no word, pushed up her riding skirt. And as the local expression was, shucked his pants to expose "the old Adam."

They were kissing wetly, his rough cheek rolling over her smooth skin, her head lolling about as she gave out gasping sounds; he didn't know if they were gasps of pleasure or protest. Her lips came back swollen to his, and he tasted her. Then he heaved himself up over her, spread-eagled her and was in her. Never a thought of Maude, then, or Solly, or the right or the wrong of this. He was letting his cock do his thinking. She was aware crude people called it *fucking*. They had lain very still, hearts pumping after the climax, laced in each other's arms. Then they sat up, looking earnestly into each other's faces. They repaired the damage to clothes, covered up those areas of their bodies that society did not approve of as being exposed in the open air. There was no regret, remorse; both had been pleased, physically pleased in what had happened. Hannah retired behind a bush for some intimate attentions and to rearrange her riding clothes and brush grass and dust from them. When she came back, Enoch was packing up her painting gear. He looked at her.

"No regrets?"

"No," she said firmly. "No regrets." She would have preferred softer, more intimate words, some tender personal comment. She was still shaking a bit, and they finished off the wine. And kissed, hard at first, then tenderly, she moving her body against him, his arms held strongly clasped along her back. She was surprised that she did not feel like a doomed heroine, or particularly dishonored, or the shame of a woman who had betrayed her husband. She felt damn good. She felt a man and woman like this were not just a man and woman. They were individuals. No man was like another man, and, as for a women, she wondered for the first time how she compared to Maude. Enoch had no such thoughts; this was a fine body he had pleasured with—and he admired her and did not question the situation.

Enoch helped her into the sidesaddle, arranged her legs. She pressed his hand with her now gloved fingers. They rode side by side slowly out of the setting of their adultery. It was the first of their many meetings. For the next two months they met very often. When the weather was bad, they went to bed in a small inn on the Rio Ronda Road run by a Mexican-Indian couple. Hannah developed a sense of sin, and somehow it added to her pleasure.

16

Much later, around the turn of the century, there would be books written and muckraking articles published in magazines that created legends and myths about Enoch Bancroft Kingston as a young man. None was close to the truth, and most made a fable of his early years in speaking of his personality, morality, and achievements. The worst mass of misinformation was the officially endowed and commissioned *History of the Western, Great Plains & Gulf Railroad*. In none of these texts is any mention made that Maude Kingston returned to her husband after her first flight from him, after a separation of over three months. In fact, none of the material ever mentioned that she had left him, and would a few more times.

The image we get of Maude from these writings is a nebulous one and more like a colored travel poster that has faded a bit, picturing her as a fiery Mexican dancer, the type to carry a rose in her teeth and stamp a fandango. The Hearst Sunday press that was to sensationalize stories of her suggested a high-living wild Amazon raised by fiery, proud, Spanish-speaking dons, riding large-balled stallions, shooting bears. In one invented episode, she was pictured flying through the night, hair unbound, holding the reins of a four-horse team of half-tamed broncos, as from the seat of a light carriage she whipped up the red-nostriled steeds, on her way to a train wreck where Enoch Kingston lay near death. Hardly based on a full knowledge of the facts.

While Maude was strong-willed, proud, and given to alternating periods of elation and depression, she was sensible to reality for all her moods, a loyal wife, in love with Enoch and her children. As for her return to home and husband, it was hardly high drama. She just appeared one morning with the baby Rawly, his nurse, Lucita Jimenez, and two rancho workers carrying her luggage and baskets of rancho products. Enoch was still sleeping, worn out from a night of redrawing survey maps; the bed, the floor was covered with his sketches and notes. Maude came in, sniffed the stale air of the bedroom, flung open the window, and went to the side of the sleeping man. He needed a shave; he smelled of whisky and funky bedding. Maude caressed his brow and kissed his cheek. He came slowly awake, fighting off facing the day, blinked, tried to focus his eyes.

"I'm back," said Maude.

"That's good," Enoch said, and smiled. "Very good."

He accepted her in his arms and she whispered, "Oh, how dull the life is at the rancho, and without you. My father, he sits in his best clothes, leans on his cane, sips drinks, talks of how now he can afford more horses. My brothers, some are regular Yankees, figuring on crops and beef prices—and some just sleep till noon, and tomcat all night. Eating, drinking, pinching the maids, talking of the grand old days. Um-um!" She buried her head in Enoch's chest. "Um, you smell."

"I sure do. Been up three nights."

"Go out to the garden. Have Miguel turn the pump on you."

"Let me wake up all the way first."

"I brought a smoked ham, a huge fish, the new vegetables, six dozen duck eggs, and a dozen jars of jalapena peppers."

"I am hungry."

He was pleased Maude was back. He would always relate well to women; some said because he was not too critical of their faults. He saw them as living up to the nature of the sex. That, to him, was what made them satisfactory women.

Rawly, growing, expanding, tottering, came in and up to the bed. He was a handsome child, not given to baby fat, attractive with those huge dark eyes like animated plums, topped by long lashes, eyes that were more Alvarez, Enoch thought, than Kingston. But the whelp had my stubbornness, my howling for what he wanted. He also

138

had Enoch's need for seeking, discovering the world—traits Enoch felt came from his gism, he had never heard of the word *genes*. He hugged the boy who yelled, *"Cuidado!"*

"We'll have to get him back to talking American."

It was a happy day. There was no comment from Enoch on Maude's leaving, and she did not question Enoch as to how he had passed the time. She assumed he had been miserable without her and had awaited her return with the bee-in-the-ear gruffness of a male deprived of his domestic and bed comforts. She was Latin enough to wonder if he had been in Madame Needle's banging shop to slack his *cojones*, and she was Catholic enough to feel a man was a man and also an animal who needed the taming influences, the grace and civilizing presence of a wife.

It was only after he had shaved, bathed, eaten, and spent the afternoon in bed with Maude, that he realized her return would mean the end of the affair with Hannah Winters. It had become a tense situation in the last two weeks, a bit strained with her romantic ardor expanding beyond his own boundaries as to what he was willing to put into a pleasurable sexual liaison. He had never told Hannah he loved her, and, being honest about these things, would have told her so if she had asked. *If* she had asked for such a declaration. She had known better than to ask. Hannah was very intelligent; she knew that what he meant to her did not relate to what she meant to him. He was respectful, grateful, but not deeply involved on any lasting emotional level.

There were no more visits to the glen, or the inn on the Rio Ronda road. It was clear to Hannah that when Maude was seen again with Enoch, it was time to write finished to their adventure; she wished there was a better word than adventure. As some said of Enoch and Maude, "They've made it up." Others said, "Been away visiting her folks." If anyone hinted at more, it was not part of public gossip.

The house was cleaner, the food better, and Rawly was a wild but charming growing child, and if Sam nipped him, Rawly bit the dog back.

The railroad project of Baring Brothers and the Texans

was progressing; too slowly for Enoch, but it was a reality, not just a dream fantasy. Later, the texts of certain books were to assume he had come from nowhere, a wild young railroad genius who had dashed out of the wilderness like a John the Baptist of the rails, and taken control and single handedly created his first big railroad system.

Actually, it was other men who sheperded his plans, his surveys. Financial men in The City, in London's money and bond issue markets—also land experts. Older men who wrote long reports and argued a lot and demanded proofs. What finally emerged was the Pacific & Great Plains Railroad, with the help of many people. Enoch was not the all-wise, knowing expert—rather the bright apprentice who was given his chance on a tight rein.

As Chalky White explained to Enoch and Pistol Johnson while they ate a marvelous dish of *sesos de ternera* under the arbor of the Kingston garden, it was a smaller version of his, Enoch's first plans, and only the germ of what was later to become a different kind of rail system.

Chalky White was sipping Spanish brandy, but was fairly sober. He had tapered off during the drawing up of the mountain of legal papers with the English and Texas backers, documents that presented the final plan, the actual pattern of how the road was to be built and financed.

"We *don't* have control; if you want a few titles, fine. It boils down to this. They are already selling P and G.P. bonds, and they watch us and dole out the money, the credits, as the line is built. I've set up the Huntington-Crocker type plan for us three. The Western and Great Plains—the mother company—makes a contract with the Kingston Construction Company to actually build the first road. Another contract—follow this, chaps—is made by Kingston Construction Company with the Johnson Supply Company to provide the rails, tools, and to contract for locomotives and rolling stock. You follow me?"

Pistol Johnson tapped his fork on a plate. "You're a cockeyed genius, Chalky."

"Legally, of course, I am."

Enoch, with Rawly sitting on his lap, asked, "And they agree to all this?"

"I put it to them as practical, and they know it. It's the way railroads—like the Central and Southern Pacific—are built in the United States. In the West, anyway. The three of us are equal partners in Kingston Construction and the Johnson Supply Company. Barings advance us money and credits to start the picks flying, the wheels spinning. They also pay in P. and G.P. bonds—let us pray for the Western and Great Plains to make money."

"How much in bonds?" asked Enoch.

"All I can jolly well press out of them. It's issued to us in ratio, in steps, according to how much rail we have down and later on a percentage of what income comes in from shipping cattle, farm products, and carrying passengers."

Pistol Johnson was thinking hard, looking over some papers Chalky White laid before him. "We make money on construction, maybe, and on supplies, maybe. If the railroad is a success, we make a lot of money, or—well, it's a poker game isn't it? We could take a few good hands, maybe even make a grand slam."

Enoch put Rawly down and the boy clung to his knee. "Tell me a story."

"Maude, get him out of here. Oh, all right, Rawly, a story when you're in bed."

With the child carried off, Enoch passed around a box of cigars. "I've got survey crews out from San Diego. I've got an option in those acres I want as division headquarters. And the survey crew from Texas is moving, mapping north to meet us. I'm broke meeting paydays. How about the two of you?"

Chalky White shook his head. "You haven't paid me a legal fee in a year. And I've been too busy to take on runaway horse damage claim cases."

Pistol Johnson touched a huge flawed yellow diamond in his cravat, turned around a six-carat ring on his left hand. "I suppose I don't have to show this flash goods to trap tinhorns—now that I'm not setting up tenderfeet and gulls to three-card monte or stud. A Chinaman will give me maybe a thousand on both."

"Keep them," said Chalky White, "There's a draft on Solly's bank due from London." The lawyer was more animated than he had been for years. Like Enoch, he was becoming addicted to railroading. As for Pistol Johnson, he was a gambler, and this looked aces to him so far. He hoped there were no jokers in the deck. Percy Johnson wanted very much to enter a respectable world, give his wife a place in the social scene, and no longer have ground glass churning in his stomach. There had been too many times when he was down to his last gold coin in a run of bad luck and the cards that were turning up in his hand could have been better. He was close then to cold decking and cheating—and had resisted the temptation so far. Unlike most professional gamblers, he knew he had peaked years ago in his bouts with Lady Luck at the card table.

Hannah Winters planned a prolonged visit to her sister Netta in St. Louis. Netta was expecting her first child, and Hannah explained it all to Sol over a Friday-night meal, lit by the two brass candlesticks Sol's mother had given him on leaving for America.

"Netta, still such a child, is all at ends, as if having a baby were such a new thing. I must go to her."

"I suppose we'll manage with you gone," said Sol Winters tasting the dish of *tzimmis*, a compote of prunes and carrots he insisted be prepared for Friday nights.

"The maids are fairly well trained. Speak Spanish to them. The children are in school most of the day."

"How long do you think you'll be gone?"

"I don't know. Get me tickets to San Francisco and from there east."

"The steamer is the fastest, but you get seasick. The Butterfield stagecoach is a hard ride."

"I want to see more of this West you men are carving up, before the Southern Pacific perhaps comes down to us here."

"We hope so. They're holding us up for a fortune in subsidies to terminate in Los Angeles—if we don't pay—" He waved off the idea. "Kingston, White and Johnson have come through with something fabulous. I'm going to bank for their companies. Enoch is a remarkable man." He continued to eat, chewing slowly.

Hannah sneezed. "This horseradish sauce is too strong."

That night after her bath, Hannah sat in her old-rose silk robe and wrote a long letter, alone in her dressing room. Then, reading it over twice and sobbing, she burned the letter in her washbasin. It was enough she felt that she had poured her heart out in a decent prose—to a man she had committed adultery with. It had all the revelations of what sex could be. Even love? It would serve no purpose having Enoch read the letter, also it could fall into the wrong hands.

Hannah left Los Angeles on the north-bound Butterfield Stage two days later, with a basket of food, a sunshade, and a small bottle of brandy "for the fatigues of the journey" that Sol gave her as they embraced at the coach station and parted. From the ache of love in his sad eyes and the way he held her hand, Hannah knew Sol *knew*.

Enoch was camped with ten men two hundred miles into wild country to the south, working with a survey crew, sleeping under the stars. The fire of piñon logs was banked, the air full of the smell of crushed sage and night sounds of small animals in the darkness. Hunting, he supposed, each other for love, or for food. He did not think of Maude or of Hannah, but of his son Rawly. And the hope of more sons, and a daughter or two for Maude. Uncle Floyd, he remembered, used to say, "A man isn't a man until he's killed someone, planted a tree, and begot himself a family." Enoch knew he liked a good tree as well as the next man, and he'd killed a Johnny Reb or two. But he saw a tree as so many cubic feet of timber to cut up into railroad ties—ties to lay across miles of land and railroad acres they were going to get free from the government for the good of settling the country, attracting homesteaders, ranchers. Enoch slept, snoring lightly, as the fire blinked with one last red coal.

Problems

17

In February of 1871, a vital railroad bill of major interest to Southern California was before Congress. If not worded properly it would, some claimed, wipe out Los Angeles as a major city, but if correctly written, it would push El Pueblo forward as the city that would become the southern giant of the Pacific Coast.

Enoch Kingston and Chalky White had been in Washington for weeks on their own project—what free Federal lands the Western & Great Plains Railroad would get for building the road. Pressuring, entertaining members of Congress, passing out maps showing the W. & G.P. plans as the hope of American transportation or, as Chalky White ironically put it, "the greatest thing since the invention of fire."

The Western & Great Plains Railroad was building rail from San Diego through Texas, and soon, it hoped, north to Kansas City. The Southern Pacific, controlled by what had been the men of Central Pacific, would meet the W. & G.P. on the Colorado at Fort Yuma.

The Los Angeles people, Canning's L.A. & S.P. R.R., and the city officials knew it was important the congressional bill included a solid, iron-firm clause that the Southern Pacific tracks *must* run through Los Angeles. If the Southern Pacific bypassed Los Angeles, then the city of San Diego, where the Western & Great Plains was to reach the ocean, would be the major Southern California port on the Pacific, not Los Angeles.

Chalky White, in their suite at the Willard Hotel in Washington, had been sober for three days and needed sleep. He was examining a list of congressmen and senators, with notes of suggestions (more than suggestions, in many cases) how they would vote.

"Rum show for Los Angeles. Good for us."

Enoch was pacing back and forth, stopping now and again to look out at what he could see of the city that ruled the nation; at clerks and others going home after a day of either work or loafing on government time. A troop of blue-clad horsemen galloped past, returning from some ceremonial duty at Arlington. They were burying more Civil War generals and officers there, with special rites and noble words. Not, Enoch thought, for lower ranks like me. It's too damp, anyway.

Chalky yawned and tossed down the papers. "It's like this, Enoch. We get what you want and some fine Federal land in thousands of acres along a lot of our right-of-way. We have contracts and funds. But the Southern Pacific, forced to run through L.A., has to be part of this bill. Now let's talk. What helps Los Angeles, helps us—and—"

"Hell, *why*? The stronger W. & G.P. is, and the weaker *they* are, the better."

"You still dislike Canning and his group—their fight with the Southern Pacific? Right *now* if they fail—it benefits us—but someday we'll want lines into Los Angeles ourselves. Los Angeles will get some sort of train connection east and north. Has to. Better they remember, my dear chap, you helped them get onto this blinking railroad bill. Get it? You kiss my arse—I kiss your arse."

"What?"

"Arse, old man, arse-kissing. We all line up for it, or do it."

"They have their people working here for what they want. Solly Winters, Ben Wilson representing the ranchers, Downey, Widney, for the land developers."

"Join with them."

"Canning has sure left a sour taste in my mouth for Los Angeles."

"Try a little whisky—I shall, and totter off to bed. This staying sober is very fatiguing. Sleep on it; do we support Los Angeles or don't we?"

Enoch turned from the window as the lawyer picked up a decanter and went to his room. Twilight was dropping like pollen on the city. It was a time of day that always

148

depressed Enoch. No one looking at his solid body, the face serious and intelligent, with the square-cut spade beard he now wore. Most observers would have thought he had no other emotions but the matter at hand, whatever it was—dealing with bankers, drawing maps, laying rail, testing locomotives. But the coming of the dusk always gave him a feeling of the end of the world, a final pitching down of mankind into darkness, the death of the sun. The premonition of death, for no reason he knew, seemed lurking at every turn; life on a dark staircase, going down. All his life in his nightmares, that was repeated, a recurring drama; his descending this steep, dark set of stairs and waiting for him at the bottom that wide-open fire-door, like a grinning skull. Actually, the open door of a giant firebox on a huge locomotive and standing there was the big fireman and his big coal scoop. Death himself.

Enoch had no idea why this bad dream came to him in moments of crisis. Hard, prolonged work often kept the nightmare away. Christ, to get out of Washington and be laying track again. He thought of what the lawyer had said. He was very close to Chalky White. They were a partnership of two men whose brains seemed to merge perfectly on major ideas, so that between them they clarified situations, triggered to get the proper answers. They were also gradually becoming involved in a deep and trusting friendship. It went beyond their solid partnership with Pistol Johnson. It was in no way what the times would have called "an unnatural passion."

Enoch spoke out loud to the empty room, "All right, Chalky, we support El Pueblo in that clause in the bill before Congress." Enoch reached for his hat on a hall tree—a Western hat, black, with not too wide a brim, and the brim pushed up a bit on the sides. The hat had become his trade mark in Washington, and he would adopt it. Western folk wore top hats in the East; the Stetson had not yet been accepted east of the Mississippi.

The journalists of the Capitol had taken to following Enoch in the streets for his comments, not just about the hearings of the bill. A tall figure in that Western headgear, a double-breasted frock coat with tails, good solid square-toed shoes, he was a novelty to the press. Young, daring, and either the coming railroad baron of the West, or destined to go down against the cunning skullduggery of Huntington, Crocker, Hopkins, and Stanford, and their octopus the Southern Pacific, also that powerful rival, the Texas Pacific Railroad. And there were half a dozen lines out of Kansas, Chicago, the Northwest, who also had desires, hopes for a control of the southwest routes to the Gulf, and up the eastern coast as far as Washington. Enoch knew he was a million miles from his biggest visions—mostly as yet only on paper. But Chalky had given him a glimmer of an idea—a pinpoint of light—and it was growing brighter. He knocked on Chalky's door.

"If Los Angeles wants my help, there is a price I can claim, eh?"

The voice behind the door began with a chuckle. "I figured you'd come around to see the advantage of helping the enemy. You're going out?"

"Yes. Need to relax, get the kinks out."

"In whose bed?"

Enoch almost answered it was a better way than taking a bottle to bed; to have a naked woman whose body one admired, used, well-used, could free a man of the day's tensions, the strains of being alert and wry and matching someone's hints, tricks, goals, and getting things done, squared away. He didn't say anything to the closed door. Never stab anyone in their weak spot if it served no purpose.

Chalky sat on the bed in his room, took off shoes, collar and tie, opened his shirt. There was very little drink in the decanter. He killed it and sat for some minutes, head down, then rose, went to his alligator-hide Gladstone bag and took out a bottle of scotch. Americans, nature's noblemen and all that, didn't drink scotch much. But it was a reminder he had been a member of a good club on St. James's Square, an Oxford Blue, and made a bugger of a mess of his life over that—never mind what or who. He was better off than Enoch, who had to relax with women. Poor sod, drawn to all that soft, warm meat—all that unlacing and uncorseting and the body and powder smell; be careful of done-up hair, pin-held. All over the damn place.

. . . The clutching and the embracing and eating of noses. Really—he took a sip of scotch from the bottle. . . . Yes, ah . . . that glow was starting. . . . And no complications. No letters, no female tears, secret meetings, no costs of trinkets to find, flowers. And those moments of final breaking off. *Hell hath no fury*—He took another sip and rotated his head in pleasure and reassurance. They never really go, the slit-owning harpies . . . they always had their wiles . . . In the feathered hats, small feet in white kid high-buttoned shoes. Formidable bitches, clinging vines. Witches with hatpins. Better the bottle than Enoch's hunt in the posh saloons, or the red velvet knocking shops of the demimonde . . . By the time Chalky White had half a pint of scotch inside him, he was sleeping on his back, mouth open, the happy smile of complete escape from reality, as he saw it, etched on his face.

The Olcott was a small apartment house "New Orleans style" on H Street. Discreet, painted white, and iron-railed front steps of marble. A small Negro in a blue coat with brass buttons (and a high gates-ajar collar showing) was always on duty to meet all visitors, but never to greet them by name or title. He took Enoch's five-dollar gold piece and nodded. Enoch went up one floor and along a worn but very good rug—up to the brown door lettered 2-B, knocked lightly. He tapped twice and waited. He heard the *tap tap* of hard-heeled slippers. Hannah Winters opened the door. She was wearing a pale blue silk dressing gown and the slippers. Nothing else.

They embraced without saying a word. The room was well furnished, solid maple furniture, gas mantle fixtures. No indication the room had been done with taste or much interest. The big bed was its main feature. The beds of the Olcott, as many senator or public official, girls of the best families along the Potomac and whores and divorcées could testify to, were the most comfortable in any safe hideaway in Washington, D.C.

Enoch smiled, took off his coat, his collar, opened his shirt and scratched his stomach. Hannah looked at him, studied him closely.

"You've gained weight, Enoch."

"Been a long time since we've been together."

"Two years," she said.

"You haven't changed," he said and put his arms around her.

"Grown older. A man doesn't grow old by years alone. But to a woman, a year can seem like three, four."

"Everything all right?" He held her closer, kissed her roughly and yet with deep feeling. She liked his vigor, his roughness. She moaned and put her head against his chest. "I wish I felt sinful, felt bad about doing this to Solly, the children."

"Balls. This isn't anything to do with them. It's you, me, what we were, what we are. Nothing more, nothing less. All the rest is kicking yourself in the ass." He got under the robe, kneaded her yielding buttocks like bread dough with his strong fingers.

"You don't think I've grown to look old? Gone flabby?"

"Get into bed."

"Tell me."

"Everything is hunky-dory."

They made love, they rolled about, he in a desire to drive out the day's doings, to come around to that peace of calmed nerves and organs that took pleasure, became sated, so he could sleep with no dream of the dark staircase and open firebox, the last final firebox of the burning out of life.

Hannah took great physical pleasure in their lovemaking. It was not just the vitality, power, cruel delight that Solly had never been, could never be. Enoch was her escape from the earnest, respectable banality of a banker's world, expected to act as a banker's wife, a mother of children she loved but found dull. A giver of parties for people who mattered socially and at the bank. *Zwei Seelen wohnen, ach, in meiner Brust.* Two souls in my bosom, ach. . . . This now with Enoch was the taste of the wilder life she had once read of as a young girl. Now, *now* as she approached a climax in the splendid bed, she held Enoch against her and she wanted to cry out to that earlier book version of herself, "I am Anna Karenina—I am Emma Bovary." Hannah came with wild bird cries and Enoch did not try to repress her. The Olcott walls were thick, made so for just such hoped-for moments.

152

Later they sat unclothed, smoking, Enoch smoking a cigar, Hannah, deeply inhaling a gold-tipped Russian cigarette she permitted herself at home only when alone.

Of course she looked older. Enoch saw that clearly in the gaslight. She had put on weight. But even so, a bit of slack here and there didn't take away anything from that marvelous, mellow body, and those great breasts were still hard and not with too much sag or droop. Hannah was the most satisfying of all the women he had lain with outside of his marriage. The tinted, curled whores, the casual pickups in the lobby of the Palace Hotel in San Francisco, even the too-thought-out theater of the Everleigh Club in Chicago, were to him only a passing through and a release. Hannah Winters was his first adultery; she had educated him in many ways—not just sexually—given him hints as how to be socially apt, what to read, how to see and partake of the bigger, outer world, see it as the everyday world of lucky individuals, as an enlargement, for bigger stakes with fancier words, of Los Angeles.

He no longer read novels, read little of anything but financial reports, what he could understand of scientific papers. Yes, he was grateful to her, and he leaned over and touched Hannah's arm. "You've been damn good for me. I don't mean just in bed."

"Coming here to this place you rented, and the dressing gown, slippers you had sent here. I excused myself by thinking you're something I helped create." She began to weep and hugged him. "You're my biggest child."

He was used to her romantic retreat to tears; he figured she rather enjoyed them, "I don't feel that young," he said.

"It's not true about my creating you. You'd have been you, done as you're doing, without me. Say I gave you a little pleasure, a little advice, and something you didn't have—call it polish."

"Haven't got too much of a shine on me yet."

He felt it was time to change the direction of their talk. He had avoided meeting her because he felt she was too much drawn to him, or rather an image of him she had made for herself. She was too much the intellectual romantic who had no idea of the danger of her situation. He did not want to wreck her marriage. Certainly did not want Hannah as a wife or permanent mistress even if he had wanted to leave Maude, which he didn't. Maude was a problem at times—but that didn't matter. He saw life as full of problems, and if not solving all of them, just disarming them. Reality crept in while he stood at the window, his back to her while Hannah piddled in the chamber pot.

"How does Solly feel about the congressional railroad bill?"

"He's fearful the Los Angeles clause will be left out."

"It will unless he and his people get off their duff and push hard."

"They have just about done all they can."

She sat on the bed putting on a silk stocking, pulling it up onto her calf, past the knee, up the thigh and as he watched, Enoch's desire for her body rose again. He took his eyes off her crisp pubic bush.

"You can tell Solly you have good information I'm backing—Western and Great Plains is, too—the Los Angeles clause in the congressional railroad bill."

She looked up from arranging the strings of her corset. "You are?"

"The people I'm with feel it's only fair."

"How can I tell Solly I know this?"

"Say you met Chalky White, he was a bit bottled and he told you."

"It's a fine thing you're doing, Enoch."

"Doing it with a long view. Two against Southern Pacific is better than one and one against them. Don't bother with the corset. Get back in bed."

Later, when Enoch had gone and the scent of him, their lovemaking, the tobacco smell, was all around her, Hannah Winters lay on the bed. *Now I'll not see him again,* she thought. *Perhaps once more in Washington. And then? Then? I could jump into the Potomac. I could get drunk (but I can't keep it down). I could be pregnant with his sperm still swimming in me (but I've stopped breeding, it seems). What I'll really do, of course, is get back to our hotel, bathe and dress up to the nines and go with sweet Solly to dinner at that splendid place where all the embassy people, State Department members and the biggest lobbyist people go and eat Eastern Shore soft-shell crab, Tide-*

water lobsters in drawn butter. Anna and Emma were af-
ter all only some fictions, men writers' ideas of what a
woman should do in moments of despair and doubt.

She dressed cheerfully, put on her hat and veil, and went out to the hack the Negro doorman had waiting. She gave him a silver dollar.

18

The spreading, thriving town of Kingston Junction had originally been a barren plateau where Indians once hunted small game, mostly ground rats and snakes, in a hungry season. Later, Mormon wagon trains that had nearly perished nearby came up through the mountains and over Outlaw Pass. There they rested their oxen, counted their dead, and offered up a prayer to their special version of the Godhead. In 1880, Kingston Junction had five thousand inhabitants, many of the adults working in the great yards and roundhouses, freight marshaling tracks of the Western & Great Plains Railroad. The town had first been called New Angeles by the survey crews on their plats of the town. However, Charles Auden White, who headed the railroad's legal staff, had scrawled on the final plans in red crayon, the words KINGSTON JUNCTION. From here were serviced the first Matthias Baldwin 4-8-0 locomotives to pound east out of San Diego and south to the plains and ranches of Texas. Cars with rosewood doors, green silk plush seats. When the rails set out freights, strings of sixty-five cattle cars—through Indian territory to Fort Smith and Topeka, the name *Kingston* became legal for all the surrounding area, and it became *Kingston County*.

The town on the rim of the division headquarters railroad junction was a hard, brawling town, more wise about Stevens valve gear and eccentric rods than sheep or crops. The train people—conductors, firemen, telegraphers, foremen, engineers—had lawns in front of their little company houses. As for the work gangs, the track workers, the migrant pick-and-shovel brigades, they lived in four-story barracks or boxlike boardinghouses, some even in old passenger coaches, wheels removed and set up, planted around the weedy rubbishy outskirts of the town. There were saloons and gin mills—crews were forbidden to drink or carry alcohol onto the trains. Two dance halls were active and six whorehouses were not molested by the law; for many of the drifting workers, the freight-handlers, caboose crews were not married, and some, if married, had wives forgotten on some other line: the Santa Fe, the Atchinson & Topeka. There were three churches, one Catholic, and the Chinese tracklayers had a joss house.

There were often killings in Kingston Junction, and grim poverty among the Mexican-Americans; poverty, too, stalked the Irish track crews who had large families and were usually divided into those who were drunkards (the shanty Irish,) and those who were respectable (lace-curtain Irish). The Chinese were not settlers in Kingston Junction, except for some cooks and servants.

It was like other towns in the Southwest living in the sun, attracting men and women (often with shady pasts), and many more with ideals and hopes of a good new life, and a faith in a God who seemed more benevolent amongst the sounds of a Western & Great Plains train whistling, dragging a mile-long freight up from the coast at a grade of twenty-six feet per mile. Good, too, the banging of locomotive repairs always present, with the clang of iron being forged or boilers being torn down for inspection over by the coal tipples.

The town had a smell of sage, of switching-engine grease, coal gas from the forges, and in every place in every room, every windowsill, a thin sifting-down of powdery cinders from the soft coal the engines consumed now that most of the wood burners had been retired or worn out.

There were grand houses: the White place, the Johnson French chateau, Floyd Denton's division superintendent's Victorian horror. But all were outshone by a structure on a regular green rising of hills to a peak, on which stood Kingston House, or, as some said, Kingston Mansion. And others, like Pat Mullaney, gang foreman, "There it is, and Himself now, he does his gracefulness fine now, don't he?"

The first Kingston House was three years old in 1880, and it was to be added to twice, expanded and raised two stories. (In 1934 it became a historical monument.) The first version was impressive enough—two stories—in part vague Italian villa style Maude had seen on a trip to Europe in 1876, and with a massive Regency roof and chimneys. It was built of a pale yellow stone gotten from a quarry that Enoch had opened a year before at Cajon Canyon to provide piers for his railroad bridges and trestles. The front and side porches had a clear view over the valley below the town, and from its western porch one could see the road up to Outlaw Pass miles away and close to five thousand feet up, where Enoch planned one day to push a rail-line through, straight to the harvest crops of the Red River Valley, the once Indian-held prairies, now corn lands, to grain fields, places where the shoats cast great litters of piglets, and the cattle were put out in feed lots for fattening for the packinghouses. The passenger traffic would create a direct, faster way into Southern California. But at the moment, the legal complications created a lawsuit that was in several courts as to just *who* had the rights to put a railroad across the mountains and through Outlaw Pass. The Central Pacific, the Sante Fe, the Greater Pacific, were eager. All were marshaling squads of lawyers in court sessions appealing to state and national courts, as their exclusive right. There was talk that the Greater Pacific was preparing to send an army of gunslingers under Bat Masterson to seize the pass and put through rails without waiting for the Supreme Court to decide who had the real rights to the pass. All to reach grain, thousands of elevators holding 100,000 bushels each, and steam gang-plows tearing up more of the prehistoric sod of the plains.

Kingston House seemed above the fray. At dawn the gardeners were up turning on the water in the gardens and on the lawns, hitching mules to the two grass-mowing machines that kept the grass neat; a special Kentucky blue stem and mixed Irish turf. The house servants, too, were up; the first smoke came from the kitchen chimneys to help prepare the breakfasts. All but for Himself, as Enoch was known to servants. He usually ate at seven, alone in the sunroom on the west side where he could look down on the Division Point of the W. & G.P. On dark mornings, red and green switching lamps were still burning. The rows of tracks and switching points gleaming, day-shift yard hogs already had steam up, were pushing the freights into order, the sorting yards and roundhouses active by sight and sound. Even up at Kingston House, the pounding of steam hammers, the striking and punching of holes in good steel, came up as a background for the expanding day. Since 1876, every W. & G.P. passenger train had installed Westinghouse air brakes.

As the maid Briggy Casey knew, Mrs. Kingston ate in bed at ten. Briggy carried in a tray of fresh fruit free of roughage, hot oatmeal and cold milk, and very black coffee with the thick clotted cream from the Kingston dairy up at Little Bear Springs. Mrs. Kingston, as Briggy put it to the cook, was a bit cranky on waking and it was better not to talk, to offer any information that it was a nice day until Mrs. K. had had a tot of bourbon in her gold and marble bathroom. From then on it was all right. She could be gay and dancing one minute, lift a piece of cake, if the mood was on her, or dark and sending for her priest, Father Pagano, if she felt her "soul was hanging from her mouth, at the end of her tongue, for the devil to pull out." As Briggy told the cook, Mrs. Royalmill (a blackie, and very British-sounding from Bermuda), "If she had in her stomach a good coating of an Irish breakfast of bacon and eggs and a kipper and scones and some good China tay, she'd be more cheerful."

For the master, Himself, liked solid food. Mrs. Royalmill had prepared a small steak, fried potatoes, fried tomatoes and two eggs sunny-side-up on all that. Mrs. Royalmill shrugged off Mrs. Kingston's breakfast. "Well, them Mexicans, now they eat snakes and 'ot chili peppers, so you kent expect them to be eating proper like us Hinglish."

"You been told Fanny Royalmill, Mrs. Kingston, she's Spanish, not Mex."

"Same thing."

The children would be up and noisy in their wing of the house. Rawly (only Nanny had called him Ralston) was the oldest, and at ten had the good looks of his mother and the feisty ability of getting what he wanted, like his father. He was, as Nanny Osborn put it, "a handful, a holy terror." Rawly had broken his arm falling off his pony and was carrying it in a cast. But it didn't stop him from tormenting his brother Willie, aged eight, and his sister Mollie, who at six already showed she would be a rather tall girl with a pretty face, the jawline and nose a bit too long. But Nanny hoped the sky-blue eyes and the red hair, the very white skin with freckles, would make up for all that. The children ate under Nanny Osborn's eye in the dining nook overlooking the hothouse, and Nanny was not beyond a slap on the head or grabbing an ear when someone threw jam about or ate with their fingers the wrong food. "Now, gentlemen and ladies don't butter a whole slice of bread. One breaks off a bit and butters it. So like. And you must use the fork in the left hand British style, and take it to the mouth, not the vulgar native way hereabouts you Americans have of cutting and changing the fork to the right hand—very infra dig."

Percy Johnson was often a house guest—a man of great dignity, a vice president of W. & G.P., in charge of finances, banking and other matters of money. He never ate breakfast, but he had that horrible habit of demanding ice-cold orange juice, some fad from down in L.A., and then he taking a walk around the estate a few times. Mr. Charles Auden White, now, he pleased Mrs. Royalmill. He liked a bit of smoked salmon, a crumpet with caviar, and a proper pot of tea. Always insisted the pot be scalded first with boiling water. He would pour out the tea, a pot in each hand, one of tea and one of milk, properly "to pour a cuppa," as Mrs. Royalmill put it.

Being newly converted to teetotaling, Mr. White never went into the den to have a morning snort of Himself's best Tennessee mash—not even a glass of wine at dinner. A bit of a dried-up frump. Thin, gray, shiny pince-nez glasses clamped to his big hinge of a nose, a proper lawyer all right, " 'ate to have 'im putting you through the cross-examination."

By noon the house was being cleaned and polished and waxed, the menus sent down to the kitchen by Mrs. Kingston, written in firm steady pencil markings (she never was known to drink during the day). Nanny was in the gazebo by the rose garden with the younger children; Mollie and Willie learning the British empire was always marked red on the maps, and whales were animals just like the dogs barking in the kennels out back. Rawly had been driven by a favorite groom in the wicker dog-cart and the farting pony named Prince, to the town's school. Mr. Kingston insisted Rawly go to a public school, at least until he left for the East and a good prep school. Willie was a good student and hoped to go back to school soon. He was recovering that year from an attack of scarlet fever that had left him somewhat deaf in one ear. Mollie just liked to draw pictures, drawings in crayons of Papa and Mama, Nanny, the dogs and the red roosters. She was rather good at it, for a six-year-old, Mr. Kingston said. "Damn good, talented." He had several of her crayon drawings hung in his office down at the division point, and he had ordered a professional watercolor painting set for her, the best imported colors from Germany through Hannah Winters.

Lunch was rarely attended by anyone but the children at Kingston House. The help below stairs fed well—Mr. Kingston's handyman, valet and confidant, Chico; two head gardeners; two parlormaids, and Briggy Casey. All below stairs were presided over by Henry Ruxton, the butler. There were, Ruxton insisted, only six true English butlers in Southern California. He met Mr. Collis P. Huntington's butler, Meade, twice a month in Pasadena, where they drank ale at Ye Olde England saloon there, and mutually shared a French seamstress in bed (not at the same time) at the monthly fee of two pounds each. Mrs. Kingston had picked the servants, and Mr. Kingston did not interfere as long as the service was adequate.

The afternoon was filled with the sound of dogs, children, and always the call of train whistles, the grind and thud of the mixed freights being made up at the junction yards. Rawly would be back from school at four, demanding great slabs of bread with apple butter topped with brown sugar. Sometimes Mr. Kingston was back at six, sometimes he phoned up not to expect him. The phone was a big oak box with a handle to turn to bring it to life. It was in the den; the county phone exchange referred to as "Hello Central" had thirty-six clients in Kingston Junction. Mr. Kingston could phone to tell Ruxton he would not be up for dinner, having trouble with a wreck at Apple Crossing, or a meeting with some locomotive designers, or just watching a Mogul & Mallet or Baldwin engine being dismantled for its yearly overhaul; burning off rivet heads, the asbestos lagger removed, chipping water scale.

Chico would either drive Mr. Kingston home in the shiny four-place carriage or one of the Negroes from the blacksmith and forge section would be at the reins of a company gig. On weekends, Mr. Kingston drove a great red-wheeled four-in-hand tally-ho coach, with the children on top, around the graveled drives, and sometimes there were trips down around the dirt roads of the town. Usually he was to busy. After he wrecked a buckboard by brooding over a union labor organizer reported in the county, and let the team be scared by a jackrabbit into bolting, he preferred to be driven. His two riding horses got heavy and old, and he didn't replace them. He was getting a bit heavy himself at thirty-two—trying to keep his weight under two hundred.

At dinner he was cheerful, and saw to it that Ruxton kept the decanter of wine at Mrs. Kingston's elbow only half-filled. They liked to chat of the day's doings, one not listening much to the other. Mrs. Kingston did not care about block signal systems or the new firebox on the mountain locomotives. He was not too interested in the flowering rare plants or the Manx cat without a tail Mollie had insisted on as a gift for her birthday. Rawly was often sent away from the table for causing hysterical laughter in his brother and sister.

Sometimes there were guests for dinner. Percy Johnson and his dark little wife. Some Eastern member of the Wall Street private bank, from Drexel and Morgan, or a division superintendent of the San Diego-San Antonio run. Very often Charles Auden White, not talking much and frowning a bit at the wineglass. Like most reformed alcoholics, he was displeased by even a white wine with the fish. Ruxton knew better than to set a brandy snifter before him in the den when the men went to smoke their cigars and sip the fine cognac.

If there were no guests, Mr. Kingston worked after dinner at his black walnut desk, sold to him by a dealer in London as belonging once to a Medici, but of course he knew better. Mrs. Kingston would be in bed early, after one last "nightcap" of bourbon Briggy poured for her.

Usually evenings at ten if there were no guests, three times a week Mr. Kingston would go out to the stables where Chico, active as a monkey—he was only five feet four, but very muscled—would have the sporting rig out and the big bay horse in harness. Mr. Kingston would be driven down toward the town, passing along the shiny tracks of the rail-line, and often a big, heavy-loaded freight would come by, never seeming to end. At 10:22, Mr. Kingston would look at the heavy gold hunter watch, its white face behind two lids. Time for the splendid shape of the *Golden Eagle* to come roaring up the track from the coast, orange-lit plate-glass windows, a glimpse of its burled walnut interiors, the dining car, a drama to him always of all crisp linen and the darkies in white handling the heavy silverware, all of it going by at a steady speed on a perfect roadbed, until all that was seen were the twin ruby lamps of the observation car hurrying south, and hell to pay if it ran behind schedule by as much as ten minutes. It was the year Western & Great Plains lines extended into New Orleans.

The sporting rig did not enter the town of Kingston Junction. It turned off at Peppertree Lane and went on rubber-tired wheels down past flowering plants and up to a small house with gothic windows, leaded stained glass, a carved front as if made of white cream turned to stone. A bit too elaborate for so small a house. It had been built by a German painter of desolate desert scenes who had died by stepping into a nest of rattlesnakes three years before.

Chico would rein in the horse under the covered porch and Mr. Kingston would get out, tap on a golden oak door tormented by chiseled work into some sort of medieval theme. Mr. Kingston had a key. Chico drove around to the stable in the back, hung a nosebag of oats around the horse's muzzle and fell asleep on a pile of blankets in the tack room corner of the stable. The shiny eyeballs of two carriage horses at first remained staring at him while they munched cracked corn, and the amonia smell was rather pleasant to the sleeping Chico for he smiled in his sleep.

At four in the morning Mr. Kingston would come out

of the house and nudge Chico awake with the toe of his shoe. They drove back to Kingston House in the crisp cold air of the usual California night, everything made unreal, all detail lost by the night mist, a halo around the lit coal-oil rig lamps. They passed Hookerville on the outskirts of the town, named after the Civil War whoremonger, General Joe Hooker, from which Mr. Kingston knew the word *hooker* came into usage. They drove past the row of cat-houses that catered to the railroad men. Usually there was a faint sound of a banjo from behind drawn curtains, the bark of a chained yard dog. Several of the doors had red railroad lanterns attached to them, hung there on hooks. They belonged to the signalmen and brakemen. Already, from Caycee to the Pennsy lines, this habit of hanging red work lanterns outside of whorehouses was spreading, along with the name "red light district."

Dawn was threatening, the sky in the east was the color of a cold oyster, and already yard boys, apprentices, were knocking on the doors where the red lanterns hung, to alert the freight crews their strings were made up and ready to roll on the rails.

Mr. Kingston rarely spoke on the drive back to the big house. He impressed Chico as being relaxed, the tensions gone.

The pleasures of the night were still fresh in his mind and body. His problems could wait. The children's education—he'd have to send them away from this wilderness. Maude's drinking was controllable. The problem of Outlaw Pass kept gnawing. Should he take Percy Johnson's advice and organize a private army and seize it? Baring Brothers were pressing him for an increase in earnings, more income, less building. The bankers were too deeply involved in Argentina, and the bond issues they were floating were not holding up in price. Charles White was hinting of some way of getting out from under the British banking control. Charlie was a great legal whale of a brain, but he didn't know you could often get as much done with a firm handshake as a legal injunction. Mr. Kingston, leaning back, closed his eyes and slept until Chico shook him and said, "We home now."

19

Enoch came awake from a night of tattered bad dreams, the guns of Vicksburg still seeming to sound in his head. He opened his eyes to discover he was not a very young soldier on a battlefield, but on the cot in his office at the W. & G.P. division headquarters. He had been up late in conference to decide what to do about Outlaw Pass and its danger of being seized by the Greater Pacific. There was another meeting called for 10:00 A.M. this morning. It hadn't seemed worth going home last night. He sat up feeling the sweat on his beard, shook his head at the dream that had awakened him. He was a boy again, charging through wild grape and oak shrub brush, up a slope into rebel fire. He had kept running forward, whole fragments of soldiers, arms, a head (still yelling), a thighbone, flying past like ducks going south. Somehow, no matter how he ran and how he sweated, ate dust and screamed, he didn't seem to gain ground, advance a yard. Then there was a break in the brush and he was falling, rolling ass-over-teakettle downhill. Ahead the fire doors of a great locomotive opened, and he fell into the firebox, turning, twisting, turning, as if he were a huge side of bacon over the red coals, and he came awake.

It was one hell of a note to have a recurring dream return just before a desperately busy day—a dream that cunningly always caught him at his worst. There was a washroom attached to his office—pine paneled—and he soaked his head and beard in cold water, dried himself on a hard rusk towel he preferred to the soft items at home. In the large mirror (rescued from a private parlor car that had been wrecked in a flash flood) he studied his head. Already the beard was touched with gray along the jawline, hair thinning on top but still enough to serve—plenty hanging down the back of his neck. The eyes with faintly bloodshot corners seemed to study him. The mouth was mostly hidden under the wide wings of the moustache, to which he now gave a few curling twists with his fingers. Enoch dressed in dark gray, picking from a closet of clothes, shoes, a shirt, a hat. He wore well-cut clothes he had tailored in San Francisco. He adjusted the gold chains across his pearl-colored waistcoat and carefully, slowly, wound his butter-gold watch—8:10—he had slept too long. Picking one of his Laredo hats—a Los Angeles newspaper cartoonist had caricatured him in it—he went out into the din of the sorting yard where strings of freights were being made up. Men probing journal boxes, switchmen turning hand brakes. He crossed a half dozen tracks full of gondolas of coal moving south, returning the greetings of crews with a wave of his hand. An asheater (fireman) commented, "Himself is a bit on the grouchy side today." Enoch entered the foundry, where in the long, high hell of the great shed fires blazed, and crooked axles, red-hot, were being pounded by steam hammers, while grinding discs were rounding wheels that had developed less than perfect circles after thousands of miles of travel. The foreman of the forge department came over smiling. He was a Negro in gray railroad jacket, wearing a flat-brimmed straw hat, wiping his hands on a wad of cotton waste.

"Morning, E.K."

"Morning, Jasper. I may want a string of flat cars for something special. That trash we got when we bought out the White River and High Haul—have you repaired it?"

"It's narrow gauge, but I can roll out a dozen flatcars with new coupler knuckles. It's not worth repairing, really."

"Keep it in fair condition. May need it in a day or so," he patted Jasper's shoulder. "Need more men?"

"Only if they're knowing engines."

Enoch nodded and went on past sparks flowing from a cherry-colored driving rod being hoisted out of a furnace. Too bad Jasper was just foreman, not full superintendent of the junction's forge and iron workings. But, to the work crews, he was a nigger, and the men were not too happy

166

with him even as just foreman. De Beck, the superintendent who ran the section, was a good enough man. Jasper
was better. Still, Jasper was in a good position, good pay,
a responsible job, a good house in the colored section of
town, a wife, four kids. Maybe when his kids were grown,
things would be better for Negroes. Enoch had no prejudices about color, but as a man with a couple of thousand
workers in his employ, a boss man had to walk wary. If
the men—the working stiffs—ever got the upper hand,
Christ! Enoch had no illusions about the goodness or honesty of the exploited—what was called the common
man—being any higher minded than the masters. He now
had more than ten years of studying men in high places:
Baring Brothers, officials, senators, congressmen, judges,
all as varied, complex as the working hands, the bindlestiffs and migratory drifters, skilled mechanics, the misfits
and the wholly or fully mad. It was quite a world. He had
a locked-away pity for mankind (in which he included
himself), but his compassion never interfered with running
a railroad system. Someday a unionization all along the
line would come—most likely before or around the turn of
the century.

Gene Debs hadn't been a bad fellow to talk to as the
head of the railroad union organization. They had spent a
fine afternoon in Chicago; Debs was a drinking man and
they laid on a few too many as they talked—got no nearer
together than a cat and dog. But you had to respect Debs,
the bald, long-headed earnest dreamer and advocate of de-
cency and hope. No wonder he was a rummy. If only life
was like Debs's idea of what it could be, and not what it
was! To Enoch, it was a planet where the strong ate the
weak, the dupe was used by the rogue, the fanatic and the
halfwit messing up progress, and with the top dogs buggering the human rabbits. He had read enough of Darwin,
Spencer, and some gloomy Germans to doubt all soft phi-
losophies.

It was not one of his more cheerful mornings. He
walked towards the road inspection section. Floyd Denton
was standing by a burnt-out passenger car attached to a
crane on a work car—his hands deep in his pockets. His
derby hat sat back on his head. His celluloid collar with its

string tie was to large for his neck. Floyd had aged too quickly in his forties, but was as wary-eyed as in his wilder days. He had retained a skeptical sense of being at variance with society.

"Seegars in the upholstery, and the whole shebang she caught fire outside of San Marino. Better use heavy black oilcloth for seats in them smokers."

"No, it's insured, Floyd. What narrow-gauge locomotives have we that can get steam up?"

"Two teakettles from that Mojave line you insisted we take over. What the hell for? They been good only for hauling borax and talc from the mines on rust streaks. Then the stuff give out around Gila Rock."

"How close does that line come to Outlaw Pass?"

" 'Bout twenty-two miles closest before she goes east to Gila."

"Get full crews and stack rails and ties. Jasper has flatcars. I may want to lay a quick twenty miles of rail to the pass."

"It's no good—it's narrow gauge."

"Remember that rebel general who said, 'Git there firstest with the mostest?' I may do just that. We can convert to standard wide gauge, later."

Floyd Denton bit off a chew of tobacco. "Going to be shootin' and a need of blasting powder, dynamite, if you're goin' to run a line up to the pass."

"Have Jasper bolt together some armor plating on three or four flatcars. And—never mind. Round up your men— get off your ass."

"I'm standing, Ennie. So I ain't settin' on my butt." He laughed, gripped Enoch at the elbow to show the work gang cleaning out the burnt car he was an old comrade in arms with the head of the W. & G.P. R.R. ("We've sat in the same privy side by side, boys, our pants down.")

Enoch had some black coffee in a tin mug from some men heating bolts in a charcoal fire, and ate sand dab sandwiches baked on a bit of boilerplate.

At ten o'clock, he was back in his office studying maps. Charles Auden White was on time, with a red leather folder full of papers, carried by his assistant; a Harvard-educated lawyer with a pink face and sandy drooping

168

moustaches. Percy Johnson came in wearing a pink riding jacket and black polished boots (The Johnsons were slowly ascending into Southern California society. Percy was Master of the Santa Barbara Hunt.)

"Sorry I didn't have time to change, E.K. Was judging some horse show."

"That's all right as long as you don't run any foxes in this direction."

Ten years had changed both their life-styles, and they were not as close as they had once been. A pile of ledgers were carried by two plump middle-aged men with the pale wax-candle look of bookkeepers, they had followed Percy Johnson in. With a rush there was McCully, a short man with little neck and heavy large-thumbed hands (telegraphy and signal towers, right-of-ways), followed by Kaminsky, hawk-nosed, short-legged, a Second Empire beard (a cargo loading expert, expediter of through trains, and fast freight.) He was actually used by Enoch as contact with the Rockefellers and the Guggenheims in secret rebates on bulk oil and ore shipping, assisted by Nat Munday, a man with the calm of a sleepwalker, the appearance of a snake-oil salesman (passenger traffic, station and depot controls, claims settlements).

They were all trusted W. & G.P. men, men of ability—some with vices, some solidly pious and faithful to their wives. All had been tested by Enoch many times in the early years of putting a working railroad together, and were what he called "lucky men." Enoch believed bad luck was contagious.

They sat around a large wooden table, pipes and cigars set alight by some. Pitchers of water and glasses were brought in by Mick Condon, Enoch's secretary and typist, a finger-pecker on the cranky Sholes printing machine. However, most of the large volume of business letters still had to be written by hand, for it was said a practical typewriter would never be perfected.

Enoch said to Mick Condon, "No need to take any notes. Go down to town and buy all the cartridges they have to fit our Winchesters and Colts. . . . What for? I *may* take us all buffalo hunting. The last herd has just been sighted in Wyoming. Get rolling, Mick."

When the secretary had gone, Enoch smiled. "This is

all, as Charlie puts it, off the record. What do you think of us seizing Outlaw Pass and putting a rail-line through it without waiting for any legal shenanigans or rulings? Speak up. *Not* you, Charlie, I know your view. Perc?"

"Do it, and go to court afterwards."

Charles White shook his head. "Easy for you to say, Percy. I have to face those old legal crooks in appeal courts."

"Doesn't Huntington put rings in their noses, have most of them on his payroll?" McCully asked.

"That's just it, Mac. They all favor his friends, like the Greater Pacific, *not* us."

"Then it's settled," Kaminsky added. He was Solly Winters's nephew. "If we don't have the courts, let's show we are in full possession. Legal delays can take years. Meanwhile, we'll be rolling trains through the pass. We should know what passenger service we'll pick up."

Percy Johnson took up a ledger. "We can run the line on tickets of twenty cents per passenger mile. But that's the least of it. Freight is the big item; once we get over the pass and get into the farm lands and ranches, we can haul the carbonate ores. The big crop farms now have the Appleby twine-binder and self-propelling reaper, seed drills, and harrows. No more rube with a hoe. We *must* go through the pass. The steam-thresher owners are just aching for direct rail-lines to markets."

Charles White again shook his head. "The W. and G.P. bonds and stock are *not* in a very healthy condition. You know that, Percy. The bankers are howling for an increase in income from existing lines. They are against extending with new rails. The costs of rails and ties, grading, new rolling stock, could bankrupt the W. and G.P."

"You said that ten years ago, five years ago, Charlie," said Enoch. "There's been three years of dry seasons in Europe. No crops. Drought from Normandy to the Danube. Russians are starving. Wheat is the answer. American wheat."

"Very touching," said Charles White.

"We'll make up the cost of a new line. Make money, not lose it," said Percy Johnson. "It costs seventy-five cents an acre to produce wheat. The gross income to the farmer is ten dollars and forty-five cents an acre."

"That's gross," said Charles White. "We can lose fortunes if we have to carry bankrupt shippers."

"Net is two-fifty an acre," said Percy Johnson, "and, gentlemen, they are plowing thousands of new acres. Why leave it all to the Central Kansas, the Salt Lake, Chicago, the Colorado & Mississippi? There are forty thousand reapers—McCormick reapers—working, and self-propelled farm steam engines are selling like fried beans at a Mexican dance. Come on, Charles—why the long face?"

"Born with it."

The talk went on for half an hour. Enoch snapped his watch shut. "Charlie, I'm going against you. But go telegraph our Washington connections and the boys in Sacramento as to just how close they are to a legal decision about the pass."

"Just promise me *no* action for three days."

"I have to decide which is our best method. I figure it's about half and half here. For and against. This is confidential, gents. It may all come to nothing. . . . Nat, how we doing with a really good automatic coupler?"

"It's still link-and-pin mostly, but Janney has a coupling he's patenting; we haven't tested it yet."

"Keep on his tail. Mac, we're running trains back with more than twenty-five percent empty freights."

"Too many half loads. We should turn 'em down."

"Never turn away a buck. Print a lot more broadsides and get them around. And Mac, put a ballast crew on the tracks south of Willow Bridge. Dances like a jellyfish on a hot stove. Tamp it solid. Hire extra crews if you need them."

After all the men but Charles White had left, Enoch unrolled a survey map and drew in a line from the old borax narrow gauge up to the pass. Charles White watched him draw.

"Very neat, Mr. Kingston, a penny pencil and ten cents worth of paper. Enoch, the W. and G.P. line can't stand the costs of any expansion. Railroad bonds are really in shabby shape. Too many small lines, too many lazy stockholders, too many family and heirs of founders sitting on their bums just asking for dividends. Kansas Pacific hit ten cents a share and no takers."

"I'd like to get the damn bankers off my back. Charlie, don't think me crazy—put on your thinking hat. How can we take over?"

Charles smiled, "You are a bloody dreamer. Me, you, Percy own *what*? Ten percent of slumping stock and bonds? Baring and the Texans own or control at least thirty percent, and the public the rest, and their proxies will go to *whom*?"

"Think, Charlie, think. The more in debt we get the line into, the stronger we can get. Phil Canning taught me that. Use other people's money for the good of a project."

"And where is he? Central Pacific swallowed his L.A. and S.P. You run a line through the pass and you'll be thinking of what to do for a job. The board of trustees, the directors, can kick us out any time they make a try. Don't rile them, old chap. Please."

Enoch rolled up the map and lit a cigar. "Charlie, you used to be bolder."

"Used to be a lot of things. It hasn't been all cakes and ale for me. It's a load. Insurance and legal rights to watch, and lawsuits over rail fences and damages in transit. And then I shrink a bit, giving bribes, I must admit, keeping so many senators, congressmen, judges, happy. It gives me a bleak desolation of the soul."

"Oh, come on Charlie. Fisk, Gould, you know about Drew, Huntington, Crocker, those bastards, Hopkins, Stanford—you name them and they all had to prime the political boodle pump to get things done, see important rail-lines pushed through. Don't they do these sort of things in England? Those rotten boroughs, those members of Parliament, those . . ."

"Don't condemn mankind's habits to me. I didn't create it. I'm an expert on sins of the fathers eating sour grapes, and the teeth of the children set on edge. Just *don't* move on the pass without telling me. At least I'd want to have blank injunctions and bail bonds ready."

Enoch sat back in his chair and clasped his hands behind his head, blew smoke rings. "Charlie, what do you do with your spare time?"

"What spare time? What little of it I grab, I read Marcus Aurelius, a bright duffer, Elizabethan poets. And, oh, yes, I raise pug dogs, like the queen. I'm not a citizen of this blasted country, you know. A very dull life, really. But life is dull, and I want it that way. You're one to go turning things over and seeking *what*? Power?"

"I don't have a label for what I want. Anyway, power isn't bad, Charlie. But what puzzles me sometimes, why this love of locomotives, rail-lines, signal towers? I tell you, I get something like a hard-on when I see a beautiful train rushing by, or when somebody brings me a model of a new engine. Why? It's just bookkeeping and carrying salesmen of shoes and manure."

Charles White permitted himself a wide smile. "You're a blighted romantic, Enoch. That's why. Also, there is something dark and hurting inside you. Damn if I know what, or you know what. Why question *what* you do, *why* you do—you can't be anybody but what you are."

"I know I've failed in my marriage. My fault. Oh, I admit it. It wasn't enough, a good wife, a solid home, and the children. I like them all right, sure. Rawly is either a genius or an outlaw they'll hang some day. But they don't really mean my whole life. Yet they're all the future I have. I almost feel it's all so goddamn unfair; they'll be here after I'm gone owning what I made. That's a hell of a way to think, isn't it? Maybe I have worms in my head."

"At least you're honest. Most men, Enoch, lie to themselves. You, now—you only delude yourself. I think women spoil you. That's the truth."

Enoch put out the cigar in a heavy glass ash tray. "Didn't you once tell me the problem with women was how to have them in your arms without falling into their hands?"

"Did I really say that? Very clever of me. Well, I'll go see what public servant has his hand out this week. There's a railroad bill before Congress we're interested in."

"Get the pass case in the courts to come to a head."

After Charles White had gone, slim, dapper, serious-faced, to his Elizabethans and his pushed-in-faced little dogs, Enoch decided to visit Peppertree Lane; he never had during the day. Worms, but not in his head.

20

The house in Peppertree Lane had been rented three years before through the Kingston Junction Bank. A young woman had moved in, a carriage with two horses appeared in the stable, and vast clay pots of azalea and fuchsia were set around. There were two elderly servants of some dark mahogany color—the woman to cook and clean it was assumed, and the man to garden and take care of the stable. These assumptions were made by a sheep man, Ortho Walley who ranched three miles from the lane to the east, and by a rather mad old woman, Inez Maileer, who collected cats in an adobe building just west of Peppertree Lane; she sold illegal distilled whisky in gallon crocks to the train crews and the town's whorehouses. These were the only people who sometimes, from a distance, saw the young woman leaving the house, being driven to South Kingston Junction to board a flagged-down train for San Diego, or change at Elsinore or Capistrano for a connecting line to Los Angeles.

She was described by the sheep man, Walley, as "a young 'un, a kinda mixture, prutty too, what you see of her behind the veil and the big flowered hat. Sometimes she rides a horse over to the shale ridges and down by Gopher Springs. But don't seem neighborly. Keeps to herself."

The female whisky seller and cat lover, Maileer, had her own ideas. Collecting two dollars a gallon in the lean-to behind her house, she would tell a buyer, "You ask me, she's some kinda fancy hurr. Late at night, you can hear some kinda rig, two, three times a week go up the lane, and mornin' when I git my ole bones up, can't sleep like I usta, there'd be these-here carriage wheels comin' down from the house."

After a year, the house on Peppertree Lane and its occupant were accepted as part of the landscape, like the white-tailed deer in the brush, the wild poinsettia and azalea by the spring, the circling buzzards seeking some stillborn lamb, or any bit of carrion. Except when the Santa Ana, the hot desert wind, came down the plateau, the weather was pleasant.

At two in the afternoon, Enoch drove down the lane in a company buckboard. The country looked different by day. He had been there only twice in sunlight—the day he went to inspect the house, and the morning it was furnished and he went out to add an oil painting of an English landscape, (once a gift from Charles White) and see the arranging of the furniture that had come down from San Francisco, shipped out in crates.

This afternoon he had felt a need to get away from the railroad for a few hours. He still sensed the keyed-up tautness of the meeting in his office on the Outlaw Pass problem. He knew he'd have to decide about the pass in the next few days. If he didn't move now, take the only properly placed pass for his needs, he could forget about his plans for a line directly east.

Farruco, the old man who was the hired hand at the Peppertree Lane house—was polishing German-silver horse gear, and he didn't seem surprised when Enoch drove up. Nothing surprised Farruco, or his wife Juana; *El tiempo corre, y todo tras el.* The old man just led the horse and buckboard around to the stable.

Enoch went to the side door and before he could reach it, it opened and Brook de Leon stood there in shirtwaist and a flowered wraparound kimono with red and yellow dragons he had brought her last Christmas. Gold-skinned, tawny hair tied off in a bun behind one ear, she let surprise show in her tight-mouthed smile, and the questioning look, as she opened her hazel-colored eyes very wide.

"Keeping gamblers' hours?" she said, and put her arms around his neck in a gracious, shameless intimacy.

"Hell, I just had so much on my shoulders, I figured I'd just drop it all for a couple of days."

She led him inside, sunlight streaking past partly drawn muslin drapes. The place was furnished in a bit of a cluttered style—Brook's idea of Turkish splendor in the form of a divan, overdelicate French furniture set around on a good Persian rug, and some of the first Tiffany lamps and vases seen in the West—the result of two weeks they had shared in New York. There were too many books, a banjo, some ornate music boxes on chairs and small tables.

"Poor dear," Brook said, kissing Enoch's cheek, "why don't you delegate work to those greedy bastards you've raised up so high and mighty?" Her voice had a husky musical quality and her accent, if it was an accent, was Eastern, touched with a slight Southern slur.

"They're all right, Brook, if I'm there to back them up. But—oh Christ . . . right now I want to chuck it all, take you to Paris, and where it is those Greeks horse around in?"

"Lotus land? You don't mean it."

"I want to."

He took her in his arms and kissed her, felt the warm youth of her, the close intimacy; for he knew every curve and muscle in that limber body. It gave him pleasure, comfort and a sense of reality he often lost in his own house, even in the affairs of the railroad. For him, she had the secret of adroit complacency.

He pulled the kimono off one smooth shoulder and down, exposed a breast and then put his head between it and its mate, while he counted her heartbeats just below his right ear. He had never decided if he loved Brook because of the wild pleasuring and sensual satisfaction she gave, or because she was clever, wise, a comfort, never morbid—in his presence—never panicky. She was always ready to listen, and sometimes to advise, and her advice was good ("for a woman," his skeptical mind reported to him.)

He knew she loved him, as he loved her. But he wondered if she fully respected him, and he doubted that she did. Some vital part of her being kept its distance from him. He wondered, too, if in those long periods of time when he was not with her, if she thought much about him. Or really liked him. For he was aware *love* is not always *like*. She was what was called, already in the 1880s, an emancipated woman. She had "unwomanly" ideas about female education, female suffrage. Her sexual ideas were very advanced he had discovered—from readings of a medical student called Havelock Ellis, and others. She took a great deal of pleasure in their bodies, and made demands in bed—some ludicrous—that as one minister had preached "no self-respecting woman should desire."

Brook de Leon, Jasper's stepdaughter, had grown from a very bright child into a crisply well-educated young woman who had a very good opinion of herself. First the Winterses had paid for her education, at a good Negro school in Alabama, then Enoch had, through some Wall Street bond-house connection, seen that she entered Vassar, where she stayed two years. She went to England for a year and failed medical school at the Royal College of Medicine, this the result of deciding she didn't like the British policies in India, a reason that baffled Enoch.

She was twenty when she came to Kingston Junction to live with her stepfather and her mother, the de Leons, to discover she was a nigger to the population there, and while Jasper had a good house and they fed well and dressed in taste, it was part of a slum called Boogie Hill. Drunken trainmen felt they could seize Brook in the street and try to rape her (she became very active and dangerous with the skilled use of a long hatpin). The county would not accept her as a teacher in any of its four schools for white students, and the colored school had burned down five years previously.

It was when she went up to Kingston House to face Enoch and demand that he do something with the county board of education, and build a proper school for Negroes and Mexican-Americans, that Enoch saw her for the first time in six years. He was amazed at what such a short passage of time had done to the bright sassy little girl who used to climb over the locomotives, her face grease-stained. She was still sassy when three months later she went to bed with Enoch Kingston in a drawing room on a Pullman car named *Southern Sunrise* on their way to Uvalde in Texas to inspect a new double-tracking of the

W. & G.P. line to Fort Chadbourne. He found her to be a girl of langour and querulous wonder.

In his early thirties, Enoch had come to one of those dry—as he called them—patches in his life, an area of time when things were progressing fairly well, he fighting to get more done, achieving much. Yet often would come a disquieting doubt and the recurring nightmare—a dry patch when he would wonder was it all worth it? did it matter? A time of thoughts that he felt were banal and harmful to his goals. But it would come—a dry patch that in the past led to a little heavy drinking, a visit for a few days to the sporting houses of New Orleans, even a trip to Europe to visit investors, bankers, and try the grande coquettes, and Suzy Masseuse, and *Les Poses Vivantes*; deciding never again.

Brook had reappeared in his life just when a particularly mean dry patch was signaling in his sleep that it was about due for a visit. Brook seemed the cure, and if not the cure, a satisfactory convalescence.

To his amazement he had fallen deeply, fully in love. The renting and then the buying (in Brook's name) of the Peppertree Lane house had followed. What she called mockingly "the establishment." Before this in all his relationships with women, he had been considerate, kind, never brutal or repulsive. But he had never tried to think of how deeply the women felt about a prolonged relationship, nor had he wondered much about what they could be thinking. He suspected that for most of the women one entertained, there was little beyond the sexual, physical act to love, little beyond body contacts and their little games, this matter of unmarried passion. With Maude the pleasures, the comradeship had been an active participation in the delights of the bed. But Maude had changed, and after two miscarriages and three childbirths, had fallen deeper into her periods of too frenzied elation and subsequent brooding moods, often actually into dark despair. He did not blame himself, but thought of her condition as unnatural, perhaps hereditary.

He saw, or had told himself, he could not help Maude. It was her nature, and in those days the excuse "you can't change human nature" was accepted as right and proper. Enoch was very active, building, expanding the rail-lines, fighting his backers, the bond and stock people, also overcoming some landscapes' bad habits of putting solid stone ridges in the wrong places, being nasty about unstable riverbeds. Also, the quality of the steel rails and the machinery had to be watched. He was never a homebody—and in time, his house had become merely a base for eating; to sleep there and leave for long periods of time.

Brook brought him back into focus, to act out an aspect of living he had not thought out. The deep relationship of a man and a woman, as a partnership in emotions, in attitudes to the wider world and even the smugness of society itself. He had had desires, attachments, lusts, but they were selfish gratifications, personal to him, based on the acceptance of his desires and habits.

As their intimacy progressed, Brook educated him to a new kind of personal life. She was cruel, she was sardonic with a perceptible raillery. "I'm not a pound of dog meat to be stuck full of your damn male tensions, to be worked off in me with your cock. I'm a human being and I'm a woman. What the hell do you know about women? I don't mean your fancy idea you're a sporting gent and you have the loot to buy everything."

"Goddamn you, Brook, education has spoiled you."

She smiled cheerfully. "Never educate a nigger. You know that."

"Oh, come off it, you're more white than most women I know."

"Blame that on all those creeping peckwoods colonels who came around to the slave pens. I'm black, going to stay black."

He had stormed out of the house on the lane that time—and swore he'd never come back. For at least two days. He suffered and brought gifts of potted begonias and zinnias. Brook had a weakness for house plants. It was all a banging of his ego, like a mad horse who had eaten loco weed, hitting its head against a wall. But he came back.

He accepted Brook on her terms from then on. He began to soften his ideas; to love deeply and tenderly was a satisfaction, the most intense even when not in bed, just thinking of it. He was able to see the streak of cruelty and

179

outrage in Brook. He feared if he probed deeper, he might turn up a contempt for him. Actually, she admired much of him, his directness, his clear vision of what he wanted for the rail-lines, the way he thought out his projects and brought them usually to some final successful fulfillment. She had no resentment that she would never be Enoch's wife; she saw marriage as a kind of slavery, an admission of being permanently owned. She had come as a virgin to Enoch, she told him, only because the men who had approached her had been disrespectful whites who felt she was a bit of merchandise they admired. Her not submitting to them, she was told, was rather foolish for a high-yellow girl, no better, no worse than the black-skins, beginner-browns and gold-skins living in luxury with adroitness and patience as kept women on the Ramparts in New Orleans. All décolleté gowns and jewels.

When alone in the nights Enoch was not present, Brook would lie awake, punching her pillow as if to pound out sleep. She suffered from prolonged periods of insomnia. Sleeplessness brought thoughts she was in a trap, there was no future for her, the society of the last part of the nineteenth century would not open up wide enough for her to creep in and play at being humble and grateful. No, not admitted for her brains, her knowledge, what she had to offer. Maybe, the dawns told her, in a hundred years, maybe more, a Negro girl would overcome the walls to full acceptance, most likely even longer before any woman of any color—snow-white or not, was an equal; before the double standard was destroyed. So she'd fall into troubled sleep as the sun came up.

Riding down to the coast in a drawing room with Enoch, they would pass the fields where the dark-skinned people, Mexicans and Negroes—a touch of Indian—worked the crops, hoed, stooped and picked the Imperial Valley cotton. Enoch had said to her, "Look at them—what the railroads did—them singing and dancing, earning their keep."

"I don't see any singing, dancing," she said and pulled down the blind.

"After dark, Brook, they'll eat, make music, make love. Not a thing on their minds but will they work tomorrow, and who has the wine jug."

"You don't really think that Enoch, that's all they want? If you did, I'd jump right off the train."

He laughed and hugged her to him. "It's the same world out there for everybody. You have to hustle and take the punches. If it weren't for people like me, this would be empty desert land. They grow crops here only because I carry them to market before they rot in the fields. I widen their world. Oh, not as much as they'd like, or maybe even *I'd* like. But I wonder, once they have a bit of a hug and some food, they aren't happier than we are.",

"Oh, shit. There is nothing fine in being feebleminded, respectful to your betters and hard-working. The Protestant work ethic is made just to go on keeping others down."

"No Susan Anthony speech, please!"

When she was with Enoch, her dark moods would not stay, and they were really rare after she and Enoch had been lovers for three years. She would be twenty-three soon, and she had an intellectual desire to see what the next twenty years would bring for her. She said she did not intend to live beyond forty; it was the only romantic streak in her. This idea she could end her existence by her own hand any time she wanted; that, she told Enoch, would teach "that white bastard of a Michelangelo who made God with his long whiskers, touching with a finger that white Georgia cracker on the ceiling of the Sistine Chapel. He isn't *my* God."

She was young enough to still believe her gods were Logic and Reason, an illusion she shared with her lover, for Enoch also saw those two words spelled out with capital letters, to which he had added a minor god: *Let the Buyer Beware*. And a high priest: *Remember to be distrustful*.

It was during that afternoon of his surprise visit that Brook told Enoch, after their making love in the big brass bed, that she intended to leave Peppertree Lane, and him, when she was twenty-four.

They were lying naked side by side, cooling in the late afternoon breeze from the open window, his tanned arms and face and white body by the Egyptian metal-toned perfection of her skin. She rose on one elbow. "I can teach at the Arapaho Indian School in Colorado. They'll take any trash there; it's *only* Indians."

"You're not leaving here."

"When I'm twenty-four, it's good-bye, Charlie to Kingston Junction, and this damn house."

"You like this house, your plants, your books."

"It's a cage, Enoch my dear. A pretty one, but lonely, and the cretins down the lane think I'm a prosperous whore with rich patrons."

"The hell with them. I'll buy them out, run them off."

"Buy *my* world, run it off." She sank back on a pillow still damp with the efforts of their lovemaking. She was in that mood of feeling power, and feeling it mixed with a sadness of knowing her power was feeble beside what the world could produce against her. But it was good to have the power of loving, being loved. They were splendid lovers. He was a marvelously endowed man—well-hung, and, as the railroad workers would express it, she was a great fuck. She knew that. Enoch had not had to tell her he thought her a marvel in physical contact, even if he often did. She felt the directness, the vitality in both of them was strong enough, and reciprocated enough to make their relationship on an emotional base, outstanding. She, living outside of the pale of polite society, didn't belittle sexual activity as was common in public, anyway. She didn't feel it was all animal and "as debasing as so many of your white Protestants say, still glued to some of those mealy-mouthed New England ways."

Afterward to her, like now, the physical sensation was already draining away, and in memory it could not really be retained unless one laced it with poetry and some neurotic padding. "I'll be better off away, teaching."

Enoch threw up his hands in exasperation. "You want Indians, have them here. There's a couple of reservations by the Mojave, up near Yellowstone."

"No, I don't want any of your Whisky Jacks—clap-rotted, housebroken Indians. I want them closer to the originals, so I can fill them with a desire to start turning your own laws against you instead of their arrows."

"You're the damndest woman."

"I am. Now, darling, make love to me again."

He did, and he kissed her, thinking: *if only I could put*

a sock in her mouth, if only I could make her see she belongs here. No, not to me, I don't want that kind of ownership, she belongs here, not teaching strangers. Because we are, we exist. He was unaware Brook had already taught him some things.

21

Floyd Denton was never at ease at Kingston House. He waited now, seated in the big wide hall, hat in hand, staring at an oil painting of moon-drenched Roman ruins. It was near twilight, and he was hoping Enoch would soon be coming home. All afternoon there had been attempts to contact him, and no one knew where he had gone.

It was a damn large hall, Floyd thought—a hell of a big shebang—two stories high, balconies on three sides, off which the private rooms of the family existed. He had never been upstairs. But the parlor gave him some idea of living high on the hog—marble fireplace, the oil paintings of folk with goat legs carrying on, sunsets, ships at sea in their gilt frames, overgilded, it seemed to him. Massive Chink vases standing right on the floor, and chandeliers bigger than in Maddie Silk's Denver whorehouse. They seemed hardly fixed properly to the ceiling.

Floyd was no judge of house furnishings; what he called "ladeedah living," but he could see Enoch had put a pile of money into the place, and was thinking of adding a wing. What the hell for, Floyd wondered. Enoch spent most of his time down at the division headquarters, banging around in his office, riding out with the work crews, cursing out some train schedule that was a few minutes late.

Floyd looked up. The feller that looked like a Barbary Coast pimp, hair roached across a half-bald skull, boiled-looking hands, that one came out to the hall and asked, "You will continue to wait, sir?"

"Hell, yes." The feller sounded as if they had poured oil down his throat and someone had a stiff finger up his back door. "It's important."

"As you wish, Mr. Denton."

As I wish? Floyd would have liked to take an oak two-by-four soaked in neat's-foot oil and swung it to the back of the head of Ruxton. A butler, Floyd reminded himself, was just a hired hand, a white house-nigger. Floyd decided he'd ask where the whisky was kept.

Floyd had grown more serious with the years, and since his locomotive-driving years and rise to traveling superintendent, he had grown more ornery too. He had hated responsibilities at first, but had grown to enjoy the power of ordering work crews around, of keeping the sections he visited on their toes. He had two nice little families: a wife Martha and three fine kids at Dana Point on the Coast; she was a onetime school teacher from New England. Very proper, very much insisting on collars and ties and polished shoes for him and the use of the china gaboon for spitting chewing tobacco. She giggled in bed, but was properly ardent in the dark. He had another wife, Bianca, "a hot dago pepper" in El Paso and a darling little child, a girl, Rita. His Texas wife was a great cook of pastas, and given to gay clothes and garlic. Her father was a plate-layer on the W. & G.P. line between El Paso and La Mesilla. With two legally married wives, Floyd called it "settling down." He was living domestically at both ends of the line. He made many inspection trips to keep his two households happy and pregnant.

He would have the whisky. He stood up and was just about to call out to the canary-voiced pimp when Enoch came in, looking as if he had been napping someplace. Ennie was sure still a cocksman; *never* ask questions.

"What's up, Floyd?" Enoch carefully put his hat on the hall tree.

"Been trying to get you, Ennie, all day. Phoning 'round. Then I figured you'd have to come home sometime."

"Fire? Wreck?"

"No, just Greater Pacific has been moving gunmen up to the pass. About fifty of them left Yucca Crossing this morning on a ten-car worktrain. Got weapons, blasting powder, dynamite."

"Heading for Outlaw Pass?"

"Heading into the Juan Cajon freight-yard. From there,

on their side, it's forty-four miles to the pass, hard all the way. They got three boxcars of mules and packs."

Enoch balanced himself on his toes and whistled. He motioned Floyd to follow him to the den. Ruxton had appeared, and Enoch told him to bring them some whisky sours and start serving dinner without him. The den oil lamps cast thick yellow light on polished wall panels, rows of unread English classics in red morocco bindings. A large framed original Audubon etching of the California condor hung over the lava rock fireplace, flanked by game heads of mountain goat, gray wolf and smaller mountain cats. Enoch had gotten these as gifts; Percy Johnson was a great and deadly hunter, and sure-shot marksman; the only hint to some that he had once been known as Pistol Johnson and in his youth killed men.

Enoch went to a wall map of Southern California, a survey map put out by the Department of Engineers in Washington. It showed the ridges, rivers, mountains and deserts, the coastline, all as if man had not touched or even been in California. On it in red paint Enoch had drawn the rail-lines of W. & G.P., and in other colors, yellow, green, blue and violet, the rival rail-lines. Now he drew a circle with a heavy carpenter's pencil around the Outlaw Pass area, and made a check where his narrow-gauge rail line came within twenty miles of it. Another check mark showed the point where, forty miles from the pass, the Great Pacific gunmen would be getting on the mules going up the west face of the broken-up arroyos that lead to the pass.

"Going to be no picnic for them." Enoch said. "Figure they'll make ten, fifteen miles a day if lucky. When can we move ten Oro Grande narrow-gauge flatcars with supplies for a hundred men, a powder car, and rifles?"

"Never mind the cars, where you going to get the gun-toters?"

"Notify all divisions to rush railroad detectives and yard guards here to Kingston Junction. We have a Gatling gun at our Fort Yuma depot, haven't we? Get Percy Johnson on the telephone line, and you, Floyd, rush your tail down to the shops and start collecting water, grub, blankets, all that about a hundred hard hombres will need."

"For how long?"

Enoch smoothed his beard by tugging on it. "How the hell should I know?" He went hunting through a small yellow notebook. "I want two flatcars of rails and ties and a grading crew to follow four hours after the first train, and begin leveling and laying track up to the pass. I don't care how badly or what the grade. Well, within reason on the grade. Move up gravel cars and all engines we have that will run on narrow gauge. Set up a camp, and I want five miles of track laid a day."

"Come off it, Ennie. In *that* wilderness?"

"The Union Pacific were laying ten miles a day back in sixty-nine."

"On level ground, and mister, they had all those Irish paddies, thousands of 'em."

"Bring in all the work crews you need."

"On that narrow-gauge line? It's just two streaks of rust."

Enoch just waved to Floyd to proceed and went to the telephone. He ground the handle to bring the instrument to life and waited for central to answer. He hoped it wasn't one of those days when central, a Mrs. Flora Moffeton, went home at five to surprise her husband, a boiler-scaler at the junction, with a hot supper. . . .

Half an hour later, Enoch appeared in the dining room, dressed in a heavy work shirt, a short leather hunting jacket, miner's duck pants pushed into boots. The people at table were just beginning on the planked salmon. Two of Maude's brothers from the Alvarez Rancho—Diaz and the one whose name Enoch never could remember—were there as guests for a week, including Diaz's wife with the one silver tooth and their three children. Maude looked very cheerful, wearing her pearls and a deep blue gown. Rawly was throwing pellets made of bread across at one of Diaz's daughters, while Willie and Mollie kept whispering "Bull's eye!" Nanny Osborn was tapping her dessert spoon on her water glass to recall order, but no one was paying attention.

Enoch waved a warning finger at Rawly. "I'll crawl a mule whip 'round you, you keep that up. Sorry, folks, I can't join you. I have to get to the junction right away."

"Emergency?" asked Rawly. "Can't I go? It's a wreck."

"Not a wreck, and you can't go; just a problem needs prompt attention. A washout on some new line we've just taken over by the Coyote Mountains."

Maude tapped the table top with her hand with the two rings on it. "Why are you wearing your gun?"

Brother Diaz smiled; he was beginning to look like his dead father Don Alvarez who, with his holding in W. & G.P. stock, had left the rancho well off. Diaz was now the Don Alvarez the people spoke of. He said, "A man and a gun, it is only proper on a journey into the mountains."

Rawly stood up, excitement gleaming from his handsome dark eyes. "It's a train robber, a train robber!"

"Rawly, I'll take that whip to you, you don't stop jumping about."

Mollie said primly to an Alvarez cousin, "It's a Smith and Wesson forty-five. Pa has three. I once held it in my hand. Didn't I?"

Nanny Osborn said, "Really, they'll have bad dreams tonight."

Enoch turned to Ruxton, who was supervising the placing of some bowls of stewed fruit and pickled watermelon rind on the table. "Ruxton, pack me some cold chicken and trimmings, and I want it right away."

"Yes, sir."

The other Alvarez brother began to talk about a cougar that was taking sheep in the canyons below the Coyote Mountains. But Enoch had just said, "Have a good meal," and was gone.

Maude put a hand to her brow, "It's always an emergency. I sometimes wish we were all still traveling in stagecoaches and growing our own sweet corn."

Diaz's wife said, "You forget, you forget the bad *calzadas*, how broken the roads were, how dirty the inns, how the *camarero*, the cook smelled."

"Smelled?" asked Willie. He was wearing his first eyeglasses and he kept pushing them up on a too-small nose.

"Stank," said Rawly. "I was up to one of the bunk cars with Daddo, and it was all feet and toe-jelly smelling, stinky." He held his nostrils shut between his fingers, *"Phew!"*

Nanny Osborn said sternly, "Rawly, I think you can leave the table. Go to your room."

"Yes," said Maude, "Miss Osborn didn't teach you such language."

"Aw, I just said feet, toes. It was the time they shot the two men that held up the El Centro express at Indio. They were just laying there, dead and stiff by the water tower, eyes open and big holes in their chests." He turned to the Diaz girl cousins. "Blood, blood, *all* over, blood!"

Maude said, "Ruxton, remove Ralston. Lock him in his room until his father returns."

"Blood!" yelled Rawly, and one of the girl cousins strained her water and wet her panties. Willie and Mollie took up the cry, "Blood, blood!" and Nanny Osborn threw down her napkin and stood up. "You two can also go to your rooms. No ice cream for a week."

"Blood, blood!"

The shaggy fur brigade of Frenchy Balbac had been the first white men to discover Outlaw Pass, then named Frenchy's Crack, in the days of the great boom in beaver pelts, when men wore tall beaver hats and the varmints still existed in the mountain streams in numbers worth going after. The mode for beaver hats died out and the mountain men, too, were often just bones with arrowheads through the rib box. There was a sort of road through the pass and wagon tracks, but the trade petered out, went north and south. The last of the mountain men settled down, died of the old rale, or hunkered down on porch rockers, toothless and fuzzy-faced, telling tall tales of fornications, killing of red hostiles, Hunkpapa Sioux, Bronco Apache, and the amount of rotgut they had drunk, or the yards of roast buffalo gut, a great delicacy, they had swallowed without use of a knife or fork.

Old Cactus Chauncey Wurdermann was still alive in Chula Vista "two years older than God." He had been involved with the two Robbins brothers, Irving and Uris, in the affair that gave the pass its second name. Cactus Chauncey had been a mountain man turned outlaw, and he and the Robbins boys, who drooled when they talked ("they wuz mouth-breathers"), held up a Wells Fargo messenger riding a stage and took two boxes carrying fifty thousand; the bandits' bad luck was that it was mostly in checks and letters of credit. The three burglars were trailed by posses and Wells Fargo detectives all the way into the Coyote Mountains. There the outlaws held out for six days in the pass, until they were rousted out by bully cans filled with blasting powder, nails and a short fuse tossed among them.

The posse found Irving and Uris with "their legs all blown to dog meat, but alive." They held the two brothers up to standing position and put nooses around their necks. "Huzus Carda was to hang them, but Uris said, 'No greaser is hangin' me—I want to be turned off by a white man.' So Nat Nailer he did the honors. They hung them from the limb of a mountain laurel."

After that event, the cleft in the mountain range was called Outlaw Pass on the survey maps. Cactus Chauncey Wurdermann said he was never captured—he found a crack a half mile up the pass and got into it, pulled loose rock over himself. Some people said Chauncey Wurdermann was a dreadful liar—"He would of confessed to planning the Crucifixion for a drink of whisky." Some say it was another Chauncey who wandered off and fell over a cliff and was pecked at by buzzards. Till the day he died, every year Cactus Chauncey wrote a letter to Washington, claiming the pass should be called Wurdermann Pass and he owned it, *not* any railroad.

The pass itself—where Percy Johnson had shot the last grizzly (*Ursus horribilis*) in Southern California, was heavy with snow in winter, and heated rock and stunted trees in summer, dwarf trees trying to stay green. The pass ran for five miles and split the mountain range. It was a natural way through to the east, past Providencal Mountains, the Black Crater peaks, then it was clear going along the Colorado River to vast grain and cattle country, the acres of homesteaders, ranchers, the silver, coal, and other minerals that were there under the shadows of the painted rocks. The mesas and gorges waiting for the men and the machines to tear apart a few million years of upheaval and erosion.

The rights to lay rail through the pass had been in legal

dispute for some years. Two lines from the east, three from the Pacific Coast petitioning, going to courts, bribing, asking for laws, and gathering their legal teams to back up the right to bring the railroads across the Southern California mountains. The Greater Pacific, its control and stock mostly in the hands of men in a loose confederation of certain railroads to control freight and passenger traffic into the southland; these were the most aggressive. Enoch Kingston and the W. & G.P. had been kept out of the confederation, and Enoch would not have joined if he could.

He was determined that the Western & Great Plains would have the sole right to run its trains through the pass. He had felt at first that it could be accomplished by his lawyers—Braverman, Otis and Jenner in San Francisco, and Walden, Weissbard and O'Conners in Washington. Both firms were directed in the project by Charles Auden White, commander-in-chief of all legal efforts of the W. & G.P. Now it was apparent Greater Pacific was resorting to full physical seizure of the pass. A common practice among Western enterprises. Huntington's chief lawyer had advised. "Grab first, then defend it in court like a mother tiger her whelp."

Dawn, that season of activities for its possession, came at 5:23 A.M., over Outlaw Pass, a gray, pearly light shrouded by mist, the cold of the night still holding the bare brown rock. The umber cross-hatching of the autumnal grass was damp, the deep dark green of the dwarf pine and cedar hiding ringtail ground squirrel, meadow vole and Townsend's chipmunk. Struggling to hold their roots in rock and in thin cracks were hardy plants. Here and there small streams ran, and enough debris had been washed down to where the birds and small animals' digestive processes had seeded flat areas in patches of hardy wildflowers, wax and mule berries, willows, and cottonwoods.

The sunlight grew stronger; the tops of ridges on either side of the pass took on golden tones and the elongated shadows withdrew quickly. Only the pass itself, wandering along with a few snakelike bends lay like a dark wound.

A thousand feet below it, red deer moved nervously

into the morning vapors, having smelled mountain lion. But the pass itself supported no permanent animal life, and by now, no signs of the charcoal fires of the outlaws remained.

22

What was later to be called "The War of Outlaw Pass" began with the march of the two armies—*bands* would be a better word—to reach the pass where no wagon train had passed through for twenty years. Because of its narrow-gauge railroad at the foot of Coyote Mountain, the Western & Great Gulf had the advantage; it had a shorter way to go to reach the pass after it left its rail-line. But the Greater Pacific had had a head start, not just of one day but of three; its plans had not been detected when it first began to move hard-looking characters armed with rifles and shotguns toward the pass. It had recruited about eighty bruisers, ex-prize fighters, fugitives on file in many courts of justice from Australia, Mexico and the slums of London, Rome. Some were dock workers, and others, at least a score, were local ex-convicts or dismissed rogue law officers.

The Western & Great Plains attack force of about a hundred gathered at the foot of Coyote Mountain's balsam and loblolly pine, backing three hundred road-graders and track-layers. Half the attack force were railroad police and detectives, cattle handlers, the rest, some Chiricahua Apache breeds and others, mainly men who had drifted up across the Mexican border in the dark, and admitted to being called a *chinga su madre*. Others were frontier misfits and men with bad records from Pacific ports and all along the Gulf.

On the second day of the start of the pass project, Enoch stood by a canvas-covered pile of supplies, looking up toward the pass, still miles away above them in barberry thorns and benzoin bush, still in morning mist. Several bald eagles were drifting in a sky "the blue of a

Dutchman's pants," as Floyd Denton expressed it. The birds circled, wondering if the new activities below them were prey.

Percy Johnson had enlisted a dozen Civil War G.A.R. vets, rather a battered lot, whisky-burned, somewhat palsied, but able to handle weapons. He and Enoch were checking compasses over a rough-drawn map of the mountain range. Enoch held to a compass direction, rotating the map in his hand until it pointed to match the compass reading.

"You, Perc, take your advance party ahead and keep going. Floyd is to follow, transporting the blasting powder, the dynamite, with fifty men, all armed. He's also surveying a rail-route. Meanwhile, Jasper de Leon has already started crews grading, cutting the ironwood and creosote bush, and is unloading ties and rails."

"How can you scrap a good grade in a hurry?" asked Percy Johnson. He was wearing two holsters containing long-barreled Colts with mother-of-pearl handles, special presentation models with etched barrels. Percy Johnson was still, as he had once been as a gambler, a dead shot. He had come up through the mining camp poker games in his youth, and had killed a man—legend said—in nearly every camp he played in, over some card dispute; at a cry of cheating, or to defend himself against some sore-headed armed loser.

"The hell with fancy grading," said Enoch, "I want track, Perc. I want it at the pass in four, five days. And there's the old wagon ruts to guide us."

Dutch Altdorfer, a big German freight-boss, whose special pleasure was beating hobos, often to death with a short hickory club, came over to Enoch, a belt of bullets around one shoulder, a heavy Sharps buffalo gun crooked over one arm. "We move now, Herr Kingston?"

"After the party under Mr. Johnson, in half an hour. Each man will carry thirty pounds of supplies."

"Is too heavy."

"You like to eat, Dutch, don't you? No telling how long we'll be at the pass."

The crews unloading rails and ties were already busy; a pick and shovel gang under Jasper was leveling the ground of wild buckwheat and silver plant, ground laid from the narrow-gauge line to a sort of path through boulders and mountain brush, marked by old wagon tracks and some ox bones.

Enoch shouted to Jasper, "If you can't roll boulders out of the way, use dynamite, if you have anyone can handle it."

A tall Chinese youth, his pigtail wound around his shaved head—smoking a small metal pipe, made an O pattern with a thumb and forefinger. "I called Dock Sing, blow up plenty hills for Centrah Prasific. Plenty good man with direnamite. Oh, yess."

"All right, Dock Sing, cut your fuses. Now, Dutch, any of your men got whisky, they take two drinks and leave the rest here with de Leon. I don't want to get any drunks killed off up there."

"We got no *schnapps*, Herr Kingston. *Nein*. Just little bit snakebite medicine."

"*No* snakebite medicine. That's an order."

The banging of rails being unloaded from the flatcars, the hoot of another locomotive coming up the grade to unload more rails, it all sounded good to Enoch; it echoed the just-gone-past. He carefully loaded his Winchester Yellow Boy, rubbing its brass section above the trigger guard against his gloves. It was not like going against the forts at Vicksburg. It was also no longer the pounding of an unsure heart, the green youth's wonder at how easy it was to die. No, times had changed. Modern times—this scientific world of 1880—were different than those primitive years of war to preserve the Union, slogging all those muddy months with U.S. Grant. A disgraced Grant now, a failure as president, and tainted by scandal, some Wall Street ruckus . . . Enoch had gone as a delegate to the second national convention for Grant.

But no more mooning over what was over. He motioned for the various parties to begin the climb and made sure his leather cigar case was in place and the silver-bound flask of bourbon was on his hip. The bald eagles had come lower and were flying in tighter circles overhead, wheeling and gliding, great wings expanded. Enoch thought, too bad that the national bird was actually a scavenger and carrion eater.

At the end of the day, Enoch was nine miles from the pass with the advance party treading down dwarf locoweed in the alkali dust. Percy Johnson was oiling a Gatling machine gun which six men had hauled on its two wagon wheels a hard way up among the rutted wagon tracks. There was still a road of sorts kept open by the mountain's surviving creatures. In the main, it had been hard going, and but for a kit fox, they saw no living thing moving at any speed.

That night seated by a fire of mountain brush and a lone fallen Engelmann spruce, Enoch said, "This is the easy side. Think of what the Greater Pacific boys are up against."

Percy Johnson threw down a spanner. "I don't think this Gatling is going to be much help. Lots of worn parts in the tubes, and I don't trust the crank gears."

"Just them knowing we have a Gatling gun is enough. All I want are a few bursts from it and a placing of the gun up front where they can see it."

A few of the men were drunk, crouching around the fire. Dutch had not been able, or wanted, to leave all the bottles behind. Enoch decided there was no use making a dust-up about it. It couldn't change anything. Dock Sing was wrapping dynamite sticks in burlap and baling wire. Enoch got under a blanket smelling of mule sweat and fell asleep.

The second day's going was harder, the wagon tracks eroded. The sun had come up strong and the day was heated up when the split in Coyote Mountain ahead of them showed clearly they were near the pass. The men cheered as they moved forward. They were suddenly met by rifle fire and Percy Johnson shouted, "Down, everybody, the bastards are ahead of us."

"We're still out of range."

Enoch, from behind an outcropping of gray stone streaked with quartz, leveled his field glasses on the pass. He brushed away insects buzzing around his face. "I don't think they have any great number of men up there now—I figure maybe five or six who were cutting trail."

"Let's test that." Percy Johnson put his hat on a rifle barrel and there was the sharp whine of a rifle firing. He lowered the hat. "They didn't come near. I counted four shots."

"Four or five. Get the Gatling in position up front where they can see it. And get someone back to hurry up Dock Sing with the dynamite."

"We have dynamite men from our leveling work-crew."

"He's got mountain explosive experience. We'll spread out now and move forward in a half-circle. Tell the men to keep their tails down and not get killed." He laughed. "If they can avoid it."

"I'll push the Gatling in as close as I can."

"We'll have the pass before it's dark," said Enoch. He felt young and feisty, as he had when bringing Canning's wagons through from Fort Yuma.

The war of Outlaw Pass lasted two weeks. There was no one-day victory. By the fourth day, the Greater Pacific had its full force of men up at the pass and were erecting timber barricades from huge planks they had dragged up to the pass on mules. Enoch had Dock Sing and three other men begin to throw dynamite clusters at all hours, but they were too far out to do more than make noise. The revolving rifle barrels of the Gatling burst on the second day of use. At the end of the first week, the Greater Pacific gang was prying boulders out of the pass and rolling them down on the W. & G. P. groups below. Enoch's men killed sidewinders and made hatbands out of the snakeskins.

Supplies, cartridges, and dynamite were brought up to Enoch's group each day after dark. Railroad ties also were carried up by cursing, sweating men—wood to make ramparts behind which all crowded during the heat of the day. Nights, Percy Johnson took out raiding parties and lost two men within ten yards of the G.P. barricades. They either deserted or were captured. Percy Johnson was having the time of his life.

Meanwhile, the rail-line connected to the narrow gauge was creeping up the rise slowly; the grades were not as bad as expected. Jasper had a knack of picking his way to nothing over a seven- to eight-degree grade to the mile on the line. Floyd, a fair surveyor, staked the way—and the railroad had brought in its top surveyors who corrected

Floyd's mark points. There was a great deal of wasteful firing, and the men tried to kill some red roe deer and failed.

Enoch went down to meet the crew laying rail. They were now four miles—a bit less—from the pass.

"It's a hell of a note, Jasper, but so far this spur line isn't going any place."

"Talk to the local sheriffs—for all the cases of likker we gave them—they're asking for Federal marshals to come in to look over all these goings on."

"I know. Had a telegraph from Charlie White. He's holding them off. But if it goes past the second week, I think we're up shit creek here. Damn it, should've grabbed the pass months ago."

"You're sure up against a mountain."

"The mountain doesn't give a hoot in hell one way or the other—it's guns we're up against."

Enoch was tired. It wasn't as if he were in his twenties anymore; besides, he was carrying too much weight on his carcass. The food, too, bothered him—camp cooking of burnt beans and suspected bacon, the strong sheep-dip called coffee, all had upset his digestion; his gut felt rubbed as if by sandpaper.

It had all looked so easy on the map. Point A *to* Point B, *to* Point C; the pass.

Jasper piled up ties and rail at Enoch's camp, and made it a depot. "So we can rush through the last couple of miles of track quick when we have the pass."

"Want to risk one of the locomotives close by on the new rails?"

"Why not, Jasper?" Enoch looked up at the Negro. (In a way, he's my father-in-law—certainly the stepfather of my love.) Christ, I'm so bushed, I'd only sleep if I were in that brass bed of Brook's.

"Might lose that engine, E.K., if the grading is bad and the ballast with these rocks up here crumbles, we'll—"

"It doesn't matter. Send up a locomotive to the end of the line and a flatcar loaded with some kegs of spikes. Keep the crew off—just the driver and fireman."

The narrow-gauge engine made it, slipping back a bit at one grade, but sand on the tracks solved that problem.

And at a turn the men called Dead Man's Drop, one side of the track sagged a bit, the engine tilting dangerously. Steel drills hammered into the rock side and then propped up by timbers fixed that, but the engine made its way gingerly, slowly. The track held.

Charles White came up to the base camp at the foot of the mountain, and Enoch came down to confer with him. Charles wore a very high starched collar, tall top hat, swallowtail coat.

"Enoch I can't hold off the law much longer. This damn thing has become another War of the Roses, between two opposing forces, each sure it's got a victory ahead."

"Just get them to see it as a local little fracas, and I'll have the pass in another day or so. It's hard going. I'll have someone drive you around the base of the mountain to show you it's not going to be like walking into a saloon."

He got Dock Sing, who was waiting for another shipment of dynamite, to drive Charles White around in a buckboard. The young Chinese drove well. He had a brightness and an alertness that pleased the lawyer. In some way he felt there they were, two aliens among these boisterous tough Americans and their hired hands. Charles White found a sort of stark beauty in the mountains—strong-colored, rough growths trying to hold on and survive. It was not at all the soft landscapes of his youth; the Old Crome, Constable atmosphere—the little streams with the punts on calm water and the stone inns with their mossy lawns. He remembered a canal trip in a house barge on the Trent and Mersey Canal, down to the Coventry waterway. The stops at the ancient locks and always a mist over the old trees, and the jolly larks with the youths from his college, Balliol at Oxford. But it wasn't worth recalling, he decided, as Dock Sing whipped up the horse—not anymore, now that he had turned away from so many things in his past. He pointed out various shrubs and herbs—giving their Latin names to Dock Sing, who thanked him politely.

On the thirteenth day of the siege of the pass, Enoch came into camp at dawn wrapped in two blankets, his face and his hands, even in the doeskin gloves, pale with cold.

"I've been on both sides of the pass, went up with some of the Mexicans who have climbed Hutchapan. We were above the pass—a quarter mile past the mouth—looked down on their camp. I'm sending dynamite crews up both sides to overlook the damn camp. At one in the morning, they"ll drop charges with lit fuses near the camp. After the first drop goes off—I want to scare them, not kill them— we attack as the first bundle is dropped."

"Why at that crazy hour?" asked Percy Johnson, unshaved but enjoying himself even if he had to scratch a bit under the armpits. "Why?"

"They're drinking and eating and later they'll all be asleep—all but the lookouts. If we surprise them, they'll most likely give up. If not, we'll have to shoot straight."

Enoch said he'd lead the attack party from the left of the pass, and Percy from the right. A few men left behind would start firing from the center and light big campfires, but that was just to make the G.P. defenders think the attack was to be a frontal one.

Percy Johnson said, "All we need are fifes, drums, and a flag."

Enoch felt just as rabbity inside as he had been in that battle when he was sixteen. A hell of a note for a leader. But as night came down quickly and a purple-blue starless sky turned soot-black, he lit a cigar and talked cheerfully. He moved forward with forty men. Dutch was cursing a knee he had banged on a rock. All the men were sober, Jasper having cut off most efforts to smuggle up whisky in the supply packs. Enoch had promised them all a big drunk once the rails were in the pass.

Someplace a screech owl sounded; a brisk wind whipped the sparse bush about. It was cold. Enoch's fingers felt so stiff, he had so little feeling in them that he wondered if he could handle his Winchester or his pistols.

After an hour's climb and some torn pants, his party was three hundred yards from the pass—if the survey crew was correct—just to the right of the pass opening. The dynamite crews, with an hour's head start, should be in position up above both sides of the pass. He whispered to Dutch to get the men down off their feet. He had trouble striking a match, shielding it from the wind and any view from the pass. He studied his watch and shook out the match.

"Twelve more minutes," said Enoch. "We move on now and stop just this side of the pass—play doggo until the first dynamite packs go off."

"Freeze *unser* balls off, Herr Kingston." Dutch carried, besides an ancient pistol a foot long, his heavy club under one arm.

"No talking." Enoch took out his refilled flask. "One tot each, as far as it will go. And see no one hogs it."

"*Goot.*"

Enoch sat shivering, then put his hands inside his jacket under his armpits, but it didn't help. The tips of his fingers had no feeling. It's goddamn cold up here, he thought, or I'm getting thin blooded. He slipped his hands out of the doeskin gloves and shoved them down under his belt, down against his crotch and around the genitalia. He had read some place an Arctic explorer (Dr. Kane?) had learned this from his Eskimo dog drivers. The warmth brought life and pain back into his fingertips and he nearly fell asleep. Rousing himself, he told Dutch to get the men moving.

He felt no reality himself, but as in one of his dreams that often led to his nightmares, it all seemed to be an unformed world where everything was made of some soft substance, and he was floating rather than moving along, bent over, a swimmer in the air. He heard the crackle of wood burning and knew they were at the pass. The G.P. gang had moved up logs for their fires; whatever brush there had been this high up, had already been used.

Enoch saw the golden glow of the flames behind the dark timber shapes of wooden barricades. He noticed the barricades were not connected together, just placed here and there in six-foot sections about ten feet wide. They'd rush in between them, or, a better idea, move between the rock face and the barricades. There seemed only two men standing up in some drowsy stance, supposedly on guard. Only the sound of the fire and some mules moving about on their iron-shod hooves came from the pass itself.

The first dynamite bundle exploded on a short fuse while still in the air over the G.P. camp. Enoch was on his toes shouting, "This way, this way." He ran forward, stumbling over rough ground, but not falling, just scraping one knee painfully raw.

He remembered the rush into the firelight. More dynamite bundles were dropping deeper in the pass. He had not planned to kill anyone if he didn't have to. From the front, below, the men he had left behind in the center, were firing. Enoch heard Percy Johnson's men attacking from the left, and he ran forward, hoping the men were following. He had a quick impression of men leaping from blankets, reaching for rifles, Dutch swinging his club among them—the *hee-haw* of disturbed mules. He couldn't adjust his breathing and kept his mouth open.

The attack had been so surprising that most of the enemy just rose to their feet and raised their hands, shapes grotesque in wrappings of blankets, buffalo robes, whatever could be added to keep warm. Enemy? No, Enoch felt—just men trying to earn a living.

Enoch cried out, "No shooting—they don't want a fight."

Someone was firing from inside the pass—two people, by the sound of it. Percy Johnson and some men ran into the pass, weapons ready, shoulders hunched. One man had kicked up a burning chunk of wood and he flung it in ahead of Percy Johnson's group. Enoch watched the fire spin and arch, then disappear in darkness.

It was all over very quickly and not too roughly but for a few broken limbs, a man lying dead, killed by a stray shot. The mules were kicking and plunging about at the confusion, and at last a dozen were breaking free. They came charging through the camp, vanishing down the mountainside, braying, striking sparks from the rocks with their metal shoes.

"Against the rock wall," said Enoch to the men with their hands in the air.

A burly man with a short black beard and with the tatooed, overmuscled arms of a blacksmith, dropped his blanket. "Hell, mate, we don't want to kick the bucket for no fuckin' railroad company. You got us fair caught."

"Collect the guns, Dutch, and send somebody back to get those men of ours out front to stop firing."

It was still the shock of sudden victory, Enoch thought,

but there was no reality to the scene yet. He tried to think just *where* the rails would come into the pass—on the most level section. Yes, by the hay and mule crap. The few miles of the pass should be easy going, beyond that he didn't want to think right now. He just wanted to get warm.

Two men came into the firelight carrying a body. It was Percy Johnson. There was a perfect circle—practically bloodless—drilled through the middle of his forehead.

"They shot 'im and run for it down the pass."

Enoch noticed that the presentation set of pistols was gone.

23

As a youth, Rawly Kingston imagined his father, six-shooters blazing, one in each hand, charging up to Outlaw Pass like Teddy Roosevelt (in a colored picture) was supposed to have moved up San Juan Hill in Cuba in a later war. He saw Enoch Kingston dominating the action for the Western & Great Plains Railroad, and by his personal courage bringing victory.

Actually, the pushing of the eastern line through the pass led to several hard-fought expensive legal actions for some years. There were several widows—a few dubious—who received some small sums of money for their losses. Six dead men were buried, and there was also confusion as to just who two of them were.

The only elaborate funeral was that of a senior vice president of the railroad, popular sportsman and social figure Percy Johnson who, the Los Angeles and San Francisco newspapers reported, met his death while acting as peacemaker among rowdy railroad workers up at the pass.

His widow and children attended services at the Pasadena Episcopalian Church, the widow in deep black on the arm of Enoch Kingston. Percy Johnson left his family well provided for, and his holdings in stocks and bonds in the Western & Great Plains Railroad and interests in railroad construction and supply companies added up to a substantial fortune. His stock and holdings were purchased, with the approval of the probate court, by his partners, Enoch Bancroft Kingston and Charles Auden White; these bought with funds borrowed from the Winters National Bank of California, the stocks and bonds held by the bank as security for the loan.

There was, of course, a group appointed by the State

Railroad Commission to sift the matter of the trouble at the pass. It took a great deal of time to study all the issues and facts. A Federal inspection by a congressional committee came out, and were dined and entertained at Kingston House; oysters on ice came down by fast trains from Oregon, king salmon from the Columbia River.

Meanwhile a standard-gauge rail-line had replaced the first narrow-gauge through the pass, and a better grading job performed, so that soon the big locomotives, in several steep places two in tandem—"double heading"—before the route was improved, went up and through the pass and beyond it. Surveyors and gangs were active, staking, scraping, grading, laying ties, swinging out the rails from the work trains in an atmosphere of steam, smoke, the clanging of iron, the shriek of whistles.

Enoch in the cab of a work train came up to the end of the line after the Outlaw Pass rail-track was laid. Irish work crews swung their spike mauls, and sang:

> Drill you paddies, drill!
> Drill you tarriers, drill!
> It's work all day
> Or no sugar in yer tay
> Workin' for W. and G.P. pay!

In time, after three years, the courts and commissions finally decided the pass could not be exclusive to the Western & Great Plains trains, that the Greater Pacific could also run track through Outlaw Pass. By that time, the W. & G.P. trains were hauling cargo in both directions, bringing passengers east, settlers and immigrants west, and a group that a California editor identified by his invented word, as "tourists," were flooding into Southern California.

It was no longer lettered as *Outlaw Pass* on the official state and Federal maps. Charles White, a vice president and head of the railroad's legal department, had renamed it *Kingston Pass*. And so it stayed. Twice a day, the luxury train *Royal Kingston* appeared in the pass, one train all full Pullman parlor cars, coming at dawn westward after a night's run up the tilt in the land that led to the pass, and at four in the afternoon, another version of the *Royal*

Kingston rumbling eastward, dining car already set for its famous menus, the nabobs and doers-and-movers of a new breed of enterprisers in the club car, tasting the last bourbon before dining. The smell of the best cigar smoke mixed with the slight scent of cinders as the special cars went through the pass, and if the wind was blowing in the wrong direction, it held the smoke of the locomotive between the rocky walls of Kingston Pass so that it emerged into the open like a speeding bullet.

There had been problems with the English bankers and the Texas stock- and bondholders, because of years of heavy outlay of money. But, after very burdensome costs in construction, new rolling stock and bigger locomotives to make the mountain climbs—Class Q-4 Baldwins, 2-8-2s with steam pressure of 120 pounds for 26 x 32 cylinders— the line began to show some profits. (The construction and supply companies owned by Enoch and Charles did even better.) The crisp cries of protest from the money people died down. Baring Brothers were expanding their rail-lines in South America, floating bonds for Argentine railways, beef ranching, and shipping plants, backing grain harvests by loans. These were their major efforts, they would get around to the W. & G.P. problem in good time.

Charles White explained it to Enoch in 1884 in his charming house on Russian Hill in San Francisco, a city where most of the railroad's legal work now centered. ("So close to Sacramento, the state capital, the state's legislators *and* the railroad commission.")

"The W. & G.P. is not Baring Brothers' major investment, Enoch; Latin America is. They're selling bonds mostly to European investors, and down there in the Latin countries, they can get better deals with the rather shady people, shall we say, who gain power in South America. From bandit to president, a few cutthroats. Yes."

It was a tall, narrow, three-story house of very fine wood paneling—teak from Burma, once brought in clipper ships—and had a splendid view of the city and the bay. There was a Whistler painting on the wall—a girl in white overlooking suggestions of a river scene—and a collection of blue and peach-bloom Sung pottery.

Several pug dogs wandered about. The only servant

206

was a young Chinese, the onetime dynamite expert at the pass, Dock Sing. Charles White had taken him on when he discovered Dock Sing could read and write Mandarin Chinese. Charles White was at that time becoming interested in Oriental art. (His collection of T'ang horses and Han bronzes was to grace a museum wing as a direct gift after his death.)

While the two men talked, Dock Sing came in with a tray of tea things. He had cut off his pigtail and wore black silk trousers and a pale yellow shirt. He was not, Charles had explained, a Canton coolie, like most railroad workers. Dock Sing was from a good family of scholars in Tsinan in Shantung province, related to the eighteenth-century Han Kan, the horse painter of the Imperial Palace. Dock Sing had been a wild and rebellious student, and been forced to leave home for some disgraceful lark. He had come to America on a whaler and, being hungry, went into a Chinese gang of the Central Pacific. Now he had taken English lessons and no longer had trouble with his *r* and *l*.

"Good afternoon, Mr. Kingston," he said.

"Hello, Dock. Like this indoor work better?"

"Dynamite more fun, but no future. You take bourbon, Mr. Kingston, not tea?"

"You know my habits. Everybody drinks a lot in California, except Mr. White."

"Ah, yes."

As Charles White sipped his tea from a Ming bowl, and Enoch held the whisky glass up to the wan San Francisco light coming through a bay window, the two men related to each other with a closeness, an understanding, that they rarely had to verbalize. Between them was a nonskeptical solidarity.

"Dock keeps the place in order and cooks what I like—the bland cuisine of Kwangtung, Peking, the best of the Orient. And the dogs like him." Charles White petted two pugs by the side of his deep-padded chair. "I was planning a trip abroad to see about some Japanese prints I fancy. Hokusai and Maranobu. So you feel we can make something good out of some railroads going to rust and ruin? I don't see why we want them—Kansas Pacific, the Denver Pacific lines."

"Because, Charlie, they run parallel to the Union Pacific and Central Pacific. *That's* why. And if we fix them up, add a few hundred miles of track, they'd look like a dangerous rival to the only other transcontinental rail lines of the northern route, the U.P. and C.P."

"You bloody sonofabitch," said Charles, smiling, setting down his teacup. "It's a mad idea. But those Kansas and Denver lines are in no condition to rival Union and Central. It's a pipe dream, Enoch, just that."

"We can pick up the stocks and bonds of the K.P. and D.P. for monkeynuts."

"And have two dismal ruins on our hands."

Enoch took his notebook out from a deep pocket and turned to a section that also held some newspaper clippings. "The Kansas Pacific and the Denver Pacific had been no assets to their stockholders, selling from ten cents to two dollars a share. Sure, the lines are dilapidated, *but* they have huge Federal land grants, even if the state subsidies, the local and foreign capital, are long dissipated, milked out by Jay Gould and his games. Yet on a map they still connect as a fairly good rival to both Union and Central Pacific, as I said. Charlie, if we pick up the run-down lines, say for a million of our W. & G.P. stock, and if we look as if we are really building up a rival to the U.P. and C.P. lines, they'll buy us out. Be crazy not to."

"For how much? And if they feel we can't pour millions into a new line, we're in real trouble."

"Go to work, Charlie, and grab hold of those two streaks of rust. We'll talk selling price when we have control. Use dummy companies and work through trusted brokers like Emerson. I have to go now." Enoch looked at his watch. "Yes."

Charles smiled, "She with you?"

"Christ, Charlie, you're lucky with only your damn blue china soup plates and bronze chamber pots, swilling tea as if it's fit to drink. It's a different thing, liking women—a hell of a lot more satisfying."

"Society insisted they were necessary when I was young. Nature needs them to reproduce the race. I played at the mating game in my youth, but I've never envied you chaps that were forced by some ridiculous compulsion to pursue them all the time."

Enoch fingered a Ching wine bowl on a shelf. "So far, I find it more interesting than mending old crockery."

"At least, Enoch, it doesn't put my arse in a sling."

Charles White was not hurt by Enoch's remarks; besides their life as business partners, they shared a friendship that needed no mutual words beyond the knowledge of the firmness of their relationship. It was a period when such friendships were normal; only later sensation-seeking historians would suggest they were unhealthy.

The Western & Great Plains Railroad maintained an apartment for its officials when they came to San Francisco on business. It was also available on loan to Eastern investors, Chicago meatpackers, farm implement makers, grain brokers—all those who had some claim on the railroad as shippers, or were merely to be politically accommodated. The large apartment was in a discreet quiet section of the city of San Francisco within sight of Seal Rock. Enoch took a hack to the address and waited in front of the place. Brook would not go into any place of their meetings, "to find me waiting for you with my clothes shucked off like a naked oyster on the half shell."

For a year now, Brook had been teaching at an Indian school in the back lands—it was all back lands of no interest to Enoch if he had no connection or hope of a rail-line in that part of the nation.

She had telegraphed him—unexpectedly—that she would be in San Francisco for some educational conference at the Palace Hotel for four days. Enoch ached for the girl. It had been a whole year since they had been together for a mere two weeks. Together—in the old days he would have said since they had been in bed. He was getting soft; *mushy* was the pitying expression—over this colored woman, and there wasn't anything he could do about it. He could toss everything away and that meant *everything,* and live with Brook in Paris or Rome or Hong Kong; he could work at something. Even build railroads in China, Lord knows they needed them. Or India, where the British Raj was laying down high iron. But it wouldn't be the same. He'd be just a hired hand; others would run and direct those rails once built—that is, if he ever even got any contracts.

209

He saw Brook getting out of a hack halfway down the block. She was very slim and he felt he wanted to protect her, feel her skin, give her great joy. That damn grace of her walk, all limbs in a dancelike motion, drove needles into his groin. What was so different from any other woman? The proud set of her head on her shoulders, the simple yet fashionable way she dressed now? In neat brown with a hat only half the size of those in the mode and the good-sized feet. No mincing on tiny toes. Feet that carried her he estimated at four miles an hour—with a sense of belonging to the earth. He must be loony thinking like this about any woman. He was no het-up boy who had handled himself into a dream world.

He took her gloved fingers as she came up to him, and he saw the little gold and ruby watch he had given her on their last parting, pinned over her left breast.

Brook smiled, a tight-muscled smile under a discipline and said nothing. Enoch also remained silent, afraid he might make too sentimental a comment. He was unused to gallantry, being too honest to express to women what he didn't mean or feel. Now that Brook de Leon was so much part of his marrow, he still could not come up with words, or a proper tone to use with them. Standing outside himself, he felt the entire situation was ridiculous. He resented most in himself the fact he had not yet decided to walk away from it.

They went up two flights of well-carpeted stairs. The apartment was neat—just the faint odor of cigar smoke that could never be removed from the heavy gold-threaded drapes. The Mission-style furniture was heavy too.

All during their lovemaking in the big mahogany bed, Brook said very little. But it was, as always between them, a fully felt, deeply emotional experience climaxing physically in a furious intensity to both their satisfactions. While he had known that women enjoyed going to bed with him, Enoch had never really thought out fully their personal participation in sex as anything more than giving the male partner the greatest pleasure. But Brook had demanded an equal role and attention to her own nuances of sex. At first, Enoch had been angry; what the hell was this granddaughter of a field-hand coon acting up, being so uppity and high-assed? It was not easy for Enoch as his power and fame in the railroad world grew, as he became aware of his full potential, his skills, his abilities, to let a yellow girl make him feel small at times. He could not fully understand what had happened to him. And Charlie, if approached for help or information would only crank out some old geezer's witty line ("It lasts only a moment, the cost is damnable, and the position is ridiculous"), and then would admit that he was one "who knew the pain, one who had taken a wound." No help there.

Enoch and Brook sat in the living room drinking wine-and-soda with ice in it; the bottles and the big oak icebox were kept stocked at all times by the janitor of the building. Below them through the windows, the waters of the Golden Gate dimpled in the bloodshot sun setting to the west.

"How's the convention?"

"The usual noble words, Enoch. High hopes, low funds, and dreamers, with a sprinkling of a few power-hunting individuals."

"Come back to Peppertree Lane. I haven't sold the house or rented it."

"No, I'm not playing your dream South Seas maiden anymore."

"I was drunk when I said that."

She was wearing only a petticoat and she wriggled her naked toes against the blue and yellow rug. She shook her head.

"I'm leaving the West. Going to teach at Fisk University down South this fall."

"Damn it, those burrheads don't need you as much as I do."

"*I'm* a burrhead, you keep forgetting. And I wish I were here in a hundred years when the burrheads—and by their birth rate alone—take over the cities, and, as dishonest politicians that control the votes, rub your white noses in the dog shit."

"What have you been sniffing, Brook? This is a white man's country. And you're no Negro. Look at you."

"I feel Negro. I won't be seeing you so often, dear, but we'll manage." She came and sat on his lap, and she buried her face between his neck and shoulder. Somehow, Enoch thought, she had the odor of peppermint, and apples stored for winter eating. He shook himself free of the spell and set her off his lap and onto her feet. He went and looked out of the window at a woman across the street carrying a bolt of cloth, at a small boy in a sailor suit rolling a hoop, tapping it with a short stick. He always seemed to be staring out of a window when he had some vital decision to make.

He turned and faced Brook, who was arranging her hair in a mirror. "I have two choices—take you to Europe where we can live well. I could turn in my holdings for a couple of million. We could be happy, everything hunky-dory—even have kids."

Her image stared back at him from the mirror.

"That isn't your choice?" she said calmly.

"It's tearing strips out of me, tearing me apart inside, but I'm taking the other choice. Brook, that one is that I'm never going to see you again. Christ, to hear myself say *that!*"

She turned from the mirror, expressionless. "You have your damn duties, obligations to your family? Not by a long shot. It's being Enoch Bancroft Kingston, King of the Western Rails."

"Let's not yammer about duties and titles—where have you been for a year? Teacher-superintendent of Dirty Hole Reservation. *There's* an honor!"

"I'm not going to cry," she said suddenly, and began to weep.

They parted an hour later, silent; faces at least under control—sharing a hack into the heart of the city. He took a Southern Pacific train to Los Angeles. As the club car jiggled over the roadbed, all he permitted himself to think of was *someday* he'd get the W. & G.P. into Frisco. Someday, too, he'd be happy, someday the moon would be proved to be made of green cheese. He discovered he was out of cigars.

24

The summer of 1885, Ralston Kingston, aged sixteen, after a freshman year at Yale, went out to west Kansas to work on the Kansas & Denver Pacific roadbed. His father and Uncle Charlie were rebuilding part of it, having acquired control of the two nearly worthless lines and combined them. They had also issued new stock and were expending a million dollars in renovating a section of roadbed between Twin Falls and Reno. New locomotives replaced some leaky teakettles and began to roar along the freshly graded track on new, straighter rails. The work crews toiled in the strong sunlight, Rawly among them, in work denims, helping to place rail.

> Patsy Ory-ory-aye
> Patsy Ory-ory-aye
> Patsy Ory-ory-aye
> A-workin' on the railroad!

Rawly had grown. He was over six feet and still might produce another inch or two. He was too slim, had none of the bulk and bone of his father. He was an Alvarez in looks and build. He had insisted on physical work on the rail-line. "No desk job, my tail on a hard chair, no shack bookkeeping either, or checking supplies." He explained to Enoch he was going out for the Yale crew and this would give him the shoulder muscles to pull a varsity oar, impress the girls, cause him to give up beer and cigarettes. He was even thinking of as yet untried sexual adventures with the factory girls down by the Charles River mills.

Eighteen hundred and eighty-two

Looking around for something to do,
Looking around for something to do,
A-workin' on the railroad.

Rawly was a born charmer—he never pushed hard to
be charming—it was natural to him. ("Charm the shell off
a turtle," said Charles White.) Rawly got on well with his
father, good enough anyway to get his card debts paid, his
allowance increased, to keep up with the sporting chaps
when they went down to New York to eat at Delmonico's,
visit with the Princeton boys at the Hoffman bar, watch
the actresses and the ladies of the evning walk down
Peacock Alley, and wonder if one were older, could one
capture such a delight for a night? As a freshman, Yale
hadn't been easy for him; when his charm failed, Rawly
was quick-tempered, witty enough to hurt by a barbed remark.

Eighteen hundred and eighty-three
Section boss a-drivin' me
A-workin' on the railroad!

The foreman blew the noon whistle and the work crew
stretched and went over to the shade of the boxcars carrying ties. They ate the heavy overdone meat sandwiches on
thick bread, drank the oily coffee out of their tin bottles.

The water boy—a bit too old to be a boy—with the
too-long chin and very large hands, who also distributed
the spikes and the rail bolts, sat down by Rawly's side.
The sweat had dried gray on the collar of the water boy's
blue work shirt.

"The goddamn sun."

"Better than rain, Jojo." Rawly was hungry, and the
bunkhouse car cook had made the sandwiches extra-thick.
There would be greasy, filling mulligan stew for supper,
and he would sleep in the reek of the unwashed men, the
bunkhouse car doors closed against the dangerous night
air tradition knew existed.

Rawly had adjusted quickly to the rough, hard work,
the crude, foul-mouthed world of the work-gang crews.
He was accepted, for he was on the pay sheet as Ralston

214

Alvarez. One didn't much question the origin of anyone's past, not on a Western railroad gang.

The water boy inspected the meat in his sandwich and pulled out some gristle. "Wanna go to town after work, Rawly?"

"Silver Bow? It's just a jerkwater town."

"They got a sporting house in that whistle-stop, and a gin mill."

"Don't want to catch the old rale. Those whores have gold teeth and more years than Rip Van Winkle. Save your money."

"We better. I hear when we reach Reno, that's the end of the job."

"Can't be, Jojo. They're going right on, alongside the Central Pacific."

"No rails being laid down in them depots, no ties being brung up. I'm gonna go buck barley in the harvest fields. Say, maybe join the navy."

"That's a bully idea," said Rawly. "Only my folks would step on it."

"You got folks?"

"Some. I'll go into town for drinking."

They were arrested after midnight by a tin-star town marshal for being drunk and disorderly on Main Street, and got ten days in the town's hoosegow. However, the foreman paid their fines of ten dollars each and set them to working the gandy irons, tamping down ballast. "Sweat out yer whisky, ya dumb sods, and it's comin' out of yer pay with two dollars extra. I ain't no bank."

> The foreman was a fine man down to the ground
> And he married a lady six feet 'round;
> She baked good bread, and she baked it well,
> But she baked it hard as the doors of hell!
> Drill, ye tarriers, drill!

Rawly sang along with the men, sweated, and tamped ballast. Jojo's idea of the navy was attractive. Better than three more years of classrooms to get the right in the end to wear a little ceramic pig on your waistcoat.

Now, the foreman was John McCann;
By God, he was a damn mean man!
Last week a sudden blast went off,
And a mile in the air went big Jim Goff,
Drill, ye tarriers, drill!

Rawly had some of his father's practical sense of values, if not his balance. Forget the navy—there was a lot of good in the East. Youths unlike the country jakes out West. The fun of weekends at Newport, and out on Long Island, the delicate girls in their white lace dresses, getting in and out of varnished carriages—all this refinement had a strong pull on him. He was no snob, but even at sixteen Rawly was not fool enough to drop the advantages his family position and money gave him.

There was an old man named Michael Finnigin,
He got drunk through drinking ginigin,
That's how he wasted all his tinnigin,
Poor old Michael Finnigin, begin ag'in.

Besides, sailors had a reputation for buggery.

Rawly went back to Yale in the fall after a visit to Kingston Junction. Willie was a plump thirteen, myopic, wearing glasses, bright as a whip, and Mollie a tall, pawky, poised lady of eleven with a rather firm complacency—a British accent that season, copied from Nanny Osborn, who was no longer Nanny but housekeeper, and putting Ruxton the butler in his place. ("He's rather common. *His* people are in trade.")

Mother was going abroad to visit some shrines with Briggy and a priest. Mother wasn't at all well. Nothing you could point to—pretty as ever, but a bit wrinkled and ready to laugh or cry—you never knew which. It was in her head, Rawly heard Father say to Uncle Charlie one weekend when the three of them were out duck shooting in the cattail reeds along Lake Lopez, near San Luis Obispo. They thought Rawly had dropped off to sleep in the chill dawn while they sat in the duck blind and waited for the bobbing decoys to bring mallard and blue tails going north, within range.

216

"Had her to Dr. Weir Mitchell in Phildelphia, and he said, 'Enoch, she's in a deep depression.' Isn't that a kick in the head for us all? He felt travel might do her good."

Uncle Charlie put a duck call to his mouth and quacked three times into the silver-colored sky flecked with cold blues. "At least she never lacks for priests."

"Fat lot of good they do her. Just get her praying and lighting candles. You remember what a fine, wild girl she was? Now she just feels hell is yawning like open fire doors on a big Baldwin. Just now, too, when she can have everything, enjoy. I tell you it's getting me down—she was always so—"

"Here they come."

Several sweeping Vs of birds, like great arrowheads were in sight . . . They knocked down thirty-two ducks in the next half hour. Rawly with his own .22 gauge shotgun, a birthday gift from Father, got a bag of six. What he didn't care for were the broken, still-twitching birds close up; feathers all frayed, eyes like fancy buttons. But he ate pressed duck slices with relish, and Uncle Charlie said, "You'll be a gourmet the way your father never was."

Rawly rode East in a private railroad car and saw Mother off on a Cunarder in New York. She was looking better than he had known her for some time.

"I may never see you again, Rawly."

"Quit the guff, Mother. Send me some stamps for my collection."

Briggy gave him a red and green scarf she had knitted for him. "The colors of O'Casey." The priest, Father Perls, kept smiling, burping a bit in dread of seasickness, and managed a short blessing.

Rawly went to Yale a second-year man and roomed with Wally Kresh, a skinny kid who had a big nose and the idea that a clean body didn't make a clean mind.

"It's biologically natural to get your ashes hauled."

They went out the first week of school to Winthrop Beach with two governesses and got a rash which they feared was the clap, but it cleared up with yellow laundry soap and showers. Rawly got a letter and pretty colored stamps from Mother. She was in Rome, staying with a sacred order of nuns near the Spanish Steps, had had an audience with the pope and visited the Sistine Chapel. "I must admit the artist doesn't strike me as a Christian—painted an awful lot of Jews."

Father wrote he might be East for the Thanksgiving football game, and Rawly wrote back he'd made the crew and would row against Harvard.

Jojo the water boy had been right about the Kansas & Denver Pacific not going much beyond Reno in rebuilding the line. Enoch's idea of causing the Union and the Central Pacific railroads to see them as putting through a rail-line to rival their own exclusive transcontinental route in that part of the nation, nearly ruined him and Charles. After much talk and conferences, there was talk of low offers and lawsuits. Enoch was prepared, he said, to take passengers from the Mississippi to the Pacific for ten dollars a head if they wanted to make a fight of it. He was printing maps of what the nearly revitalized line would be. It took time and standing pat, with costs mounting. In the end, Charles White and Enoch sold out their holdings in the K. & D.P. to the Union and Central Pacific for five million dollars. They had put two million into construction, engines and payments "to friends" here and there, so they divided three million between themselves. They had expected to make ten million.

They sat with a balder and more wrinkled Sol Winters on the great porch at Kingston House, twilight bringing on the fireflies. Below them the forge fires at the junction work-yards glowed where some special repair work was going on. Enoch looked at this watch. "We had to sell at their figures or declare bankruptcy." He shut the watch case. "The *Golden Eagle* is four minutes late."

"Here comes your heart's delight," said Charles White, closing his eyes and listening to the express train's whistle for a crossing. To Enoch and Rawly, it was always a grand sight; in rain, clear dusk, fog, or desert sand—this rushing by of mechanical beauty, luxury and comfortable speed.

Willie came out carrying a red hound puppy. "Can I ride the *Eagle* next time you go to New Orleans, Uncle Charles?"

218

"If your father is liberal enough to give you a pass, and if he permits the journey."

"You're going to prep school, Willie."

"I'd rather not. I want to dig in some Indian mounds."

Willie was stubborn but polite, and the shine of the silver-rimmed glasses he was ordered to wear because of his nearsighted vision, gave him a serious, scholarly look which he exploited as a role to play in the world. Willie was a sly humorist not, Enoch felt, as witty or sharp-edged as Rawly, more placid—and the boy thought things out, even at thirteen.

"All around here, Father, you find Indian pots and stonework. They worked chipped flints, you know."

Far down the line the *Golden Eagle*'s whistle echoed back from the hills.

"You're going to get educated. Railroads aren't going to be run by rough muckers anymore. There's a new century ahead."

"Only the calendar says so," said Uncle Charles.

Willie rubbed noses with the pup. "I don't really want to be a railroad man. You know, this puppy is part wolf."

"Don't be a darn fool, Willie. He's the best pedigreed hound in the West." Enoch laughed. "His mother was stolen from the Huntington kennels, I think."

"I suppose," said Solly Winters, "dogs were all wolves at one time. Don't like railroads, Willie?"

"Not that much. I want to be in a bank. Uncle Sol, you said I could start in a couple of years. Didn't you?"

"Up to your father. I said perhaps. You have a good head for figures, and you are curious."

"Don't put ideas into his noggin, Solly. He'll do what's best for him. Charlie, while you're here, I want you and Solly to look over some bond figures on the major ownership of the stocks of W. and G.P."

Enoch went off to his den. Willie held the puppy tighter in his arms and went down into the gardens. Charlie crossed his legs and drawled, "E.K., he's in an itchy state these days."

"It was a near thing; liabilities in millions if that coup with the junk railroads up North had failed, and it was by the skin of his teeth he did it."

Charles White made a gesture of pulling a rifle trigger.

"He's already after bigger game. He's blooded. Now he's the hunter who brought down a bear."

"What does he want now?"

"He wants the Western and Great Plains as his very own—that's what our friend wants. Lock, stock, and barrel."

Sol Winters whistled softly. "That's no bear—that's a tiger. That's *all* he wants?"

"That's all."

"Charles, talk him out of it—not to tangle with Barings. The W. and G.P. line is making money. He's kept the rolling stock up to snuff. The rail-line is solid. London and the Texans want more income—but they'll be satisfied if things stay as they are."

"Enoch isn't. He's got ideas."

"Ideas? He'll ruin us all. Charles, the bank can go only so far. I have to say no when it's a risk to the depositors."

"Enoch calls it the right moment. When market conditions, bond prices, economic charts, and a bit of panic all come together, that's what he calls the right moment. Don't wager on it, Solly; it's not this year or next year. Maybe never. You're right, of course. He's dangerous."

Sol Winters recited:

> Gefahrlich ists den Leu zu wecken
> Verderblich ist des Tigers Zahn.

Charles White translated slowly:

> It's dangerous to wake the lion
> Danger lives in the tiger's tooth.

"Correct, Charles. That's by Schiller."

"Would be. Shakespeare had a purer ear."

From the gardens they heard the puppy bark and there was a threshing about in the flower beds—beds now somewhat neglected since Maude had gone to Europe. Below them a long freight train was pulling out of the yards, double-headed, two locomotives in line for the climb up toward Kingston Pass. In the deepening twilight, they saw

Enoch standing in the shadows at the other end of the porch, watching the train switch onto the main line. For a moment Charles White got the impression his friend was a stranger—a figure of impenetrability.

The Costs

25

The name that came up the most often in the best Western clubs and at hunt breakfasts in the 1890s, up to the turn of the century—in talking of the great days of the sporting life in Colorado, and a reputation which carried on into contemporary life—was that of Ralston Alvarez Kingston. He was one of those remembered figures so encrusted with gossip that one has to move carefully among the fact and fictions. He had a personal uniqueness, a love of excitement, a psychic urge for enjoyment, and a demanding only of the best.

At twenty-one, he was some few years out of Yale, almost dismissed from that college, suspected of presenting a gold-plated chamber pot on the bottom of which was painted a large eye to Lillian Russell, on her visit to New Haven, in the name of the Yale president. That, and the affair of a winning racehorse he had dyed dark brown and entered as an unknown maiden at great odds in a race near Boston, caused him to leave college without appearing to accept his diploma. The ringer lost the race by two lengths, a fact that kept legal action from being taken against Rawly.

He was actually not the senseless playboy of the lobster palaces that the Sunday supplements of the Hearst and Pulitzer press were to present. He was a good student, and worked summers for his father's railroad system. He only stayed in college because of a promise to his mother who was living in Europe, at Baden-Baden, later in the south of France, with a nurse, several doctors within reach, her maid Briggy and usually a priest or monk or two in residence.

Maude had taken to religion "like a diver into a deep

well," her husband claimed, "and will never find any bucket to come up in."

In his senior year, Rawly had visited his mother and spent two weeks in Paris, often at the fancy bordello, The House of All Nations. He had promised Maude to drink only wines and to graduate from Yale. He returned to Kingston House saddened by her condition.

Rawly listened to his father as they ate breakfast with Willie on the side porch. Willie was slimmed down but still plump enough at eighteen, in his second year at Berkeley, working that summer in Winters National Bank of California in San Diego.

"Why the hell, Rawly, don't you want to work in the division headquarters right here?"

They could hear the hooting of the yard hogs as they moved freight cars about in the sorting yard below.

"Because, E.K., I don't want to be under your fat thumb."

Enoch looked at his son with a frown on his face. Enoch, portly now—to quote Charles White—had cut off his beard. The time of the Civil War beard was 'way past. He had retained his thick reddish moustache. He had no paunch, but he was heavier. Near his mid-forties, he had lost some of his humor, but none of his vitality and drive.

"I ought to kick you down the hill, all the way—talking that way to me."

Willie was amused and poured cream on some breakfast food that was growing in popularity. "Bug Slop," Rawly called the corn flakes Willie enjoyed. Willie was trying to grow a moustache on his short upper lip, and he fingered the fuzz there now. "I tell you what Rawly wants; he wants a little railroad of his own."

"Let him go find one," said Enoch, looking over some cables from England.

"I can," said Rawly, "but I'll stay with the firm. One thing a noble Yale education does: it teaches family loyalty to the family money."

"Did you make Skull and Bones?" asked Willie.

"It's just a drunken bunch of bastards with society names. 'Skiddo,' I said when they asked me to come on up."

Enoch put away the cable messages, his mind mulling

over their contents. He looked up to catch Rawly watching him closely. The damn dude in his high masher's collar and pompadoured dark hair, striped silk shirt, a stickpin in a poplin tie, white flannels, and white shoes. Add dark maroon socks with a yellow clock on them. On the extra chair lay a kiss-me-Charlie straw hat out of a George M. Cohan show. Rawly had become what was called a nifty dresser.

"All right, I'll give you a little railroad. The White Water and Colorado. Up by Denver, hauls ore on a narrow gauge and hasn't made a penny in years.

"Why do you keep it?"

"Promised Senator George Hearst and Horace Tabor I'd keep it running."

Willie spooned sugar over his second bowl of corn flakes, sliced banana, and strawberries. "Father, you also have a lot of holdings in carbonate leases in Leadville and Central City."

"Willie, I catch you reading my personal papers again, I'll have Charlie write you out of the companies."

Rawly winked at his brother. "Anyway, what you lose for the stockholders, father, on the Whitewater and Colorado, you make up by shipping your ore at cut rates to the smelters."

"Take it or leave it."

Rawly stood up and picked up his straw skimmer—at Yale it was called a boater. He set it at a cocky angle on his head. "I'll take it, E.K., and I'll see it makes money."

"You do that," said Enoch, putting the telegraph messages into a pocket. "Don't come to me for help. It's sink or swim."

"Very noble motto," said Rawley.

Enoch looked from Rawly to Willie and saw his two sons were amused at him, the louts, and he laughed and joined in. He was proud of his children. Willie was some kind of a goddamn mathematical wonder—like a horse that could add. Willie, with his fingernails bitten off short, and as nearsighted as an owl in daylight. Rawly was a dude and smart aleck, too handsome for his own good. But anybody that would dye a race horse to try and fix a running, would bear close watching. *Very* close.

Enoch felt he had tried to raise his children with certain ethical values. He once wrote out his ideas for them to study. Along his own lines of morality, not the one the Hebrews got on Zion. Keep your word was Enoch's first rule. Reward good work done. Be loyal to those who have faith in you. Use the political system, which is corrupt and greedy, to advance needed progress. But don't feel more virtuous than the people you bribe to get the laws and ruling you need to build railroad lines, move products to market, keep stockholders satisfied. Love your country; it's the best system around, for all its faults. Treat women with respect, go to church if you want to, but it's all mealymouthed platitudes. "God wouldn't waste much time listening to the Reverend Coleman or Father O'Hallahan or Rabbi Kisselbraut's bullshit, giving out with stuff they can't prove or back up."

Respect the working stiff, Enoch always said. The blue shirt gink. He's smarter than you think and he has the muscle to do what we plan. "The worker's no more honest than anybody else in business. But he is usually dependable, and he's got feelings. If you jolly him along and don't let him get too hungry, he's all right. And he'll stay away from Debs's American Railroad Union. Other union leaders are about as honest as a trolley conductor ringing up nickels ... one for him, one for the company. Debs's wasting his time. Money is a great thing unless you get to love *just* money. Old Phil Canning taught me one thing, he said 'The way to do business is with other people's money.' Credit, loans, stock issues, getting mortgaged, having debts is all to the good for a company. But it's rotten for an individual to get into debt. I'll allow you enough to live well, but not too fancy, and if any of you get bankrupt, don't come to me for help; but I'll always have a coal-shoveling job for you—to start with. . . ."

But Enoch was aware his children were a different breed than the men and women of his generation. Rawly, Willie, even Mollie; the country was going soft. He had never had much interest in food beyond the fact it had to be a thick, well-hung steak spiced enough to be felt. He drank whisky, sour mash, but even he was taking to French champagne. He didn't care much for clothes, just somber grays and blacks, well-cut solid fabric, and that black Western hat that was his trademark. But nothing else fancy. He liked comfort, but didn't see much in being bedded down in posh suites, fancy furnishings at Saratoga, Atlantic City, Hot Springs, and Palm Beach. He was becoming a well-known personality in such places, often with a charming but ever-changing woman. The kids must think him a backwoods country jake. They were sophisticated, knew about lobster thermidor and Bond Street tailoring, gold and ruby cufflinks, while hardly out of puberty. Liked people who drove sporting rigs, went to the theater twice a week, and Rawly waited at stage doors for chorus girls. Enoch wondered if Willie wasn't just aping his older brother. Willie was solid timber underneath the blubber; already cool, calculating, amused.

Enoch wasn't a father for them to recall too often—his own hardships early in life, the tumbled-about years, the frustrations of a self-education, the callow boy in the Civil War, the dreadful journey west, the hard times as wagon boss for Canning's freighters. ("I see a bronze statue," Rawly would whisper.) What it meant to be broke in a new town and not have two bits for whisky or a meal, not even a jit for a beer, in order to get your hands on the free lunch. What did they know of living unwashed, in reeking clothes, of wondering how did one escape, get out of the world of mean, put-upon men who just ate, slept, worked too hard, had lost hope of betterment. (Willie said, "Make that statue hollow; fill it with hot air.")

No, no use talking to his children about much but the everyday banalities. They were healthy; they didn't seem addled or feebleminded. The rest, well it was their life; maybe if Maude hadn't gone off to Europe, lost what horse sense she ever had, and hadn't settled among the crucifixes and pictures of saints being fried—maybe the children might have been different. He tried not to think too much of his own life, his private life. He got a limited amount of contentment from it. Since Brook, no great passion, but certainly pleasure, in moderation now.

On the afternoon he was promised a small railroad, Rawly asked, "Can I take the rig and the team of bays down to town?"

"I gave Chico orders to let you use a buckboard and the gray gelding."

Willie sipped slowly on a glass of milk. "He's got a toot-sie in town. Visiting the Emersons. Very ladedah. Needs good horses to impress her."

Rawley said, "I promised to pick up Mollie and Wilma De Groat visiting the Emersons, show them the mesa and the hills."

"All right. Don't overdrive the bays."

Willie began to whistle "Oh, You Beautiful Doll."

Rawly threw a porch pillow at him, and started for the stables.

The Emersons were jack Mormons—lapsed Latter Day Saints—and Crane Emerson was a stockbroker specializing in railroad issues and trolley and utility bonds. Enoch used him for certain buying and selling as a front when he didn't want his name or the railroad's to be used. Fanny (Faustina) Emerson suffered from asthma in the low lands, so they lived in Kingston Junction in a big bungalow built of native boulders, with a roofed porch. Here Mrs. Emerson could breathe better than in Los Angeles. Crane Emerson had branches in San Francisco, Denver, and Houston. He also was on call by Drexel & Morgan of Wall Street in the gathering of information on Western railroads. J. P. Morgan disliked shoddy small companies; *consolidate* was his advice.

Mrs. Emerson's niece, Wilma De Groat from Boston and Pawtucket, Rhode Island, was just out of Miss Miller's Academy for Young Ladies, visiting the West this summer. She was a big blonde with small, graceful hands and feet, wore fashionable clothes and talked of "the theaateer and doncing—don't cha-know" at Newport during the season. Actually, she was a very sensible, intelligent girl; Miss Miller's Academy was to blame for the affected accent. Rawly found Wilma amusing, not at all stupid for all her fashionable accent. She had a healthy laugh, frisky limbs, and "the face of Liberty on the 1878 silver dollar" (Willie).

Homer, the Emerson's son, was sweet on Mollie. Homer was going to a new college opening up north next year— Stanford, at Palo Alto—a school that Homer told Rawly was created when a fortune teller had insisted that Mr.

and Mrs. Leland Stanford spend their railroad-made fortune in memory of their son, who died of drinking germ-rich milk in Florence, Italy, "while he was being taken by his parents on a tour of the culture spots of Europe."

Homer was a husky boy, a bit too communicative as to his ideals. He had told Mollie he respected her womanhood and would never trifle with her honor; certain areas of her body were sacred to him, which wasn't Mollie's idea of fun at all. At sixteen, Mollie felt trifling was all to the good, and she enjoyed hugging and pressing herself against Homer. She enjoyed seeing him blush, get hot under his stiff, high collar, and turn away to pant at times and adjust his trousers. His glands had no respect for his ideals.

Rawly drove well; he never performed a task he didn't do well and gracefully. The spirited, matched bays, the pride of his father's stable, knew they had a master at the reins. Wilma, in pale blue with lace-edged sunshade, said there was certainly a lot of land in the West. Rawly agreed; yes, horizon to horizon. They drove past two loblolly pines guarding a narrow lane. Rawly pointed his buggy whip at it. "My father used to keep nigger girls in a house down that lane. A dozen dusky beauties, a regular harem."

"How you talk," said Wilma. "A harem and your *own* father."

"There's a moat around the place and alligators and when E.K. he'd had his fill of a favorite, he tied her up in a bag and threw her into the moat for the 'gators to feed up on."

"I like the way your mind works," said Wilma.

"You're fibbing, joshing Wilma," said Homer. "Dad says it was only one girl. The de Leon one who went off to be a schoolteacher. And she isn't a nigrah, she's Spanish; she's only Jasper de Leon's stepdaughter."

Mollie nodded. "Bet her father was a white as we are."

Rawly touched up the bays with the whip, winked at Wilma. "Why, Homer, I remember her when I was little. She was black as coal, shiny as stove polish. Had a gold bone in her nose—my father made it for her."

Homer said, "Respect your father."

Rawly said, "But she didn't file her teeth to points. *That's* a lie. E.K. also says she didn't eat her meat raw—she warmed it a bit."

"You are like nobody I ever met," said Wilma. Rawly found her very desirable.

They got out of the rig and walked down by the spring where, Homer told them, some old woman, now dead, used to get water to run an illegal whisky still, and she was suspected of shooting two husbands, one fatally.

Wilma said, "Oh, I love this country. Rhode Island isn't like this." There were cottonwoods and willows by the iron-tasting spring. They had sandwiches and cold punch set in half-melted ice, and a rather too-rich cake. Homer took Mollie off to the springhouse built of old adobe bricks from a ruined mission. Rawly mussed up Wilma on the traveling rug they had brought along. He blew in her ear, felt her legs, pressed her breasts and she said he was a naughty boy, but not as naughty as *some*. They kissed, and she pulled back when he put his tongue between her lips. Wasn't *that* nasty? It was, by Miss Miller's Academy morality, Rawly said, but wonderful, like some snow put down the back of your neck under the collar.

Wilma said, "That was just it, that's how one went down the primrose path." At that, they both burst out laughing and he kissed her neck and shoulders.

Rawly said, "Aren't I the devil?"

She said, "Yes and no."

Mollie came up, calling out, "We must be getting back."

They drove back, singing old college songs and some ragtime. It was a beautiful afternoon, Rawly thought—to be alive, young, in all this shining landscape, to see the distance crayon-blue haze over the mountains. And beyond the far horizon, someplace up there to the east, was Kingston Pass, where he had once thought his father had single-handedly, with a few cheering workers, destroyed an invasion of evil men determined to ruin the W. & G.P. He put one arm around Wilma. "Isn't this driving dangerous?" she asked. He told her yes, it was.

Roadrunners—strange birds that seemed part lizard—crossed in front of the horses, and a desert turtle came slowly on scaled claws across the dust, its stone armor clattering as it went its clumsy way. To spare the creature, Rawly reined in the horses who reared up at the sight of the dusty turtle.

Mollie said, "I don't like to see them run over. The shell breaks with a noise like firecrackers."

Rawly steadied the horses by talking to them tenderly.

He left a week later for Denver, as managing director of the rather worthless White Water & Denver narrow-gauge mountain railroad. He had one of Wilma's pink garters in his Gladstone bag, and—such is the nature of man, he decided—an introduction to Maddie Silk, who ran the best sporting house in town. Unlike his father, Rawly understood women, could emotionally feel with them a relationship full of joy, if not respect. He had little of Enoch's attitude of treating them kindly and well. Rawly preferred the whirlwind approach: "Sweep them off their feet, but don't knock them down."

26

Rawly Kingston had his father's driving sense of purpose,
the determination to get things done. Besides, he also had
a sense of play, a wider horizon of interests lacking in
Enoch Kingston. While Enoch had gambled and whored
some as a young man, he was never dedicated to pleasure
seeking so much as his son. In his first three months in
Denver, Rawly reorganized the railroad to some sort of
order and competence—realizing it was a rather worthless
property, that it would not do more than just pay its way
under its present condition and rail routes. He set up
bachelor quarters with Leopold Ball, a young man from
St. Louis, five years his senior. Ball came of a good
family, rather rigid and atrophied in social aspic. He had
decided that the placid life of a top-drawer society family
with safe investments in lumber and coal was not for him.

Leopold, known as Leepole, was a smiling aggressive
young hedonist with a high-pitched voice, a short but wiry
body, black curls falling down on a domed brow, his hu-
morous foxy face suggesting ironic wisdom. He was a
deadly dangerous man in a barroom brawl for all his
small size. Leepole Ball could drink until he fell
(smilingly) unconscious. He smoked a bent-stemmed briar
pipe, had been to Cambridge two years, and had been ap-
prenticed to a Scottish engineering firm for three more.
People learned not to mock his British accent. He was
wealthy and a cheerful spender. Leepole was a very skilled
engineer; he ran a family silver mine at a place called
Noodle Flats (so named for no known reason) outside
Cripple Creek.

Rawly and Leepole first met at the Pickax Bar in Denver. Leepole had ordered a drink in his accented, high

voice, and Rawly said, "Cambridge—know that slurred 'A' anyplace."

"Yale," Leepole had answered, "Can smell that nasal superior drawl."

"Sonofabitch," said Rawly, cheerfully putting an arm around Leepole's shoulder. "My treat, sport."

"Not likely." Leepole lifted a finger to the bartender. "Mike, me good man, pour two more. I'm Leepole Ball. Have some mining leases and run the family hole in the earth. You interested in mines?"

"No, I'm Ralston Kingston. Rawly. My old man has me working a toy railroad up here, the Whitewater and Denver. A junk yard really. Takes a day a week of my time. What does one do in this town after they roll up the sidewalks?"

In the next week, the two new friends tested the tasty doings at the Antlers Bar and the gay life of the sporting houses of Colorado. Leepole put Rawly up for the Cheyenne Mountain Club, and the young man proved himself the first night by having a fight with a local hard case, and in happy truculence tossed him through an expensive plate glass mirror.

Leepole was impressed. He sent Rawly out to run things at the Ball Mine at Noodle Flats, a gunshot from Cripple Creek, a very tough place. The town was wild and mean, game for anything, Rawly wrote Willie:

> Gunplay, cards, the rustle of silken taffeta skirts. Madams and whores coming in by every train and stagecoach; poker sharks, shady lawyers, con men, saloon owners and miners hard as the rocks below, making Myers Street of Cripple Creek as tough as the Barbary Coast of Frisco.

Leepole liked fancy girls and he liked them wild. And he got them. As for Rawly, if sometimes he attracted the attention of some mine official's wife and was involved in furtive privacies, well, the women agreed he was handsome. Rawly stood out by his attire—well-cut Eastern riding breeches fit for polo and boots that cost as much as a good horse. Within six months, as a lark, he and Leepole had evening clothes and top hats; they defied gunmen to take potshots at them for their habit at times of dressing for dinner. Those who made snide remarks about the tenderfoot dudes were often shown college boxing was superior to barroom rough and tumble, aided by a fast right hand and a good uppercut.

Rawly and his friends cut against the grain of the popular conception of the West. It wasn't only the history of sourdough prospectors, frontier whores, flashy saloon owners, and poker-faced gamblers. Trained men, educated experts, also made places like Leadville, Virginia City, Goldsmith, Austin, Eureka, and the various Frying Pans, Dead Man's Gulches, the hell-on-wheels, and often departed with their boots on.

Rawly ran the W.W. & D. Railroad, but his best friends were wealthy young men involved in mining: Spencer Penrose, Charlie Tutt, Albert Carlton, Horace Devereaux (Princeton), Harry Lenard (Columbia), others, too, college-educated men, members of good families from as far away as Boston and Charleston, who didn't act ashamed of having learned something at Ivy League schools. These men, as Rawly wrote his father, were

> the managerial forces, vital experts who ran things, made fortunes, and spent them with no parvenu awkwardness. The great smelters, the combines, and building of new cities are their tasks. I feel *this* is my world. They know the workings of the connection with gold, silver, copper markets and Wall Street's setting up of corporations and holding companies.

They also knew the swish of voluminous silks scented with sandalwood, the set of an ermine tippet. Rawly and his friends sported bowlers and canes and their long-tailed coats at the Palace Bar, or with an armful of parlor-house girl in red corset and camisole. Nights were spent dancing at the Tropics Dance Palace. All this, too, was part of Cripple Creek.

> These men are taking from the earth or earning through speculations and investments, $200,000,000 from Cripple Creek. So, E.K., I'm resigning from your

railroad, I'm going to manage some Ball Mine property and buy into leases. . . .

Your son,
R.

Enoch sent Rawly a wire: YOU ARE FIRED. E. B. KINGSTON.

Rawly celebrated by changing enough of his tailoring to wear a wide-brimmed Stetson with his riding tweeds. His white bulldog, Storm, learned to rest by the hitching post at the Ironside Dance Hall or Johnny Nolan's place until dawn. The dog was rewarded by Rawly from time to time, with a steak soaked in gin, and, so the story went, the animal became a noted lush.

Rawly was a fine dancer, and the jack-strutters just stepped aside and watched him whirl the fancy tarts in their voluminous ruffled skirts. He wasn't much of a poker player and knew it, proving wiser than those who didn't—and played. He could drink as well or better than anyone that ever stood at a bar testing his capacity. Rawly wasn't just a playboy, a pleasure-seeking idler. He had a good head for business. "A genius touch. He could smell money coming out of the ground," said Leepole Ball. But he also wrote his brother Willie: "Any man who works after lunch is a damn fool."

As to his hours of play, it was testified to in a court case. "Rawly Kingston never rolled in until dawn." Pleasure, he advised his friends, was the escape hatch from the unhappiness the world had an oversupply of.

In politics Rawly was a solid Republican, and in one local contest he threw one of the biggest parties ever seen in Noodle Flats; a hullabaloo; wild, wooly, boozy, and loud, to the jingling rowels of spurs and champagne corks popping. When the newspapers wrote up the event, with some gaudy invented details added, Enoch told Willie he hoped Rawly would change his name "before he gets killed."

Enoch was like so many men who had worked hard for their success, Charles White suspected. He resented his sons' having life made too easy for them. While Rawly was sporting and becoming an expert on the logistics of ore producing and shipping, going down into the heat and damp of the mines in which he and Leepole were buying shares, Enoch and Charles White were facing, they sensed, the opportunity of their lives, *or* something that could send them down to ruin.

"Nature, God's irony, and man's greed," as Charles White put it, "are producing conditions that have to be met head on."

"You sound like a train wreck."

Baring Brothers' bank, the principle dealer in W & G.P. bonds and stock, had become overextended in South America for a period of years. Three years of drought in the Argentine had destroyed the vast wheat farms, burned out the mortgaged crops and acres. Then an attack of anthrax and black-hoof rot, both deadly cattle diseases, attacked the great beef herds that were that nation's major exports. Beef, financed in many cases by Baring and their bondholders; in turn bankrupted shipping lines controlled by Baring interests. The hope in 1890 was that the rains would come again to the Argentine, flood the parched fields, the millions of acres where the seeds died and the earth turned to iron clay, or the wheat never rose more than a few inches before it perished. The grasslands turned brown, the anthrax spread, was fought by killing off vast herds and burning the bodies in ghastly hills of piled-up carcasses. Still the epidemic spread, and no Argentine beef was given entrance into European ports ... Enoch and Charles White subscribed to private cable services for overseas news.

Soon the Baring-backed Argentine railroads began to fail for lack of shippers of grain and cattle. Baring Brothers in Latin America had taken on millions of dollars in railroad bonds, paying five percent interest until the bonds were sold. Then they were to take an added two and a half percent commission on the bond sales. But, as Charles White pointed out, "Maybe they'll be good just for wallpaper."

Baring Brothers insisted it could weather its disastrous investments in Argentina railroad stocks and bonds, government securities, and industrials. "But in an economy

238

based on grain and cattle," Charlie noted in a private report to Enoch, "weather was a factor they overlooked. They also bought (the crazy coots) gold at 140 on the world market and invested it in Argentina—invested it all in that country's grain and cattle economy. Stand by. *Bad show.*"

Baring Brothers became insolvent. They had liabilities of over $100,000,000. Enoch and Charles surveyed their cables from London. "Bank of England has tried to bail B.B. out by a $7,000,000 loan. The Rothschilds added $15,000,000 gotten from the Bank of France. . . . Baring Brothers' hopes were mostly in their holdings in Argentine government bonds. The Argentine government has *just* defaulted, the bonds are valueless. . . . The English firm of Baring Brothers has collapsed."

It was clear that even the Bank of England and the Rothschilds could not put Baring Brothers together again.

The Grand Turk Baths on Sutro Street were, for San Francisco's best-known, most prosperous citizens, a place to steam out a hangover or get a black eye skillfully painted. It was a sort of club, to just pop open one's pores after a season of overeating or sweat out the fat from the many dinners the nabobs and the socially ambitious wives were giving. Charles White and Enoch Kingston sat naked on a high seat in a small private steamroom, hoping the fatigue could be drained out of them by wet vapors. They had been up for two full nights with just some catnaps of an hour or so, studying the stream of cables arriving from London, Paris, Buenos Aires, telegrams from Wall Street, then penciling in charts of the wheat and cattle prices around the world and the market in railroad stocks.

"The British move slowly," said Charlie White, feeling his lungs full of steam, wiping his face and neck with a towel. "This collapse will take time to settle the dust, seek out assets, try and get a true picture of the debts."

Enoch tried to focus a tired brain, "Their holdings in W. & G.P. are an asset. Of course, the bondholders can't recover their costs just now."

"We haven't been earning much for them—lots of road

building, buying locomotives, cars; oh, solid—but for the future."

Enoch grasped Charles' arm. "The future is that we take over the road."

"How the devil can we? We need a big wedge. There are still bond and stockholders."

Enoch was rubbing his hairy chest, draining the moisture away with the palms of his hands. "Put the line in debt. Begin to throw *our* shares on the market. Dump them in big lots through Emerson. Panic the European holders, the Texans, to dump, too."

Charlie stood up and draped himself in a sheet. He said softly, "I'll be blowed. It's a blinking good thought. We depreciate the line, the bondholders begin to dump their holdings when we start throwing piles of shares we own on the market. But do we own enough to put the fat on the fire?"

"Sell, sell short, sell what we haven't got on top of what we have."

"Then, when they hit bottom, we buy, *buy*."

"First we poor-mouth the road, then arrange, Charlie, to take it over as reorganizers. The trick is to avoid bankruptcy, just get a reorganization: then, when the stocks we buy back for peanuts go up—"

Charlie pulled Enoch to his feet, grabbed his hands and did a little dance. Enoch joined in, a large man with the beginning of a paunch, and the slim, fish-belly-white-skinned beanpole, Charlie.

Bathhouse Billy Simon, the Grand Turk's best rubber, coming in with an armful of towels, stood open-mouthed at their dance. "You gents celebrating a winning horse?"

"You might be right, Billy," Enoch said.

"Who of you do I take first for a proper rubdown?"

But the two men hardly had time to dry themselves before they were dressing and with shoes not buttoned all the way, collars ajar, cravats not firmly knotted, were off yelling for the doorman to get them a hack.

The collapse of Baring Brothers caused panic in every stock exchange and bond house in the world. Cunning operators and speculators also saw a wheat and beef shortage, but the public saw only ruin. Stocks and bonds issued

240

by other banking houses felt the loss of faith investors developed, doubts in the solidarity of their investments. A depressed market developed.

Nothing on the Pacific Coast fell faster than the value of Western & Great Plains' stock. Emerson and three other brokers acted for Enoch and Charles. Huge blocks of holdings were thrown on the market. The railroad issued a gloomy report of its future. Bridges had to be rebuilt, locomotives that had been ordered by the W. & G.P. were behind in the payments to the foundaries and factories.

But the scheme that Enoch had put together, so simple in the Turkish bath, ran into serious problems. Enoch's construction companies had built well, had extended lines into prosperous regions. The reports might show little income, but railroad speculators and boards of directors of rival lines had looked at maps. They counted the number of passenger trains, freight cars, rolling stock, locomotives. They measured the Federal land grants along the right of way and saw the W. & G.P. was not yet a corpse.

Two months into their scheme, Charles White very gloomily sat facing Enoch in his office one night, the Santa Ana desert winds blowing from the east. He looked paler than ever, a tic repeating itself on his right cheek, giving him, Enoch thought, an obscene wink.

"We're in too deep, Enoch."

Enoch tried to cheerfully light a cigar and leaned back in a new-type swivel chair he had bought in St. Louis.

"If we go under, Charlie, we'll make a pretty big splash. What the hell—I haven't had so much excitement since Vicksburg. At least nobody is shooting at us with real bullets."

"We're down twenty million of our own assets. We've borrowed from Solly Winters on watered stocks of the White Water & Denver and others. We'll ruin him, too."

"No, Sol knows we can cover his loans with our holdings in land, ranches, mines, leases. Rawly has put me on to some pretty good mine assets that are paying off. We'll protect Solly. We can't protect ourselves."

"And there was a splendid Turner oil I wanted to buy—made of reflection of gems and air."

"Buy it, Charlie. Owe them the money; get a loan on it."

"Enoch, we still haven't brought W. & G.P. stock down far enough. It's twenty-two this morning."

"Nineteen, I'll bet, by this afternoon. How much did we have of the whole shooting match."

"Ten percent. We need to buy or control twenty-five percent at least—should control thirty percent in any reorganization. I'll have to play patacake with a few courts and legal procedures, but even so—we need a lot of shares to act like a majority. Oh, proxies help . . . but . . ."

Enoch looked up from a report in his hand. "Charlie, do you know Baring sold three hundred million dollars worth of stocks and bonds of their various enterprises, sold them in Europe from Switzerland to the Czar's court in St. Petersburg. To merchants, widows, peasants, grocery store owners . . . three hundred million, and today the stuff is hardly worth holding on to. How much of what Baring sold over there was W. & G.P.?"

Charles White seemed to inflate—color even came back into his face—not good color, but color.

"I can find out."

"Let's start buying secretly, cheap, in Europe. You get on a special flier east for Chicago, New York. Telegraph for any fast boat—Hamburg-Amerika, Cunard, White Star—leaving for Europe. I want you—Emerson goes with you—to set up dummy companies to start buying up W. and G.P. holdings in Europe. Contact anybody with anything over fifty shares. We sell small here, buy big there. Have your men cry when they make an offer."

"I need time to pack."

"Not *this* trip. Wire ahead to New York for what you need. I have to fix up an open track on other lines for you with some railroad superintendents. Meanwhile, we'll cable Robbins, Weiss and Godoff, our brokers in London, to start the hunt for stockholders. When we think it has hit bottom, we buy back our shares here."

"You can't get a special train rolling by morning, Enoch."

"Make it four o'clock in the afternoon. Go get some sleep on the cot in my back room here."

Enoch went to the door and yelled into the courtyard for Chico. "Chico, wake up. Whip up the horses. Go wake Floyd Denton, and MacMonn of the Pullman division. Oh, stop the *Golden Eagle* at the Pine Tree crossing. Flag it down. I want the locomotive and tender and the club car and diner detached. . . . Never mind, I'll get that part done myself. The passengers can go with whatever slower engine is in the yards."

27

The great transcontinental record attempt across the United States came to be known much later as "the Kingston Caprice" first by the *Brooklyn Eagle*. By noon of the start, the borrowed engine, its tender, club car, diner, and Pullman car *The Fairy Queen,* were standing at the junction, steam up, conductors, dining car steward, waiters, cooks, two firemen, and an engineer, the last reading new schedules. Enoch had wanted to drop the club car, but Floyd Denton had shaken his head. "Look, I'm goin' as extra relief engineer, and I need that extra car to keep enough weight on them tracks I know nothin' about."

"Blow the boilers out of her, Floyd. We're calling it a U.S. Mail contract test."

"I don't care, Ennie, if you call it a jumping frog contest. I'll decide on the weight. You got water towers mapped, and coaling crews, and a clear track into Caycee and Chi? Too bad Jasper isn't the fireman he was.

"He understands. All I want is to beat Mojave Mike's record run."

"Get me extra coal boards up the sides of the tender, three more feet. Mojave Mike's record? Shootin' high. It's like tryin' to piss to the moon."

In 1876, an eccentric desert miner who was supposed to have a fabulous secret gold mine someplace in desert sands, had come forward with bags of gold coins. He wanted to hire a fast train to beat the eight-day record of crossing the United States by four days or less. That train had carried four cars, thirty passengers at five hundred dollars a head, and eight sacks of mail, on a run of over three thousand miles. And in what clocked time? Enoch went indoors to seek out the figures. Charles White with

Crane Emerson and his son Homer were inspecting their luggage. Mollie and Willie were going along for the ride. They were so excited they were almost walking on tiptoes. Mollie asked Enoch, "Can I stay over in New York for a week? I want to see Homer off on the boat."

Willie tapped his father on the shoulder with a small notebook. "The 1876 run went 3,306 miles in 83 hours, 35 minutes, seconds not given."

"How many days is that?" asked Crane Emerson.

Enoch did some quick mental arithmetic. "About three and a half days. The normal time is just over eight days."

"Can we beat it?" asked Homer.

"We'll see."

The whole damn run—somehow the event had leaked out—was getting too much notice. Perhaps it was a mistake. Newspapermen wanted to go along, some to join the train in Kansas City, in Chicago, Buffalo. It had been hard enough to get track clearance from lines whose rails they wanted to use. It was Charles who spelled it out on primitive phone connections, telegraph keys, to several top officials of rival lines. "It's going to advance railroad travel fifty years. Yours could be the only line left out—its name not reported big in the headlines splashed across the world's newspapers. Pictures of the run over *your* rails, through *your* stations. . . . Impossible? Of course you can clear the St. Louis rails. Barnum & Bailey circus train? My dear chap, sidetrack them and have them parade with the bands and clowns to play the special train through. Marvelous."

His voice grew a little hoarse, but as the special tooted its whistle to start its run, he could say to Enoch, "Only fifty miles of track line to clear out of Abilene, and on the Hudson. The Vanderbilt swine say they can't give us a clear track from West Point into Manhattan. Have to take our chance."

"I'll get it clear. I'll telegraph J. P. Morgan. He's got the muscle to get us track on the New York Central *or* into Hell."

Charles White and Dock Sing carried two well-filled suitcases aboard the special. Jasper de Leon, his wife, and six daughters stood by cheering. Mollie kissed her father,

Willie set his eyeglasses firmly on a rather too-small nose, and with Floyd at the throttle, the special rolled off toward the grade and began to gather speed for momentum to get over Kingston Pass. Floyd had pulled the throttle lever, opened the cylinder cocks, and the exhaust bellow's roar was loud and good. Jasper tried to keep his expression happy; he was just too old to work the banjo (scoop shovel.) Enoch accompanied the special on another train on parallel track, watching the special's piston work the driving wheels as they connected to the slide rods; all worked together, the crossheads, the side rods that sped the big 2-8-2 engine taken from the *Golden Eagle,* and now was outdistancing him. Floyd leaned on the whistle lever, gave two long blasts and one short at a crossing where two muleteams pulling hay-loads waited, ears alert, hooves in panic.

"Damn Floyd whistling when he should conserve steam."

Enoch's escort train fell further back as they crossed an arroyo on a truss bridge. He figured Floyd had the steam gauge up to 310, a full head, and was nursing the blower valve.

He knew the train was too light. It would be going over seventy miles an hour over straight runs—maybe eighty. He had told Floyd, "The limit *all* the way." If the special was wrecked, he had a son and daughter aboard, an uncle, and the only man in the world he fully trusted in a close friendship. Floyd was—in railroad terms—an expert ballast-scorcher, and the cars of the *Golden Eagle* did not have hotboxes, broken coupler knuckles; the draft gear and air-brakes were always kept up to snuff. Still, trains *did* derail, run off bridges, collide, burn, explode boilers.

There was some trouble on the special's run. After crossing the Mississippi outside of Cairo, a wagon was destroyed, while taking on coal. A deck girder span on an was to pay to rebuild it.
old iron bridge was found to be torn loose after the special roared across it outside of Erie, and the W. & G.P.

The last few hours of the run had been a problem. J. P. Morgan was appealed to by Enoch; they had met twice before when Morgan was thinking of consolidating some of the bankrupt rail-lines—forty-five thousand miles of track were declaring they were running in the red. Morgan demanded and got the New York Central to clear track for the special down the Hudson into the city.

On his first trip east, Willie stared out at the flowing, placid river, so unlike the burnt-out stream beds, or the roar of mountain cascades he knew. He tried to imagine redmen in birchbark canoes, Dutch settlers being scalped, the stories of Washington Irving. What Willie really looked forward to was what he still called "the temples of money," the Subtreasury on Wall Street with gold bricks stacked under its sidewalk, the cool interior of Drexel and Morgan with which E.K. had been so impressed. Willie was still young enough to think there were answers to all questions. Mollie and Homer were holding hands and had their noses pressed against a window. Charles White and Crane Emerson sat at a linen-covered table in the deserted diner, going through lists of European brokers and exchange bank officials. Floyd Denton came through the car from the Pullman car—he had been sleeping for four hours after eighteen hours at the controls. Now he was not fully awake, but determined to take the Kingston special into New York City himself. He was still dressed in grimy railroad jacket and greasy pants, but wore a tall gray top hat, had a length of red silk, a scarf, tied around his neck instead of the usual bandana sweat rag.

"Mr. White, get ready to send E.K. a telegraph. We're going to break Mojave Mike's record." He looked at his big silver watch attached by a heavy chain to a brass button of his jacket.

"Holy cow, the poke-ass up front has lost me twenty-two seconds!"

He ran forward to take over the controls, climbing over the tender with only a few hundred pounds of coal left now.

There was talk in New York of building a great rail station to be called the Grand Central, but Floyd was just as happy to slide the special into the old depot—all steam vents open—to cheers, a crowd, newspapermen, flash powder-lit cameras on stilts.

Over three thousand miles away, Enoch, sleeping on the cot in his inner office, was awakened by Chico, who shook him with no respect and handed him a blue-crayon-written telegraph,

BEAT M. MIKE RECORD SPECIAL RUN 3,306 MILES 82 HOURS 6 MINUTES. C. WHITE.

Unfortunately the exploit caused such a sensation it sent W. & G.P. stock up four points that day and two more that week, but no further.

Enoch was always to feel that his plans for gaining control of the W. & G.P. was betrayed by Willie to his brother Rawly. The truth was that while Willie had hinted that E.K. was involved in some changes in the running of the road, Rawly himself figured out what actually was going on. His mind was sharper than his father's; not more intelligent, but he had less of Enoch's worn-out traditions (as he saw it) to "dump overboard," and Rawly's world was more sophisticated than his father's. He sensed at once that Uncle Charlie and his father were depreciating W. & G.P. stock after the news of the failure of Baring Brothers to gain personal control of the railroad. Rawly decided it could be useful knowledge.

He put it to Leepole Ball one noon as they sat under a stuffed head of a mountain goat at their club, taking soda water for lunch after a night of celebrating Leepole's thirtieth birthday.

"It's this way, Leepole, my mother, my Alvarez uncles and cousins, me, Willie, Mollie, we all have big chunks of W. and G.P. stocks and bonds. My father, he called it dividing up the nest eggs, and he being able to feel how warm they were at all times. Control of voting rights of course."

"He wanted you to sell too, as he's doing?"

"Not a peep. He expects it to rise in value soon." Rawly motioned to the Negro waiter leaning against the wall. "Sam, some clear soup and crackers and a double bourbon. You, Leepole?"

"I don't feel up to that heavy a meal. Just the dessert, Sam, a double."

"He's driving the stock down to gain control."

"The way I see it, Rawly, your old man has a good chance of getting the line."

"Do I sell or buy more?"

248

Leepole groaned and held his head. "Must have had too much birthday last night. Can't get the ol' brain to spark. . . . Don't sell your stock just yet. But let's you and me sell short a few thousand shares, just at first. If it keeps dropping, we'll make a pile on more selling orders."

"The damn stock has gone up since E.K.'s train race out of Jules Verne."

"Dropping again. Thing is, old buddy—" They each took up the glasses set before them. "Thing is, we'd have to figure out at what point the stock is at its lowest to start buying it up to cover our short sales and pile up a batch of it for ourselves when your old man takes over."

"Suppose the road is put into bankruptcy?"

Leepole sipped his drink. "Hm? I figure your Uncle Charlie is one smart corporation hombre. He is shooting for reorganization. Then he'll send out some good news. Rate of carloads up, big profits coming in, and so stocks go up."

"It's a damn gamble." Rawly seemed amused. "What the hell—all we have to lose is a fortune."

It was a week before Enoch found out that Rawly and Leepole were selling W. & G.P. short. Willie was blamed, but he just shook his head. "Rawly—he's your son, E.K. Got his savvy from you."

"He'll come a tumble living high."

Rawly liked show—unlike his father—and champagnes, insisting on Mumms, Pol Roger or Moët & Chandon when he was treating the house. "Not the horse brine and vinegar the establishment usually serves, but Beaujolais, Chateau Latour." He even dared talk to mine owners of pheasant *en plumage* and imperial caviar, in a world raised on sourdough and camp beans.

A sartorial perfectionist, Rawly liked braided morning coats and white piped waistcoats. If he went Western, his high-heeled boots were hand-stitched by Herman Hieser of Kansas City, and he paid $125 for a Stetson. Later, much later, he explained to newly rich Westerners the need of a Briggs umbrella in London, the discreet pleasures of Rosa Lewis's Cavendish Hotel in Jermyn Street. In time he did much to teach the rough pick-and-shovel miner in dirty red flannel long johns, or the half-mad hunters of the legendary Dutchman Mine, that once they got rich they could try to be gentlemen. Not all listened, and many continued to eat with knife in mouth and turn away from fawn-colored spats. Even during the Baring Brothers crisis, Rawly did not neglect his appearance. He remained part of the game of the hunt for wealth and part of the gay life sandwiched in between the making of fortunes; in the next sixty years, Noodle Flats produced two score very rich men and half a billion dollars in bonanzas for Rawly's crowd.

Rawly and Leepole did well with the mine leases, but they saw that digging ore was hard work and expensive. The big money should be in smelting and refining. You had to find a mine and hope for gold or silver in it, but smelting was pure business. Ore, no matter whose, had to be refined.

As W. & G.P. stock went down and they sold short, Rawly said, "Gotta idea—let's build some smelters if we don't go broke."

"Too many smelters now. It's ore that's short."

"I've found some. Got my eyes on that huge mountain of low-grade copper ore discarded, lying around, worthless stuff, millions and millions of tons of it not worth refining."

"The discarded tails are low grade, they just ruin and fill the landscape."

"Found a man called Bixby who said he could show how to refine this low grade stuff into pure metal by a cheap-jack process."

"Every night say the Lord's Prayer that your old man wins."

They put a half million dollars—most of it Ball family money—into the first low-grade ore smelter and called it the Rawlee Copper Company. (Rawlee, not daring to call it Rawballs Copper.) The process worked beautifully, and as they had bought up all the Mount Everest of tailings left by the Guggenheim holdings, they dreamed of becoming copper kings. But they needed capital and they depended on Enoch's scheme's working.

The morning they broke ground for their first smelter at Frying Pan Creek, they stood on a mountain of tailings and Rawly said, "Leepole, I'm about to make an even bigger leap over a cliff."

"I know, that girl Wilma in Boston you've been writing to."

"My problem Leepole is I'm a thinker. Can't help it. And I see myself in ten, fifteen years, a busted-up, clapped-out womanizer, still sniffing at a whore's petticoats, still waking up smelling drunken breaths in a hired bed. I'm sorry to disappoint you as a rounder, Leepole, but I want a home and children and somebody who isn't asking me for a flask of perfume and a pile of gold coins from a morning mouth. I want to be loved. My mother couldn't love—she was too—" he fluttered his fingers in the air. "E.K. has no life but his rails and his engines. I bet he's never loved any woman as much as his timetables. I want—"

Leepole slapped Rawly's back. "Grab her. So what if the smelter fails, if the W. & G.P. goes under, and you'll be mucking with pick and shovel like poor old Horace Tabor after his bubbles burst."

"Not us—we'll be taking half a million a month out of the tailings in ten years."

Leepole said that called for a drink.

28

For all their planning and maneuvering to take over the W. & G.P., Enoch and Charles White were running into problems that they had not expected to face. Many of the European bondholders were willing to sell as the prices fell sharply, but enough of them were canny peasants, shopkeepers come to wealth, and were hoping to hold out for higher prices. This delayed Enoch's agents' buying up the shares because of the time-consuming dickering. Also, several Western rail-lines were considering forming a combine attempt to get hold of the W. & G.P. for dividing among themselves. What splintered their ranks was the bickering of *how* the various W. & G.P. tracks and mileage were to be appropriated. So as they met and fought to decide who should get what section, a final firm agreement to move was delayed. Later it was discovered that to sabotage the raid, Charles White had planted officials of some Texas and Utah lines among them.

What brought the final climax to Enoch's plans was not the doing of any group; neither Charles White or Enoch Kingston, nor the bondholders or the hopes of the rival rail-lines.

It was the destiny of the *Coast-Mountain Express*, a daily train that Enoch had created for the Kansas City-San Diego run—with passengers wanting to enter Los Angeles, changing for a Southern Pacific train at Tujunga Junction. On a cold, snow-stained January night in 1891, the *Coast-Mountain* was approaching Kingston Pass from the east, first moving up the grade to 2,754 feet, then going toward the 4,980 foot pass at the summit. Twenty-eight miles from the pass, the train halted at a depot to take on an added locomotive for the needed extra pulling power to get it over the summit, with its load of two baggage cars, U.S. Mail car, three Pullman sleepers, club car, and diner. Excluding the crew, the train carried 122 persons. The depot men uncoupled the engine K-12 that had made the run from Kansas City and inserted from a spur line between it and the first baggage car, the second locomotive, K-28. This engine was a bit less powerful than the K-12. The two engines would take the train up to the pass and there the K-28 would be uncoupled, run off on to a turntable, and when the *Coast-Mountain Express* was on its way down to the flatlands, K-28 would return to the bottom of the eastern side of the pass, to wait until the next train needed assisting over the pass.

The night was not too dark, but it was stormy with snow flurries and the intense cold. The temperature, as conductor Crowell had noted at the depot, was dropping and would be below zero when the *Coast-Mountain Express* reached the pass. The sleepers were heated by coal stoves and they gave warmth, comforting the passengers as the train slowly ascended towards the pass in a cold, blue world. Among the stone sides of the pass's wilderness, it was a wind-tormented world, desolate to see beyond the frost-rimmed car windows.

The passengers were asleep, most of them, but for a late storyteller boring three people in the club car. The efforts of the two engines echoed in the pass, the cars swaying as the train took the several rather sharp curves that led to the top.

On the summit, the train came to a stop with steaming and puffing. Well-bundled-up but still shivering, the work crews came out from the brick hut and telegraph post that serviced the pass. The front-end brakeman went forward to help uncouple the extra locomotive K-28 and get it onto the turntable, leaving the original engine for the moment unattached to the train. Conductor Crowell swinging his red lantern went to the hut to report the time of his run as ordered by Enoch on all pass trains. The rear brakeman, Eli Carmin, was approached by a gentleman in a great brown cape and a gray bowler hat tied down over his ears by a wool scarf.

"I must send a telegraph back to Kansas City."

"We're not standing here for long, sir," said the brakeman.

"I'm a friend of Mr. White, head of the line's legal department, and this is vital."

Carmin looked about him as a new snow flurry thickened in the wind. "Well, sir, you better follow me in this here gale you could get lost, blow over a cliff."

It was against regulations for either brakeman to leave a train during the cutting out of an engine on top of the pass. After Carmin had taken the gentleman to the hut, the wind blew out his lantern and he had to go back inside to relight it. When he came back to the *Coast-Mountain Express,* he was shocked to find the engineless cars were moving slowly backward down the slight grade—going past the siding switch, lamps burning behind the car windows, some waiters moving about, yawning. The original engine K-12 was standing by itself, and the spare engine K-28—uncoupled—was just moving onto the turntable. It was a runaway engineless train, rolling backward down the pass and gaining speed all the time as the grade grew steeper and steeper. Carmin knew at once what had happened: the engineer had neglected to fill the compressed air-brake hoses with air just before the engines were uncoupled, which meant there was no air pressure in the train's brakes to stop it from rolling down grade. The brakeman made a running leap at the handrail and steps of the club car and dragged himself aboard as the train's speed increased. The hand-brakes were not set because air-brakes were there on the grades to hold the train stationary when needed. Carmin began to twist the hand-brake on the club car. He could not make it grip very firmly. He ran back to the first sleeping car and worked the hand-brake tight; meanwhile, Conductor Crowell and the other brakeman were moving from car to car as shaken passengers, awakened from sleep, began to wonder and some to shout, "What's happening?"

"Why are we going backward?"

The train was gathering speed and the curves grew sharper as the train came out of the pass, plunged down steeper grades.

As he took a quick look at the passing ridges and brush, Carmin figured that they were moving at a speed of at least seventy miles an hour. The cars were being severely shaken—lamp glass was breaking, bags cannonading about as if fired from guns. Several passengers in nightshirts and one in red flannel underwear were falling down and rising, and some were helping trying to tighten the hand-brakes. The cars began to tilt dangerously to the left as they reached a sharp turn known as Devil's Leap—on top of a twenty-foot embankment. The passengers and crew could hear the screeching of the steel wheels as they ground against the rails. There was a shaking and tearing of metal as the coupling between the club car and one of the Pullmans tore away, and two cars rushed separately down the mountainside. The remaining cars seemed to pause for a moment, as if undecided, then leaped over the embankment. Like a snake of steel, wood and glass, the train fell with a great shattering crunching together. A folding up of car undercarriages, wood, interior furnishing, hot stoves, lamps and flying bodies, to mash together at the bottom of the embankment. The two cars that had broken free, with men hanging onto the hand-brakes, came to a stop four miles down the track.

What remained of the train crew led by Crowell and Carmin fought their way in wind and rain back to the scene of the disaster. They saw flames shooting up, great tongues of red and black smoke. The stoves heating the cars, and the hanging oil lamps had set fire to the smashed cars. The party clambering down from the embankment could hear cries for help, voices highly hysterical and screams, the breaking of glass. Some passengers were trying to escape from the crushed and burning interiors.

By morning Enoch was at the scene of the wreck with a relief train of four coaches, two flatcars of road crews with jacks and cutting tools (and a dozen coffins.) Twenty-eight people were dead, forty were injured, some of them seriously; with loss of limbs, broken backs, internal injuries. Enoch raged among the still-burning smoldering remains of the cars, stormed up and down the embankment.

Crowell, the conductor, with a bruised face, several teeth

missing in a badly cut mouth, could just say, "Mr. Kingston, it's terrible."

Enoch in his heavy wolf pelt coat shouted. "You're goddamn right it's terrible. What the hell kind of a report is *that*?"

"It's like, suddenly—" the conductor just shook his head.

"Why? *Why*?"

Many of the dead were being wrapped in canvas—not enough coffins were on hand. Two cars still burned with a smell of what Enoch could only feel was flesh. The hurt passengers who could walk were mostly weeping. The badly injured were silent. They lay in snow and charred earth waiting to be lifted up the embankment.

Enoch yelled, "Carmin! Where is Carmin?"

The rear brakeman still holding his lit lantern glowing jewellike, turned a haggard face towards the dreaded E.K. "Yes, sir."

"What happened to the air-brakes? Why didn't they stop the train?"

"I don't have no idea, sir."

"You sonofabitch, you know." He turned to face the surviving crew. "You *all* know. The engineer didn't put any holding pressure into the air-brake hoses before they were uncoupled. True?"

"You'll have to ask him," said the conductor.

"The sonofabitch swears he did. He's a liar. Crowell, why wasn't there a hand-brake setting as soon as she began to stir?"

"Well . . . now . . ." The conductor felt where his teeth had been and spat blood. "The rear brakeman, he weren't on the train."

The brakeman turned down the wick in his lantern, "It was this way, sir, I—"

Enoch swiveled, swung his gloved fist into the brakeman's face. The man fell, both from the blow and slippery ground. Enoch turned away, burrowed his head down in the wolf collar of his greatcoat. He knew the Kingston Pass wreck would enter railroad history. The brakeman's dropped lantern rolled away to shatter its chimney on a boulder.

Enoch sat the next day in his office—bulky, tired, soot smudge on one cheek, facing some journalists, local men and two who had come down from up the coast. He had not slept all night, and he wished Charlie were there so they could talk things over. Floyd had suggested they get up a posse and shoot the engineer and the brakeman. Enoch had said, "You work up any mob action, Floyd, and I'll shoot *you* down myself. This is an act-of-God accident. You've heard of them."

"The Lord he sure used a lot of careless fellers to get done what he wants done."

Just before the first reporters came up to the junction office to get Enoch's version of the wreck, Enoch had snapped his fingers, touched his chin lightly with a closed fist. *He wished he could smile at what had just occurred to him.* For bad as the deaths and wreck and the injured, the closing of the pass to traffic to replace displaced rails, it *was* in a way a solution—at least if used properly to break the bottleneck that had so far hindered the taking over of the W. & G.P., the stocks still held by owners and which he needed for control. Enoch turned to the journalists very seriously. He had not shaved, and he wore a dark railroad shirt. He spoke slowly and calmly, not raising his voice.

"Gentlemen I am about to make an official statement. Take it down. The record for safety of this railroad has been good. Our roadbeds, our trains, engines, have all been maintained in good working order. But there are unlucky times, some of you call them acts of God. Those things no human being among us can foresee. The accident in the pass. Some people who put their lives in our hands are dead; more are injured. I'm not going to talk of the losses to the road."

He looked around the men writing rapidly on pads or some sheets of paper. He felt the palms of his hands go moist; he swallowed air. He hoped his features didn't overdo his looking sad.

"This may mean the end of the Western and Great Plains Railroad. Its stocks, as you all know, have fallen in value, fallen greatly. There are outstanding debts and many creditors. There will be lawsuits by the relatives of the dead and by the injured. Judgments will be made against the line. I fear we shall go into bankruptcy. That is all I have to say."

"Is this connected with the failure of Baring Brothers?"

"It certainly does not help us to face all our obligations if they pile up all at once."

"What actually caused the wreck? Why did the train roll down through the pass without any locomotive. Why didn't the air-brakes hold?"

"Gents, all good questions—they will be answered by a committee of investigation."

"Mr. Kingston, was it human error or failure of some mechanical part?"

He looked stern and answered at once. "We have, so far, not found any evidence of human error. If there was, it will come out in the investigation. As for mechanical failure of some sort, on that, too, at this time we have no information. That's all, gents."

He turned away from more questions and went into his inner office. He felt ill as his tensions still held him. He seemed to have difficulty breathing. He took a big gulping drink of bourbon and coughed because of swallowing too quickly. He should feel dishonored, guilty, but all he felt was the tired long-distance runner getting his second wind.

The Kingston Pass Wreck made headlines in most of the nation's newspapers. The cables carried it to Europe. The value of W. & G.P. bonds and stock fell away to the lowest they had ever been. As lawsuits were filed against the railroad, the stocks fell to being quoted "in dimes" as Charles White put it; and his agents had no trouble in acquiring all they needed to control the line. Rawly and Leepole stopped selling short and began to buy W. & G.P. stock.

Charles rushed back from Europe to face committees of investigation, to make arrangements with creditors, suppliers, to talk to lawyers. The line must avoid bankruptcy, he advised, instead, a form of reorganization would be best. And after some interesting sessions with committees and commissions, with bankers, and the larger creditors, the W. & G.P. was voted into a reorganization headed by Enoch Bancroft Kingston and Charles Auden White, major stockholders. They refinanced by selling some of the land grants; they settled with creditors for twenty cents on the dollar, the rest in promissory notes. They avoided most of the lawsuits for damages from coming to court, by insisting they, as reorganizers, were not responsible for the events created by the old W. & G.P. Railroad. They sent agents around to inform the people suing that their cases were hopeless, but the new people—feeling morally but not legally obligated—would make some token settlements. In most cases this line of talk was enough to shake off most of the large damage suits. Those who insisted on their days in court found it took years of playing the usual lawyers' tangled games, and then was hardly worth the effort. Enoch was not very proud of this kind of dealing.

The rest of the taking over was legal maneuvering, getting judgments they needed from the courts, and in the end, turning the original stock and bonds into real assets by getting courts to approve the use of them for new credits. Historians were never able to fully track down the methods, nor how for all its seeming defects, the Western & Great Plains emerged in two years as again a fully functioning railroad system. With the majority of the controlling stock held by its president and chairman of the board, Enoch Kingston, its vice president, Charles White, and the Alvarez family, Ralston Kingston, and Leopold Ball.

If the W. & G.P. position was shaky for some time, and if the earnings were slim, it was again solvent, or so the bookkeeping proclaimed. And its lines were back in full service, at a time when 45,000 miles of railroad in all parts of the country were bankrupt, many never to recover.

Kingston House was a lonely place. Enoch no longer heard from Rawly. Rawly who was getting married (Enoch had been too busy in court to go to Boston for the wedding) was becoming a rich mine and smelter owner. Enoch had hoped speculation would break the young bastard; he had even envisioned the day Rawly came back asking to be taken into the railroad business. But he knew Rawly had done well in W. & G.P. stock. Willie was fininshing college at Berkeley, would pass the bar and go into one of Solly Winters's banks where he worked summers and was, Solly reported, "smarter than anybody. He feels the pulse of money and credit, smells a good mortgage like a camel scents water."

"The hell with that, Solly; I wanted him with me. But I suppose a banker is better than being a fiddle player or painting barroom nudes."

"Unless he's a very *great* fiddle player."

Mollie, too, was gone. She had married Homer Emerson and was living in San Francisco. Homer and his father were involved in trolley franchises, talking of connecting every American city by networks of big red cars. Maude was an invalid in the Convent of the Blue Nuns in Rome. . . .

Enoch went down to the kennels to see the dogs fed.

29

Willie and Mollie had gone to Boston to attend Rawly's wedding and had been very impressed by "the Puritan codfish-and-beans society pomp," as Willie called it. "And the bone-dry manners of people who thought themselves humble enough to feel so solidly superior that they did not have to point that fact out." Willie was developing a sharp tongue and had stopped biting his fingernails.

The De Groats were an old New England family going downhill financially from their inherited once-substantial fortune. But still with a Bulfinch house in the best part of Boston and a Copley portrait of an ancestor who had been the owner of a slave ship and deacon of the First Congregational Church of the city. He had also been a collector of Greek texts, a sponsor of one of the first presses to print books in the colonies.

Godwin De Groat, the father of Wilma, was a serious-faced Bostonian, a bit on the bony side, director of the family's hide and leather business, a firm going back four generations. It had been declining for at least two of those generations while the De Groats endowed chairs at Harvard, built up a well-filled corner of a first-class cemetery, and broke the basic rule that was the sacred creed of most of Boston's old families: *never* to dip into your capital. For De Groat investments in cotton and woolen mills (the Crompton loom for figured cloth), shipping, Maine potatoes and Chinese tea, had all turned out disasters. The cotton mills were already hearing talk of how much less trouble it would be to relocate in the South, close to the cotton fields and cheap, hungry labor. There were signs that the children of the poor below the age of ten were going to be barred from New England mills. Once De Groat was heard to ask what New England had fought the Revolution for!

Godwin De Groat was not pleased to have Rawly as a son-in-law, even if the young man's grandfather was said to have been a Boston mechanic who had worked on steam engines for the mills. Still, Rawly was the son of Enoch Kingston. Godwin De Groat, active in the hide market, in corn futures, hog bellies, and a dreadful foray into hemp rope imports, was aware of the hundreds of W. & G.P. freight cars shunted through by New England carriers to local yards. Those weathered, dark yellow cars with the large red letters under the wingspread of an eagle:

WESTERN & GREAT PLAINS R.R.
Reliable, Swift, Safe

After the ceremony, Godwin De Groat, a widower (his wife had been a Standish of a less-known branch) took his son-in-law into his black walnut-paneled library and said seriously to the young man so neat in his formal wedding attire, "I have great belief in the future of the West, and I'm sure Wilma looks forward to existence there."

Rawly, a bit woozy from the brandy before the ceremony, also sherry and port, looked very handsome in morning coat and striped trousers, his dark curly hair combed back and to one side. He nodded. "We have the Indians pretty much under control, sir, and running water inside the better houses."

Godwin De Groat felt Rawly must have a Western outdoor humor, but he added, "I have not been able to give my cherished daughter all I had intended. But," he took a velvet jewel case out of a desk drawer and handed it to Rawly. "These are the De Groat emeralds Captain Abner De Groat brought back from India in the clipper *Flying Star*. I pass them into your hands for Wilma."

Rawly opened the case and saw a gold chain and two emeralds attached.

"We are grateful to you, sir," he said, "and should you ever feel you need them for some dealings where you need a pledge—" His son-in-law didn't finish, he just smiled.

"Wouldn't think of it, not at all. Family heirlooms."

"Well now," said Rawly, "Dad—and I never called *my* father that—I know De Groat and Company has been somewhat harassed of late. My best man Leopold Ball tells me the hide and leather business has been invaded by European buyers, and you are not getting the raw supplies from the Chicago and Kansas City packinghouses."

"I don't think Ralston, this is the precise time to—"

"Of course not, of course not. I thank you for the family emeralds. Just know your little girl is in good hands."

"Oh—of course."

(Is he mocking me? thought his father-in-law.)

"My partner Ball and myself, we have the rights to certain cattle ranches and we ship steers to—"

The door to the library opened with a bang and Willie, a bridesmaid on one arm and a tray of De Groat family crystal held high, in danger of shattering, filled with champagne.

"Lordy, lordy, see how the bridegroom tarries. And the honeymoon coach awaits."

Rawly put the jewel case into a jacket pocket. "I must go up and change." He shook his father-in-law's hand and left the room. Willie, who was not used to drinking, pushed his plump face close to Godwin De Groat's and grinned. "You're getting a prince, Groat, my man, a regular twenty-one jewel prince. . . ." He turned to the bridesmaid on his arm, "I think, honeychile, I'se gonna be sick. Where's the indoor privy?"

The rumor for many years was that Godwin's son-in-law's brother William was sick all over the De Groat waistcoat and cravat. The truth was that Willie, quick on his feet, threw up into the Wedgwood umbrella stand in the hall.

The honeymoon was done in style. A senior partner of Starkweather & Company—Howard Harrison Starkweather himself—a friend of the Ball family, was delighted to let Rawly have the use of the Starkweather private railroad car, *The Sea Witch*, for his honeymoon. It was a magnificent palace on wheels and even had a marble bathtub, which was not to be used while the train was in motion as it splashed itself away. The cook and a waiter-steward went along with the car, as did the private wine cellar.

The first night of their honeymoon on wheels, attached to the Pennsy's crack train *The General* and heading west past the smoking mills of Pittsburgh and down along the Monongahela River, Rawly decided Wilma was the perfect wife. He was not surprised to find her a virgin, but an ardent novice. They drank champagne before the deflowering, and again after the event. They made love when *The Sea Witch* was switched to the Central Mississippi, conceiving their first child on the Northwestern Oregon.

For three months they toured in the private car, seeing the nation or those parts of it a train could reach, and Rawly talked business with certain men.

Wilma became aware that Rawly lived in a world of men who took delight in owning private railroad cars, and often in New Orleans or Arkansas Hot Springs, three or four private cars were settled side by side in some private siding, music and partying going on. The age of the motorcar was still to come. The luxury private cars—three hundred of them—were on the right of way, carrying as Rawly expressed it, "high livers and heirs and prodigal sons, Presbyterian dowagers from Newport to Churchill Downs, to the Carolina hunting fields, and from Saratoga's waters to—ah!—the Eastern Shore's turtle soups." To Wilma it seemed sinful—private railroad cars used as showcases of material and social success on wheels, moving inherited wealth and divorcées, playgirls and actors, steelmakers, meatpackers, and newspaper publishers about in grand style.

Rawly told her, "Too much Boston in you still. The private railroad car is a kind of super-caboose. Oh, to carry the president and his cronies. E.K. never wanted one—others did—to haul about the big stockholders to inspect the line, and to shoot at some gamebirds, to drink, play draw poker. Dream up schemes too, and skim off millions in Wall Street in some raid. The old George Pullman company built most of the first private cars—painted them a discreet goose-turd green, but fitted them royally. Look: rosewood, teak, and mahogany, and mother-of-pearl trimmings."

"It's still too, *too*—wasteful, Rawly."

Most of the private cars were built by the American Car and Foundry, the Wagner Palace Car Building Company, and Harlan & Hollingsworth. All of them working at making the private cars heavier, more ornate. A year before, Rawly had ordered a car—still in work—from Harlan & Hollingsworth for the Ball and Kingston Company.

Rolling across the plains of the Texas Panhandle as they ate breakfast at fifty miles an hour and watched the umber dust beat across the seared landscape, Wilma said, "I want to meet your father."

"Do you?" Rawly peered out at a small herd of bony steers by a dried-out waterhole. "You know, dear, General Sherman said if he owned Hell and Texas, he'd rent out Texas and live in Hell."

"You afraid E.K. will not like me?"

The newlywed couple spent four days at Kingston House. Enoch seemed cheerful enough. He was cordial to Wilma ("a hefty chunk of girl"). They did not inform him he would be a grandfather. Father and son remained cordial to each other, but it appeared to Wilma as a kind of walking-around-each-other truce. Riding with his father on frisky horses up a trail to shoot sand hens, Rawly suddenly asked, "You don't think I'm trying to rival you, do you?"

"Never gave it a goddamn thought, Rawly. Beat you and young Ball in any raid you plan, if any, on my stamping grounds."

The honeymoon continued. At San Francisco they joined the around-the-world cruise ship, the P & O's *Golden Dawn*. Wilma began to have morning sickness in Japan, while Rawly was interviewing the bowing, hissing little men who looked over his blueprints of smelters and said, *"Ah so,"* They'd been building battleships, a whole fleet, and could perhaps give Ralston & Leopold's *Ball & Kingston* so honorable company an order. *"Sonno joi."*

Yes, the American firm could have the rights to erect a plant in Japan for the Zaibatsu. Rawly was invited to the Yoshiwara, where he refused the offer of a grand courtesan, but drank *sake*, ate *nasu no miso-yaki*, and next morning left for Shanghai to comfort Wilma, who said the city smelled so. The Sassoons entertained them, explained the blighted condition of Chinese railroads, and gave Rawly letters to Sassoon relatives in the jute transport trade in India. By the time the Rawly Kingstons were in Europe, Wilma was feeling better and had a neat little melon under her Worth gowns. The Rothschilds and de Herschs gave them some small dinners, and in Berlin Rawly was shown a map of what would some day be the Berlin-Baghdad Railroad.

It was in St. Petersburg that the parties and entertainments became hectic. After a palace ball, taking off her emerald necklace and Leepole's gift of a diamond tiara, the tall handsome blonde Mrs. Kingston turned from the pier glass of the Pushkin Hotel suite and said, "I want to go home, Rawly."

Rawly stood out on the balcony overlooking the Nevsky Prospekt, smoking a cigar, seeing the mist come up around the islands that made up the city, and hearing the curses of a droshky driver lamenting his horse and his fate (or so Rawly thought). He turned and said, "Of course. All this attention here is just because the Kingston name means railroads. And Russians are savages who want to learn to use iron."

"I wouldn't want to have our baby born in this place. There is ice all along the Neva."

"You're right. We've been seeing a lot—too much to digest."

Rawly was thinking of their stopover in Rome and their visit to his mother at the Convent of the Blue Nuns. No American, he felt, should become *too* European. Certainly not like Maude. At the convent they had been shown into a pleasant enough room, small, but whitewashed a pale ivory. It contained a comfortable bed, a huge brass crucifix, and little other furnishing. Briggy, looking very old, had whispered to Rawly, "She's not having one of them bad days, but she may not know you."

Maude did. She was seated in a deep chair with a pale olive-colored traveling rug across her knees. She looked too thin, her hair gray and cropped short, almost like a boy. There was still a hint of beauty in the bone structure of the face, Rawly thought, but the skin was parchment, the hands thin and long. One hand held a rosary, and on the black too-loose gown hung a silver crucifix with a rather overrealistic tortured Christ, His face twisted in true physical agony. There was the smell of damp walls, of a sick woman, and spread horse dung from the garden beyond the windows.

Rawly introduced Wilma, whom Maude mistook for her daughter Mollie.

She said to her son. "Rawly, there is a dreadful time coming. But as a good young man—*defiendame Dios de mi*—you are in a state of grace, I'm sure."

"I try to be as good as I can, Mother."

"Your father is a sinner, a mocker." Maude suddenly laughed. "Remember the time he bought you that Indian paint pony and you fell off and he was going to show you how to dominate it, and it bit him." She made the sign of the cross. "May you both be protected; may the mercy of God be upon all you love. You're not Mollie, are you?"

"No, I'm Rawly's wife, Wilma. We are just married a few months."

"Married? In the Holy Mother Church?"

"All properly married," said Rawly, "We're going to take you out for a carriage ride tomorrow, Mother."

Maude smiled—her teeth appeared in splendid condition—and took a glass of milk Briggy brought in. "I have always loved family life. Don Alvarez, your grandfather, was a good family man. I had many brothers. And Enoch, how we enjoyed ourselves. We sinned, but it was not meant as evil—*sato olvidado*. Our bodies ruled us, and I went to confession every month. Yes, I have had a wonderful life. Yes."

She sipped the milk, some dribbling down her chin, and smiled. Wilma was observing the wrinkled stockings on Maude's thin legs. "Is there anything we can do for you? Do you need anything?"

Briggy wiped Maude's mouth. "Herself has God, and her appetite is improving. She hasn't missed a morning mass this whole month."

"What?" Maude asked. "Who missed mass?"

Rawly leaned over and kissed his mother's cheek. "Would you like to go out? I can rent a carriage."

"The Borghese Gardens. That would be fine, wouldn't it, to see the pines?"

But it rained hard, a cold, bone-chilling Roman rain—rained for the next three days. When Rawly went to say good-bye, Maude knew him, but Briggy explained it was Maude's day of fasting and silence. Briggy said, "Don't you fret now, Mr. Rawly, after two or three days' fasting, she eats like a horse."

Now in St. Petersburg, thinking of his mother in her self-imposed exile, he said, "Our child is going to be born in the West, in a dandy house Leepole is getting ready for us. It was to be a surprise."

Wilma sank her head on his shoulder and sighed. "Europe's all very fine, dear, but I'm just a big American girl who doesn't want any more caviar or French *coquilles St. Jacques.*"

"We'll take the Warsaw express in two days. I've got to see Baron Gunzberg. He's putting together a railroad idea that can some day be the Trans-Siberian. Nothing as solid and safe as Russian investments. They need everything modern. Leepole and myself, we may put up a lot of the capital—a good chunk, anyway." (Thirty-five years later, Rawly's holdings in Russian Imperial Bonds were selling for three cents per thousand dollars face value.)

The journey home was pleasant and personal. No business meetings, no talks of steel, smelters, processes, rolling stock. Just luxury transportation to Hamburg, the boarding of the *Kronprinzess Victoria.* Wilma and the unborn child were rather grateful for a calm sea all the way to New York.

There in the Hoboken rail yards was a brand-new private car owned by the firm of Ball & Kingston, the *Morning Star.* It moved west on the more steady roadbeds, took them to Boulder, then by a private spur line up to High Hills where stood the magnificent new house, rather too much in the French chateau style ("Thank God, no slits in the towers for archers." From Willie.) It was modern enough to contain the best Victorian fretwork, gargoyle chimneys, and Prince Albert decor. Here in November of 1890, Benjamin De Groat Kingston was born at two in the morning, Wilma having an easy birth. ("That's a man's version," she said.)

Benjamin weighed nine and a half pounds and proved a greedy feeder at Wilma's splendid breasts. He was a howler and fast gainer of weight, which delighted Fraulein Erica Holtzman. She was scientific, fully and rigorously trained, and a humorless German. As a nurse she took Benjamin over as her own and he thrived and always smelled pleasantly. As she wrote home:

Lieber Mutter,

The Crown Prince himself does not get better care. I have full charge, and the Father and Mother resent my domain. He is a *lustig* young Siegfried and has the Aryan blue eyes and the blond hair of his Mutter. The dark strains of the father, Herr Kingston, are said to be of Spanish origin, coming from his mother who died last month in holy grace, *Gottes will,* in Rome. She had been ailing for some time, and the end was expected. The *Amerikaner* do not go into full respectful mourning here in the West. But *Mein Herr* Kingston wears a black mourning band on one arm, and *Grafin* Kingston has put away the most colorful of her costumes. While the native *Junkers* here lack our disciplines, our own feeling of duty, they do manage to get much done. Their manners leave much to be desired. I miss the *Kaffeeklatsch,*

Auf Wiedersehn,
Erica.

The last years and the death of Maude appeared to Enoch to be a kind of fantasy that had never taken on full reality. He had for years insisted on the idea that she was not seriously ill, that it was a mental condition—depressions that overcame her from time to time because of some pious overloading of her mind. He knew, in time, as her European journeys from spa to spa, from Swiss sanitariums to Catholic retreats were prolonged, that she would never return to America. He wrote a dutiful letter once a month, and Maude (or Briggy or some nun or priest) wrote back from time to time. Maude would perhaps once a year fill a dozen sheets of notepaper with her letters written from some grand hotel or sanitarium. Pouring out an incoherent attack on godless America, the need for Jesus to return and punish the evil, the sins of Protestants, and copulation for pleasure. There were lamentations for the lost divine rights of kings, and an answer to everything to be found in the secrets of the Great Pyramids of Egypt. In time, Enoch stopped reading the letters.

Maude had died suddenly in her sleep in the Convent of the Blue Nuns. She died without leaving a will, which caused great confusion and certain legal problems. She had in her name large holdings, not only in W. & G.P. stock and bonds, but also in the railroad construction and supply companies, in ranch lands and coal mines. The Church presented an unposted draft of a letter by her (gotten from Briggy) in which she had promised two-thirds of her estate to the glory of God's Church and the Vicar of Rome. But the letter, as Charles White pointed out, seemed to have been a very rough first draft and was not signed.

Charles White, and the firm of Calvalcanti, del Testa and Morandi, successfully fought off the Holy See's claims. In the end, Maude's holdings and estate were divided in equal shares among her widower Enoch Kingston, her two sons Ralston and William, and her daughter Mrs. Homer Emerson.

Enoch was deeply touched for the first time, at her death, when he got the final legal papers. He got down from the attic at Kingston House an early portrait of Maude Alvarez, painted by an English sailor who had jumped ship in Monterey and gone to work on the Alvarez Rancho as a cabinetmaker. It was a rather good portrait of Maude, painted just before Enoch met her. He sat down at his desk and looked at the young girl so vital, so full of youth's bloom; he restrained tears with difficulty. Her strength and joy appeared to almost escape from under the varnish on the picture. He marveled—not with pleasure—at what time did to beautiful women. He wondered at the biological change. Enoch could not put any special blame on God, for he had read Herbert Spencer, Charles Darwin, Thomas Huxley, and the other great skeptics in his youth (perhaps—he thought—now old-fashioned ideas of the world, but he'd stayed with what he had read in books borrowed from Hannah Winters.) He felt Nature was not fair to so misuse, warp, and finally destroy Maude—she who was once so alive, so passionate, so much part of his best years. Damn unfair! What if he ran a railroad the way Nature did—so wasteful of its products?

30

The solid, no-nonsense house on upper Fifth Avenue was daily pointed out to rubbernecks—the word *tourist* was not yet popular in the East—as the den of that expensive lion, J. Pierpont Morgan, "the money master of the nation." Costly looking enough, the structure was certainly expensively produced, but not in the showy ornateness of the city palaces of the steel masters, Frick and Carnegie, the various residences of Vanderbilts, Astors, and Goulds. It had the aspect of a Renaissance fortress, for J. P. Morgan was not just a solemn gadabout; he relished club fellows, his yacht, and he ignored the aura of mystery, power, and sin that the popular journalism and gossip had erected about him. His ability to make and keep huge sums of money in a material society made him a celebrity.

Drexel & Morgan, the original firm, had become J. P. Morgan & Company, on Wall Street, and as a private bank it organized the financing of industries, set up corporations, taking over bond and stock issues, selling them at home and abroad to investors. Rawly Kingston was among those who said Morgan was by inclination "a goddamn Englishman, enjoying that country's setting and patronage, selling a great many bonds to old British families." He was an unforgettable sight, as Willie Kingston once saw him, huge, with the great red-knobbed nose, solid in banker's broadcloth, topped by a square bowler hat and that day swinging his cane at some aggressive photographers and their cameras daring to try to take pictures of the great man while he was out strolling. "He never just walked, he strolled," said Willie, "a Viking God whom you could believe had fed on human flesh."

The cartoonists did, and the radicals wrote that he

drank blood. ("He preferred the best whisky," said Enoch.) The coming age of the muckrakers would malign him.

His love of great, sweeping victories, the combining of corporations, naturally touched the untidy conditions of the railroads. The crisis in the Western & Great Plains Railroad management was just one isolated incident in the vast web of growing transportation troubles in the early 1890s.

It was clear to J. P. Morgan in his Fifth Avenue mansion this spring morning that a crisis existed and there was need for a railroad trust. He was a large man with a humiliating, spoiled nose—a diseased feature that made him look like his caricatures. He sat surrounded by paintings by William Blake, overcarved bookcases he no longer saw, cases that held rare editions of books he had not read. It was as if he had run beyond the boundaries of his acquisitive habits and had no brakes. Morgan was getting old; he had saved the nation from panic and depressions in the past, his private banking firm controlled the bloodstream of industry, money and credits. Active in combining smaller companies into huge profitable trusts in steel and copper, he was now planning to solve the problems of over thirty-five railroads floundering in debt, some already bankrupt, others going listlessly to ruin with outmoded locomotives, faulty, neglected tracks, roads, involved in damage suits, embezzlements, in many cases, major crimes—out-and-out stealing, dishonest bookkeeping.

Morgan had been a great womanizer; there was still a mistress in Paris, Enoch had heard. Morgan was also a religious man, a powerful force in his church to which he fed money, like tidbits from the dinner table to a family pet. If he had the morality of a shark, as some claimed, he also had an honesty of purpose which impressed both Enoch and Willie; to keep the nation's industries on an even keel, to see that efficiency and skill were kept on a decent level, that stocks and bonds paid their stockholders and investors a fair and safe return, he earning his fee (off the top) for his efforts.

He let no man judge his moral values, and he wondered at times why he collected early Christian texts, the ink-stained original pages of Dickens's manuscripts, rare books, art in various forms. He had an eye for beauty in a woman, in the hull of a yacht. Perhaps, he mused this morning—he was expecting Enoch Kingston—it was because he worked hard and most people were such fools that he liked to indulge himself in inanimate objects, picking here and there among the historic trash the dealers brought him as something unique; one of a kind connected to a valued event. He despised dealers as born thieves, liars, and often fakers of the objects offered. Morgan had an eye for the authentic, but still had hired an Englishman, an art critic, a writer, an expert on the genuineness of things, who passed on items for him. It was clear the fellow despised Morgan, his wealth, his power, his ability to buy whatever he wanted. But the fellow was also greedy for money, his pay. Morgan chuckled. He'd not discharge the fop, but kept him on to see him suffer.

The butler came in and said, "Mr. Kingston is here, sir." Morgan nodded. Enoch came in and the banker rose from his chair and extended his hand. He had a firm grip, but applied no pressure.

"I knew you were in the city, Kingston; felt we should chat."

"Always good to see you and talk, Mr. Morgan." Enoch had to admit the old bastard was the only man who ever awed him.

"I hear you've become a grandfather."

"You get good reports." Enoch smiled. He understood this old man, still powerful, with that spoiled face, the heaviness of him. The hand grasping one arm of the chair, almost a fist, a dangerous weapon; the shine of the arm of the chair highlighted in the shaded room to look like a broad-bladed dagger in the powerful hand. The butler came in, set down a tray with glasses, a bottle of whisky.

As Morgan poured two glasses, there was some talk of the weather, (it had been raining) and the stock market (sluggish).

Morgan leaned forward. "You happy with the railroad situation? I mean the whole national scene?"

"It's never been worse." The aged blended whisky had a mellow flame to it; the room was as impressive as the old man.

"We can both swear to that. Nearly three dozen rail-lines in financial difficulties, the target of stock speculators. Most of the common stock is in the hands of a few families, eh? Too ripe, rotting on the vine. Now there are people who want me to do for the railroads what I did for steel, for copper, huh? What do you think, Kingston?"

"Would it work? Can it really keep the roads going?"

"I could do it. But for the Western and Southern lines, I need a strong railroad man who knows all the tricks and games of railroad boards of directors. Are you that man, Kingston?"

Enoch laughed. "I'm available, but who knows if I fit your plans? I still don't fully understand what you think can be done!"

"Don't play country boy with me, the barefooted farm hand. You know what I plan."

"I can guess, Mr. Morgan. May I smoke?" He took out a cigar case, offered one to Morgan who shook his head. "Tell me more."

"Most of the common stocks, Kingston, of about thirty-five lines are in the hands of blockheads, a few men in some places. I will demand the delivery of their stocks into our hands while the reorganization is going on, to make sure the men would not speculate on the shares while the new organization of the lines is being set up."

"One big new good line out of many poor ones?"

"Tell me how you see it."

"Richmond, New Orleans, St. Louis are good profitable junction points, Mr. Morgan, that have been mismanaged. Here are lines, regions that should show great profits, but the heads of the roads have speculated and drifted into bankruptcy, or close to it. Most of the roads are in receivership and have come to you for help."

Morgan grinned. "Your information service is also damn good."

"I've sent out *my* own experts to estimate what the minimal earning capacity of some railroads could be if combined. In thirty companies, securities of two hundred fifty million dollars had been issued. Now if they were turned over to you—I say *you*, not *us*—so no one could speculate while the reorganization was going on, I'd say yes, you had a chance of saving the roads."

"They'll scream. I'll insist the fixed debt be reduced by

devaluating securities, reducing fixed charges, forcing stockholders to accept common stock. Preferred stock and bondholders will have to take lower interest on over one hundred thirty-five million dollars in floating and bonded debt. This I can cut down to maybe ninety-four million."

Enoch nodded in admiration. "Bold, very bold."

"The result would be the companies' earnings meeting the cost of operating the lines and paying the interest on their debts."

"Right as rain. Will they agree?"

"They'll have to. Even accept assessments against their stock—refill your glass—so as to provide capital to work the lines. Of course they could sell their stocks—to Morgan and Company handling the reorganization. Well?"

The two men drank, staring at each other.

"As the saying is in the West, Mr. Morgan, you have them by the short hair—their balls are in your hands. You have a strong hand and can squeeze. Knowing you, you have a damn good reason to be explaining all this to me."

Morgan stood up and went to a bookcase, running a finger over a row of leatherbound books. "You're going out for us—for me—to sweet talk a lot of the Southwest, Southern and Southeast coast railroad people to agree to the whole shooting match."

"Whoa there, Mr. Morgan. I don't mind picking up hot chestnuts for you; you've proved a hell of a friend to me before this. But where does this leave the W. and G.P.?"

"Your line is a relic of the past, a grand one, but a relic. You proved that by the ease with which you gobbled it up."

Enoch said nothing. The wily old wolf was grinning. "Kingston, I propose to form a new longer, larger railroad for you. Say the Western, Great Plains and Gulf. Give you lines all along the whole Gulf, some in Florida, the Eastern Seaboard, the Eastern Shore. Right into Washington, D.C. You'd like that?"

"Damn right. Western Great Plains and Gulf? You're giving me all that *if* I go out and get it. You'd hold not only their shares and bonds, but also mine? I'd be working for you."

Morgan came away from the bookcase and slapped Enoch on the back. "You understand perfectly."

They eyed each other, neither angry or disrespectful of the other. Enoch held out his hand.

"I'll take it."

"I knew you would."

"If I'm going to get my ass kicked and my clothes ripped off, I'd just as well it was done by you."

"You'll come out of it smelling of millions, Kingston."

"I have millions—mostly in debts, of course. Do you like trains?"

"I have a private railroad car; if the roadbed is good, the chef passable, I don't ask much beyond that."

"There's something goddamn beautiful about a good, well-run train. The engines on full steam, the signals on the right-of-way blinking green, the sound of the whistle and knowing the road is on time. . . . It's like nothing else, Nearly nothing else, Mr. Morgan."

"Yes, well, I suppose it's like holding a rare book—the very first book ever printed from movable type."

"I was thinking of women," said Enoch blandly.

The butler was back. His voice seemed to come from a pocket in his clothes. "Lunch is served, sir."

It consisted of pale broth, a salmon in aspic, a white wine, rusks, strong coffee, and a rare brandy. They parted with a quick, strong handshake.

Enoch had been in New York for a week as a guest of Diamond Jim Brady, the greatest railroad supply agent the nation had ever had—a fact Brady admitted himself. Brady's firm had a new hardened steel undercarriage it wanted to sell to the W. & G.P. Brady had invited Enoch to Saratoga for a few days at the Grand Union Hotel, "for the horse races and the entertainment," which with Brady could consist of tips on the horses, gifts of cases of whisky, champagne, tins of caviar, and the keys to the bungalows of certain ladies. Hardly the right term, ladies, but bright and pretty, brought up from New York.

The summons from Morgan had come while Chico, who now traveled with Enoch, packed for the trip to Saratoga at their Waldorf-Astoria suite. Brady's special train, with other guests, would be leaving at five o'clock.

As he left the Morgan mansion, Enoch thought over the conversation with the banker, felt the parting drink of good brandy. He looked over the avenue spread before him. New York did not awe Enoch. It had to exist, he always said, and you could get used to it "if you had to." It was acceptable on a sunny day, but now the weather threatened to dampen the city again. Still swinging his cane, he walked briskly—he liked the find carriages, enjoyed seeing the well-dressed women, the men in their top hats, and even the clatter of wheels was exhilarating—not all the hacks and carriages had rubber-shod tires.

He smiled. The old pirate Morgan hadn't turned a hair about their mutual interest in women. He hoped Morgan's satisfaction in the pretty creatures was stronger than his own. It wasn't that there weren't attractive complaisant women in Enoch's life, it was just they seemed not to matter, but for those few moments of getting your ashes hauled. Maude was dead, Hannah Winters was a fat old lady living mostly in Baden-Baden in Germany with Solly, who had developed a bad heart and rheumatic stiffening joints and needed the hot spring baths and the sipping of stinking waters. . . . As for Brook de Leon, that had been a complete and final break. He never heard from her. (The newspapers of the period did not report Negro educational or social news with any detail, if at all . . .) My only golden tropical girl of the early adolescent dreams, dusky memories.

He would never fall in love, be in love again. Besides, if he was to put the Morgan reorganization ideas into force in the Southwest, on the Gulf and Southeast coast, he'd have plenty to do and not mourn old bedrooms. He would never—sure as shooting—fall in love again.

It was at Saratoga that he met the woman who was to become his second wife.

31

Lucy Wallingford was the widow of George Harmon Wallingford, an associate of Charles T. Yerkes, P. A. Weidner, William Elkins—men who had created gas lines, brought water into city mains, set up trolley lines to connect the suburbs of new, growing cities. There were those who said they were all thieves and corrupters of municipal and state governments by bribes and by buying politicians. Others called them empire builders, making life possible in the metropolitan centers of the nation; certainly George Harmon Wallingford was mentioned in all histories of the expansion and exploitation of many cities.

At thirty-eight, Lucy Wallingford was still a striking woman, shapely in the style of the times, often to be mistaken for Lillian Russell, but more tasteful in her dress, more mannerly in a social climate not at all theatrical at her estate *Green Brook, Saratoga Springs* (as her stationery read) not merely Saratoga as the vulgar mistakenly called it.

Her hair was a striking shade of brownish-red, not dyed. She used only the slightest touches of cosmetics, having been in her youth, it was whispered, a minor opera star when George Wallingford married her in London. Actually she had been an assistant voice teacher and coach, and not English at all—an American, born a Barraclough of Hawleytown, Maryland, on the Eastern Shore. And while she kept up the Saratoga Springs estate of her late husband—dead six years—with its grooms and gardeners, housemaids and other servants, the Wallingford great fortune was really a myth. It had been dissipated in a tobacco-importing project, and finally on the commodities exchange in Chicago, in Wallingford's last effort to corner the wheat market by buying up grain futures. He had died muttering, "Autumn hard ... sell. ...." Still, there was enough left for Mrs. Wallingford in stocks and bonds to keep her afloat *if* now and then she dipped into her jewel box and sold some vulgar gem in its atrocious setting. George Wallingford had no taste in jewelers' shops in London or Paris.

It was Hamilton Ormsbee, her lawyer—a rather shaky but respectable old man—who brought Enoch Kingston to Green Brook for dinner. A well-served, discreet meal on the candle-lit terrace, for eight guests: Dungeness crab vinaigrette with watercress, bluepoint oysters, soupe de légumes, Guayamas shrimp, a New York State sauterne, scooped-out cantaloupe with strawberry ice. Enoch, who usually liked simple, overspiced dishes, was impressed by the flavor of everything.

After dinner and a stroll in the gardens where they sighted a doe and her fawn among the dogwood blossoms, Mrs. Wallingford turned to Enoch. "Hamilton says you would like to have some private talk with me."

"Not if it's not polite socially. I'm a roughneck from the West and don't know all the rules." It was a taciturn game he played in the East, even here among the crackling voices of the cicadas in the night.

She gave him what he thought was a cool smile. "Come into the library."

It was not a command, and it was not casual. Enoch followed her fine, erect back and wondered just what she thought of him. He was no roughneck and he knew it, but, as with Morgan, he was prone to play the rather simple role.

The library was satin-lined, a rather pale rose, and the books were bound mostly in blue leather. The chairs were delicate and gilt: in petit point, shepherds hugging farm girls. Enoch sat down carefully.

"You may smoke," Lucy said, as she saw Enoch tap himself for his cigar case.

"No, I don't think so. Mrs. Wallingford, I never met your husband."

She nodded. "But you appear to have known of him. He was a very remarkable man. Lots of people didn't approve of him. There were times I didn't. But life with him was interesting—very few sublimated moments.

"I understand from Mr. Ormsbee he had certain holdings in railroad stocks, among them bonds in one I control—actually one I built up: the Western and Great Plains."

"Excellent food on the fine train to New Orleans."

"I try to keep up a standard. Mrs. Wallingford, I wonder if you still have those bonds?"

"Not much left I'm afraid. George tried to corner the Chicago wheat market, you know, one winter, and when he thought he had it all, some smart person dynamited the ice on the Great Lakes and brought barge loads of Canadian wheat through to dump in on the market. George had to cover millions in short sales. He couldn't—we went to live in France."

"He was smart enough to hold back something."

"Will you pour us both a little sherry, Mr. Kingston?" She indicated a cut-glass decanter and some small V-shaped glasses.

As he held a filled glass out to her well-cared-for hand, she opened her mouth and gave a surprisingly loud laugh. "The truth is, George was a man who when he sank touched bottom. I can't keep up this house, afford the carriages in the stables. The house and grounds are mortgaged to the hilt. If you want candor, Mr. Kingston, *there* it is."

He shook his head, relaxed for the moment. "It's healthy to know you're not fooling yourself . . ."

"For a woman alone it's—" her eyebrows went up as her gaze searched his face. "I suppose you wonder *why* I'm saying all this to you?"

"I give people confidence." He *almost* leaned over and patted her knee. "You're a wonder, Mrs. Wallingford, to give a dandy dinner like tonight and carry if off in style. I like style."

"I want to raise all I can on what is left, sell this place, and go live in Europe. Hamilton Ormsbee is a good village lawyer, but he's old; thought you might help if I had bonds. But he's not worldly."

"I'm not worldly either, just get about here and there a great deal. One thing don't do—don't settle in Europe;

don't shake off your grass roots. I can tell you what it does to people traipsing round from place to place, living out of steamer trunks, floating on their money. . . ."

She seemed to take a new, a different interest in him. "You sound like Henry James. You'll have to convince me there is any reasonable future for me on these shores. Another sherry?"

"I'd rather have whisky."

She rose to go to get a whisky decanter from a small cabinet.

Jesus, Enoch thought, she reminds me of that painting in Florence. First trip to Europe being taken to see that picture of Venus rising from the sea. Damn exciting, a nude woman served up on the half shell. As for Mrs. W., even in her flaring gown he imagined Lucy Wallingford's body as pink, as firm; even close to forty (at least that age), she was holding up splendidly. Had grace in movement, and she stood straight—free from the too-casual slump of Westerners. He had never known such Eastern women (the ones you don't pay for); not skin to skin. Now in his middle forties, he felt a reawakening of the old Adam—the female as special, not merely a vessel. He had not been celibate this last year. But it had been routine, pleasant enough, comfort more than pleasure, bought and paid for, but no relationship with the human being under the skin, only, as Charlie had told him, "with some anatomy in sagacious quivering."

She was standing beside him, a glass of rye in one hand. "George liked scotch. It always tasted too medicinal to me—mixed with burning rags."

Enoch didn't drink the whisky at once, but watched the beads near the rim, a test of a well-aged rye. He lifted his eyes to hers. "I'd be happy to look over whatever stockholdings you have left and advise you. I have a humdinger of a lawyer, and my daughter's father-in-law is a real expert on bonds and stocks."

"You have children?"

"Three. All grown pretty much. Just me now in the big house in California. You been to California? You should visit it." (Lord, what banal chatter.) He took a sip of the drink. "Tomorrow why don't I pick you up in a carriage,

Mrs. Wallingford, and we'll go to the races, have dinner, gamble at Canfield's, and I can look over your holdings?"

She shook her head. "I don't think so, Mr. Kingston; the races, dinner, and Canfield's Club. Would cause gossip. Saratoga Springs is a gossipy town. I'd rather not be the cause of public debate with any—" she made a graceful gesture over her head with her left hand—finished the sentence, "with any man."

Enoch swallowed the drink slowly, stood up. "I'll call for you at one. There's a horse running. Bet-a-Million Gates took an oath that it's set to win the third race."

They were married two weeks later, in the parlor of J. P. Morgan's mansion on Fifth Avenues under a huge tapestry of a unicorn hunt by men in white doublets, aided by greyhounds whose tails made the letter O. Lucy looked very formal and beautiful in pale blue; a bit matronly, perhaps, Morgan's trained woman-analyzing eye decided. But then Enoch Kingston most likely needed this poised, settled type now that he was moving up to a wider field of activity. She would look fine as a hostess of a dinner table—and delectable in bed, a rich family background (the minister was reciting something), well-mannered; even that bastard George Wallingford hasn't dented her calm appraisal of the world seen by those deep blue eyes (vows were being exchanged). Yes, Kingston had picked a winner to run in double-harness with. (Lucy had lifted her veil and was offering him her cheek to kiss.)

There was no honeymoon trip; Enoch just took a bigger suite at the Waldorf Astoria. The wedding night was no novelty to them: they had been to bed together for a full week and had found it very satisfactory. Later he knew there had been a tall handsome Irish groom at stud service most of the years of her widowhood. Uncorseted, unupholstered, combed out, freed of whalebone, calf-reaching shoes, stockings, garters, slips, and petticoats, Lucy became that woman painted on the half shell for Enoch—only more animated and vocal, and with no shame at all. In day attire, trussed up, veiled, hatted, she was the very proper Mrs. Enoch Bancroft Kingston expectant of service and good manners in the better shops. Enoch was delighted with his wife's cool acceptance of her new status, her realistic view of the social scene—and he was a little awed by her but tried not to show it.

They spent the season in New York—the Diamond Horseshoe at the Met, the dance at the Morgan's Yacht Club, the private dining room at Delmonico's. Enoch worked with Morgan and his staff on the merging of over two dozen railroad systems into the one that would become the Western, Great Plains & Gulf. Then in the Morgan private railroad car, husband and wife, the two of them began to move around to the cities where Enoch preached the gospel according to Saint Morgan, who would save their hides, bring back value to their holdings, mend their roads, and see that dividends would again make their cup overflow. Enoch's message was not delicate or subtle; as he told Lucy in Charleston, "I lay it on the line."

If the officials and stockholders balked at turning over their certificates to Morgan's care, Enoch talked of doomsday for any individual who didn't enter the reorganization plan "for the benefit of all."

Lucy, traveling with her maid Olga in attendance, proved an asset in Lexington (Kentucky), in Cleveland, in Pittsburgh. She rode well in a fox hunt in one of the Carolinas. She danced at an exclusive club in Atlanta ("Yankees as rare as nigrah members, ma'am"). She was hostess at dinners Enoch gave at some gourmet inn, usually in one of her favorite blue silk gowns, her hair and wrists jeweled with taste by Enoch's and Morgan's gifts, and her favorite dog collar of pearls on her firm neck. Some thought her cold, others a damn snob; "an international thief's widow, now with a new operator." Lucy never lost her poise, and by the time they reached Kingston House Enoch regretted it was dangerous at her age to breed her.

So the Western, Great Plains & Gulf Railroad system came into existence, and it was to grow by absorbing and swallowing smaller lines even past the turn of the century.

To effect Morgan's plan, a great deal of new stock was issued, at least 30 percent more stock, Enoch learned. "This is done, Kingston, to increase the capitalization of the new road." Morgan and Enoch each took $400,000 in cash for their work on the merger, and $4,700,000 each in common stock of the newly expanded Western, Great Plains & Gulf. With such holdings, the two men controlled full voting power and set up a tight board of directors they could control with Enoch as president and chairman of the board. All this, Charles White pointed out, had to be done before the teeth of the Populists could put burdensome restrictions on business by an Interstate Commerce Act. Already the Sherman Antitrust Act was looming up.

Lucy rebuilt Kingston House, added a story, imported furniture and paintings (a splendid Gainsborough, a poor Corot). She insisted that Enoch join the best clubs in the East; in time he was a member of Links, New York Yacht Club, Century Association, Pinnacle, and the Bohemian in San Francisco.

As Enoch entered his fifties, he assured himself that he did not feel or show his age, and only his mirror did not seem to know the fact. His hair was thinner, gone on the top of his head, the moustache was colored at Lucy's insistence. His neck was somewhat wattled, his stomach a bay window, and he had to keep his shoulders from hunching over. Time had him by the ass, he had to admit, and wouldn't let go. People were dying who had never died before. It was a poor joke, but it would have to do.

32

People were still yelling "get a horse" at motor cars when Rawly Kingston was burning up the dusty roads of Colorado and California in a Delauney-Belleville with its big brass gas lamps and barrel-shaped motor hood—the sound of it like a battery of Chinese firecrackers on a San Francisco Oriental New Year. He wrecked the car in January of 1902 on a curve outside Sacramento, and himself, too, a bit. The left leg broken, two ribs cracked, and loss of some skin on the right side of his face. The motorcar in America was no longer a novelty, but as a toy for the rich it was good for headlines and news stories with no subtleties but hints the rich were sinners given to Greek and Roman vices.

'RECKLESS RAWLY' MILLIONAIRE SMELTER
PLAYBOY
SURVIVES AUTO CAR CRASH
RAWLY KINGSTON DOES IT AGAIN!

Ralston Kingston, known to his intimates as the richest thrill-seeker of Western society, yesterday at 2:20 in the afternoon ran his monstrous motorcar off a curve on the Placerville Road, completely wrecking the machine and injuring himself to the extent of a broken leg, some cracked ribs, and various cuts and bruises. Treated by Dr. Marcus Beeninstock, the 33-year-old president of the Ball-Kingston Company Enterprises was taken not to a hospital, but on his insistent demands to a suite at the Palace Hotel in San Francisco. At his side was his wife, who rushed to the hotel. She is the former Wilma De Groat, daughter of a prominent old New England family of Mayflower stock. Also present was his partner, Leopold Ball. The Kingstons have three children: Benjamin aged ten, and twin boys, Nicholas and Howard aged nine.

From his bed in the hotel's Gold Coast Suite, while champagne was being poured, Rawly Kingston told your reporter, "No reason for all the dust my little accident stirred up. H—, I was in a hurry rushing to a sale of the furnishings at auction of Nell Kimball's grand old place. I wanted particularly to buy the fancy gold-plated spittoons for my new hotel, Greenhills. I suppose now, d— it, I've lost them."

(Nell Kimball, we hasten to inform our readers, was the madam of a notorious and a la mode bordello in the Uptown Tenderloin on Larkin Street. She has now left town, and it is rumored is back running a sporting house in New Orleans' Storyville).

Rawly, in a plaster cast, bandaged and bruised, said he was not giving up driving fast motorcars, and that he had a Pierce-Arrow touring car in Oakland, and also had on order a Stevens-Duryea. Offering your reporter a glass of bubbly, he said, "I'll be driving in six weeks when Greenhills opens its doors."

Greenhills is a very lavish, very expensive hotel Ralston is building at Deer Springs, to be "the most posh and luxurious vacation hotel in America" (to quote Rawly). The hotel is a pet project of Rawly's, and it is widely written of in the press as one of those rich men's follies. One story is that Rawly built the hotel to revenge himself on the famous Antlers Hotel, that had reasonably objected to his riding his motorcar up its steps and into the bar, with Rawly armed and shooting glasses of whisky and mixed drinks from the fingers of thirsty guests. It did seem a dangerous eccentricity to men needing a drink. There are those who swear the story is true; your reporter did not get a yes or no answer to the question.

Ralston Kingston is the son of Enoch Bancroft Kingston, president and chairman of the board of the Western, Great Plains & Gulf Railroad, and the brother of William Alvarez Kingston, managing director of the Ranchers and Growers Bank of the

West, formerly the Winters National Bank of California but now a Kingston bank, investing in and controlling family holdings of farmlands, ranches, orchards, vineyards, and oil.

The relationship between father and son Ralston is said to be strained, even stormy. The Ball-Kingston Company, with its vast smelters and mine holdings is also deeply involved in a combination of several raillines, merged as the Western Continental & Blue Water, which is a rival in many sections of the rails of the family's holdings in the W. G.P. & G.

Your reporter left the cheerful invalid being tended by a nurse and his beautiful blonde wife, with the wine still flowing. Asked as to the effect of the spreading national coal strike, Rawly did not think it would cripple the Western railroads his company owns as they have their own coal mines and are unionized. "Besides, Teddy's in the White House, isn't he? He'll crack skulls before he'll let the wheels of industry stop turning, or the chimneys of American industry go smokeless."

There were several more such newspaper stories about Rawly and his motorcar accident and his new hotel at Deer Springs, his gay, wild way of life, much of it distorted and overcolored.

The press was not too interested in his industrial abilities, knowledge of Western resources, except for the money it gave him to appear flamboyant and reckless. Ralston was actually a remarkable businessman driven by a sense of the transience of events, with a vast field of interests: from telephone lines, city public transportation, major holdings in smelters, mines, and railroads. He was more daring in the business world than Enoch, and more given to prolonged talk in dealing and compromise, whereas Enoch's way had been usually direct physical action by a self-made man who trusted few besides himself. Rawly never had to seize a pass, send a train across the nation for a record run; he never tore up rival tracks and laid his own across a right of way without legal permission. Rawly felt himself fully a twentieth-century man. The hard, crude ways of a Fiske, Gould, Sol Winters,

Morgan, Canning, and others his father knew or talked about had all done their work in a different kind of nation. The Civil War veterans growing old and persnickety were a bore and a menace to the U.S. Treasury. Teddy had licked the Spaniards in Cuba; Dewey had done the same in Manila Bay. Soon the Great White Fleet would go around the world. Rawly had been a lieutenant of Volunteers in Cuba for three supremely mad, heat-rashed months, then been invalided home with malaria and dysentery. He left behind a reputation for poker playing, rum-drinking and organizing raiding parties that brought in barefoot prisoners whom he fed and gave cigars and drink to. "Salud!"

It was Colonel Teddy Roosevelt who had ordered Rawly shipped home, and there were those war correspondents—Richard Harding Davis, Stephen Crane—who felt Teddy did not like Rawly Kingston's stealing part of his thunder. "Mr. Dooley," a popular newspaper creation who commented on the news, wrote in the broken Irish brogue of his character: "Shur now thim two boyos, Teddy and Rawly sees thimselves in the limelights and find that in bein' quoted there just ain't enough press space to shine on thim iv both is heroes. I'm suggestin' whin they are a buildin' a triumph arch for the lads to pass thru to build it of bricks, that good auld Irish confetti, so the people kin have somethin' to throw at thim heroes whin their fame grows cold."

However, President Roosevelt had the Ralston Kingstons to two White House balls, and the president had talked to Rawly for ten minutes without once saying "bully" or "by Godfrey."

Rawly was up about five weeks after the auto accident, driving the Pierce-Arrow for the opening of Greenhills. The first version of Greenhills was presented at a gala with fireworks, a great deal of wine, fine food, and some scandals in the kitchen among the staff until the graft and kickbacks on supplies were brought under control by Leepole Ball, who had a nose for finding out the swindles of employees. "I have that kind of mind which I keep honed by imagining what not-so-trustworthy minds are up to." Leepole had not changed much as a hell-raiser, drinker, hedonist, or ironic observer. He was just becoming a bit shopworn as he became richer.

Wilma, who had spread out a bit, was delighted with the three months a year they spent at the hotel. The rest of the time there was the Boulder house, the flat on Fifth Avenue, the place on the Champs-Élysées, a fishing camp in Utah.

It was not until after the Great War, 1914–1918, that Rawly enlarged and rebuilt the place into the famous Greenhills that most people who remember it at all— "that's the place" a sporting generation thinks of when they think of Greenhills. The original of 1900 was reasonable in size, surrounded by lofting hills, mountain ranges; there were streams, a forest and bridle paths.

Benji, a too thin, too tall, delicate boy with blond hair, "growing too fast," was to remember it all his life as the place where his father swore marvelous oaths, hurling glasses into the fireplace after some toast to King Edward, Anna Held, or Ralph De Palma, as his father hopped around with one crutch to aid him. As for the twins, when they were bad, Nick would cry and Howard would bite people, kick at shins. *They* were not whipped, but Rawly would sometimes tell Benji he was going to get the whipping of his life, and he would bend a slender bamboo in his hand and swish the air with it, but actually never struck a really painful blow.

Benji was prone to colds, sore throats, runny ears, digestive upsets, while the twins were healthy hoodlums who could play in the rain and slide down banisters. The worst scene at Greenhills Benji could remember was the morning he was on his way to take a beef rib-bone with some meat on it to his Boston terrier, Beans, a dog he had earned by taking cod liver oil twice a day. He passed the room called the Frontier, where there was a real buffalo head on the wall, and large paintings of Indians by someone called Catlin that Dad admired. Daddy was there talking to Grandfather, and Grandfather, a big man, face very red, was pounding a table made of redwood logs. Daddy was laughing, making Grandfather shout even louder.

"Rawly, you goddamned high-collared dude, you'll ruin every railroad in the West if you permit full unionization of your roads. Engineers, all right, some of the mechanics, but the rest—"

"It's my damn line, E.K., and Leepole's, and our stock-holders, and we do as we please. I'm sorry you find us aggravating."

"Sorry! *He's* sorry! Cock of the walk, aren't we! With your fancy friends and your high-and-mighty ways. Well, I'm still the biggest railroad man in the West, thank God, and I have behind me thirty-six lines that say we fight the union demands, the new wage demands that can ruin us in this time of crisis. Thirty-six lines, you jackass!"

Daddy had stood very still in that extremely calm way he could maintain when others were angry. Benji, just outside the door, holding the greasy rib-bone against his clean sailor suit, heard his father say, "You can shove all your thirty-six rail-lines up your hairy asshole, and it's big enough for them all, I'm sure."

Benji was never sure if Grandfather actually struck Daddy. A Tiffany lamp was overturned, certainly, and the glass shade broken. Grandfather stormed out of the Frontier Room almost running Benji down, roaring and waving his arms, his white hair in disorder, his bald spot flaming red. Benji had licked his fingers—the rib-bone was very greasy—and he walked into the Frontier Room. Daddy was standing facing the fireplace, hands clasped behind his back as though his shoulders ached and he seemed to be flexing his shoulder muscles.

"Why is Grandpa angry?"

Daddy didn't turn around as he said very softly in that dead-level cutting voice of his, "Grandpa is getting old and he hasn't got good control of himself."

"Does he wet the bed?"

"I don't know. Now run along, Benji. I'm expecting some people."

Daddy didn't turn around, so Benji never did know if Grandpa had "laid one on him," as Mike the motorcar mechanic put it. As for just what was control, the eight-year-old twins still wet their beds from time to time. No control, Mother called it, but somehow Benji couldn't see Grandpa lacking that kind of body discipline.

He went out onto the east porch, which was now in

shadows made by the striped awnings and the wisteria and trumpet vines. Mama and Grandmother were having what Daddy called "a Presbyterian high tea." Lucy wasn't actually their real grandmother, Nick had said one morning when it was raining hard and they were playing Three Days at Gettysburg with their lead soldiers. Nick was very nosy and liked to pry. He said Olga, Grandmother's maid had told Zelsmith, the *maître d'* at Greenhills, that Grandma was Grandpa's second wife, and not the mother of Daddy.

Oh well, Grandma smelled very nice for a lady, and she brought Benji windup tin toys that danced and balanced balls.

Mama looked up from the Spode tea things. "Where are you going with that bloody bone. *Look* at your new white sailor suit!"

"I'm feeding it to Beans, He's my dog," he said to Grandma, "a Boston bull."

"Don't sit in the sun without a hat. You get headaches," said Mother.

"Boys and dogs," Lucy said as Benji went down into the grounds before he could hear Mother explain he was delicate—growing too fast.

"Even grown men take to dogs," said Lucy. Enoch raises hounds you know."

Wilma nodded. "I was almost chewed up one time at Kingston House. That was on our honeymoon. They don't get on at all, Rawly and E.K."

Lucy lifted her teacup. "Rawly and his father? It's natural, isn't it? They're both overendowed with spacious tendencies to survey and rule."

Wilma shrugged her shoulders. "You mean they're both bastards in business, and one can't get the other to kowtow or kowtow back."

"Kowtow, my dear?"

"A Chinese word of Uncle Charlie's. Says it means to bow down or take a secondary position of respect to what one is facing."

"All over coal? Or is it unions this time?" Lucy, like Wilma, had broadened out just a bit more, but her skin still glowed; her hair was now a color more splendid than it had originally been, and frankly, Wilma saw there was rouge on Lucy's cheeks and on her lips. Yes, Wilma decided, a bit of crimson lard laid on skillfully. You had to give Lucy credit for retaining a majestic spaciousness, a sort of well-coiffured odalisque look (Wilma had been reading the *Rubaiyat*).

"I think it's not that at all, Lucy. I think Willie is E.K.'s favorite and he shows it. Making him head of those banks he took over when Mr. Winters died, putting Willie on the board of directors of the W. G.P. and G."

"Now, now Wilma," said Lucy briskly. "Let's not you and I get caught up in any of *that*, the agonies and dislocations of family feuds. Truth is, Rawly," she leaned over, her magnificent bosom touching the table top, "Rawly is so much richer than Enoch it galls him. Mines, smelters, and that railroad he and Leopold play around with. Well, Enoch doesn't see Rawly as a son at all at times, but as a rival."

"As a rival! Oh, Lucy, they're not boys playing games anymore."

"It's been my experience the more successful the man as a *flâneur* in business, the greater his intellect and instinct for his special field, the *more* he *is* a child—often a cantankerous child in everything else. That's why rich men collect art, it's as close as they can get to trading frogs and marbles as boys. Come, show me your fountains."

Wilma decided Lucy, the old guileful charmer, wasn't so far wrong.

Out on the lawn by the public drive Beans was barking and tossing his rib-bone around, and Benji was reading the funny papers. Uncle Charlie sent him a big wad of them every week. Benji's favorites were "Little Nemo" and "Buster Brown and Tige."

33

Kingston House had entered the twentieth century with a third story insisted on by Lucy, a new heating system, a croquet lawn, and an added wing shaded by acanthus trees which served as a ballroom. For the second Mrs. Kingston now entertained; the Prince of Wales before he became Edward VII, roly-poly, with his spade-shaped beard and a plump mistress among his party—she who dropped some crushed ice down his royal back once, to shock Ruxton and the staff; William Randolph Hearst, who invited the Kingstons to a hill up the coast where he was raising a strange collection of styles into a bizarre castle; President Roosevelt on his way to make a speech in Los Angeles, a bit too heavy for the horse he rode around the mesa with Enoch, and spoke of his ranching days and the time he captured a cattle rustler and was undecided; "to hang him *or* save him from a posse."

Enoch seemed to remember these events, and some guests rather vaguely; invited mop-haired violin players, piano pounders, prissy Englishmen who lectured in various places but who proved themselves remarkable drinkers of Kingston whisky for all that, even if one or two *did* molest some of the stable hands.

Lucy was a remarkable hostess, he told Charlie. A good wife, and if she insisted on their being active in what passed for society in California, "What the hell—I want her happy and laughing." But Enoch, as he struggled with a boiled shirt, a collar stud, for some high society shindig, would often recite:

> The miners came in '49
> Married the Barbary Coast whores
> And sired the Native Sons.

The truth is that Enoch rather enjoyed showing Lucy off. They were seen at the opéra in San Francisco, at the exclusive dances in Santa Barbara, were present at the Huntington dinners in San Marino, at the California Historical Society (*Mrs. Enoch Kingston: chairlady*), when some old adobe pile was favored as part of the state's heritage, and a bronze plaque was affixed.

All this social assumption gave Enoch an excuse that having done his duty to his wife's ideas of status, he could go on a two-week tour of the rail-lines, ride in the caboose of freights—he needing a bath—or sit at ease in the club car of the *Golden Eagle*. To smoke, drink, gamble, visit sporting-houses along the right of ways. Nell Kimball in her fancy place in New Orleans, after her moving back there from San Francisco, kept for many years a Laredo black hat Enoch left in her bordello in 1900, after a wild night's spree with some members of the board. That was when the W. G.P. & G. opened its biggest railroad junction and workshops just north of the city. The hat proudly hung on Nell's hall-tree with a bowler left at the house by John Barrymore's father and a cap John L. Sullivan threw up on a chandelier—or so Nell claimed for these relics of male vitality. ("Every girl is sitting on her fortune, if she only knew it.")

For all the vitality Enoch showed in his early fifties, he wanted no problems, no crises; he hoped to avoid a crippling railroad strike. He had survived two major strikes to unionize every railroad worker from barrow pusher to bridge builder. He liked his men; he understood them. It was not that he was against unionization of specialists. It was the lack of personal control, loss of company rights, raw power he feared if the entire rail system could be called out on strike as one unit. He was ruled by the rigid laws of necessity and consequence.

He disliked waste and disorder. There had been broken heads at Kingston Junction in the past—armed strikers burning a freight yard, and Pinkerton men came to guard Kingston House (that was when certain windows were broken at the house) and ride shotgun on the fast luxury trains. For he had kept the best runs open and nearly on schedule. He disliked using the Pinkertons, perhaps because he remembered stories from his youth of their tossing a bomb into the house of Jesse James' mother and blowing off her arm.

As the coal strike spread across the country, he was returning from an inspection trip, a loser of six hundred dollars in an all-night poker game in Dallas. He was aware that the strike was a huge, growing menace to his raillines, for his trains, like all others, ran on coal. The days of "Old Sal," the wood-burners, was long over. Unlike Rawly and Leepole Ball, he had no coal mines of his own. His coal came mostly from Southern mines, and he hoped they would continue to produce the shiny hard coal chunks, and not listen to "the Yankee socialist bastards undermining the freedom of the worker to be his own boss within the limits of loyalties to the railroad!" The mine owners were blue-balled bastards, Enoch admitted, no doubt of that. His Eastern and Southeast lines were already short of coal from the Pennsylvania, Ohio, and Illinois mines. The mine owners were greedy, indifferent to trouble on the rails, and had combined into the Penn & Reading Coal & Iron Company, under the wing of an operator owner, George F. Baer, who was lifting the price for anthracite sky-high, all the traffic could bear.

On the way home, Enoch had stopped off in San Diego where Willie was managing and running things for the banks. The final name of the bank on those eleven branches at the time, from San Francisco down the coast pleased Enoch—The Ranchers and Growers Bank of the West. Poor Solly was dead; his widow, a fat deaf old lady, was living someplace in Austria. As for the Winters children, washouts—not worth their salt. The son a professor with stringy whiskers, yes, a professor of Spanish literature at Rutgers; the daughter a concert pianist struggling for success, touring India, Australia, South America. Neither child wanted anything to do with their father's hard-fought ideas on banking, or tried to save the banks from closing during the bad years. It was Willie who had acquired their depreciated bank stocks, their leases, buildings, and with loans on Enoch's stocks on Wall Street, had established the new banks, bought up some charters, to create the Ranchers and Growers Bank of the West.

Willie, fat, bald, nearsighted, proved to be a solid and clever presence in Western banking.

The San Diego bank building was new and, for its period, the usual Greek-Roman granite temple with plate glass lettered in gold, bronze grilles and Pompeian designs on its tile floor. On the main wall was a mural that Willie (when drinking) would describe as "a buxom Anglo-Saxon virgin discreetly draped, but exposing strong legs and arms, and a bosom like blacksmith's bellows, holding a cornucopia from which issued rails with trains running on them, ships loading in a flood of oranges, cotton bales, tuna, tall palm trees, a Pony Express rider, a Canning stagecoach, even several motorcars." The artist had delighted Willie by topping all this with a huge sun pointing its rays like protecting spears in all directions.

Enoch had never cared for the mural. But Willie, who had a good eye for art and disliked paintings of sad sunsets, shipwrecks, and nudes that seem inflated with air pumps, felt the mural was the right overripe ironic touch. Willie was a bachelor; not celibate, but not really taking sex seriously in the mutability of human affairs.

Willie greeted his father in his office, which was large, well-furnished in what Willie said was Art Nouveau, and contained on pale green sackcloth walls, a simpering angel by Burne-Jones, and a Boudin seascape painted so thin it was already fading. Willie, his humor as always bubbling forth, offered his father a cigar and a deep brown leather-covered chair.

"Damn it, Willie, why don't you come visiting? Lucy is hurt."

"I love Lucy—you know that, E.K.—but I can't stand the stuffed shirts and political windbags she usually has in tow. I have to deal with the fat cats in politics and business and that's enough. Now, you know the coal situation is serious?"

"Don't I know it! I'm piling up tons of it in the yards, but there's just not enough being mined."

Willie leaned back in his chair, almost disappearing from sight, the lit cigar in his mouth pointing up at the ceiling. "The coal people are destroying the country with their meanness. You know what a miner makes a year? He gets what they call subsistence pay of three hundred eighty-five dollars a year, *if* he's lucky. No human being, no family, can live on that. Unions have to come to the mines—no matter how many miners the owners' private armies kill. In the end, the men who go down the mines will wreck them if they don't get a living wage."

"The hell with that. Think of me, Willie. The owners have added a dollar thirty-five a ton, and it's going to be two dollars more a ton if the strike spreads, more as the shortage continues. Sure the miners are kicked around—but if the economy fails, where are they?"

"E.K., this union leader, John Mitchell, is going to call out one hundred forty thousand miners. That means no coal this winter for the cold Northern cities, and as for the railroads—" Willie flung his hands up into the air. "If the railroad workers join them in a strike of their own—it's ass-over-teakettle for the whole economy."

"Christ, Willie, aren't things bad enough? Don't go scareboogering the whole country."

"I think it's coming. So go kiss the behinds of the railroad union leaders, and head it off on the W. G.P. and G."

"Like hell. I'll be fair, but no more."

"Your idea of fair is outdated, Father." Willie nodded and studied Enoch's face.

"I give work to thousands. I build houses for them. I have three generations of families working on the lines—grandfathers, fathers, and sons. I'm no bastard like George Pullman or John D., putting the guns on men, women, and children. Christ, boy, I came up from those people."

"They're not going to thank you for that endorsement. They want a good life, things they see in magazines. The common man, he's no better than anyone else. He's just too common. If he were in short supply, he'd do better."

"Willie, you sound like some goddamn socialist professor at Berkeley, poor-mouthing the American system. Nothing is perfect, but show me something better."

"I have to see all viewpoints to manage money and property. The system—in basic ideas—is good. But right now, E.K., why don't you work out something with Rawly? He's a smart negotiator, a wizard at conciliation."

Enoch put out his cigar in an ash tray shaped like a lily, mashed the tobacco out with a crunch, as if breaking a neck. "I wouldn't touch his ideas of railroading with a mile-long pole."

"Think of his coal mines. He and Ball have control of a lot of anthracite and in case the strike comes, your gondolas could freight coal down to you and you'd not be dependent on Eastern or Southern mines."

Enoch stood up and buttoned his coat. "I wouldn't ask Rawly for a drink of water if I were dying of thirst, crawling on my hands and knees in the middle of Death Valley . . . and why the hell don't you get married and give me some decent grandchildren?"

Willie smiled, took off his glasses, blinked like an owl in daylight as he polished them with a silk handkerchief. Put them on, peered through them as he reset them on his tiny nose. "Because I'm having too much a grand time as it is—I sleep alone in a big bed and like it. I don't see any marriage—forgive me, Father—not any around me that I care to get stuck in, like a wolf in a trap. Marriages that I see really pay no interest rates I'd care to invest in. Look at poor Uncle Floyd."

"Sad," said Enoch, "damn sad. But Lucy and me, we have a good life—anyway, a pattern that harms nobody."

"Good . . . I'm seeing Rawly next week in Denver, so if—"

Enoch shook his head, clamped his hat on. "Just keep my goddamn name out of it. Where they bury Floyd?"

"The widows are still fighting over the remains. He'd have liked that."

They agreed he would have. Floyd Denton had died of gunshot wounds inflicted by one of his wives. It had been predicted that if the two wives found out about each other, about Floyd's two ménages, it would be the hot chili pepper of an Italian wife in El Paso who would reach for a weapon and drill him. But instead, Floyd was gunned down by his schoolteacher lady at Dana Point. She shot him down with a small silver purse pistol of which he had insisted once, "you couldn't kill a cockroach with that." But the respectable New England Mrs. Denton had managed to press off six little bullets, all of which hit a vital spot, and Floyd died at once with an expression of his face asking *why this?*

There had been a court trial, but the West Coast Mrs. Denton, testifying on the stand, insisted she had merely been showing her husband the little toy to impress upon him that she was a delicately balanced woman upset by the discovery he had another wife and children in El Paso, and she was going to destroy herself for shame. Somehow, she blacked out and her lawyer agreed the pistol went off six times without her knowing it. It was play-acting anyway, Mrs. Denton not knowing the gun was loaded, and that her actions were the result of grief, her way of defending the honor of her home, her children and sacred institution of marriage. Her lawyer, in summing up, quoted Shakespeare and the New Testament about casting the first stone. But mostly the defense was the "unwritten law," which did not exist. Every lawyer in California used it—domestic killings were rather common—giving his own version of it to excuse his client's actions.

Mrs. Denton (West) was set free, the jury not leaving the box, and she was soon engaged in a pension fight, and a contest to claim the body of Floyd Denton for interment in California.

Enoch felt the loss of Floyd deeply—even if he was accepting the fact that so many people who were once part of the drama of his life were dying, and those not already dead were falling away, drifting off into senility or worse.

A loss as great as Floyd's took time to get used to, that scatterbrained, wily, boozing, womanizing uncle of his—his last kin, the man who had raised him from a pup. It was a loss as great as the departure of Jasper and his family from the United States. He had heard that Jasper de Leon had handed in his notice at the forge, not even asking for his pension.

Enoch drove down to Boogy Hill where the Kingston Junction Negroes lived. They still hadn't paved the streets, he noticed, and the houses needed paint. It seemed unfair that a foreman of the W. G.P. & G. junction forge and rebuilding plant should live like this. Backyard privies, so near the wells, no street lights or curbs. Jasper's house looked cared for and the front lawn had flower beds, now

300

a bit neglected. Enoch found the front door open and Jasper seated on a packing case in the empty parlor, eating an egg sandwich. Christ, Jasper is an old man. He is only a few years older than I am, Enoch thought. Jasper went on eating. Enoch got a kitchen chair and sat down facing the Negro. "What the devil do you think you're doing, Jasper?"

"Pulling tracks."

"But why? You can stay. Nobody I know is pushing on you. You'll get a pension. You still can be the big man at the forge if you want to."

"Don't want no part of it, E.K. They lynched two more black boys out San Jose way last week. But you might not have noticed."

"Damn peckerwood sheriffs don't try to hold the mobs off."

Jasper said without noticeable rancor, "They lynched forty-two Negroes last year in the United States, twenty-six so far this year. No place this here America for me and my children."

"Where the hell will you go?"

"Brazil. The wife and the girls already there, setting up house in Macapa."

"You might have asked for my advice. What can you do there?"

"Gonna build a railroad and they got no color bar down there. They have black folk in the government."

"A railroad—you, Jasper?"

The Negro put down the sandwich, held up a coffeepot he took from the embers in the fireplace.

"Coffee? No? There you are, E.K.—you, too, don't think this nigger can build a railroad. Gonna build one from Bragança to Fortaleza."

"I didn't say you *couldn't* build a railroad. But I need you here. My sons have their own lives. Floyd's gone. Now you. And Charlie? I don't know if he has all his marbles anymore. Christ, a man goes along living and suddenly he's deserted. Did I ever poor-mouth you, treat you like a field hand?"

"You always treated me like—" Jasper laughed. "Was going to say like a white man, but I've seen how you treat white men sometimes." Enoch walked around the empty room, peering into the other rooms. The furniture was gone, just a few packing cases mostly already nailed shut; all but one open box that contained calico gowns, pewter candlesticks, a skillet and a few photographs mounted on gray cardboard. He picked one up and looked at it.

"Isn't this Brook?"

Jasper looked at the photograph showing a woman, some white men, and a small boy, in missionary dress, and four Zulu natives with feather headdresses pulling rickshaws.

"That's Brook. Taken someplace in South Africa. Durban."

"She looks older. When was this taken?"

"Two, three years ago. She been going round in South Africa with that Boer trouble. Nobody cares what happens to the natives. She's going to make trouble for herself."

"The people she's with—who are they?"

Jasper looked at Enoch. "Just people, Bible pounders."

Enoch put the photograph on the fireplace mantel. "You don't have to go to Brazil, Jasper. You think Brook is happy gallivanting around? I'll pay to bring your family back. Look, I have this big fancy coach house at Kingston House. You move in; there are a few acres all yours. Raise dogs, horses . . ."

"Watermelons, chickens?"

Enoch frowned, then laughed. "You sassy bastard. Go if you have to go, go. I'll get some railroad money for you."

"I've saved. I've invested. Got land in Brazil, got a nice ranch, some cattle. This is no sudden thing. Been thinking it out a long, *long* time."

"Come up to the house before you go." Enoch looked toward the fireplace mantel and went out. Jasper sipped his coffee, now tepid. He chuckled. Just for a minute there he, E.K., he wondered is *that* his son? His and Brook's child. Well, he'll never learn it from me. I could see he had a little thought that way soon as he saw the picture. Well, now, he'll never know for sure. Brook, she had said he was never to know. *Never.*

34

When the problems and pressures of the times grew too heavy and Enoch needed a breakaway from planning, he would go down to the junction and the forge and see the actual working of the yards rather than face the paper work, debates and arguments as the coal strike spread and the railroad unions began to breathe out the first threats of a strike to stop the trains.

In the back shop they were giving a Mallet 2-6-2 locomotive a cleaning, all parts being sprayed by kerosene and steam, and the firebox being cleaned out over the ash pit, the tender filled with coal and water, loose bolts being tightened on the water-feed pump. Two men were filling the lubricators, forcing grease into rods and valve gear bearings. This was real, this was, Enoch felt, understandable, like serving a good working horse.

The foreman waved a gloved hand at Enoch. "She's goin' to be ready on time for the Kansas run, sir."

"Fine, Eddie, fine."

Eddie Hayes was an old railroad nut-buster, as machinists were called. He had been with Enoch at the laying out of the first roundhouse of the W. & G.P., been a donicker—a brakeman—and not one to listen to union organizers' talk of pie-in-the-sky. Just a man to go about his work with the dinky, the switch engine used to pull freights into order. But now there was talk Eddie would lead the strike if it came. As Charlie had said, "Every event waits for the first gesture."

Christ, he loved these men, he had been greasy alongside of them. He went out to the yard where a rattler with a string of reefers was being made ready. It couldn't be delayed, had to redball its farm products east as fast as it could. The men were polite enough, but they seemed to turn to their work as if presenting their back to him. Just to make talk, Enoch examined some transverse bolsters, read some waybills.

"How she making up, Murray?"

Murray, a short Irishman with a jaw deformed by a chaw of tobacco, spat and nodded. "Oh, she's a big string, Mr. Kingston. Eighty cars and she's rolling out five-ten at sixty-five miles per hour."

"What's the makeup?"

"Reefers, caustic soda tanks, grain, ten cattle cars."

Enoch knew all that information, but he patted Murray on the arm. "You're doing a fine job, Murray. Be sure the caustic soda is in the nickel-lined tank cars."

Murray gave him a look as if to say, "What the hell kinda fool do you take me for, you auld duffer? Enoch went back to his office. He was just a pain in the ass to the work crews at the junction. They knew their jobs and did them well. He looked at some figures. It would take 15,000 freight cars to carry the Southwest's crops, and he had hoped to have a major share of it. Could he collect enough empties and keep them rolling? Always 25 percent of his empties were floating around on other lines—some not reported by the Silverton, Gladstone & Northerly, the Denver Longmont, and the Virginia & Truckee. He'd have to build some fire under division checkers. For a moment there was the thought: *borrow cars from Rawly's lines.* But it was the thought of only a moment. *That* would be the day, asking for Rawly's icers and ore cars. He could imagine the jubilation that would cause in Colorado.

He'd have to go up to San Francisco and see Charlie. Charlie was getting old and brittle. He was developing young lawyers to run things in the legal department. Charlie had the shakes a bit, needed to get out more and get around. Not hidden away in that old house of his, a place full of chow-mein Chink junk, the rooms smelling of joss sticks, sandalwood punk. With that soft-shoed Chinese servant, Dock Sing, just standing there giving you that big slant-eyed stare. Still, Charlie would know how best to get injunctions against strikers, pickets, how to legally protect the scabs he'd have to move into the yards, and arm if the strike got mean. Charlie still had a good line to the ears of the right judges and courts.

Enoch began to draw a dream engine he hoped to see in production, a 4-6-4 switcher for yard work. Four small wheels up front, then big driving wheels, and small wheels in the rear with a shay gear, a boiler to superheat steam to 2000°, and fit a fifty-foot turntable. For two hours he was away from the problems of the day, the troubles ahead. Lucy had to send a servant down to get him up to the house for dinner when he ignored the telephone. Some Italian opera singer was on his way to San Francisco, and Lucy had bagged him for a dinner at the Huntington Hotel, with several of the opera company, to meet some of the culture and society of the Southwest. Hell, as Mark Twain had once said over some glasses at the Hoffman House, "opera is better than it sounds."

The day had been misty in San Francisco—rain at two o'clock, with an attempt of a wan sun to come out in late afternoon. It was dusk now, a gray hood descending on streets, still reflecting the scene in the remains of the rain in worn slate walks.

At Charles Auden White's house the blinds remained drawn, and a damp cat lurked under the front porch, too miserable to go out into the wet, and too hungry to sleep. It had once been fed for some months by Dock Sing—but for the last six weeks, no plate of chicken remains, no saucer of milk had appeared at the back door. The cat's pale orange fur was speckled with beads of water, and one ear was frayed from some amorous encounter in the past.

The blinds were seldom raised now in the big room with the bow window, overlooking the city and the bay. Inside there were, in this twilight, some glowing embers in the fireplace. The electric bulbs set under red silk shades with bases of Ching pottery gave just enough light to show a low rosewood table with volumes of the *Mustard Seed Garden*, a row of Yenan plates on the wall, a Tai Sung scroll of two water buffaloes fighting, besides a Buddhist monk's painting of a tiger, Dock Sing's favorite.

Charlie White reclined on one of the two sofas upholstered in blue silk. He was thin and drawn, his features stretched tight on the thrusting bones of his face. But he looked contented enough, as if beyond all subtleties and intuitions. He watched Dock Sing leaning over a low table, preparing the first smoke of the night in the *yeng tsiang* pipe of orangewood. Dock Sing set down the pipe and looked into the blue flame coming up through the perforated glass globe of the *ken-ten* lamp. The Chinese lifted a small dark pill of soft matter from the round silver box, rolled it skilfully between thumb and forefinger, rolling the bit of opium, *gow hop*, carefully, slowly. Charles White watched and waited. There was no hurry. When the smoke came, to become part of his all-peace, it would be his all-contentment without any heightened perceptions.

The two of them had been smoking opium now for some years and, being wise and careful smokers, they felt it had done them no harm, just created a trance free of malevolence. Dock Sing put the *gow hop* pill onto a *yen hauch* needle and held it in the blue flame of the little lamp until it sizzled. Charles White had insisted on knowing the name of each individual tool used in the cooking ceremony. He was once very interested in details about many things. The cooking pill gave off a sweet odor. Dock Sing felt it had baked just enough. He removed it with the *tsha* knife and deposited it in the bowl of the first pipe and handed it to Charles White. "Diverbuchi." (Pardon.) Charles answered "Ha yung chi." (Good luck.) He took three long pulls of the opium smoke into his lungs, into his being, and began to drift placidly away from the always encroaching world. Three times more he took deep draws on the *gow hop*. Just before he felt the universe rolling at his feet like a puppy, and the release into the great peace, he heard Dock Sing speak as he prepared the pipe for himself. "You must talk to E.K. He had been sending telegrams since we took out the telephone."

Charles White tried to think of some answer of amity and complacency.

> Brightness falls from the air
> Queens have died young and fair. . . .

If it didn't fit, it didn't matter: nothing had to fit anymore except the smoke.

Dock Sing was inhaling the last of his pipe and then he too slipped away to meet the goddess Kuan-yin, the guide of souls with whom he had been having a debate on the paragons of filial piety. The room was filled with the too-sweet heavy odor of opium. Below, at the front door, a telegraph messenger was banging the front-door knocker. After a while he gave up and slipped the envelope into the bronze slit of the mailbox opening set into the wall.

The mail receptacle in the hall was filled with an accumulation of old mail and the overflow was spread on the pale green rug. There were several pounds of mail. No one in the house, for some time, had made any attempt to open it.

Enoch's telegram had been direct and short.

STRIKE ON W GP & G SET FOR TOMORROW 6 A.M. ON ALL BRANCHES IMPORTANT YOU ALERT STATE GUARD AND RESERVES FOR DUTY TO KEEP TRAINS OF U.S. MAIL RUNNING CONTACT WASHINGTON FOR FEDERAL ACTION

E.K.

The strike began simply enough with all trains stopped from leaving or entering Kingston Junction. The *Golden Eagle* was left standing, steam escaping, just outside New Orleans; the *Royal Kingston* at a desert water tank. Miles of freights were deserted by their crews in various sidings. Most of the dispatchers, signal men, inspectors joined the strike. Enoch at once organized supervisors, office workers, foremen, the railroad police to keep what trains they could, moving. Pinkerton began to move in its men, and the Mentrex Service was recruiting strikebreakers; hoodlums on skid rows, ex-convicts, and pug-uglies, anyone who could handle a club, fire a pistol or shotgun, slug and stomp at ten dollars a day and board at the W. G.P. & G. junction points. By the next night, a pitched battle had taken place at Silver Falls, and freight cars were burning on the Kansas City run. Several million dollars' worth of farm products spoiled, and the poor came to pick up spoiled oranges, apples, and hams, along the rail-lines. Reefers could no longer get ice, and miles of fermenting egg crates marked the outskirts of cities. A whole herd of steers were turned loose near Salt Lake City to go seek their own water and grass when a scab crew was beaten trying to run the locomotive into a packing plant.

In a week, the entire system of the W. G.P. & G. was running at about 15 percent of its capacity, and there was no coal to move the luxury trains at all. Enoch having decided it was the freight that had to move *and* the U.S. Mail. Mail was, and had been, a key item used to smash strikes in the past. The railroad owners could cite the strikers for stopping the Federal mail and demand troops to escort the trains.

The reserves, the National Guard, were turned out; gawky young men in ill-fitting uniforms, fearing their own bayonets. In the second week of the strike, Federal cavalry units from Arizona were marched into the yards at Kingston Junction to prevent strikers—so the Pinkertons claimed—from burning out the roundhouses. There was no proof they had ever intended to do that, but it was an item to make newspaper headlines in journals whose publishers owned railroad stock.

Enoch lived and slept in his office, surrounded by the ex-convicts and riffraff he had hired. Lucy had been shipped off to friends in Santa Barbara, after insisting she wanted to stay.

"Enoch, I don't want to leave you here. With just men—and such depraved-looking men."

"There are angry railroad workers, even women helping the picketing out there. I want you to go. Hell, I don't want you on my mind if they burn down Kingston House."

"They wouldn't dare. Just a few weeks ago it was all so normal." She had great pride in Enoch and was a proud woman herself. She must not press him too far.

Enoch reached for his cigar case, but didn't take out a Havana. The tobacco didn't taste right these last few days. "Take any paintings, any trinkets you think valuable, that you might miss. Take them with you."

"Oh, Enoch, that is just expensive trash." She leaned her head against his chest as in the early days when they had first been attracted to each other. She said, "No, my dear.

If it goes, let everything go. House, china, art, silverware, antiques. All I'd miss would be you. Don't be heroic—take care."

"I know, I know, old girl—we've really got no one else, have we? Just each other, really."

She didn't weep; she didn't raise her voice. She was a real lady, Enoch felt, as he hugged her to him. Nothing like breeding and manners, and she worried about an old man like himself. He kissed her cheek. "The Pinkertons will see you down in a motorcar convoy."

"Can't this thing be settled, Enoch?"

"Not the way they want to settle it. Union control of too much that belongs to management. They'll get hungry, poor bastards; their wives will jaw them to death, the kids will cry. Common sense will show them in time I'm not their worst enemy. I'm representing farmers, ranchers, miners. Christ, haven't I been fair, haven't I paid good wages. Built houses and a hospital in town as good as any in the big cities?"

"Yes, dear." She patted his unshaved cheek. He was growing a beard again. "They want certain rights, foolishly, perhaps, but that's human nature. Why don't both sides arbitrate?"

"I would if the keyed-up organizers and union bosses would listen to reason. But they like turmoil. And I haven't got enough coal to put the pressure on them by running the trains, or the engineers, for that matter. But the Federal troops will show them you can't go against the government."

"All I ask is that you take care." It was such a maddening travesty.

When Lucy was gone, Enoch sat drinking hot tea with rum in it. He hoped he wasn't getting pneumonia, working in the yards in all weather. His chest didn't feel right. But he'd have the strike broken as soon as he got that injunction against the stoppage of the U.S. Mail. Charlie had at last come to life, or one of the young lawyers in the railroad's employ. They were moving in the right direction, keeping it as legal as they could. And there were few labor-loving judges. Sock the strikers with injunctions, torts, bribes, accuse them of going against the welfare of the consumers, the farmers going broke, the hungry cities needing beef and grain, stopping machines that made jobs, needing oil and industrial chemicals. And the national defense: wasn't there still rebellion—American soldiers dying in the Phillipines? Also needs for navy supplies at seaports. Even revolutions in Latin America, in those banana republics where United Fruit made progress, got things done, sometimes backed up by a few marines. Enoch was a product of his era; there was something reprehensible about people he supported with jobs questioning *his* way of doing things.

The railroads were the veins and arteries that fed the heart of the nation. He rubbed his chest and coughed, and it hurt—he swallowed more rum than tea. All he had was his integrity, his word, his record; let some of those anarchists try and run a railroad.

The Federal troops were withdrawn when the unions announced they would man the mail trains, also any army and navy supply freights.

The radical and liberal press around the country applauded that action. The conservative newspapers hinted of un-American ideas and sinister foreigners. Some nervous California reservists, hunting rabbits up near Kingston Pass, fired at some movement in the shrub-oak brush and killed the wife and two children of a track-layer of the W. G.P. & G. who were living in a lean-to up there.
TROOPS KILL RAILROAD STRIKER'S FAMILY IN COLD BLOOD.

That was the mildest of the headlines.

The financial page of the *New York Sun* reported on a rumor: J. P. MORGAN & CO. WILL WITHHOLD NEW W. G.P. & G. BOND ISSUE FROM THE MARKET AT THIS TIME.

Enoch was running a rising fever. The fire in his chest seemed held in the grip of a tightening chain. He sat in his office drafting a cable to J. P. Morgan in England, at the estate of Lord and Lady Sackville-West. He never finished it. He dropped the pen when a massive heart attack overcame him—he feeling the shattering of the world into shards of great agony. He fell to the floor, lay staring at the dusty cinder-soiled rafters of his office ceiling. In the outer office, Chico heard him fall and rushed in to find the large body motionless on the floor. It took ten minutes to bring Doc Mercer from the emergency hospital set up in the yards to service the strikebreakers. All he could do— Doc Mercer was an ill-trained mining camp medico—was to send for a heart specialist. Enoch spent the next two weeks in the general hospital with specialists and Lucy, Willie, and Mollie waiting, hoping Enoch would survive the damaging coronary. Lucy sat expressionless, dry lipped; the son and daughter now seemed strangers; her Enoch wasn't their Enoch.

Charles White came, a bit tottery. But no one was permitted more than a glimpse of the big figure lying still in the bed. He was not permitted to talk; no one could talk to him, certainly not about the strike still in progress. Willie had taken over some controls and telegraphed Rawly to come down. He made it clear the strike had to be settled before the entire W. G.P. & G. system was in bankruptcy or sent up in dynamite and flames. . . .

Enoch was walking barefooted in a glade on his mother's farm, avoiding the cow flops. He was carrying his copy of Melville's book, and his head was awhirl with South Seas islands, palm fronds waving, deep pale-blue water, deep but crystal clear. He could see clear to the bottom, the stone-armored scurrying of lobsters, starfish stretching. The naked girls, brown-skinned, swimming and waving their arms for him to join them. He dived into the water. Brook swam around him, laughing that throaty, ropy laugh of hers. He caught her, and the waves all turned to smothering bed linen. He tried to tell Brook to stay, but painted Indians with long, feathered headdresses, waving schoolbooks, were carrying her off and she didn't seem to mind at all. Enoch wanted to follow, but it seemed he couldn't walk and the world had a carbolic smell; a woman he had never seen before, in a nurse's uniform and cap, was looking down at him. He drank from something she held to his lips and shook his head, for Uncle Floyd was driving "Old Sal" with loads of contraband cotton and Maude was fireman, tossing pine chunks into the firebox as the *chug chug* of "Old Sal" became like a heartbeat. He called out, and Phil Canning, at the controls, pointed to the firebox and he knew he had to jump in. He dived in, headfirst, and it was not at all the hot fire he had feared in all those nightmares. It was a pale pink coral seabed, and he was swimming hand in hand with Brook, and he was saying *you've come back, come back*. Swimming, swimming ... never coming up for air, breathing the air right from the water, after all ... wasn't water two parts hydrogen to one part oxygen, or was it the other way around? And he heard Brook's voice, rather gruff, whisper ...

"There is a good chance now of his recovery. He's also had a mild stroke. We don't know if there has been any permanent damage to the speech and the right leg and arm."

35

The gathering at Greenhills in the fifth-floor private quarters of the Ralston Kingstons should have been—Willie supposed—gloomy, serious-faced, perhaps even tragic. Yet, as Willie looked around the big table, there was no false Uriah Heep facade of oh-this-indeed-is-a-tragic-moment. Actually, only Uncle Charlie White seemed a morbid ghost rather than a person, very thin, eyes vacant, as if filled with colored water. He was assisted by two young lawyers who weren't people either, Willie felt, but actors in minor parts in one of Shakespeare's plays—he thought of Rosencrantz and Guildenstern.

Rawly and Leepole Ball looked serious but not pompously dignified, not at all. Sister Mollie had become a bit bony, and after bearing three children could talk of little else but them, and her husband's views of the Republican party. She was now waiting for explanations for the meeting.

Julio Alvarez, a grandson of the Don, was there, representing the Alvarez holdings. He had come with a lawyer, a dark, jowly man with a long black moustache, who kept whispering in Spanish.

Rawly stood up and leaned on the oak table; from below on the front lawn of Greenhills, they could hear some of the guests knocking wooden balls about with mallets. Rawly put down some papers. "We regret that Enoch Kingston himself cannot be here, but his doctors insist he stay at Kingston House and continue his progress which, I am happy to say, is good. He'll make a fairly full recovery, they say. Yes. Very little impairment, a bit of thickening of the speech, a small stiffness in the right leg. But it can all go away."

Willie was doodling with a gold pencil on a bit of paper, turning a fish into a bird, the bird into a landscape. "Get on with it, Rawly; we're all happy Father didn't die. Lucy sends regrets—she'll not leave him. The matter before us is already almost too late to bring to a head, a solution. Go on, Rawly."

"What Willie is talking about is the Western, Great Plains and Gulf railroad system. The whole procedures of E.K. have been wrong, out of date. And they now menace the survival of the holdings we have in the line's stocks and bonds."

Mollie said, "He was so sick and didn't know it."

Charles was raising a finger and shaking it slowly. "Most irregular. E.K. is a shareholder. A big one. You have here *what* majority of voting stock?"

Willie said, "Now, Uncle Charlie, we sent you a report." (One of the young lawyers held some sheets before the old man's eyes.) "You agreed that to save the situation, for the line to continue solvent, certain things had to be done and quickly."

"Yes, yes. Go on, go on."

Rawly looked at one of the sheets of paper. "We have power to vote nearly twenty percent of the holdings of the W. G.P. and G. stock. We represent stock here or hold proxies that bring it to that count. There are not only the Ball-Kingston shares, Willie's, the Alvarez family holdings, what shares are controlled by Mollie, Uncle Charles, and also by shares of H. H. Starkweather and Company that handles some of our bond issues for their Eastern and Wall Street clients."

Willie nodded and folded his doodle sheet. "I had the bank's accountants check, and we do at this meeting consist of a majority, enough to control and vote. To save the railroad, to protect our investments, we plan to elect a new board of directors, a new chairman and a new president, and end the strike at once. The unions have agreed to meet with us."

Mollie said, "I think we should wait until Father can be in on things and know we're doing it for his own interests, too."

Rawly said dryly, "He'll know when it's the right time."

Leepole Ball stood up and looked at a list in his

hand—the new board. "We shall take over control, settle the strike, and begin to ship coal from the Ball-Kingston mines directly to the W. G.P. and G. division junctions. We nominate, in full respect, Enoch Bancroft Kingston to first vice president in charge of future planning and engine design. Now, before we get too damn formal and legal, we all know this is the only way to keep from tossing the road into bankruptcy and destroying most of our shareholdings. Remember, E.K. has a hell of a lot of shares himself, so we're also keeping his holdings valid, it seems to me. If you agree, I shall take over a chairman of the board, and Ralston—" Leepole wiped his lips with a finger at calling his partner by his full first name, "Ralston as president and managing director of the line."

Charles White mumbled, "Meetings aren't run this way."

The Spanish-speaking lawyer lifted two fingers. "It is agreed, of course, that on the board Julio and one more Alvarez be seated, *si?*"

Rawly smiled. "*One* Alavrez, and we will welcome Julio to the board. Also, the board will consist of Homer Emerson, several of our mining group, and two people Charles White will nominate. Unless, of course, he himself, as a major stockholder, would care to continue? I have already had a meeting with the old board—I have their resignations in case we need them. Uncle Charles?"

The old lawyer shook his head; it seemed so loose that Willie felt it could be attached by a thread. "No, no more."

"All right, Uncle Charles," said Willie. "The banks are ready to advance costs and funds to revitalize the line. Millions have been lost by no movement of freight and loss of through passenger trains. So you will all be asked to turn in some of your holdings to the bank as security against certain loans. They will, of course, belong to you, not to the banks."

Charles White, who had closed his eyes, opened one and mumbled something to one of the young lawyers that sounded like "Young fox, he's saved the old wolf. E.K. will *never* forgive him."

The meeting went on for three more hours and Charles White departed first, between his two young lawyers, almost carried to a waiting motorcar and driven off. . . . Charles Auden White was to survive for many years, but his active connection with the W. G.P. & G. ended with that meeting. From then on, he was rarely seen in public. His Oriental art collection went to the proper museum, his large portfolio of railroad and industrial stocks was set up as the Charles Auden White Foundation, and still functions. ("As with most foundations, to give well-paid jobs to its officers." Willie.). Many years later, the Chinese Communist forces executed a rich landowner in Kwangsi Chuang province—a landowner named Dock Sing Tai who spoke very good English, kept several concubines, dealt in opium and currency exchange, and claimed to be an American citizen.

As for Rawly's reorganization of the strike-bound W. G.P. & G., the newspapers in New York, Chicago, and San Francisco carried front-page headlines of the transferring of power and control. Featured were short biographies of Enoch Bancroft Kingston. "More in the nature of an obituary," Lucy observed, "than the story of a living man." There was a great use of the words "pioneer . . . great builder . . . empire maker . . ." and phrases "from poverty as a farm boy . . . to one of the most aggressive of the railroad kings." There were also a few items, none of them fully true to the facts. It was claimed he had been decorated at Vicksburg by Grant in person for leading a brave charge (not any mention of his being a deserter) and Maude Alvarez's name was printed as Marion in two papers.

The coal strike was being pushed to a settlement by the president of the United States and, as Willie was to add, "with that vigor and attention to his public image that made his terms in office so memorable." Rawly, as a coal producer, went East to attend a series of meetings that were to agree—mine owners and unions—on the settlement.

J. P. Morgan—as a most visible target—was under attack in the press for his dealing with the coal kings.

Going East, Rawly looked over the newspaper clippings about his father's associate:

Is J. Pierpoint Morgan greater than the people? Is he

mightier than the government ... Morgan has placed
upon us universal ruin, destitution, riot and blood-
shed. ... We appeal from the king of the trusts to the
President of the people. As for those magnates, the
Vanderbilts, J. Pierpont Morgan, and Cassatt of the
Pennsylvania Railroad, they are squeezing out smaller
capitalists and adding most of the anthracite mines to
their railroad domains. Mine owners have found ways
of altering the weight of a ton of coal which the
worker must dig, from 2,340 pounds to 2,700 or even
4,000 pounds.

Stupid bastards. Morgan had brains, but like E.K. was
old and blind to facts. On the train, Rawly watched the
fields of the republic flash past. As a child he had ridden
with Enoch on several long trips and had been puzzled
that while the foreground of fields, trees and poles went
running by, way in the background, the landscape was
standing still it seemed, and he wondered about illusion
and reality and the magic of perspective caught short and
having to move at different speeds. Of course, he did not
then think in those terms, but in a child's idea of the
world in which he lived. There had been good times, of a
boy and a man, his father, living together, eating chocolate ice cream in the train diner with three Negroes standing around doing the *yok, yok* act, play-acting Massa's
loyal servants. Maybe they were like that, then. But these
were newer, harder times of Krupp steel, the Russian po-
groms of the Jews, the Kaiser's moustache. Rawly didn't
fully trust the twentieth century, so shiny and new, and he
felt guilt about Enoch. They had grown far apart, but he
respected the old boy (Enoch was only fifty-two). No one
could build up what he did, from bare rocks up, or do
it so well. Yes—presently we'll build him a private railroad car. We'll keep him busy. No figurehead kicked upstairs. E.K. knows more about how a locomotive, a club
diner, or a freight car should be designed and built than
any firm in the business. As he had said to Rawly on one
of their trips, "You can load up some fancy dan of a
galoot with educated degrees and T-squares, and formulas
on how to make steel, sure. But it's all theory and little
games out of books. When you have to make a railroad

317

run on spit and baling wire, the rules and formulas have a way of turning impractical. It's in the doing, *only* the doing, that you learn."

Yes, a beautiful private luxury car all E.K's own, done up in satinwood and inlays, and carvings—painted the colors of his favorite train, the *Golden Eagle*.

In several all-night sessions in the Fifth Avenue Hotel, as ordered by the president, the stiff-necked coal operators and the United Mine Workers' Union heads heard the truth from bankers and Wall Street houses that handled railroad stocks and from Ralston Kingston and others. Rawly didn't spare anyone. "We, as big stockholders in coal mines can raise holy hell. We have the money connections, the Wall Street connections to do it if you don't settle the coal strike and give the nation, and companies outside the coal trust, fuel." The president also threatened to run the mines with Federal troops. The operators huffed, then gave in, but made it a point of acceptance that they would *not* seal the agreement directly with the miners' union.

"We agree, Kingston, we will hear the men's demands, but *not* as union members, and we'll accept impartial arbitration."

"You had damn better. Arbitration by a presidential commission."

It was a rather unbalanced commission, dominated by mine owners. Rawly got one union man added: the president of the Order of Railway Conductors.

The Western, Great Plains & Gulf Railroad became one of the seven giant American railroad systems. Roads dominated, controlled by Rawly, E. H. Harriman, the Vanderbilts, J. P. Morgan, Jay Gould, and James J. Hill.

For Enoch those were perfect days at Kingston House. When the summer had passed its zenith the Spanish dagger was in bloom. The days began to cool after nights when one needed blankets, and the sun was good but did not burn off the mists over the far-off mesquite flats. With the pleasant heat of the day, there came the scent of the orange and lemon groves below, from some late blossoming. And the giant eucalyptus (once six-inch saplings he himself had planted) made a kind of leaf music in the wind.

The distant mountains were the lavender and faint violet of some paintings his son Willie had been collecting—all dots and dashs of paint. If you half-closed your eyes, Enoch discovered, you could find the world was like the pictures, not at all solid but an atmosphere of particles and reflections of bits of light on stone and plants, walls, even people.... Aesthetic subtlety was beyond the man, but he had an intense feeling of the rhythmic nature of things.

Sitting wrapped in blankets in the wheelchair on the west porch of Kingston House, the sick man did not feel ill—more an indifferent tranquillity. He did not feel anything much but a regret his body had had that weak moment during a crisis. His right arm and leg were slowly responding to manipulation and to his will. If he spoke slowly and firmed the muscles of his mouth, Lucy hardly noticed the slurring of a few *b*s and the sliding sound of the *s*.

He saw that they were busy again down at the junction and in the yards. The big 150-ton forge hammer was at work on red hot steel THUM! *THUM!* The freights were moving out. With his left hand, he dug under the blankets cocooned around him and dragged out his watch on its chain, snapping open the double lids. In seventeen minutes the *Pueblo-Fort Wayne Express* would come by, one of the Rawly line of fast varnish, now merged into the newly reorganized W. G.P. & G. Cock of the walk, Rawly was now. "Napoleon of the rails," the *Los Angeles Times* had called him. Taken over as ramrod of the whole outfit—frontier style. Made his peace with the unions and the coal sharks, he and that goddamn four-eyed Rough Rider. Well, it was, as Chico said, *their* ballgame now. He couldn't—mustn't—think of past agonies and dislocations. From old readings of Spencer, he remembered: Nature is never economical.

They could take their offers of first vice president and director of construction and design and could shove it all, everything ... yes ... But he mustn't let it get his dander up. He had to stay alive for Lucy's sake. He had to heal, had to get the limbs kicking out properly, the voice back.

Eat their slop—it looking like clean pig swill—swallow their pills, sip their Indian swampwater and snake-oil mixtures. He'd lie wary and waiting. The time had to come when he'd spring out and show them how a real hell-lifting, half hoss, half 'gator (as Uncle Floyd used to shout out) got things done. The rigid laws of necessity and consequence would catch up with that young prick, Rawly.

There was a sudden feeling of weakness as he thought of his son, a wanting to weep. He shook it off as Lucy came out on to the porch carrying his one small thin cigar of the day, all he was permitted by the expensive quacks.

"Can't we cut it in half and save the rest for after supper?"

"No, and you are to only smoke half of it anyway. No chewing soggy ends."

Lucy held the silver lighter to the tobacco between his lips and he inhaled slowly, carefully, feeling all wasn't yet right with his inner machinery. He smoked with relish, holding Lucy's hand as she sat beside him in a gracious intimacy. Must have given her a hell of a bad time when I was off my feet.

"I want to get out of this hand-driven buggy."

"In a week or so, Dr. Norman says."

"That's what he said last month."

"You became querulous, had a bit of a setback. Now you're producing a good pulse. He wants the leg stronger. You'll look very dignified with a cane in London, pacing down Piccadilly, Bond Street, St. James."

"London?"

"We sail in two months if you keep up your progress. Young Dr. Stockton is going along with us."

"He play a good hand of poker?"

"Whist. I never understood the lure of poker."

She noticed his right arm made a gesture as if to pat her, but never completed it.

"No, Lucy, there's a lot about me you never understood. But you got the hang of the vital side. What I had that was worth more than a penny a pound—you got that clear. I've been happy with you. In my own way, I've been a damn good husband too. As Rawly told the new board of directors, I was outdated, a toothless gear, a worn brake shoe. Belonged in Barnum's side show with Sitting Bull and Zip-What-Is-It."

"He didn't say you were out of date or anything like it."

"In his own way, he meant it. Hell, I know they all did what was right as they saw it. But, Lucy, you know I'd of preferred to have gone down, to wreck the whole shebang, to sink it and go live in the old soldier's home they have at Sawtelle."

She took the cigar from his lips. "They'd have shot you as a deserter. Now, close your eyes and don't work yourself into a bad state." Lucy took a newspaper out of a workbasket. "Let me read you Mr. Dooley. You usually agree with him on the state of the world."

He wasn't really listening. Yes, of course he liked Mr. Dooley's comments on the day's news, but his mind was going back, back in time, and he was wondering how it had all happened and how foolish and gawky he had been as a boy, and how hard-nutted, nerve-tightening life was on the wagon trains and in card games. And supple-as-eel whores and the whisky made those wonderful exciting little dramas, goosing life to look bigger, seem wider, and all lit up by fireworks.

He didn't like growing older, or his body being such a sack of impersonal mechanisms. He didn't like what he saw age do to people—that automatic mysterious appearance of wrinkles, sore joints, rotten breaths and liver spots. All the melancholy road to the bone yard. Whoever it was up there didn't do much of a job to stand close inspection on people, certainly had no sense of how to make up a timetable.

Lucy reading on was having a little trouble with the brogue: " 'I'll niver go down again to see sojers off to the war. But you'll see me at th' depot with a brass band whin th'men that causes wars starts f'r th' scene iv carnage. . . .' "

A month later, Mr. and Mrs. Kingston were listed on the Cunarder *Aquitania* sailing from New York. Enoch was very tan from sitting in the sun at Kingston House. The way he handled his blackwood cane, people hardly noticed the slight drag of the right leg. On the ship, Lucy was delighted by them being invited to the captain's table, where Enoch told the story of how he helped steal six hundred bales of contraband cotton.

The crossing was rough, but neither one of them was seasick.

5

Dynasty

36

There still exists an essay Nicholas Kingston wrote in prep school at the age of thirteen, while greatly addicted to the style of Rudyard Kipling:

THE GREAT WAR

How easily it all began—like a ballet of toy figures in uniform falling down in a row, domino style. There was the Dual Monarchy, a mixed language nation called Austria-Hungary "made up of eight nations, seventeen countries, twenty parliamentary groups, twenty-seven parties." The name of the Bosnian town where the war fever incubated is remembered even by the casual newspaper reader: Sarajevo.

The leaders of the European nations were eager for warlike gestures, some even earnestly hoping for battle, a short pageant of power. So the Great War began. . . . Using the excuse of an assassination, the Austrians saw a chance to punish and grab off more of Serbia, and even when Serbia offered to meet all terms, the Austrians wanted war. The Russians came proudly to the aid of their Slavic brothers in Serbia—Russia still so medieval, autocratic. The Germans announced they must aid brother Austrians if the Great Slavic Bear moved, so the French gave notice they held a treaty of aid to Russia. England stood firmly proud in its assistance alliance with France. Doomsday had come.

Sir Edward Gray stood gloomily at his London window. "The lamps are going out all over Europe. We shall not see them lit again in our lifetime."

All the nations had plans, all had long studied charts,

maps for victory. In the main it was to be—as they saw it—a war of foot-slogging infantry, flanked by fine horsemen with a great deal of artillery. Of the new air forces, little was expected—perhaps some scouting of the weather and the roads.

So far, the Great War has produced four major innovations in warfare. They were the airplane, the machine gun (based on models fifty years old), chemical warfare (poison gas and the flamethrower), and the land tank, moving like a metal turtle on an endless belt, a road it laid in front and picked up behind itself. But the railroads carry the full burden of keeping this war supplied. . . . ("Just like a Kingston," Wilma had said as she put the essay into her scrapbook.)

Nick's father, Ralston Kingston, had been in the war zone since January of 1916, having been asked by an Allied commission to inspect the railway systems of France, which were beginning to break down. Worn and battered rolling-stock, patched rail-lines that fed supplies and the men for slaughtering on the western front. That ghastly zigzag line of trenches that Rawly visited; it ran from the English Channel to the Swiss border. He rode the trains which carried back the wounded and the mad, the leave trains—others escorting a *capitaine* or *pilote de chasse,* an ace.

Rawly had also been commissioned by his brother William to check on the ability of England to continue the war. For Willie, in a small way, like so many bankers close to J. P. Morgan & Company, was involved in the billions of dollars in credits to the Allies. And while great profits were expected as commissions, there was always the danger of the Germans breaking through and winning the war and voiding the Allied loans. Incompetent British generals were wiping out England's young men in front of Passchendaele, Ypres and in one battle on the Somme, the donkey generals sent 60,000 to their death.

Rawly, worldly and experienced at forty-eight, still blanched at the murderous frontal assaults that changed nothing. When America came into the fray, as he thought it would, he might wangle a colonel's rank and help end this stalemate. Was he too old to be a warrior, he asked himself. He was graying, still a dapper, slim figure, wrinkled under his eyes. But he didn't expect to fly a Spad with the Lafayette Escadrille. He entered middle age a bit frightened of time passing. Thinking of decline and senility ahead, he felt a touch of madness. He had shaved off his moustache and looked his age, which was good; he had led a hard, sporting life, been active in a dozen corporations, climaxing knockdown and drag-out proxy fights.

He worried about Benji—sixteen, turning to literature and radical ideas. And the twins? Nick and Howard. Nick had been kicked out of Culver, and out of Groton at fourteen. Still, he was a brilliant student when he put his mind to it. As for Howard, well, being born ten minutes later than his brother had given him a mean streak, but great skill as a hard-hitting football player. He must try and see more of them—he was a rotten father and knew it. Get them into Princeton in a couple of years. At least they'll be spared this intrinsically hideous war, *if* it ends soon.

Rawly was staying at the Ritz in Paris, a rather shabby Ritz, a gloomy Paris in nearly the third year of the war. Sad *estaminets* and soldiers on leave *en fin de compte*. Rawly had the Egyptian suite. He was accompanied by Waldo Gaylord, the most promising of the young lawyers that had replaced Uncle Charlie's group of legal experts. Waldo was average in looks, average in size, but a fanatic about the Kingstons. He had specific qualities and no reticences. Waldo came from genteel poverty among the lesser aristocrats of South Carolina, had been the brightest of his class at Yale and at law school ("worked as a waiter nights"), and remained average in looks and size. Blue serge suit, a high starched collar and just now, in the hotel suite, a red nose from a cold caught in the unheated troop trains they had traveled on to inspect the rolling stock.

Rawly was eating a brioche. "Waldo, I think the French are on the balls of their ass. I can't see much choice but to advise somebody to send them lots of locomotives and a few thousand freight cars."

"Goods carriers, they call them here."

They were having breakfast, a fairly good one considering the war, and better than what the French women in black got, or the thin children and the hungry whores prowling the Quartier Saint Paul among the men and officers on leave.

Rawly sipped the bad coffee. (You couldn't expect the French to ever know about coffee.) They sat at the window facing the square and the big bronze column on which Napoleon stood, as if daring the Germans to come this far. Ambulances were unloading bodies on stretchers across the way. The thin wail of an alarm siren sounded far off across the city in the Fourteenth Arrondissement.

Rawly inspected a small notebook Waldo had handed him listing appointments for the day:

Fancy frock coats offering handshakes, too much drinking, a lunch with the British transport general—a *soufflé a l'Armagnac* again—too much dinner with some of the French steelmakers.

"Waldo, they're going to get caught, pants at half mast. The Germans are planning a big push. The Allies know it. But they're tired and the generals are old crocks or sadists."

Waldo took back the notebook, flipped some pages. "Yes, we had information out of Switzerland last month through our holdings in the Hamburg-Berlin Railways, of shipments of men and supplies reported—all very heavy, to the Woever Plain and surrounding depots."

"The French seem to know that. Still, they haven't taken care of the rail-line leading up to the Meuse, to Fort Douaumont. I think they treat my reports as a joke. I might as well sound impressive. Draw me a map of our inspection routes."

Waldo was too clever to draw maps of *any* section of France; he dreamed of being shot as a spy, and Rawly refusing a blindfold.

On the morning of February 21, 1916, Rawly was alerted by the American embassy that the Germans had begun their attack on Verdun after the crown prince had addressed the soldiers of his Fifth Army. The embassy prided itself in having the text of his speech. "The iron will of the sons of Germany is still unbroken, and the German army's attacks will be stopped by no obstacle."

On the six-mile front, 2,000,000 shells began to fall along the triangle of Brabant, Ornes, and Verdun. Rawly was at Ancemont, inspecting a railroad repair center, luckily escaping most of this fire as the shrapnel, high explosives, and gas shells began to fall. The French front line trenches disappeared as 100,000 rounds an hour fell and continued for twelve hours. The Chasseurs were cut to bits and at twilight of the murderous day, the German infantry came probing among the ruins of French outposts. They found the surviving French still holding out among the rubble; these, too, died. In the morning the shelling began again, and the faces of high-ranking officers turned gray or, if brandy drinkers, red. Rawly and Waldo Gaylord were moved by command car to observing some action from Fort Michel.

By February 24, the town of Verdun was in danger and Rawly was ordered out of the battle zone by the high command at Chantilly under General Chrétien of the XX Corps. The Germans were four miles from the town. Waldo sustained his courage with several *café arrosé rhums* at a canteen. The Germans had taken 10,000 prisoners and 65 cannon. Whole French divisions were down to one-third, and thousands and thousands of French infantry lay dead. The smell of death and the smoke of high explosives filled the air.

Rawly was ordered away and provided with a large Rolls Royce; the Brandenburgers of General von Luchow were attacking. They took Fort Douaumont.

"I hope the French railroad lines stay open. The Huns are going to keep driving until something gives." Waldo felt the bumps in the road jolt his spine. "Nothing human can last that long."

General Philippe Pétain was up from Noailles to organize the defense of Verdun. In three meetings, Rawly had not been very impressed with Pétain. "He's the type in a saloon fight stands back and counts blows. He'll kill a million Frenchmen—and for what?"

On the train back to Paris they sat with a British major in a compartment. The major seemed to suffer from a neurotic inertia; he had a tic in his cheek.

"Not the war of the horse and saber, is it? The one we chaps expected. All this digging in, bad."

"It's all that's left to do," said Rawly.

"Think the French will hold?"

"I suppose they'll try. Costly, however."

Waldo said, "It's like Grant in the Wilderness before Richmond."

"Is it, now?" said the British major. "We've been moving a yard at a time on the Somme. Grinding up a whole generation of young Englishmen. Been in the line myself nine months."

It was clear the major had been at the brandy in the big silver-bound flask which he passed around. Rawly took a good swallow, Waldo a sip. Rawly felt the brandy warm him. "Why doesn't someone work on a peace plan?" The landscape, the train were icy cold, the sour smell of decay and rotting wood; dust filled the air.

"Can't, old boy, say the governments. They say unconditional surrender. Break the Boche. Only way, I suppose, or in twenty years the Hun is back. It's the French I wonder about. I think they'll break, toot sweet. These generals of theirs, *monstres sacrés.*"

Rawly needed a bath, perhaps even later something else. He smiled. "Hardly the talk for a railway carriage, is it, major?"

"Quite, *quite* right."

Some company histories of the W. G.P. & G. give the impression that Ralston Kingston was decorated, awarded the Légion d'Honneur and a few other medals for being one of the saviors of Verdun. Rawly felt such texts were sheer invention. He knew he had done very little; gotten some rails sent over from England and put in better systems of dispatching trains and truck convoys supplying the murderously prolonged battle.

Entertaining a one-armed *capitaine* in a *maison de tolérance* on the rue de Fourcy, he heard despair: "Whole squads drown in mud, to die there in mud."

By March 6 the Germans were west of the Meuse, and important rail-lines were lost. All through March Rawly followed the horrors of La Mort Hommes and Hill 304 as the slaughter went on. Paris began to pack up. Fort Vaux fell in June, and by October Rawly and Waldo were in England seeking rails and goods trains. Then the French counterattacked, taking two miles back and Vaux and

Douaumont. Both sides were too deadly injured to continue the battle.

Rawly had a suite at Browns, and was expecting Willie over on the matter of more loans to the Allies. He hoped Willie survived the U-boat-infested waters. Rawly was feeling he had enough of war and wanted to see Wilma again and the children, and insist that Benji stay at Harvard. Meanwhile, he was giving parties at Browns for War Office chaps and marvelous English actresses, offering Russian caviar by the pound from the czar's embassy in London, and buying antiques for the new version of Greenhills he was planning to build.

A November morning rain was falling in tea-green dampness on London. He was in bed with Gwen Burlton who, whatever her talents in musical comedy in *Chu Chin Chow*, was rather entertaining in the well-known privacy of Browns.

Waldo came into the bedroom with a dispatch case, and said cheerfully, "Morning, sir, morning, Miss Gwen."

"Be a good poppet, Waldo darling, and see if they have Irish rashers this morning, and I'd give my soul for an egg. Really I would."

She put a naked foot out of the bed, and Waldo hardly lowered his eyes. He treated himself to a barmaid once every two weeks. Magnificent flanks. He handed her a pink robe trimmed with feathers. He admired Rawly's taste in women (a bit too grand and costly), in food, wine and the ability to handle complex details, even after a night of it. Gwen disappeared into the bathroom and its Victorian plumbing.

"Thought you might like to see some secret files on Verdun." Waldo winked without smiling. "Out of the War Office, hush-hush."

"Later—just give the gist."

Rawly was feeling lazy, and a certain edge of sadness. Was it a sign he'd soon be fifty? Damn it, he could still enjoy a good shaking with a woman, still know a good wine from a bad. But just this morning he wanted to forget war, Allied loans, the danger to Willie still at sea. The war was so dreadful that it was becoming for him an insubstantial pageant of skulls.

"The French, sir, lost half a million men, dead, wounded, missing and prisoners, that sort of thing. The Huns lost nearly as many. One statistical expert in the War Office—a mathematical wizard—figured forty million rounds of shells were fired in six months of the battle. Amazing."

Rawly lay back on the pillows, eyes closed. "Figure it out, Waldo. Roughly, I'd say it took two hundred artillery rounds to remove one soldier from the battle.... Poor business. Will you get Gwen out of the bathroom and tell her to come back to bed?"

Waldo already knew that any flip gesture or remark by Ralston Kingston was not to be taken at full value. He was really touched by the waste of manpower, the death of soldiers; not merely the waste of rails, rolling stock, steel. Waldo never forgot their last sight of Verdun—the gas-coated yellow marshes, mud over all, with men dying there because no one would bother to pull them out. Dead horses and mules rotting and swelling, bursting with the smell of Hell. Places where only bayonets stuck out of some caved-in trench. These dead would stand on their feet for eternity.

Waldo was a man who figured the course of the future as if by a chart, and he judged men by their ability to understand forces before they tried to use them. Like Rawly, he saw war as a grandiose swindle, but he also felt the shock of outrage missing in Rawly's nature.

"There is a letter from home." Waldo didn't like to say "from your wife" while a woman was douching just six feet away.

Rawly sat up and read the long letter, reading at a glance whole sections as he'd trained himself to do, stopping to reread with care only those parts which held his interest. He commented out loud to Waldo. "Nick has been sent back home from another school—Exeter this time. My sister Mollie's boy, Hank, is thinking of volunteering as a Red Cross driver; it's all the rage at Harvard. I hope he doesn't infect Benji. Contractors are demanding inflated prices for rebuilding Greenhills. You're to pick up some perfume called l'Harlequin."

"'I will." Waldo went up to the bathroom door and knocked briskly. As he saw sex, stand the best-looking woman on her head and you couldn't tell her from a barmaid.

37

If you are seventeen and have been at Harvard for two years and there is the Great War, the Germans set for *Volk* and *Vaterland,* the English for King and Country, it's all the great adventure waiting. You are tall and thin and blond and can pass for twenty. So there is only one thing to do: go, young *Américain,* get into it. Of course the United States would get into it in the end, but it wasn't the same thing as being with the British or the French in those splendid uniforms. And there was always the idea if you were a young intellectual who had read Ruskin and Rupert Brooke and had been weaned on H. G. Wells and Bernard Shaw's ideas of a better world, and were alert, good, and clean, full of justice, that you *had* to do something dramatic. Strike a blow against the Hun. Eyes too bad for the Lafayette Escadrille, but do *something.* It was bad enough that your grandfather was a robber baron according to *McClure's Magazine* and *The Masses,* and your own father an exploiter of the workers. "As Karl Marx had put it so well in *Das Kapital,*" insisted your roommate, your cousin Hank Emerson (which book you can't finish, but people say it has a lot of meat in it).

Hank had been taking flying lessons for a year, had a nose bent by the crash of a rickety plane, was broad and not too tall, red-haired. He came into their shared room with newspapers—*Great Battle on the Somme—Huge Casualties.*

"You see what they need, don't you, Benji?"

"More replacements." Benji was writing a poem. Everybody at Harvard who was not a jock who smelled of stale socks, was writing poetry. Dos, Cummings, others of the literary set. Dos had even edited a volume: *Eight Harvard*

Poets. Benjamin Kingston would have made it with his sonnet suite "Frozen Stones," *if* there had been room for the book to be called *Nine Harvard Poets.*

Hank was very logical. "They need ambulance drivers. Lots of college men are going over. Then maybe it's easy to swing over to a flying unit. You apply to the Norton-Harjes offices."

"Where are they?"

"In Paris. Oh, it's a posh volunteer Red Cross unit. What you say, Benji?"

"School has two more months."

Hank said, "Fuck Harvard," which was a term never reported in any of the daring college novels of 1917, or later in the 1920s.

Benji gave up the poem. It was too much like someone else's.

> And purged with tears
> God's image reappears.

"I bet it would rile the folks back home if we go."

"Can't let them know, Benji boy. They'd have us hog-tied and sent home. Too bad you wear glasses for reading—you'll never make the *Escadrille des Volontaires.*"

"How are the cattle boats out of Canada?"

"Romantic but stinky. Dad has connections with shipping-line brokers in Boston. Get ourselves jobs as deck-hands on some truck cargoes going to France. What do you say?"

"Paris! Villon. *La Bohème,* Cezanne!"

Hardly, Hank felt, the version of France-in-agony as one read it in the newspapers.

Benji and Hank (Henry) Emerson were like so many other young idealists, yearning for excitement, grads of Roxbury Latin, Dartmouth, and Yale Law School, going to war and driven to the depots at St. Louis, Santa Barbara, New Orleans, often in the family Pierce-Arrow, Franklin, Stearns-Knight, Packard.

Since the start of the Great War, Americans had gone over to drive ambulances, fly with the Lafayette Escadrille, serve in the Foreign Legion, learn names like Sopwith Camel, Fokker, Nieuports. In 1917, Harvard men

Kingston and Emerson had gone with other Americans to join the Norton-Harjes Volunteer Ambulance Service and drive Model T ambulances on the Western Front. It was in part a country-club war service; very fashionable with lots of Harvard and Yale and Princeton men, left-wing intellectuals and poets. Benji, trying to make concrete a transcendental experience, wrote home: "The fellows are frightfully decent—all young men are frightfully decent."

The frightfully decent fellows read Henri Barbusse's *Le Feu*, dreamed of running a better world than the "swagbellied old fogies." How Benji loved it all as they rode the drafty, war-worn train into Paris—*je n'oublierai jamais* —stopping at stations to buy wine and rolls in the station *buvettes*, and were cheered by widows in drab black and old men bent over canes, as *"Les Américains!"*

Hank had been snapping pictures with his box camera from the dirty train windows. "The French trains are really charming. Intimate, you know."

"But sloppy," Benji said. He was thinking of the trains his father controlled, the splendid luxury all-Pullman runs his grandfather had created. The French wartime trains were dirty and rattled, the goosey train whistle rather sissy. There were hints of bugs in the plush, and, as for the lavatory section, better hold your breath. But, as he wrote in his journal:

> "It is a country racked by war and great losses and much sorrow and therefore even to be here is ennobling. For all its past epochs of luxury, gaiety, the saraband of *pétroleuses* lives again. For me it is better than drinking Boston beer and singing "The Whiffenpoof Song." As the landscape kept running by and the stone houses huddled under a dark rain that fell and fell, we saw the fields were worked even in the wet by women in black and by skinny kids. It all translated itself into what is called experience and learning about life."

Benji, as they approached Paris, recited Dryden's lines:

> Arms and the man I sing, who forced by fate
> and haughty Juno's unrelenting hate.

Which didn't exactly fit, he knew, as the rain gave up and they began to move among troop trains and Red Cross carriages from which came a smell like a remembered childhood odor of a butcher's shop on a hot day. It was clear they were engaged in some great crusade, a project that would be marked down in history. To have missed it, Hank said, as they began to crawl through the outskirts of the city, "Why, it would be like missing getting born."

The rolling stock around the station, Benji saw, was in pretty bad shape. Battered flatcars with only half-covered seventy-fives on green-painted gun carriages. Some rusting tanks, two with jagged holes of shell hits. The roadbed needed ballast-tamping; the windows of many cars had lost their glass and been repaired by cardboard.

Benji and Hank entered Paris through the Quai D'Orsay station with ten other volunteers, all carrying their baggage in the dark, moving toward waiting cabs in a Paris dank and tired of three years of war. Benji knew Paris from family trips abroad. Now the Paris of his memory of childhood in green French gardens, horse-cab-filled streets, had become this unpainted, war-damaged town; the Germans, lovers of *Kultur* still firing their Big Bertha shells into the city. . . . Their hotel had blackout curtains, and there was little of the room service Americans used to get in Paris. However, he wrote home, "this is a true effort for a crusade to progress in the human condition."

Next day he and Hank went to the Norton-Harjes offices on the Rue François Premier. Here in a happy huddle were others of their Harvard classmates; the *cercle littéraire*, they had been called by some. It was a jolly reunion of the decent chaps coming over to join them. Benji wrote to a favorite professor, beginning *"Cher Maître . . ."*

They still lacked uniforms, and the French, slaughtering their hundreds of thousands of citizens, were arresting all young men out of uniform. The French, Benji heard, had over a million casualties, and there was talk of mutiny of entire divisions of weary French soldiers. Why, he felt, couldn't the French die with the grace of a Rupert Brooke?

As a man who already knew Paris, Benji led his friends down along the Seine to the towers of Notre Dame. It was all a sort of dress rehearsal for the Americans who would come to Paris for the emancipated life, a life that the waiting Red Cross drivers hoped to be living in post-war Paris. To find rapture during a cruel war, Benji felt, was most likely a sin. Puritanism kept seeping back, he decided.

38

The ambulance men and the soldiers in full battle gear lying in the woods of the Ypres Salient could hear the nightingales singing in the trees. The ambulances were drawn up in the night just behind the wood, and to the drivers, the singing of the birds seemed to be a kind of interlude of pure fantasy when all along the line from the Yser Canal, Hooge, Wytschaete, Messones, they had passed thousands upon thousands of soldiers moving up, all pointing towards the objective of Passchendaele they were to take. Men were packed together on every road, lying in ditches, massing past the canal locks. Those facing the Messines Ridge where the going would be the hardest were apprehensive under their tin hats. The nightingales continued singing.

It was 2:20 ack-emma as the British read it, and resting under the earth deep down, rumor was that a million pounds of TNT and dynamite were packed in long tunnels under the enemy lines, to be set off before dawn.

Benji leaned against his ambulance and listened to the birds. He turned to Hank, who was lighting a cigarette, his back to the night breeze, the tiny flame making a bloom in the dark.

"Do you hear the damn nightingales?"

"Benji, how the hell do you know they're nightingales?"

"A captain with General Plummer of the Second Army told me."

"How would he know?" Hank was a bit keyed up as in the next hours men went listlessly, or in fear, to their expected deaths.

It was clear as the dismal battle ground to a murderous

standstill that the British had gotten nowhere. General Haig boldly issued a distorted official version of events.

Walking down Bond Street, Rawly bought a newspaper from a shouting newsboy:

> YPRES SALIENT WIDENED TWO MILES IN ADVANCE!
> *"We have broken the German Lines on the whole front."* Haig.

Rawly found Willie in the Edwardian hotel lobby where tea was being served. He was with a neat young woman in uniform whom he introduced as Lady Jessica Brett-Tyndal. She was a tall plain girl with a marvelous peach skin, large feet, and small hands. She was about twenty-eight years of age, Rawly's expert eyes told him, and one of her sleeves had a black mourning band on it. The way Willie handed over the watercress sandwiches made Rawly suddenly stare at him; fat, bald Willie at forty-four. Look at him—just from his posture, the way he hovered over the woman with a feeling for the amenities, it was clear Willie was in love.

"What do you think of the news, Lady Jessica?"

"A bit thick, rather."

Willie said, "She's at the War Office. It's all lies, Jessica says. Sir Douglas is faking the news."

"Would he dare?" Rawly asked.

"Would he not," said Jessica Brett-Tyndal, "Would he bloody not, the bloody barstard."

The ambulances were no longer serviceable. Even if functional, they were in horrible condition from their constant transporting of bodies, flayed bloody tissues. It seemed best to burn them, but no one would give the order. So they were abandoned one dawn, and Benji took over some lorries.

They asked for and were given leave, as the burial squads continued their work. Benji and Hank went off to Paris. Hank was to go to join an air wing—his permit had at last come through. Rawly would meet them in Paris. It was no secret among the officers that the Third

Battle of Ypres was a major disaster for the British. They had gained 9,000 yards at a cost of 245,000 men.

Benji and Hank sat with Rawly in a little café on the Boulevard Montparnasse looking out at the blustery November day. Now that America was in the war, there was some animation among the Paris gendarmes, waiters, doormen. There were even a few American flags on the Rue Cardinal Lemoine and the Place Contrescarpe.

"Your Uncle Willie thinks the horror of Passachendaele Ridge is the beginning of the end of the British empire, even when the war is finally won."

Benji was looking out at the taxis sounding their Citroën horns, at the whores and *poivrottes* with whom he wanted no more adventures.

"He really think that?"

"He's not in his right mind. He's fallen in love, and at his age. Some long-toothed titled English widow, Lady Something-or-other."

"The British Empire," said Hank drinking Pouilly Fuissé with his oysters. "It will always be there."

"Of course," said Rawly. It was to be one of two major international misjudgments of a brilliant life, vastly wise and knowledgeable in worldly matters. Rawly had paid little attention to what was happening in Russia, feeling, as he had told Willie, "Those damn Russkis are always flogging each other with whips or birch branches and reading Dostoevski. The same cocksuckers will run things badly as usual in the end."

"Will they continue the war?" asked Benji. "My friend John Reed, a Harvard man, thinks not."

"That settles it. A Harvard man . . . Oh, *garçon*. I don't suppose they have Scotch. No, make it a bottle of Gevrey-Chambertin. How can anyone drink that *vin cassis* and *marc*."

Benji, to show off, said *"Garçon, double fines à l'eau."*

Hank was wearing a Burberry military raincoat he had bought from an English officer. He held up his glass. "I'm going to be flying soon, Uncle Rawly. Here's to victory for our side."

"Damn silly thing, Hank, you flying. Those crates—that damn Sopwith Camel is made of toilet paper and toothpicks."

"Spads, Uncle Rawly. They're fine machines. The best in the air."

Rawly shrugged. He was fed up with Europe—the misery of it, the ruins, the sodden, hungry, sad-eyed people. He wanted to be home at Greenhills. The new version was being worked on while he was here with these wet-nosed kids who talked big and fancy. "Benji, you come back with me. I can get you out of the ambulance corps. And it's time, if you don't want to finish college, to learn something about railroading and mining. The Ball-Kingston companies need new young blood."

"Don't say 'blood.' And I'm sorry, Dad, but I'm thinking of staying on in Paris when the war is over."

Rawly looked calm, but surprised. "What the hell ever for? Oh, sure, it's a place of fun and games, or was. And they certainly made screwing easy and pleasant here. But I'm not *too* crazy about the French. I mean, of course, I'm sorry for them, the war and all. But in nineteen-twelve and nineteen-thirteen when I was here with your mother, they were nasty. They are real bastards."

"I want to write, seriously."

"Write in Denver, San Francisco."

"You don't understand. There are Americans here, been here a long time. This Leo Stein is a brain. I mean a modern mind, new way of thinking about art forms, and—"

Rawly grimaced. "Stay away from Jews, Benji. I like them. You can trust them in business, and they really keep their word. And this artist writing thing is just an excuse for lazy living for trashy people. I mean you're somebody, a Kingston. We build railroads, we dig mines, we own banks. Stay in your own pasture, Benji. Hell, I collect first editions; you'll be able to afford it."

"I think I can be a great writer. A good poet, perhaps. You have to understand that—"

"So we're Philistines? Listen, your Uncle Willie is a real picture collector. Lucy's been painted by Sargent. And me and Wilma have collections of Catlins, Remington, and Winslow Homers we're proud of."

"Provincial dabblers," said Benji. "You ever hear of Matisse, Vlaminck, Picasso?"

"Why shouldn't I? I'm no horse's ass, you know, Benji, so you better stop making me out a dope before I knock you down." He turned, winked to Hank. "I don't know what your snotty generation is coming to. No manners, no respect for values. I'm a bit of an outlaw myself, but you all think you know the answer to everything."

"Uncle Rawly, there's a way of life here we find different and exciting."

Benji said earnestly, "I don't say it's better, but it's less material, not lived on such a dreary buck-grabbing level."

"Spare me," said Benji's father.

Later Rawly remembered that his son Benjamin had been among the first, perhaps the very first postwar American expatriate in Paris of the Lost Generation, although Benji never used that expression.

Willie in love, even in war-worn London, was an animated, delighted person. If love had come so late, it had come to him with a force, almost a fury, that to an onlooker might appear somewhat ridiculous. In his middle forties—good tailors never successfully fitted him, his hat never seemed just right—he was as pleased as a schoolboy with his first crush on a teacher. He had not denied himself an occasional woman in the past, but he had none of the sensual urges, the itchy needs of his father Enoch, his brother Rawly. His sexual experience had been pleasant enough, but not particularly vital or ecstatic. Frankly, to himself, he admitted at times, *what* the hell was all the agony, shouting and lamenting about, that people put into this sort of rather tacky nonsense. It seemed to consist of smells, sweat, pores, moles, clumps of hair, long toenails. Sex was to remain for him a dreadfully overrated game arranged by Nature to produce reasons for sending birthday gifts to nice nephews and nieces.

What attracted Willie to Jessica Brett-Tyndal was an awareness of his loneliness. For he had, as he thought of it, like Dante's traveler, in the middle of his life, and perhaps a bit past it, found himself in the dark woods of being along. The life of a banker, he sometimes thought, but not too often, is full self-abnegation. And yet, being so much himself, it had begun to frighten him. Like most fat people who seemed to others so jolly and amusing, so well adjusted and delightful to be with, inside lived another being—a Willie neither witty nor forbearing—one who knew the clown was sad—a trite but true condition of those who amused others and made them laugh.

In Willie's case, there was also a realization that he had reached the ultimate querulous pleasure of being an art collector. It is a sterile game—he had decided—to buy paint plastered on small panels. For the object possessed, its cost, its rareness, had replaced for him, as with most collectors, the beauty or wonder, and the skill of the picture or print itself. Besides, the dishonesty and greed, the lies of dealers, self-serving critics, the limp-wristed museum staffs—all had made the game even more indecent and a swindle. On the trip to England on the matter of the credits and loans to the Allied war effort, he had been reading some of Freud, just translated into English, and had agreed that the rich collector was a kind of flattered slob, the kind of person who disliked to go to the toilet and give up anything to flush away.

He had met Jessica when she was detailed by the War Office to show him about the city of London and take him to meet certain people interested in loans to Middle East countries, the Greeks and others, who were being courted to fully support the war against the Central Powers.

She had an attractive voice that some found too distant and crisp; an anchored serenity, Willie felt. She was well-built, but long in face with the blue eyes of a Siamese cat, taffy-colored hair and that marvelous English country skin. She was, she told Willie with a distracted smile, a war widow. Captain Anthony Brett-Tyndal—son of a good family—having been killed (she always referred to his end as "fallen") very early in the war in the retreat from Mons. There had been two children after nine years of marriage, and an existence at a not too flourishing farm in Surrey. (The idea all titled people were rich was wrong, Willie soon discovered.) Young Tony was eight, and Rosemary, six. They lived in a flat in a mews, the children taken care of by Jessica's Aunt Nina, who, in a long yellow smock, amber beads, and a cigarette in one corner of her mouth, painted lampshades made of a parchmentlike paper for Harrods. Painted dragons, knights in armor—"Castles, my dear, and eagles," as Aunt Nina put it, "for the American trade." She could play the tambourine and the bones, having at some time in life been in a minstrel show in Blackpool.

They were all delighted with Willie and his food packages, his humor; he had a fine, easy way with children. When Tony came home for the holidays from a famous but second-rate school, the boy was delighted to have a man take him about to reconnoiter the war-busy city. If the appearance of Willie and Jessica together amused some people (she was nearly a head taller, he a foot or more wider), they didn't care. He was round—even his head— but not at all unattractive. He had handsome features a bit overpadded, and a nose just a bit too small. But it was soon clear that they found themselves entertained and amused by each other. Jessica, sunk into an introspective emptiness, had had a hard time of it, and the future seemed grim. Besides the pension as a war widow, and the little paid her at the War Office where she was really a hardship case, she had nothing to offer office or business. She could not type, or work codes, or trace plans. She served mostly to prepare tea trays for hush-hush meetings or to drive some stuffed shirt War Office visitors, vital to someone in the government and if invited for a drink, keep their hand from creeping up her splendid leg and thigh.

She, like Willie, was not a sensual person, and had always felt the sexual act a sticky carry-over from the aborigines. The late captain was a feeble performer who felt his duty was to produce heirs to the family's coat of arms, a bit of the nasty, but to Jessica, a wifely duty.

"We are a matched pair," Willie told her one night in a pub called The Three Crowns, as they drank pink gins and enjoyed a kind of cheerful insouciance. They were making a night of it with the theater (*The Importance of Being Earnest*) and a supper later at a club to which Willie had a guest card. Willie made no improper gesture, had not gone beyond holding Jessica's hand, and a delightful quick kiss of thanks on her cheek as she took her latch key out to let herself into her mews flat. Aunt Nina, cigarette smoke in her eyes, was reading a thriller and drinking 'arf and 'arf. "I'd have him if he asks you, American or not."

"Don't be preposterous, Auntie."

On his way back to America, Rawly met Willie at the American embassy in London to receive certain documents which were to be turned over to Morgan & Co.—papers pertaining to some unpublished State Department aspects of Allied loans that had to be kept secret from the public. Enoch's friend J. P. Morgan had died in 1913, but the son and the firm had arranged many of the loans and credits for the Allies, acting as purchasing agents for France, Russia, Belgium, Serbia, Montenegro, even Japan.

Seated in an Embassy office done with too many eagles and rather overheated (the embassy got extra coal rations), Willie hastily explained he was staying on in England for a few more weeks, "In London, that is."

Rawly lit one of the long thin cigars he favored over his father's fat Havanas. "I suppose it is this long-legged bit of fluff."

"Now, Rawly, be as bawdy as you like about anything else. I'm damned serious about Jessica."

"Jesus, man, the irrational in human behavior—at your age? And how serious is she?"

"I amuse her, entertain her. We like doing things together. Not what you think."

"Wasn't thinking of any slap-and-tickle. What the devil is getting into the family? You like a simpering schoolboy. Benji thinking a Paris attic and dirty feet is productive of great literature. And Hank going up in those tissue-paper planes. I think the war has unbalanced the whole frigging world."

Willie let his laughter shake his belly. "Yes, yes, and you, Rawly always building some kind of Xanadu among the deer spats. It's hopeless with Jessica, I suppose, but—"

They shook hands and parted. A U-boat trailed Rawly's ship for two days and then lost it in the fog.

39

The butler Ruxton—not the original, but a nephew ("They breed them over there in England—butlers, like prize show dogs," Enoch had claimed)—came across the sun porch Lucy had added that year to Kingston House, and where she and Enoch sat at breakfast. Ruxton II carried an envelope on a silver tray.

"Pardon, but this was just brought up from the town. A cable."

Lucy, as if in some sudden fear of bad news, put a hand up to one cheek. "No, I hope not."

Enoch took the envelope off the tray. At age sixty-seven there was a slight tremor in his hand to which he paid no attention. His grip was still strong, fingers powerful as ever, he insisted; he tore open the envelope. "I hope it isn't Benji. Why the hell do they send these things . . . Oh." He looked up at Lucy over his gold-rimmed glasses, "Isn't bad news at all."

"What then, Enoch?"

"Nobody dead in battle."

"Very gratifying," said Ruxton II.

"Enoch. No games."

"I'll read it. PLEASED TO REPORT MARRIED THIS DATE TO LADY JESSICA BRETT-TYNDAL (is that a name for real?) VERY HAPPY KNOW YOU BOTH WILL BE TOO SAILING USA NEXT WEEK
WILLIAM

Ruxton II put the discarded envelope on the tray. "Congratulations, sir, madam." He went out. (Brett-Tyndal? Once a rather good house. He must check in *Burke's*.)

Lucy laughed, a pressure off her ample chest. "Oh, that Willie. You think it's a joke?"

"Christ, no. Figure that—at his age putting his head in the noose!"

"His age? You weren't actually senile at his age, dear."

"But Willie? I never figured he was much interested in women. Now, Rawly—"

"Spare me the Kingstons' high scoring—as it's crudely put out here—in horniness."

"It's more fun than the preacher who said, 'He who loves his fellow man plants trees.' "

Lucy was not angry, but amused at how casual Kingston men were about some things. She and Enoch had adjusted well into a set pattern of living together that pleased—or at least adjusted painlessly—to the life of both of them. She knew of Enoch's sexual adventures, but as long as he carried on away from Kingston House, she made no issue of it. ("Don't bring the feathers home," as Willie had once put it.) Enoch and Lucy loved each other; he never mentioned how much he disliked her sense of duty as a social matriarch, a pillar of Southern California society—those people she liked to entertain at Kingston House. She was still beautiful—if one did not come too close to her to see the crinkly, crepy skin, notice the high-collared dresses that hid a rather plump but raddled neck. One was impressed by Lucy's carriage, her poise, her never abdicating from a responsibility.

Enoch was grateful to her for all the years, the bad years, since Rawly had taken over the railroad. They had traveled, he so bored by Greek ruins, rotting Gothic cathedrals, and ancient castles with cabbages growing in the drained moats. "All those views of the Swiss Alps, a country stood on end, made of chocolate, cows, and goiters on the women. Hardly seemed worth visiting." He had been inspecting what was the start of the Berlin-Baghdad rail-line when in 1914 war clouds had sent him back to America the day France mobilized. And Enoch read of the Schlieffen plan and the stand on the Marne in a cottage they had rented on Ochre Point at Newport.

The years had not been merely travel, sitting at Kingston House being served hot coffee by Ruxton II, or Enoch's getting drunk with discretion in some sporting house, or buying some tart a flask of perfume besides leaving two gold eagles on the mantlepiece, after having trouble lacing up his shoes.

Enoch had remained active in the railroad junction yards, working with a bright young Scot named Randy MacDonald on plans for a new kind of train engine being talked about—a diesel, an oil-burner. They had German and Swedish blueprints—stolen, most likely. From these he and Mac were working out a practical design of a diesel for American tracks. The right size, the proper weight, the ability to pull passenger varnish or sixty to eighty freight cars and a caboose, with no strain.

In the yards at the foundry the men, behind Enoch's back, (he knew) called it E. K.'s Trolley Car. But the Blessinger Foundry at St. Louis was building him a sample set of wheels and platform, and Westinghouse had a contract to build an actual diesel train motor. All going slowly, damn it. War orders came first, and certain steels and precision-milled parts had to be bought with no questions asked as to price or where procured. But maybe with the war over in a year or so, the Blessinger-Kingston Diesel Company could begin production. Yes, *then* let Rawly come begging for the engines.

Enoch had never really gotten over losing control of the W. G.P. & G. Now the line was more prosperous than ever, carrying troops, supplies, wheat, and secret cargoes along its thousands of miles of track. The trains serviced by monstrous-sized junctions so much bigger than the backwater Kingston Junction. It was overshadowed by huge acres in Louisiana, Texas, and yards in Charleston, St. Petersburg. Just across from Washington, the Kingston Division spread was now the headquarters of the entire system. The damn modernization caused by war had made Kingston Junction a kind of historic relic, but it still serviced the trains through the pass and the special sleepers going south to Texas and New Orleans. But the W. G.P. & G. was not merely the Southwest, but a larger system in the South, and the Southeast from Florida up the Eastern Shore. The Western divisions were only one-third of the system now. The bulk of the passenger service, the freight handling, tank cars, steer shipments, belonged elsewhere. Only the war need for cars had kept the Kingston yards and shops from laying off a good half of their workers, mechanics, forge, and repair crews. (Willie pitied Enoch; "Poor bastard, he's like Napoleon on St. Helena, scratching his balls and telling everybody how smart his failures were.")

The war's end would see many changes; Enoch knew that. But his diesel would save the junction. He'd open a Western division for diesels in the old sheds—revive Kingston Junction, the town. Already many of the workers' houses stood empty, the abodes of stray cats, kid gangs smoking butts in the empty rooms and breaking out the windows. Most of the Negroes had departed for the big money in the shipyards. The younger men were off to become part of the AEF. Singing those crazy songs as he heard them one day when the troop train in the Kansas through-service stopped to take on water. "K-K-K-Katy." "Pack Up Your Troubles in Your Old Kit Bag." And "Smiles?" Nothing as finger-snapping as the old ragtime tunes or that jazz the darkies were playing in Nell Kimball's sporting house in Storyville.

After breakfast, Ruxton II discreetly brushing some crumbs off his master's vest, Enoch left for the junction, driven down in the Franklin, a motorcar he liked. Biff O'Hara was at the wheel, a young reform school mick two years from Ireland—Enoch had guaranteed him a job. He drove rather too carefully. O'Hara was small and dark ("Sure me great-great-grandda, he swum ashore from the Spanish Armada when, as is well known, it was wrecked off Galway.") Actually, O'Hara was a particularly inept house burglar. Biff's uncle—granduncle, really—had been a ballast tamper on the old L.A. & S.P. line—so Biff had received a chance for honest work in Enoch's employ. Enoch figured he really never stole more than ten gallons of gasoline a week, at fourteen cents a gallon.

"My son Willie got married in England."

Biff O'Hara made an O of thumb and forefinger. "The best to him and the missus. I'm sure he'll be happy."

"I'm only sure I got up this morning. Get rolling."

O'Hara drove well, with a kind of controlled natural grace. He took curves skillfully, just a bit too fast while passing the packing plant, a branch of a Chicago firm.

"*Phew*, sir. They really brew up a reek in the morning, don't they?"

They were passing a huge structure surrounded by cattle corrals and rows of high chimneys pouring out a thick, evil smoke with a smell that seemed to creep across the mesa like a cloud and curdle the earth.

"They're canning meat for the war," Enoch said. "I suppose it is necessary. But I wonder anyone could eat the stuff."

"You have too. I did me time, three months at Dix, before they found me bad record. It's whale shit, sir, they're putting in the tins."

Enoch was aware the bribed Federal inspectors didn't mind the diseased condition of the steers, even a few horses and mules, if gossip was true, that went into the bully beef the Allied soldiers ate. As the car came abreast of the main gates, Enoch looked over at some rock formations that hadn't been blasted away, and saw that right here had been Peppertree Lane, and nearby a crazy sheep rancher, and a witch that sold damn bad whisky. And the house was *where* . . . ? It was painful to recall . . . not easy to bring up memories. . . . *Say it, think it.* I had come here so many times to make love to Brook. Oh, God, oh, Christ, I was damn happy then. Crazy happy.

He allowed himself the one cigar he was permitted at noon, and lit it now in the car—as a kind of burnt offering to his great love. Yes, much as I had loved Maude, and now love Lucy, it's nothing to what I felt for the gold-skinned girl, that crazy, feisty, angry little bitch. All I have left of that time to stir my groin is a witless dream. I was wrong not to have taken her, gone off lickety-split to live in Europe. What am I now? A crackpot with a ticker that races or slows up, and I have to swallow pills to keep me on an even keel. Nothing, nothing, a vault full of engraved paper, a set of blueprints. I'm a bucket of ashes, that's what I am. Sons grown away, and one as mean as a polecat. Grandchildren—just names and faces and little asses to pat and send a check to on birthdays. Mollie embalmed alive with the better people of San Francisco. Benji? Hell, some kind of a nut, up to his navel in radical Bolshevistic thinking. Maybe the twins—Nick and

Howard—would be something along the line of the old Kingston stock.

For all these gewgaws I gave up Brook, gave up myself, me, that dumb kid with his ideas of tropical islands and golden girls on white sand. A bucket of ashes, a goddamn bucket of ashes.

Down in the big shed at the junction they were stripping a locomotive the K-2B, a Mallet ten-wheeler, sixty tons, one of his favorites. Giving it the yearly tear-down, removing the wheels, the running gear being disengaged, and bolts burned off.

Enoch stood outside the range of the sparks of the cutting torches, smelling hot steel, inhaling, he felt, his own life, his past. Pipes, pumps, and cylinder domes were unscrewed, asbestos lagger removed and when the boiler and frame were sandblasted, Enoch moved out of range.

That old teakettle, the K-2B, and he had made many a run, and if it weren't for the war, K-2B would be rusting at some siding, horned toads in residence, or cut up and shipped in bits to Michigan to be turned into flivvers or manure forks. The war had given old K-2B new life. He liked to spend hours here watching locomotive parts being lowered into the lye vats for bathing clean, watch flues being loosened and chipped for water scale. This had to be done once a year on the W. G.P. & G. Enoch made the rule and they hadn't changed it; maybe they cheated a bit. Rawly ran a good railroad, but wasn't too watchful, didn't know work crews or foremen like his father. Now the crew often skipped a need for a new firebox, new plate steel where it was necessary, or air pumps, valves, gauges, properly cleaned and restored. No, the war had made full repairs and strip-down work scarce and far between. It was no way to run a railroad, even if it was making a hell of a lot of money and paying fat dividends. He walked out to the yard where a Baldwin engine, reassembled, was being tested by a breaking-in crew. The engineer, his white hair sticking out from a high crowned rail cap shouted "Want to take the throttle, E.K.?"

"Some other time, Walter." (Walter had been at the Battle of Outlaw Pass. Walter *what*? Memory getting dusty.)

He waved off the invitation and went back to the small machine shop that he had made his own. Here was his true past, some models of early locomotives, a Spanish saddle with silver mounting, a relic from his days as a young sport. Living at Irish Agnes's boardinghouse in Los Angeles, and popping his *cojones* at Madame Needle's knocking shop, gambling with Pistol Johnson, a fist full of gold eagles, a cheroot in one corner of his mouth—and hoping for another ace. Christ, am I really nearly seventy, in three more years? Yes—that's the bad hand dealt you—you have to play it. Somehow it has been a crowded life, and yet it lacks climax, a fitting finish. I'm not much different than a cinder-dick knocking bindlestiffs and boomers off freight cars when they steal rides. Only difference I have more money—money I don't need or care about. What a lie, still lying to myself. Money is a good thing—only a love of money isn't. Who the Sam Hill said that to me?

Enoch drifted off to sleep in his big chair, a chair with the buffalo robe seat and back. He dreamed he was riding the caboose of a long freight, drinking cowboy coffee (eggshell in the pot to settle it) while the train slowly went by stations and crossings he hadn't seen in two generations. Dominguez, Monte Vista, Red Cliff, Vesta Pass, and Pagosa Junction. Pagosa Junction, where he had lived a week with one of the Carson girls. Hayes Carson was depot boss there, with a redheaded wife and two redheaded daughters—in time I'd managed to sleep with all three—the wife, too. (Ruby?), the most beautiful of them all. The sweat drying on our bodies in the night wind, the honeysuckles in the yard smelling up the world. Hayes Carson became division superintendent that year.

Enoch came awake with a bit of fast pumping of his heart, to find Mac, the Scottish engine designer shaking him. "E.K., din' ya want to see the final plans for our diesel?"

Enoch clawed his way up from sleep into full awakening. "What? *What*, Mac? Damn you, I wasn't asleep. Just thinking of the dead-man-control lever on our project."

"You allus snore when you think?"

No respect. No respect at all, Enoch thought, as he followed Mac into the shed behind the machine shop. On the west wall, over a three-foot mock-up of the Blessinger-Kingston Diesel, was tacked the cross-section plan of their project—the IOA, the final version Enoch was sure, once built, would revolutionize railroading in America. He admitted there had been diesel talk for a time and some models built, but nothing like this one which he and Mac and the foundry back East in St. Louis had decided to risk building as a prototype.

"Thirteen hundred fifty horsepower, three units to a train. Hell, the Pennsy, they tried a gasoline car in nineteen-oh-five, but this one is an oil burner."

"Rockefeller will rob more, get richer."

"Four times as much power from the fuel than from a steamer, Mac."

"That would be about it."

Mac was a cautious Scot, and the burr in his voice was never cheerful or full of hope. Biff O'Hara came in carrying a big tin lunch bucket. "Shall I be laying a cloth?"

"Runs on pistons and bearing shells. No firebox, Mac, no boilers . . . Oh, spread it on a table, anyplace."

"Anyplace?" Biff pushed away some papers.

"No boilers."

"Thats the hull idea, sir."

He, Mac and O'Hara sat on a workbench eating fried chicken sections. "We'll make a tender to hold three thousand gallons of fuel, eight thousand gallons of water for the Pullman compartment sinks and toilets."

"A bit on the large side for our diesel."

But Enoch just put a thumb to a crumpled corner of the plan drawing and smoothed it out.

O'Hara said, "There's pie, but missus say not for you, E.K. There's cheese and an apple."

"I'll attach my private car to it, plate glass and burled walnut, crystal lamps, onyx lav fixtures—attach it all to the first diesel out of the Blessinger St. Louis shops. I'll hand out cigars and bourbon on every line across the continent, taking orders with both fists."

"You're eating pie, E.K."

Mac looked up at the model. "Well, there's this woor on and we haven't built or tested anything on wheels yet,

354

have we? Westinghouse says they can't build the engine until woor orders slack off."

"I'll put a hot coal up their prat and get them working on it right away."

At dusk, as O'Hara drove him back to Kingston House, Enoch felt it had been a good day. He was no old doddering fool. He knew the future belonged to a practical diesel, and he had it within reach. Let Rawly put *that* in his pipe and smoke it; he snapped his fingers—*see*, hardly a tremor . . .

On a clear afternoon, Lieutenant Henry Kingston Emerson made his fifth kill over Ponte Mousson, downing a single-seater Albatross. Later he received a report that a German plane was over Mont Mihiel guarded by *Jagdstaffel* interceptors, very high above the Archies trying to reach it. When it got within range and was hit by antiaircraft fire, it went spiraling down. It looked like a goner, but it recovered and, like a wounded goose, began to labor back to its base. Lt. Emerson, like a good sportsman, decided to go up again and put the wounded creature out of its misery. His own ship was not fueled. He asked if a plane on the field was ready and armed. He was told by a mechanic there was, and set off in the Nieuport.

It was a seven-mile chase. Lieutenant Emerson got up to 2,000 feet, ducking the *Jagdstaffel*. He began firing at the enemy photo-reconnaissance plane. Some observers on the ground said they sensed that his guns jammed and that he circled while he cleared them. Then he came in on the German plane again, from the rear. The enemy gunner got off one quick burst. The Nieuport showed flames and went into a shallow dive straight ahead.

Lieutenant Emerson felt he could reach his airfield in the gathering twilight. Darkness was thick as he circled twice, trying to study the murky field and its smoky flares set up to light him down. He came in for a landing with a banging, jolting sound. The plane had snagged its wheels on a high tension cable, slingshotting the machine onto the turf, smashing it down on its nose, then somersaulting it across the field. In horror, men ran toward the wreck. Lieutenant Emerson had been rocketed from the cockpit, his safety belt tearing loose. His legs were broken and he had fearful internal injuries. He was still conscious. In great pain, he heard another plane overhead and muttered to a Captain Tanney, who was helping carry him, "If that fellow gets down all right, he can thank me for taking the goddamn wire out of his way. . . ."

Captain Tanney rode with Lieutenant Emerson in the ambulance to Gerardmer. They sang favorite songs as the pain grew worse. The hospital doctors did not think the injuries were too serious, but by morning Hank was in a coma and the doctors had changed their views, saying it was a blood clot in the brain. Unconscious, he was never to come out of his coma. Fellow fliers stood by as the dying man was given the rank of captain and the Légion d'Honneur to add to his Médaille Militaire and Croix de Guerre. Hank received the full military dress parade burial at Luxeuil, with a firing detail, and the bugle dirge of a very slow taps.

40

Finally, in shattered misery, the war ended. The Great War—Benji remembered—as it was to be called for a generation, until he saw it given a number, as the first of a series. Rawly came back in 1918 to draw plans for a new wing to an already fresh section of Greenhills. Then he went back to the Peace Conference with Woodrow Wilson, and later assisted Herbert Hoover, a mining engineer, with relief trains for famine and epidemic-filled nations in Eastern Europe. Relief sent over broken rails and weak bridges to feed the typhus-riddled, starving victims of defeat and revolution. He wound up in a quick visit to Paris where Benji was living in a drafty studio on the Rue Dupuytren. Benji wearing corduroy pants and a Basque fisherman's shirt. He was writing a novel, but the few sheets he pointed to, as his father sat on the only studio chair, didn't look impressive. "I'm influenced by Dada, the music of Ravel, but it's American in its background."

"You'll need more pages that that to make a book, Benji."

"I've some out being retyped."

Besides a continual draft, the studio was dusty, the ceiling rain-streaked.

"You enjoy this mess? No heat, a cot to sleep on, a privy two flights down that announces itself. Your grandfather houses his hound dogs better."

"It's what I want, and you don't have to give me a big allowance. The rate of exchange is favorable."

"I don't intend to starve you out of here. You'll stay on or come home. You can go to the devil in your own way. Aunt Mollie wants to know about Hank. Write her a long letter."

357

Benji looked at an unframed cubist painting on a wall, done by an Italian girl he was trying to get to move in with him. "Bad luck, I guess. Running into those *Jagdstaffel* interceptors. Bad luck."

"It certainly is, getting shot, going down in flames."

"Truth is someone got a lucky burst in—and he hit a wire in the dark . . . Two more days, I mean, and the war was over. He already had the Croix and the Médaille Militaire. He insisted on flying and the Aviatik photo plane got him."

They went to the Dôme, father and son, for drinks, to sit on the terrace. It seemed all the Americans did it. Benji introduced Rawly to Ford Madox Ford and a Romanian prince, and both let Rawly pay for their *marc-cassis* . . . Rawly left Paris and after a quick trip to Rome to buy some marble statues and red and gold damask wall covering for Greenhills, he was back home to add still another wing. Wilma had developed a talent for interior decorating. It took her mind off the problems of the adolescent twins, Nick and Howard.

All through 1919 and 1920, Rawly kept insisting the place was ready, but it was not until June of 1921 that the formal opening of the new Greenhills took place. Willie came up north with his wife and her children. Willie had adopted Tony and Rosemary legally. The sun had destroyed Jessica's pink skin—she was a good solid tan and had taken up tennis seriously. The kids were called Kingston-Tyndal.

Mollie Emerson didn't come; she was going into menopause, and was more than a little mad, cursing Rawly over the phone: "You and yours killed my son Henry. It was that damn Benji let him go up in those planes. You were there, had influence. I'll *never* forgive any of you. My little Henry."

It was no use explaining that Hank wanted to fly, so between brother and sister a silence took over, with now and then some reports that Mollie still insisted to all who would listen that the Kingstons had encouraged Hank to become a war flier.

Greenhills was popular and almost showed a profit. In a smoke-filled room, as the press reported, with a dozen others, Rawly helped nominate a likable fellow named

Warren Harding as a good and honorable man for the White House ("Besides, he can be handled.") Later Rawly turned to Al Smith, who was for bringing back alcohol as a beverage and meant it, and Rawly was to vote Democrat for the only time in his life.

The hotel he built—his dream idea of comfort and splendor—Greenhills, was run badly because he saw it as an ideal, and not a business project. He always had a love of living in high gear and was not ashamed of his way of doing things: *"Quelle élégance, quelle distinction,"* as one of his chefs once put it.

He became a member of the Pacific Union Club on the top of Nob Hill. It was a very exclusive club, the privileged male nook of the best coastal families who, as Enoch's song had it, had clear ancestral lines of miners and whores.

Actually, Rawly hardly ever entered the Pacific Union Club. Asked why he retained his membership, he said, "I might want to have a drink there someday."

The visible signs of Ralston Kingston in the 1920s were his clothes. He was always remembered as a fancy liver and a nifty dresser. He bought his clothes from Henry Poole of Cork Street, London, silks at Sulka, jewels and gold cases at Shreve's, San Francisco; Mappin & Webb, Burlington Arcade, London; Van Cleef & Arpels, Paris, or from Stronitherm's, the royal goldsmith on Dover Street.

When his partner, Leepole Ball, died suddenly in a Turkish bath in San Francisco—keeled right over in the steam room with never a sound—Rawly had a special London black coat made to mourn a dear and close friend.

Willie, living simply but spaciously in Santa Barbara, said, "Rawly makes of his life a work of art. He sees existence as a fabulous chain of possibilities. Life is art to him in the sense Marcel Proust—whom he's never read—expressed it:

The great quality of true art is that it rediscovers, grasps, and reveals to us that reality far from which we live . . . that we might die without having known and which is simply out life, real life, life finally discovered and clarified, the only life that has been really lived—that life which in one sense is to be found any time in all men as well as in artists. . . ."

Jessica said, "I find Proust not up to Virginia Woolf. He's rather a cad, a climber, isn't he?"

Willie had expanded into a good husband in a bland and respectable marriage—rather dull to others, but very satisfactory to Mr. and Mrs. William Kingston. The children called him Daddo.

Wilma felt Jessica was "a frigid bitch with ice water in her veins," but Rawly rather like her. She played brilliant bridge, and Rawly was a bridge fiend. He also kidnapped the manager and the chef of the Palace Hotel with promises of great rewards. The chef de cuisine, Bouie, and he hunted wild game in Utah seated in a Pierce-Arrow— Bouie steering with his elbow, and both popping away at the deer and the antelope with twelve-gauge shotguns, Bouie still able in a few days to supervise a *fête champêtre* for Rawly and guests in the evening.

Rawly was no tinhorn piker. The hotel cost him three million dollars in a period when a million was still worth a million. The young people coming back from the ritual trip to Paris in the 1920s—who had read Freud, Jung, and maybe Marx, or had met Hemingway, Fitzgerald, they liked Greenhills, and Rawly was to them fun and odd. As Waldo Gaylord explained, "Class, he has *that*—the kind that called for clean, starched shirts, and diamonds in the ears of the girls. None of the old Noodle Flats roughhouse. No, Rawly Kingston, he's turning with the times." He was certainly turning more eccentric.

There was an ice-skating rink, a riding hall with fifty horses ready for saddling; and Rawly in his best riding breeches, tweed jacket, and hard collar with a stick-pinned cravat. Outdoors he had pools built for real seals he imported from California and Alaska. But the seals, intelligent animals, preferred the animated social life of the lobby, and were often there flapping flippers and barking for herring tidbits while shaking water onto the guests and the velvet sofas.

Waldo was to insist the World War changed Rawly; its sights close up threw something in him out of balance. To

Waldo, Rawly's efforts at Greenhills was a tragic charade, a sign of a deteriorating interest in major projects, he felt. Rawly's interest in the railroad, the mines, the smelters was growing less and less. He said he had perfectly reliable managers, clever accountants, engineers, time-study experts. He felt he had created a perfect system for producing wealth. He was unaware that the 1920s was a period when practically every project made money, every corporation's assets were overvalued, watered stocks seemed to be always rising on the stock exchange. Rawly neglected to contract for Enoch's Blessinger-Kingston Diesels which, by 1925, were being used successfully on rival roads. Waldo had met with Enoch several times, and he felt the old man was more stable than Rawly.

"I like steam trains," Rawly told Waldo in the Frontier Room where once his father had (or had not) slapped him. "I don't care for diesels, even E.K.'s—I'm pleased the old boy put them over."

"Diesels get four times as much from fuel as steam locomotives."

"But they're ugly. Look like suppositories on wheels."

"Ralston." Waldo never called him Rawly. "This country is held together by great family fortunes. It's the job of lawyers to see these fortunes continue to exist, expand, from generation to generation, by investments in land, in patents, in grasping the future value of things like diesels, and setting up of funds, now that income taxes are rising."

Rawly disliked talking of "after-I'm-gone," of heirs.

"There will be enough for everybody—Nick's cars and Howard's gambling. The only lawyers I ever liked where Uncle Charlie and you."

"Thank you. I value that statement. But will you let me set up trusts and funds in various ways so the family will be like the Astors, Vanderbilts, Guggenheims, Morgans—still solid to change or panic?"

"Let me see some ideas you have on paper. And keep it short."

"Heirs by profligacy and sloth can do great damage."

"So can seals."

Rawly exiled the seals as alien to the mountains of the West, and brought in pink flamingos which were supposed to stand around in the pools and look beautiful. Wilma said, "Rather Alice-in-Wonderland decor." They were worse than the seals. Animal life didn't seem to be the right note at Greenhills, so the birds went. For sporty riding, Rawly bought half a dozen yellow Stutz Bearcats, autos that, like predatory leopards, endangered life on primitive roads.

Back when Prohibition seemed a gloomy cloud on good living, Rawly had already begun to stock on alcohol in freight car-sized shipments, in truckloads, buying wines and whiskies by the hundred-case lots. Charles and Company sent out a thousand cases of champagne, bringing it to Greenhills on the W. G.P. & G. freight cars, gunslingers riding shotgun to protect it from highjackers. Rawly bought out stocks of existing liquor from hotels without vision of the desert ahead. All went down to a mine tunnel under Greenhill. Wines were of the best: madeira, port, sherry and brandies, all protected by locked vaults and tough mine guards. Rawly felt he was giving élan to a dry milieu. Truth was, Willie said, "Rawly at fifty is bored to death."

Nick Kingston at twenty-two, one of the twins, had met Julie Walters, a charming woman stunt flier at a country fair, took her to an El Paso club dance. When Julie scooted off to Nice to make a film serial, Nick followed. They were married by a cardinal—Julie being a Catholic, and, like his grandfather Enoch who became a convert to marry Maude, Nick entered the faith, but fell under its spell and became in time a papal knight. Nick was a vice president in the Los Angeles branch of the family bank. Julie got pregnant very frequently. She had a wild taste for good living, sports, motorcars, the côte fleurette of grand parties and Escoffier-class food. They shared an all-encompassing vision of life on the sensual level. Rawly liked his daughter-in-law. He had sold Ball-Kingston to Anaconda—his mine smelter rights, making $40,000,000 in the deal, and at Greenhills he built an icebox to store tropical North Africa watermelons, so that in January he could give a melon party. Willie figured out each slice of melon cost his brother ten dollars.

Rawly grew more eccentric. He lost $500,000 in a town named after him—Ralston, New Mexico. While burning ranch grass at one of his holdings, he turned nearly all of Arrowhead County to ash, and had to pay the losses. He thought of building a canyon bridge and told Waldo Gaylord, "Don't spend more than a million on it! Damn it!"

Waldo was wondering if the family might not call in a consultation of medical experts and neurologists. Rawly was always building and remodeling Greenhills, planning to tear out or add. He employed a staff of 300 Indians (Sioux, Blackfeet, Apache) as carpenters, glass men, cabinet makers, rug-cutters on full pay, and kept them busy. He moved his herd of horses after a bronc bit a child—moved it halfway up the mountain, and it was a *big* herd. Wilma told Jessica he did it to protect the animals, not the visitors, and Jessica did not understand the remark as a joke.

Rawly could always spend money with a dash. When Wilma was offered a Charles II silver service at $150,000, Rawly said to the dealer, "Send us three—I like things in threes." It was not difficult—the sets were remarkably clever fakes.

Waldo was wrong to think Rawly was losing all of his mind. Rawly was merely amused at the way the world reacted to his behavior. It was certainy odd: he felt he was perfectly sane when he was drunk; sober, he was not so sure.

Animal life dominated the hotel park; twenty zebras roamed there, and some giraffes as well as Hereford bulls.

At last Waldo got him to sign a proper will; he left enough money in his will to the Railroad and Ranchers Club to hold a yearly Ralston Kingston Cocktail Party in memory of *la belle époque* of the Rockies. He listed $105,000,000 in special bequests in his will, and, as he signed it, he said to Waldo and Willie, the witnesses, "It all seems printed on water."

Time was passing. The huge spread of mine tunnels spoiled the wine by overaging it and by bad handling. Rawly refused to recork wine when the old corks shrunk. "We're not drinking fast enough." Wilma was trying. Returning from a party at Kingston House the year Enoch was seventy-five (Rawly had suspended the father and son feud for the event), Wilma, a bit looped, fell fully dressed into the shallow goldfish pool in the lobby. As she explained to Rawly later, "I couldn't just seem to get out. It was so late I hated to yell for Lola ... I mean, it was warm water and I spent the night in a good soak. I was entirely comfortable, and I think it was good for a head cold I felt coming on ..."

Willie, when he heard of it, said to Nick, "Such, too, were the pioneers."

The only member of the family who hadn't been present at Enoch's seventy-fifth birthday, besides Benji in Paris, had been Howard, the other twin. Princeton had expelled him in his second year. He took to gambling at New York card clubs, signing vouchers for losses until Waldo gave notice no name on an IOU or check signed *Howard Kingston*, would be honored. New York was in its best-remembered decade—a legend that was to be called "Roaring" and Howard became one of those rather drifting young men about town of the 1920s, with larded hair parted in the middle, wearing in season a racoon coat, high Arrow collars and in summer white linen with wide trouser bottoms or plus-fours, for which F. Scott Fitzgerald was to be blamed later, a style—Benji insisted—the writer himself never knew. When Howard insulted a minor gangster from Larry Fay's gang at "21," over escorting the hoodlum's girl around the speaks, Howard got slugged in a Fifty-second Street hallway, and was taken to Bellevue with a broken nose and three shattered teeth. His allowance was stopped and he was ordered to report to Bronco, Arizona, to learn how to run a desert railroad junction. There was neither good nor bad company in Bronco—just some starving sun-baked Indians mooching cigarettes, six tourist cabins, two gas pumps and a sign: Red Devil Battery: *Free Air*. He took to going down the line in his white Packard roadster to visit the wife of the Wolf Crossing telegrapher.

Harvest

41

Visitors from the United States crowded Mediterranean palazzos, American Legionaires visited Chateau Thierry, Belleau Wood. In the spring of 1926, Enoch and Lucy went to Paris. The doctors had insisted that for a man of seventy-six, he had been too active as chairman of the board of Blessinger & Kingston. They were worried about his heart, which Enoch felt was nonsense as he told Lucy, who was now arthritic. "I'm eating good but careful. I'm drinking some, and I can still kick higher than my head, *if* I want to. Besides, Lucy, I want to take my boy Rawly down a peg or two."

"Boy! He's in his late fifties! You need a good coat. We'll go to Brennans on the Champs Élysées."

So there he was in Paris with a new camel hair coat, staying at the George Cinq, sneaking a terrapin stew and filet de boeuf when Lucy was out shopping, and finding that you could still get a stein of the real Wurzburger at Jimmy's Bar.

Benji was living in a flat on the Rue Rousseau with an Italian painter, Camilla Comparetti, a tall thin woman with fine eyes, rather long face, and just the faintest suggestion of a dark moustache. Her fingers were usually holding a brush or a cigarette. She had a habit of gesturing when excited by bringing all the fingers of a hand to a point and waving them in front of one's face while talking rapidly. She orated, rather than spoke, in a combination of Roman street slang, English, and French.

There was a two-year-old baby girl, Bianca, that everyone assumed Benji had fathered. Others said they were actually married; a rumor that was to cause great legal problems years later over Camilla's claim to a share of

the W. G.P. & G. stock Benji owned, or rather was held in
trust for him.

Benji had talked to his grandfather on the phone and
said it would be better if they met for lunch someplace
else, not in his flat. He was speaking from the phone in
the concierge's apartment, but Camilla, returning with some
marketing and dragging Bianca—a beefy, pretty child—
by the arm, overheard the end of the conversation. All the
way up to their third floor flat she harassed Benji.

"Sonamahbitch, *mi rammento!* you think I not good
enough to meet you family. What am I, a housekeeper?
Just for the *fottuti!* Bianca! Don't drag the feet. *O Dio!*"

"It's just the place is such a mess, paintings, I mean, the
baby's nappies hanging around—"

"That you want a washerwomans? I am creative artist.
I am the maker of newness in paint. To you maybe cul!
Potta. You want-a I should wipe you arse, light you pipe.
Good. But meet the family, no! You chile here hide him.
Keep still Bianca, my heart, or I slap you."

In the flat Camilla did the fingertip gesture under Benji's
nose and just before she delivered to him the slap Bianca
didn't get, she cried out. "You think you are a artist, a
writer? You are nutting, hear me good, not even a *gran
cazza*. All of yous. That fat Jew Signora Stein, that cowboy Ernesto, all you think Americans are so special. Very
bella, bella?" Camilla spit. "You are jokes. I taking Bianca. I am leafing you. No more a bit of potta for you use.
I am of the Castelfranco and dall'Ongaro family."

Bianca sucked on a sweet and looked from her father
to her mother. They always played *so* loud.

Benji hunted a tie for his meeting with his grandfather.
"Castelfranco? Ongaro? Balls! Your father was a Sicilian
tobacco smuggler; your mother sold fish in Naples."

That was how Benji got his scratched nose. *Mamma
mia*, these misunderstandings in life are so unpleasant.

He loved Camilla, loved Bianca. What he didn't like was
his failure to become an important writer, to make real
progress on his cycle of novels, the use of American society since the Civil War, done in a prose world of Balzac-
like detail with the minute jewellike subtile nuances of
Proust's *A la Recherche du Temps Perdu*. He was aware

Camilla was a true artist, an original, that she was the only important woman Cubist. Juan Gris had said so, and even Braque had once come to her exhibit at Bertha Weil's. Only Pablo had been ironic and merely pinched her ass. Benji tried not to resent Camilla's small success, her mention in avant-garde publications.

The best Benji, aged thirty-six, could do in the Paris of the mid-twenties, was as a publisher and editor of *SALT*, a small magazine, very avant-garde.

So—nose damaged, covered with a little baking flour to hide the scratching—Benji went to have lunch with his grandfather at La Coupole.

Both were somewhat shocked—but holding back—as people do who haven't met for many years. Enoch was still large, but his skin hung loose on his big bones, almost like a hound dog's. The doctors and Lucy had dieted him, and he had chin wattles like a turkey gobbler. What was left of his hair was white and combed forward around his ears, his beard neatly trimmed. The eyes in their nest of crows' feet were still very much alive and his voice had come back; the slight slurring of speech cured, either by nature or willpower. Enoch agreed to two cognacs.

"*Oeufs en cocotte* very good here, Gramps. Eggs."

Enoch found Benji a puzzling object. Perhaps it was the way he dressed. Baggy tweed pants—hell, you couldn't kick out knees that baggy unless you blew up paper bags and tied them over each knee. The lumberman's shirt was frayed at collar and cuffs, the hat, a brown felt, had been creased in the wrong shape once and never recovered, and the plaid tie had wine stains. The heavy horn-rimmed glasses added a professorial touch. One thing sure, Benji would never be bald. His blond hair was no longer shiny gold, but there was a lot of it and it overran the back of his collar; in front was combed down nearly over an eye. Benji had cut himself shaving and some soap was still on one ear lobe, and a bit of newspaper stuck to a cut on his jawline. From the way Benji swallowed his drink, Enoch figured he was a booze fighter—just look at those burst capillaries on that scratched nose.

"Christ, order what they have best here. I once ate a great *coquilles St. Jacques*—that's baked scallops—at the

Chatham. Cognac is good for the old heart, the doc says. Imagine me knocking back anything but bourbon and rye. I'll have the leg of lamb."

"You're looking well, Gramps." To the waiter he said, *"Gigot d'agneau."*

"Fell pretty good, truth is. You, now, look like you don't get around, not much exercise."

They talked of city life, of art. "Well, you know, writing, editing a magazine ties you to a desk."

"Lucy, she keeps waiting for that big blockbuster from you—what is it called—yes, an epic?"

"I'm revising a work in progress. The magazine needs a hell of a lot of attention. I sent you the last three issues."

"Lucy says they were interesting, but dirty. She didn't say dirty right out, said obscene, erotic, really. In my time we just chalked up the words on barn walls, privy doors." Enoch sliced the meat on his plate and looked up. "Listen, Benji, why not come home?"

"This is my home. Paris is the twentieth century, Gertrude says."

"That's expatriate crap, and you know it. Let's talk turkey, boy. Your father, as the doctors and head thumpers put it, is showing pathological traits. Like that damn fancy dan of a hotel of his. And not paying attention to his holdings. Our holdings."

"There's Nick, there's Howard, Aunt Mollie's kids. Willie's boy, Tony."

Enoch wondered if he should order a rich dessert dish forbidden to him. Baba au rhum with cream. "All of you are needed. Nick is with Willie in the banks, wife always pregnant, and the damn laws now don't allow too close a tie-up with the railroads. Nick, he's just a banker, like Willie. The dollar signs, not the rails and the high iron rolling and the signal-board green for the express on the right of way ... Christ, it's a sight—it's just—" Enoch broke off, hands in the air, not being able to express the wonder of it all.

"Howard is in the railroad."

"Just on payday. He's cunt-crazy. I don't say some of us haven't got a failing for skirt lifting—perfectly natural. But we didn't spend a lifetime at it. We did our work and

370

enjoyed ourselves along the way. Willie's Tony is a good young fellow. But he's *not* ours. He's a stepson. He's in bonds and stocks on Wall Street with Starkweather and Company. Mollie's got only girls left. Yep—lost Hank as you know in the war, and Martin, he drowned in a sailing race off Catalina. Homer, Mollie's husband, a good, decent man." Enoch tapped his forehead. "He just hasn't got it up here. Goes chasing God's shirt-tail down at the Angelus Temple. Believes in original sin, Judgment Day, all that. Benji, I always felt you had the brains . . . God, you sit on them and turn out this fancy crud. Lucy reads it to me from that magazine of yours. Hell, I read Defoe, Melville, Dickens; *they* had *balls*."

Benji ordered another brandy, his second on top of the wine. "I can't give you an argument, E.K. Maybe it's all nonsense, and we're second-raters. Who's to say right now? But you can't overlook Cubism, the Fauves, Dada, the Surrealists, Freud, Joyce, *The Waste Land*. Most important names in our times."

"Benji, I wouldn't name a shit-house after them, let alone a Pullman car. Could be, if you and Lucy are right, these people, their stuff, will mean something, but they're a handful, boy. There are what?—twenty-five thousand Americans living here in Paris expatriating, all horsing around with paint, words and music. Nearly all just playing with themselves. Little cliques. That's all. They haven't got it, and Benji—you're no fool—I think you know you haven't got it either."

"That's to be seen. I'm a late starter."

"Level with yourself. You'll be dead of booze in ten years or jump off a roof. Come work in the family holdings."

Benji looked down at the half-filled brandy glass. He thought, *This old man—he's on my back, eminently illiterate, deep in profligacy and duplicity. The whole family is on my back. I'm weak, maybe, not up to sex or the material conditions of his dying world. But if he's right? If I don't have that spark, that voracious fire that comes so easily to others, to make literature, create new things, does that mean I have to be what this old cantankerous bastard of a grandfather wants me to be?*

"I don't like ostentation, E.K., or anything else your world can offer. I sound pompous. I don't mean to be."

"Listen, Benji, I've made a big thing of diesels. The Blessinger-Kingston unit is being tried by at least half the railroads of the world. The steam locomotive is finished soon. Your father—he's a romantic, thinks everything old is best. And, well, something else. Benji, I'm offering you and the boys the whole shooting match. You want to collect art, want to screw the most beautiful women in the world, don't think money doesn't help. Or set up foundations if you feel a duty to mankind, to end war, cure cancer. . . . It's all a bigger challenge then making marks on paper for only fifty other people to see. What do you say?"

"E.K., just look at me. You know I can't be anything but what I am." Benji laughed. "Suppose I can't handle the most beautiful women in the world?"

"Practice. Look, I have this legal genius, Waldo Gaylord. He can school you, back you up. You can buy brains, skills, even Congress, the Senate, the courts. It's called campaign funds now. In my day it was plain bribery. I never liked it—but I was building big." Enoch decided he'd had too much brandy, was talking wild. "Doing it your way, Benji, is living in a barrel."

"That's what I mean, what you condone. The decline of the American ideal."

"Oh, bullshit. We're the greatest country on earth, the best run, and men like me, even worse bastards, we built the roads, laid out the cities, dug the mines. In the end, boy, we all die off, Goulds, Morgans, Rockefellers, Belmonts; sure grabbers, stealers, worse, and what's left? What we built. *Everything*."

"Marx has it that—"

"I know Marx, better than you, maybe. I read *Das Kapital* before you were born. I also got him quoted from union field organizers, and the IWW boys. They were real fighters, terrors. But look at Russia—the murders, the millions who were starved to death. . . . What's a good dessert here?"

"A nice cheese plate." Benji turned to the waiter. *"Les Fromages."*

"Maybe you're right. Whipped cream and that goo is bad for me."

They looked at each other and Enoch grinned, and put out a hand, ignoring its tremor, grasping Benji's; nicotine-stained fingernails, nails so bitten down. "Think it over. You have this woman, this Dago girl."

"We're living together."

"Married?"

Benji shrugged. "That's middle-class morality, philistine thinking. I have a beautiful daughter, two years old, named Maude."

"That's fine of you to remember your grandmother."

"Camilla calls her Bianca . . . I'll really think of what you said, Gramps." He motioned for another cognac. "Really will. You offer to do what for me? Whatever you have in mind. But I don't think so."

"I think we need a walk. We been hitting the hooch hard."

Their meeting ended with a walk along the river. Benji was suddenly aware that they liked each other. As for Enoch, he was old enough and wise enough to make no full judgment on people—outside of business. It had taken a long time to prove it all, but he now felt each man was a world of his own, with his own habits and mysteries. You accepted that part of him (or her) that served you best, that you could get along with. Life is lived in boxed-off episodes, sometimes with no windows. In Benji he saw slackness that could become fatal. Benji was an independent thinker, a searcher—or had been one once. Now he was high and dry on the beach, going through the motions, acting like he was swimming towards some goal. But it was all just motion, and by the looks of him, his talk, not much of that. He'd give up soon, sink with that woman—most likely more man than Benji—and that child, into what you saw in New York's Greenwich Village, or on the café terraces. Talkers, sitters, drinkers. The smug mediocrity of followers who spoke the language of their messiahs.

It was, he figured as he walked to his hotel, a fifty-fifty chance Benji would come over to him—would work with him. The steel was there. Just as you take any old class Mikado 282 locomotive that had been in storage for years or rusting on a spur line, and if the honest stuff was there, built in, you could paint it and scale the boiler and refit busted parts—and have a blaze in the firebox, and 220 steam pressure in a matter of time. He told Lucy that night, "Too bad humans don't have replaceable valve gears and cylinders."

42

It was good to get away to London, to an empire that ruled over palm and pine—even if Lucy feared it was going to be too damp for her aching joints. Lucy was stiffening some, and walking was an effort even if masseurs tried to keep her limber. But she never complained. Instead she treated herself to a good coiffeur, Anthony himself, before they left Paris. She insisted Enoch buy some gay shirts at d'Ahetze. Enoch muttered, "The older the face, the younger the clothes."

They had a good corner suite at Grosvenor House in London, and they could see the Horse Guards ride by in the morning to take up their ceremonial posts for the day. Enoch hired a Bentley and a careful driver who took Lucy to visit the Harley Street specialists for her arthritic condition and other pains.

Enoch was busy cabling Waldo. He was preparing for a coup—nothing less than taking back the control of W. G.P. & G. In the present stock market with his holdings in many enterprises, he was doing very well. Why not? he told himself on his walks, swinging the furled umbrella he had gotten at Briggs on the Avenue de l'Opera, and wearing one of the gay shirts. But he never would give up his black Western hat for a bowler. "Damn it, Lucy, it's my trademark, and anyway my head is too big for one of those silly iron bowls."

Lucy came back on a Friday afternoon, a good sunny day, from looking at some cabochon emeralds Enoch insisted she inspect.

"A lovely bit of weather, isn't it madam," the maid said to her, pulling back the bed covers for her daily nap. Lucy agreed it had been a really fine day. Enoch, coming back from a walk to Hyde Park Corner, found her sleeping. He touched her arm and it was cold. It didn't take him but a moment to know Lucy was dead. One touch. Another, longer. God! Yes. His reflexes were still good. He just stood, leaning over the bed, an old man in shock. Below, the Horse Guards were returning from duty, the *clop clop* of horses' hoofs somehow transporting him to another time and place. His tremor was very bad, and a slow shaking of the head from side to side was uncontrollable. She had kept some very serious symptoms secret from him, he later learned.

Waldo came over to take care of matters, and Lucy's body began the long journey back by boat train, by ship, and by special club car to Kingston Junction. The last part of the journey in Enoch's own private car, the undraped casket swaying on a stand. He, Waldo, and young Nick, who had met them in New York, riding behind the special train that Rawly had arranged for. Enoch's memory all the time delineating, dissecting their long life together, all across America.

Enoch didn't say much, didn't shake more than usual; he'd control his tremor by putting his thumbs deeply under his belt.

Lucy was buried in the Kingston Junction grave site once reserved for Maude, whose remains were underground in a Catholic burying section of Rome.

Enoch never knew just who of the family had come to the burial. He and Waldo left at once, entrained back to New York, as if fleeing the just-gone part. Enoch was going to see their major stockbrokers, H. H. Starkweather & Company on Wall Street. Enoch was beginning to make his first move to return to power. He did not feel lonely, for actually he felt Lucy's presence near him. He was not a mystic, not one to fall into strange, traumatic experiences, but he accepted her being there and she *would* be there, he knew, for the rest of his life. He knew Lucy always had such a strong sense of duty, of doing the proper thing. He was grateful to her.

There is a folk song in the Lomax collection in the Library of Congress, "The Ballad of Howard Kingston," written in 1927 by a Texas chain-gang prisoner of Hudspeth County jail, identified by some as Ransom Smith, and by others as Claphands Turner. The refrain in this version goes:

> He had ten million dollars
> And Mary Welton died among the flowers.

There is very little truth in the ballad. Howard didn't have ten million dollars. He was an heir to part of a trust fund set up by his father, Rawly Kingston, but Waldo Gaylord, who had drawn up the details of the fund, knew Howard's share did not exceed five and a half million dollars. Also, the woman's name was not Mary, but Mabel, and her husband Josh Welton, stationmaster, ran a sheep-loading corral at the Gila Ridge station of the W. G.P. & G. in southwestern Arizona. Howard had been moved down there by his father after some trouble over a railroad telegrapher's sister elsewhere. Howard boarded in Gila Ridge with a half-Indian family—Chiricahua Apaches—whose younger members herded sheep for an Oklahoma combine and shipped wool and sheep on the W. G.P. & G. Mesa Freight Line in a world of alkali dust, creosote brush, and barberry thorns.

Josh Welton was a grumpy ex-soldier who had taken a German bullet through the right thigh at St. Mihiel, so that he limped some, worse when he was in likker, or in dark dissatisfaction with his life. His grudges, he told to Howard, who was railroad division manager from Dragoon all the way down the line to Huachuac. "I got frigged out of my rights, my army bonus, my old job at Carsontown waterworks, and six bucks a month for this slug in my leg, frigged by them bastards in Washington. And your grandfather, too, he never paid enough for the land my pappy sold to the railroad up on the Bowie Mesa. Yes, sir, skunked all along the line."

"You'll get a railroad pension, Josh."

Howard used to visit the Weltons a lot, as there was no town of Gila Ridge. Just the depot, the corral, a water tank for the locomotives, and some six adobe huts where the sheepherder families lived when they were not up on the plateau fattening sheep, aiding the ewes dropping lambs, and shooting at the hungry coyotes skulking in the wild buckwheat.

Mabel Welton was later reported as being a gum-chewing waitress from Tulsa and the Arapaho oil fields where rotaries were bringing in gushers or dry holes after spudding in the last of the boom towns. But actually Mabel was from Lima, Ohio. Her father's hardware store had made money—enough money left when he died for Mabel, at seventeen, to go out to the West Coast to try to become a movie star. She had sung in the Baptist Church choir, and acted in the Lima High School in a version of *The Bat,* playing a frightened comic servant.

Mabel was a beauty, a bit on the heavy side, but her butter-colored hair done up in finger waves, and her good teeth should, she dreamed, get her someplace in films. They got her into bed with several agents who made whispered promises as they undressed her, but only two days' work as an extra in a De Mille Bible picture. Mabel was a very simple but basically decent person, her head addled by reading motion picture magazines. She often slept with *Photoplay* under her pillow. The Bible picture brought back a Baptist fear of sinning and the anger of God. She gave up seeking stardom after three years, and met Josh Welton when she was a salad mixer (not a waitress) at Victor Hugo's, a very-well-known eating place in Los Angeles. The American Legion had proposed a fresh attempt to assault the U.S. Treasury and Josh, a decorated vet, had come out for a meeting of a planning committee. Being paid expenses, he was eating a steak at Hugo's when Mabel passed with a fresh bowl of avocado salad.

Josh neglected the meetings of the Legion to court Mabel. What appealed to her was his version of the honest, decent life of the true Wild West, its sunsets, mountains, canyons, clean air. "God's country," Josh called it, and it led to her accepting his offer of marriage.

Gila Ridge was a blow to Mabel. It wasn't at all the world of Tom Mix and Buck Jones, the excitement of *The Virginian,* of *The Covered Wagon.* In their hut behind the depot, Josh turned out to be a soured, maudlin grouch, blaming the government, the railroad, and the poor quality of whisky the sheepherders distilled. He rarely bathed, and his limited sexual assaults twice a month were hardly

378

worth the effort. "It's the damn heat, and your cookin' gives me dyspepsia."

When Howard Kingston arrived in his Packard roadster with pigskin luggage and a case of Old Crow store whisky, both Josh and Mabel welcomed him, and Mabel sobbed less in bed at night after Josh was deep in sleep.

After two weeks, Mabel began again to curl her hair and use lipstick. Josh drove his old Dodge truck up onto the plateau to load wool fleece from the fall shearing, a plateau event usually celebrated by a week of firewater, barbecued mutton, Apache war dances and hell raising. Howard and Mabel, who had been under growing tensions, got into bed the day Josh left, and Mabel said, in her fan magazine prose, "We've found each other."

Later press coverage pictured Howard as a seducer, a suave city dilettante taking advantage of an innocent wife left alone while her war-hero husband was off earning their bread and refried beans. This text didn't jibe with the version of her as a tramp waitress debauched in the oil fields and on the couches of Hollywood. Neither version of her would be the truth: that Mabel and Howard had found a hope for a better life. Both were a bit battered, both had lost self-esteem, had sunk into a doubt of any solution of their despairs. Howard blamed it on being dominated by too strong a family background, a family favoring his twin Nick, the family expectations that he could not fulfill. Mabel was not a stupid woman, but her orientation to life was conditioned by motion pictures. God-fearing and weak-willed, one reporter wrote, would be a fair way of explaining her. A person desiring love, knowing from the pleasures she felt in sex that Josh had been short changing her. She saw in Howard, not a mere affair, but a hope of a better, fuller life.

After six days, when Josh Welton came back from the plateau with a truck full of bales of stinking wool, he found the house behind the depot empty, and a note in Mabel's labored handwriting:

Josh, it's for the better. I'm gone off and not coming back. Don't go looking for me. Mabel Anderson Welton. Perhaps she felt writing out her full name made the document legal. The emotional level of simple people is as deep-felt as for the greatest lovers, but their expression is usually banal when put into words.

It was old High-Tail-Under, the grandfather of the part Chiricahua Apache herders who, for a half-pint of Old Crow, said "You squaw, she gone off las' night with the tall fella in Packard with bags and all they varmoose."

"Which way?"

"Likely they go to Taco Flats making for Meekheego, you bet."

Josh went back to the depot, smashed the rest of the whisky, got out his Smith and Wesson forty-five, and a twelve-gauge double-barreled shotgun. He cried for a good ten minutes and took off after refueling the truck at the railroad's rail-cart gas pump, for which he had the key. He dropped the wool bales down a gully and drove south raising up a cloud of chrome-yellow dust behind him that reached a hundred feet into the heated air. It was mean country, dwarf locoweed, broken buffs. He had been born here and lived here, but for a year and a half in the army. Unlike visitors, he didn't see the beauty of the cliffs, the amazing mineral color in the rocks.

He kept driving south, patting the .45 jammed under his wide leather belt and dragging a boot heel across the floorboards to make sure the shotgun hadn't been jolted out crossing some dry arroyo. In six hours he was in Taco Flats, a town which had at least twenty-two houses, stores, a gas station and a Chinese eating place. Beyond the town there were what were known as dude ranches. Two of them where there were barbecues, folk dances and fancy roping lessons. Taco Flats was also supported by a talc mine. The W. G.P. & G. ran a special passenger train during the summer twice a week up from New Orleans and from San Diego.

Josh Welton parked behind the Owl Diner on Main Street, had a bowl of chili and went to sleep in the cab of his truck. He awoke at midnight, dry-mouthed, tacky-eyed. He drank a cola and drove out to the first dude ranch, The Spanish Spur, and saw no Packard roadster. He almost cried again; maybe they had moved on to Mexico, driving all night. But more likely the horny sonofa-bitch and that itchy slut would be fucking their heads off right now in a good clean bed when they could hire one.

Josh drove on to the Hundred Horses Ranch. There at the second cabin, right in front, was the Packard. Someone had washed it and it shone banana yellow under the night moon. Josh took up the shotgun, inserted two shells, and went behind the second cabin. Sure enough, by the sound of it, the two of them were screwing away. Disgusting happy time talk and sounds, having their jolly sport in it. He peered in through the small window. Gave him the grue. Josh watched and listened for ten minutes. Holy Mary and Joseph, he himself never got the hots that stud was having right then, or any reaction with all that moaning and thrashing around and happy crying Mabel was giving out. Josh choked back a weepy spell, feeling a poor, unlucky, put-upon-bastard and with a lump in his gut because he too had ideas about love and companionship. He was a man as good as any. Now humiliated, outcocked, feeling the world was down on him, he busted the glass of the cabin window with the shotgun butt. The moonlight over his shoulder showed Mabel rising up naked and indecent on the bed, tits bouncing, and that million-dollar prick on his feet standing by a dresser pouring something from a bottle over some ice in a glass. Not a hair on his belly—shoulders like a barn door.

Mabel screamed. Howard turned and threw the glass at the figure in the window. Josh got off one barrel—the left—a shotgun blast at his wife. She turned all red and tattered in the light of the twin light-bulbs in the ceiling. Heavy deer shot is damaging. Josh turned a bit and fired at Howard, who had dropped down behind the bed, then got up and bare-ass was through the cabin door, taking the screen door with him, then dropping it. Naked as a plucked rooster, he was streaking down to the big hall and main ranch house where there was blue grass band noise and a caller getting a square dance going.

Hang up yer coat.
Spit on the wall.

Josh reloaded the shotgun as he cut around a corner of a Paige sedan, and having a bad leg he wasn't as fast as Howard, who was moving on a loping run desperately trying to get out of shotgun range.

Choose yer partners
And promenade all!

Doors were banging open. Perhaps Howard wasn't thinking properly, maybe he wanted to talk to Josh, explain how things really stood. None of the dozen people who came out of the other cabins, the ranch house hall, they, too, were never sure why Howard did what he did. To stop. He turned to face Josh and waved his hands held at chest level.

Meet the gal and hug her tight
You both got a date goin' tonight!

Josh dropped the shotgun in the dust and pulled the Smith and Wesson from under his belt. The gun butt felt damp in his hand, sweat was in his eyes. Carefully, with the back of his left hand, he wiped his brow. Then he shot Howard—who never uttered a word—shot him five times at the range of fifteen feet. Howard just put both his hands first on his burst stomach, then on his bleeding chest. He made no effort to feel one side of his head where the last slug had gone in and come out behind in a mess of brain and skull bone.

Josh turned the gun on himself to absorb the last bullet, but by that time two people had reached him and they disarmed him. He put up no resistance. All he said very politely was "I could use a real drink now."

The *Phoenix Sun* broke the story first. KINGSTON HEIR AND RUNAWAY WIFE GUNNED TO DEATH BY AVENGING HUSBAND.

For no logical reason, W. G.P. & G. shares fell four points the next day, but recovered. Josh Welton's trial in Cochise County for the double murders lasted just three days. Public opinion ran toward a "Not Guilty" verdict, but Josh was convicted of second-degree murder. ("In Arizona," wrote one reporter, "that meant the party killed didn't have the guts to reach for a gun.")

Josh Welton did three years at the Walls—then went off. No news of him was reported after that in the press.

The railroad paid for Mabel's burial in Taco Flats.

Howard was interred in the cemetery a mile above Greenhills, in the best place, where you could see the mountains spread across the sky. Rawly had built a magnificent tomb of marble above ground; room for several caskets—with old English letters outside spelling in bronze: KINGSTON.

Waldo had tried to gather a full burial party. Enoch didn't want to be haunted by memories and wanted to leave after the services, but Wilma felt he should stay and talk to Rawly. "He feels maybe he either neglected Howard or was too harsh."

Back at Greenhills, Rawly said, "It seemed a small crowd. Good to see you, E.K." He was looking around him, Enoch saw, as if someone was coming at him with a twelve-gauge shotgun or a rim-fire .45.

Enoch said, "Come down to Kingston Junction sometime; we'll talk."

That night Enoch came into Waldo's room before retiring, winding his watch. "I don't suppose dying for a woman is such a bad way to pecker out. Of course I'd like to pick the woman I'd die for. If you're going to ask me *which* one I'd nominate, I'd say that's what you lawyers would call a privileged answer."

He went out without saying anything else, leaving Waldo with the thought there were some gestures in the world he didn't mind missing.

43

Waldo Gaylord did not despair in "the bad years the locusts ate" (his words) between 1929 and 1933. Rather, he sank into a kind of observant fatalism. He lived alone in three rooms at the El Royale in Los Angeles (not even a dog) and took to making notes on the conditions of the nation. Along the way charting the Depression, he developed a philosophy that no matter what happened to the individuals who had built up the huge enterprises, falling and failing, somehow the physical evidence of rail-lines, factories, processors remained. He wrote during the worst years of the nation and the W. G.P. & G. history:

"One becomes aware that the malaise of decline cannot be postponed or stopped. Nothing is invunerable to fate, no force or method (in times like these) is insulated against change. You cannot defraud destiny."

In middle age, Waldo was as ordinary-looking as before, ("He's skipped his youth." Willie.) as bland-appearing as in his first days as a law student. His clothes cost more but didn't fit any better; he never seemed properly pressed or brushed, but was always buttoned. He took to wearing piped waistcoats after his sexual urges grew weaker and then departed. He always carried a pocket watch, never wore a wristwatch, even after Rawly had given him a thousand-dollar Swiss one. It was Enoch who presented him with the pocket watch, the antique gold turnip, twenty-one jewels, three inches across. The outer lid was engraved, aided by a bas relief of an oncoming locomotive, its headlight a large diamond, one side lamp a ruby, the other an emerald. Across the train's cowcatcher had been added the engraved words: *To W.G. from*

E.B.K. He's the whole team and the little dog under the wagon . . . July, 1929.

Yes, it had all looked so good, the impregnability of an era before 1929. E.K. was about ready that summer to make his move: take back the Western, Great Plains & Gulf. For the Blessinger-Kingston Diesel stock was selling for $210 a share, 2,000,000 more shares were going to be voted in December—an issue planned to be offered to the public by Starkweather & Company, and backed by Willie's banks. But first, could Ralston Kingston be declared a man too sick to handle his own affairs, and Wilma and son Nicholas appointed trustees to administer the estate?

Mollie Emerson was a holdout. She still felt Rawly and Enoch were responsible for the death of Hank. Her husband Homer had invested heavily in the Florida land boom. That bubble was bursting and he was involved in the Palm Tree Land Company of Inlet Sound, liable personally for $2,000,000. So if Enoch bailed Homer out, it was only a little time before their shares in W. G.P. & G. would be voted in favor of Enoch Kingston's taking over control of the railroad he had founded. It was clear Enoch was in a mood of being impervious to past disasters.

Waldo had fairly earned his presentation watch. He had served for some years as the transmission belt between the failing Rawly and the aged, but active, Enoch. There never was a full reconciliation between son and father. But Waldo made it easier for them not to clash or bump together, grinding down resentments that could upset the running of the affairs of their estates.

Waldo visited Rawly a week after the doctors' final reports were written. Waldo found Rawly wearing a red dressing gown, seated at a window of the War Room at Greenhills. It was called the War Room because it housed a huge collection of lead soldiers, mounted men: Royal Dragoons of Balaclava, Chasseurs à chevaux, Grande Armée Curassiers. Whole battles of miniature cannon existed, various color bearers of empires long gone, of corps and divisions that had been led by Frederick the Great, Cromwell, Wellington, Napoleon, Grant, Lee, Foch, Pershing (all present in metal). Rawly had made the collection, he always insisted, for Nick and Howard. But actually for several years he had been arranging Agincourt, Waterloo, Gettysburg, on the big teak table using hundreds of lead soldiers.

As Waldo came into the War Room, he saw by the dust on the table and on little mounted or standing figures, there had been no war games lately.

Rawly looked up. His feet were bare. His hair was gray, uncombed, and needed cutting.

"Morning, Rawly."

"Oh, 'lo Waldo."

"Enjoying the view?" Waldo set down his dispatch case on a smoking stand on which stood one mounted lead Tobolsk Cossack rider at full gallop, swinging his saber.

"Always a fine view, Waldo, just fine. I've ordered a bowling alley, also going to put a piano in every club car of the Kansas City-Washington, D.C. run. Liven things up, you know. Been very dull. Dull."

"Very interesting. Now Rawly, listen carefully."

"No business details. Please. I've a goddamn headache."

With a twinge of contrition, Waldo went on. "As you know, you've been involved in too many projects. Here, in Europe, in South Africa. Dissipating your interests."

"It's a bull market, itsn't it? The goose hangs high, Waldo, with cranberry sauce I hope, and truffle stuffing."

Waldo opened the dispatch case and took out some papers stapled together. "I have here preliminary reports on your treatments by some well-known specialists and neurologists."

"Treatments? I was just bullshitted by those jaspers. How they come to decide I was abdicating responsibility?"

"It is felt you are in no condition to run the various enterprises like the railroad, the assets, the holdings of your family."

Rawly smiled. "Well, well."

"I have here legal papers signed by three medical men that if presented to a judge will certify you, Rawly, as incompetent to handle your own affairs, and so ordering you to be confined for treatment under careful medical conditions."

"The booby hatch?" Rawly fingered the silk fringe on

the end of the belt of his dressing gown. "It's gone that far, Waldo, *that* far?"

"Legal-medical language isn't overfastidious." Waldo stared expressionless at the man he loved, respected, a person with whom he had spent so many years in travel, confidences and friendship. He felt suddenly as if he were in a deep-sea diving helmet under the ocean and his air were being slowly cut off. How does one practice candor without pain or irony?

Rawly shook his head. "Tough tittie. Very tough. Living calls for such delicate calculation. Waldo, remember those days at Verdun, that war? And all the French infantry fodder under their tin hats, muddy up to their arse, marching to sure death, and they knowing it every poor son-ofabitch. Nobody fell out. Not one trapped *poilu*. They just marched down the road to be blown to bits. All we could hear—remember—from them, thousands of them going by like the sheep they knew they were, to the slaughter, was them making that sound. 'Baaa, baa, baaa.' "

"The only protest they could make, Rawly."

Rawly stared out of the window at the rolling lawns of Greenhills, the lofting hills and the dented outlines of blue-violet mountains beyond.

"You tell me what to do, Waldo."

"If you sign certain documents I have here, the certification of legal incompetence will *not* go before a judge. You will be admitted of your own free will to Robin Farms in Palo Alto for a rest. And Wilma, Nick, and Willie will administer the family holdings."

"Shall I sign?"

"Yes."

Rawly leaned over and patted Waldo's blue serge knee. "Old buddy. I'll do what you tell me to do."

Waldo nodded and laid out a deck of papers on the wide windowsill. "A good rest at Robin Farms is what you need."

As Rawly finished signing the papers, he looked up smiling, and for a moment it was the wild and clever young man of the Noodle Flats days as he spoke, "Baa, baa, baa."

Six months later, the market collapsing, Waldo was writing in his notes: "The idea of an impregnability of an era is always based on blind fate, a mood of being impervious to past disasters. We were all tempting the gods . . ."

October 1929, had by then come and gone; the Depression lay like a sour gaseous layer of air over the nation. Everything—all the fine and carefully laid plans of Enoch to recover the W. G.P. & G.—had gone wrong.

To begin, Blessinger-Kingston Diesel stock had fallen forty points in one day—kept falling even after Enoch and Willie and some favored shareholders had poured millions in to bolster it with buying orders. In the end, the new bond issue H. H. Starkweather & Company was to put on the market was called off. Mollie's shares of W. G.P. & G. were no longer hers. Her husband Homer had pledged them as collateral in his Florida land deals, and there were heavy claims against them. The W. G.P. & G. could not pay its dividends to its stockholders as freight hauls and passenger traffic fell off. Baldwin, U.S. Steel, Pullman Coach, seventeen other corporations put liens against what was owed them. A reorganization for the railroad had to be arranged, and Eastern shareholders and operators formed a new board of directors on which no Kingston served.

Willie's banks had closed. All across the nation banks were closing, some to open again in time, but the Kingston banks never opened again—not as Kingston banks. Willie had been involved in loans to big Midwestern utilities corporations, dealing with Samuel Insull and other manipulators. These loans were never to be met, and banks held watered utilities' stocks, worthless by several billion dollars.

Willie had an exquisite sense of perception; he was no longer a banker. He and Jessica decided to live in England. Their income would be cut down, 'way down, to some few shares, interests in Swedish iron mines. But they would manage to live on it. Tony Kingston-Tyndal, Willie's stepson had come out of the collapse of the stock market, as Willie put it, "smelling like a ton of roses." Tony had dreamed one night the crash was coming and had closed out his own portfolio. He warned Willie, who scoffed at any dream idea the Great Bull Market would fail. Tony had also sold short RKO, General Motors, Goldman Sachs, and some other stocks to retire a very rich man. He went to Jamaica and took to sailing. His sister Rosemary was married to a naval officer stationed in San Diego and was content.

Tony came out to Santa Barbara in 1931 to help Willie and Jessica pack for the trip to England. It had been a good home for him and his sister: a two-story white stucco "Italian" villa—open, airy, a good view of the bay. Jessica had grown a bit too bony, and her tennis tan was like good smoked leather. The nose longer, the salt-and-pepper hair cut too short, dressed in tweeds, sensible low-heeled shoes, and a loose-knit pale yellow sweater. She was packing the Spode dinner set into a crate, wrapping each dish in layers of newspaper (headline: ARMY BURNS HOOVERVILLES.) Tony, a bit too stooped for a Noël Coward stance (just a touch of Leslie Howard), came into the living room with a bundle of old newspapers.

"Why take it all, Mums?"

"Sentimental reasons. Will and I have lived a happy life with these things."

"He's taking it well. He's down in the garage sitting in his old Mercer runabout on its blocks, smoking a cigar, going through some old picture album."

"Is he? Odd. Will used to say nostalgia was a rash that silly people scratched."

"I remember him saying to be rich is not enough—to be *known* to be rich—that is the true desire."

"It's all he has now, his wit and us."

Tony opened the glass doors of a cabinet holding silver cups, medals; sports awards. "You'll take these, of course. Lord, you won the West Coast Women's Tennis Finals three times! Didn't know that. Shall I pack the lot?"

Jessica shook her head. "No, I'm selling them to someone who is coming to make an offer for all of what we're not taking."

"But you trained so hard."

"Just pot metal really, mostly with some silver plating,

some engraved bad prose. They spelled my name wrong in the Carmel series."

Mother and son continued wrapping and setting objects firmly in place into crates. Willie came in before lunch—a cloth fishing hat with hand-tied trout flies in the band. He was wearing a tweed jacket with leather patches on the elbows, disgraceful trousers he used for gardening when working in his rose bed, on his own variety of flowers which never won a prize.

"Oh, Will, please don't pack what you're wearing."

"No, I suppose not. The English swells would begin to copy me. I'd sink the empire's tailors."

Tony was inspecting a set of steak knives with bone handles.

"I hope you got some of your post-Impressionists out of the vaults."

Willie looked amused as he put his hand into his jacket pocket. "Not a paint stroke. Hocked them all to H. Bleinheimer & Fils in Paris when the market broke and I was trying to cover. Old Hans, that pirate, owns them all now."

Jessica sighed. "I thought you had lent them to museums."

"Well, I had a good eye. Someday they'll be worth a few millions for somebody. I'm taking a seashell E.K. sent me on my tenth birthday. It says ATLANTIC CITY—HOME OF SALT WATER TAFFY. Worthy of Walt Whitman, don't you think?"

Willie went out to get the shell; it was someplace in the hall closet. He was not feeling sad or numb. After all, as old Hegel had written, "In turning our gaze to the past, the first thing we observe is ruins." For all his ridiculous bulk, shiny bald head, William Kingston was a very brave man, a character firmly philosophical, and a stoic. Of all the Kingstons, he claimed he had a closer understanding of the true value of the world and the forces that debased it, a wider education in life and its patterns. Outwardly witty and happy in the comedy of conformity, he was a pessimist inwardly; he pitied the condition and misery of most of mankind. Its cruelty and savagery gave him little hope mankind was a satisfactory product.

The seashell was there—a bit chipped—behind his golfing jacket. A big, vulgar, foot-long white shell with a pink interior, and the gold letters, what was left of them: AT-LANTIC CITY—HOME OF SALT WATER TAFFY. It had been one of his treasures as a boy, with a copy of a book on training hunting falcons, and a glass cat with green eyes, one eye lost.

Here he was in his fifty-ninth year—a disaster area—remembering a glass cat originally with green eyes. One eye had fallen out (he had swallowed it by accident). Was it the right or left eye? He didn't remember and, as he carried the seashell down the hall to be packed, he decided that was abou the only important question he had left to decide.

(A London fire warden found the seashell unharmed in the remains of a house blown up by a V-2 during the Blitz, on Hamilton Terrace, St. John's Wood. He took it home for his grandson.)

44

The Sabbath is a bride, the twilight the wedding hour.
What of the night? Enoch had heard an old Hasidic Jew
recite that text at a dinner Sol Winters had given long,
long ago. Enoch had no idea how long ago, for he was—
he touched his brow—eighty-five? No, eighty-six years old.
There were spaces in his memory now—then a gush of
knowledge, a rush of remembering. When all he wanted to
do was sit and not think. Not brood; just exist, become
part of the landscape. Nothing querulous, spiteful. What a
good thing to simplify oneself at last.

He had taken a taxi in the village to drive him to Kingston House. He had no idea how he had come to Kingston
Junction, or why. Had it been a homing instinct? The
lost dog one reads about who walks two thousand miles to
rejoin family that have moved away? He didn't have a
dog anymore. No more. He, himself, had been in storage in
a rest home in Battle Creek. Eating ground straw, asked
daily about his bowels. Then he was on a train, and changed
to another train . . . The taxi driver drove up the neglected drive. Enoch saw all the elms had died and light-
ning had taken the top off the Engelmann spruce by the
porch of Kingston House that faced the junction and the
dilapidated railroad work-yards.

"Want me to wait?" asked the taxi driver.

Enoch nodded. Waiting was old age under a curse of
one's own making. Waiting was wondering at the reason
of everything, with very little answering. The porch was
unswept, and some hardy vine had forced itself up between the planks from below. A lonely rocker waited for
a passenger, but its rush seat had burst through and wasps
had built a brown paper hive on the top of the dead ivy

stalks. Down below, the junction was nearly dormant, a string of six freight cars loading some local product—and beyond stood row on row of derelict passenger cars, flat cars, and coal gondolas. Even an isolated caboose, its tin chimney leaning to one side like the "Toonerville Trolley," a cartoon he and Lucy had enjoyed. It was a sad sight. Who had said, "Old men grow hard to please as they grow more unpleasing!" Don't remember.

He heard footsteps—heavy shoes and a short, feisty man with very broad shoulders, legs too short for the torso, came up to the porch, a black pipe smoldering in one corner of a thin mouth.

"Who the hell do you think—*oh*, Mr. Kingston. Had no idea you be comin' up."

"Yes." Hunt memory for this face, stir the name file. Oh yes, O'Hara. "Just dropped by."

"Had I known, I'd a got some room ready. Nothin' much left inside, you know. No lights, no water in the house, just turned on for the garden lines, and they're rusted out mostly."

"You're the caretaker?"

"And lonely it is. Can't keep the place green, and no winder glass in lots of rooms. The roof in the ballroom leaks."

"Never mind. The place isn't meant to be lived in no more. It's just—just a survivor. You have a key? I mislaid mine someplace."

From a ring of keys, O'Hara selected one and opened the front right-hand panel of the two weather-worn oak doors.

"Would you like something to drink, sir. A beer, maybe?"

"No. Just go about your duties. I'll be all right."

O'Hara pursed his lips, rubbed a soiled hand down the side of his jacket, an old one of Enoch's, a once-bold plaid now worn and faded. He touched the porkpie hat with a hackle in the band and went off muttering to himself. *The old bastard,* O'Hara thought, *thin as a rail but still with that mean and nasty look all them Kingstons have, like they own the world. Them eyes under the caterpillar eyebrows still could hold you in their gaze like you was*

*dirt. Snooping around like I was stealing something valu-
able, when I'm just saving some old clothes from the
moths.*

Enoch walked slowly through the hall; his tremor
seemed to leave him, as if not daring to invade this great
house, this now-empty house. It gave off a mindless menace, smelling of old layers of wallpaper and dry rot some
place. Dust everywhere, the gray linen covers limp over
the few bits of remaining furniture. Not much left. Willie
and Mollie and Nick had carried off a lot, even several of
the great glass and crystal chandeliers he and Lucy had
seen blown for them in that island factory near Venice;
even these had been taken down and just some wires left
dangling from holes in the ceiling, like a hangman's ropes.
He had once seen an outlaw lynched, hanged from the
Canning corral gate. What *hadn't* he seen? Christ, why
wasn't the past lost irretrievably. Charlie White had said,
"We must learn to eat time." The tremor was back, and
he could feel the slight shaking of his head from side to
side. Still, he smiled; it's been a full life, a plenty of everything. But say what you will, a man can't go into the
W. G.P. & G. repair yards and get stripped down and
scaled, have the old bolts burned off, get a new firebox
and reforged driving rods put in. That was where he was
one up on whoever or whatever had made man of frail,
soft stuff. No use to get het up about it. He said out loud,
"Serenity, detachment, that's the trick."

He walked into the den. His eyes grew accustomed to
the dim light. The bones of a little bird lay on his old
desk. All in order, a skeleton as if etched in a book. It had
flown in and never gotten out through some break in the
windows. Ants had carried off most of it, all but the delicate design of bones. It was like a statement left by the
Messiah's messenger. Again the memory of that Old Testament talk at the dinner of Sol Winters's, which recalled to
him the handling of Hannah's body in the glade. . . . *I was
something in those days. We all were. Nobody was over
thirty-five in the whole damn world, food didn't taste like
sheep dip, and breathing was easy as pie*—not this choking
effort and pain in the chest.

The horse halters, bridles, hackamores were gone from

the den wall. O'Hara's work, most likely. But the old black leather couch was still against the wall, and above it rusty thumbtacks showed where once there had been on display his hand-drawn map of Outlaw Pass. The couch wasn't worth taking away. Sagging, spring-sprung, leather torn, some gray, curly entrails showing.

He lay down on it and began to laugh at something he remembered. He had found Rawly at seventeen, home from Harvard that summer, belly down, on the couch, screwing away on his old nanny, Miss Osborn. Yes, prim, correct Miss Osborn, then the housekeeper. Miss Osborn's naked legs, remarkably fine legs—hairless as an egg—in the air, and she giving the proper English accent to her moans of pleasure as she came.

His laughter turned to a coughing fit. Rawly had inherited his love of women, his lust for living. He didn't remember if Miss Osborn screamed or not, when she saw him . . . Rawly, now? Sitting in slippers and a dressing gown in some walled-in park, sipping buttermilk, his brains turned to cat's meat. . . . Listen to my barking bronchitis. Nothing really turns out the way you wanted it to add up. Grandchildren, great-grandchildren—he no longer kept count of them or knew them by name. Nick's kids, the Emerson girls filling whole nurseries. Well, it's share and share of all my holdings. Waldo has the papers.

There was the hoot of the freight leaving the yard. Most likely it ran only once a week now. The big W. G.P. & G. yards were elsewhere. The lone survivor of the mile-long consists; the great engines doubled to make the top of the pass; the roar of the luxury specials. The *Golden Eagle* going by at seventy smooth miles an hour on the best tracks west of St. Louis. No more, no longer. Newer, shorter routes, and planes and goddamn trucks. Twelve-wheel rigs were cutting in on the haulage business in these dark years of depression. Every string of freights now carried deadheads; hundreds of homeless bastards, broken men. Okies, migrant workers, and dispossessed bankrupt tractored-off men, not the old time hobos and their gunzels, the fat and dirty jockers of the 'bo jungles. Just jobless, hopeless men. How many had once been W. G.P. & G. workers?

No matter, the whole system was now in other hands.

Run by a high-assed Eastern board of directors, controlled by Manhattan banks. The Kingstons and the Emersons and the Alvarezes were just stockholders. A lot of shares were still in their hands, but with hard times, a falling away of dividends . . .

It didn't matter. When Enoch had sons in their sixties and grandsons turning forty, what was the sense of it? He forgot *what* was the sense of *what*? He lay back on the black leather couch, hearing the rattle of the old springs that had burst loose from their moorings, and he caught the smell of disturbed dust. Outside there was the shrill sound of starlings in the overgrown shrubbery.

It was all a great piece of nonsense letting himself get this old. But he had enjoyed it; he had never had any of the fashionable despair of the intellectuals, not even when the depression deepened the Dust Bowl, blew it away and seemed more than a calculated impudence of Nature— why had the plows broken the plains? And as for the stupidity of men too big for their breeches, bureaucracy ruled the world, badly. He would vote for that sonofabitch with the superficial charm, Roosevelt, because the man had a head on him, a feeling for the people, and made sense. Christ, it was the first time he would cross the party line since he voted the Bull Moose ticket for Four-Eyes, the goddamn Rough Rider. In those years the country all around Kingston Junction still had blue grouse and a rare black bear and cougar . . .

. . . he turned on his side and slipped off into the crystal-clear water and began swimming towards the white strand of beach, the fronds of the trees touched by the trade winds, making a rattling, crackling noise. He was young and strong of limb, and he laughed. He had come awake, was aware he had only been dreaming he was an old man, weak and shaky, lying among dust and cobwebs. It was all a bad dream he had been having. One of his nightmares. He kept swimming and a shoal of angelfish scurried by. The palms beyond the surf were waving and brown girls were singing. He lifted himself up in the rolling surge of the sea and waved back from high on a blue crest—then riding it down, a surface like pale green glass. A brown girl waved and as the wave crested with a hiss of

396

white foam, he was engulfed, yet just for a moment there he saw the girl launch herself toward him. He just had time to cry out in delight, when it was as if a giant jellyfish had burst inside him and he tumbled over and over deep inside the moving wave, holding his breath until everything around him was purple-black, for the wave would never throw him up into the world . . .

"What do you know—the old boy come back here to die."

"Who's gonna pay me for the taxi ride?"

"I better try phone some of his folks."

"Nobody wants you when you kick the bucket."

"He was old, real old."

"Maybe you better cover him with something."

The freight engineer far down the line was blowing twice at a crossing. In the ruined garden the bees were buzzing about, seeking out some last flowers, indifferent to events that had nothing to do with their own tasks in nature.

Epilogue

Federal Judge Nelson Jason Deleon was satisfied with
his work on the problems which had hovered like a hallu-
cinatory presence over him for three months. The judge
was a portly man in his middle forties, a handsome man
with a round face, his dark, curly hair already mixed with
much gray. He was married twenty-six years to Emily Del-
linow of the Main Line Dellinows. They had a son who
was at Princeton, a daughter who was a successful interior
decorator; her husband, Stanley Adams, a very successful
corporation tax lawyer. There were three sassy, bright
grandchildren, and the judge was looking forward to three
weeks of golf and sun with Emily. In Palm Springs, where
he usually took his yearly vacation unless he was attending
some international lawyers' conference (next year he
would be a main speaker at the Worldwide Legal Conference). His book *The States and Colonial Law* was not a
best seller, but at several law schools it was recommended
reading.

He was decidedly a man on his way up. He still had a
long way to go, but he had a reputation for penetrating
acumen and an innate aptitude for writing quotable briefs.

The big shiny Lincoln was in his special spot in the
parking basement of the Federal Court building. Harold
touched his chauffeur's cap with one finger in greeting, got
the judge set in the car, and wrapped a rug around his
legs. It was a chilly Philadelphia day, and there would be
snow for Christmas this year. Harold handed him a copy
of *The New York Times*. The judge didn't care much for
the local newspapers.

"You made the front page, sir. Got more space than
Kissinger."

"Did I?"

398

The car moved into the traffic and began its skilled run to Germantown at the hands of Harold, and the waiting tray of cocktails and the guests arriving for the special dinner. It was Emily's birthday. He read the newspaper's version of his yesterday's decision (as he touched the inner pocket of his topcoat to be sure Miss Shapiro, his secretary, had placed the jade earrings there, the packet from Tiffany's. Emily liked jade.)

WESTERN, GREAT PLAINS & GULF CAN'T JOIN NEW U.S. RAIL SYSTEM, JUDGE RULES.

Surprise Decision May Force Nation's Largest Line to Liquidate.

A Federal judge ruled Monday the bankrupt Western, Great Plains & Gulf Railroad should not join a proposed new federal rail system set up by Congress. The order by U.S. Dist. Court Judge, Nelson Deleon, could lead to the liquidation of the nation's largest railroad.

W. G.P. & G. was expected to become the major part of the Consolidated Railway Corp. (ConRail,) which was created by Congress to bail out financially troubled railroads.

Judge Deleon said the Regional Rail Reorganization Act "does not provide a process which would be fair and equitable to the estate of the debtor."

Besides the W. G.P. & G., the Penn Central, Lehigh Valley and Reading, other ailing railroads involved in the ConRail network are the Central of New Jersey and the Ann Arbor of Michigan.

The Rail Reorganization Act was passed and signed into law by the President. It provided $235 million in interim financial help for the seven bankrupt roads, a $1 billion fund for creation of ConRail and another $500 million to upgrade the passenger system.

ConRail would operate only freight trains, would be a semipublic corporation, partly owned by private citizens and run by a government appointed board.

Fair enough—the judge decided—trimmed a lot of the legal decor. Perhaps he could have used a bit more of an attitude of passive responsibility. His father had a soft spot for the W. G.P. & G. The judge's great-grandmother was—in family legend—supposed to have been related to someone who helped survey the route of the first rails the road put down. A man named Jasper or Jackson ... the judge thought—someday he must get one of his clerks to search the old reports of the forming of the W. G.P. & G., if they still existed. People were very careless in those days with records and documents. And the original Jasper or Jackson had emigrated to Brazil.

His great-grandmother, according to family stories, must have been a very wonderful woman; as a widow she raised a son—his grandfather—in still wild country. Started schools for Indians. There was a very fuzzy old photograph turned yellow and brown with age—of great-grandmother standing behind some miserable shiftless-looking Indians, Oglala or Nez Perce at Chadron Creek Reservation. She sun tanned and weathered, a huge hat shadowing her face, tensed as for the ordeal of the camera, yet full of vitality and determination.

It was her son, the judge's grandfather Bancroft (there were hints he was illegitimate—Great-grandmother may never have married) who had changed the family name *de Leon* to *Deleon*. He married three times and produced one child that survived; two others were drowned in some accident. Bancroft was given to paranoid fantasies. You never were sure most of his stories of the family weren't lies.

It was Judge Deleon's father, Baxter, who had tried to trace the family to the de Leons of Georgia, but that was intense vanity, Judge Deleon always felt. No Jasper or Jackson de Leon was listed in the de Leon family documents now in the Library of Congress. Besides—the judge mused as the car moved through diesel exhaust— Father had been a bit of a snob, retiring from the Deleon Printing Corporation, joining the Foxdale Country Club, insisting on a restricted membership as president, building a private railroad car for himself, supporting Goldwater and approving of Truman dropping the atom bomb on those "little yellow Jap bastards." He always, till the day he died, referred to all natives of Asia as gooks and wogs.

Well, Father had come up the hard way, a poor boy delivering paper to printing offices, slowly getting there, growing, fighting unions, being forced to employ minority groups, and hating the Welfare State. "Raising slum bastards just to get child-support handouts."

The judge picked up the newspaper and read a story relating to the railroad case:

> A special court kept ConRail from certifying a final plan for taking over the bankrupt Western, Great Plains & Gulf. The panel ruled that certain parts of the law are unconstitutional because they fail to protect creditors and stockholders by guaranteeing adequate compensation while the new system is being put together. That is likely to take at least two years. The trustees indicated that they would appeal the ruling to the Supreme Court.

> Congress did recognize that there would be losses for the railroads while ConRail is organizing, but it only provided $85 million. This sum would cover only about a third of the W. G.P. & G. losses at its present rate of operation.

> The giant railroad, which operates 20,000 miles of tracks in 16 states and two Canadian provinces, reported Monday a net loss for the first five months of $97.6 million, an increase of more than $7 million or 7.8% over the similar period of last year.

> As for Judge Deleon: "It may be ... apparent that even if all the authorized, guaranteed bonds $500 million were issued consideration would be inadequate," he said. "The same does not follow so far as Reading is concerned."

> "Until there is some information about the precise valuation of the specific assets that will go to ConRail and the exact mix of the proposed payment, I am unable to see anything for the W. G.P. & G. but to fully liquidate."

Well, it was a dramatic three or four generations for the Kingstons. Ralston—never met him—an eccentric, certainly, but the last of the real firecrackers in running the railroad, and even *he* lost control. Blame the Depression, or the stories you heard about him. Died at seventy. Maybe it was a suicide. You know how they cover these things up in those sanitariums. Rumors are he just starved himself to death. Didn't really matter how—the rest of the Kingstons were all more or less inept, just stockholders spending their dividends rather conspicuously. No control to what happened to the W. G.P. & G.

You see them now sometimes in public print. The middle-aged and the young ones. The old café society faces—remember them?—and the already stale jet set moving around from Monte Carlo to St. Moritz, to the Islands as guests on one of those Greek yachts with millions of dollars in paintings. Not all were drones; there was a Dr. Kingston in Boston at the Leahy Clinic, a corporation lawyer in Houston. There was one who made a sort of literary reputation as a discoverer of new talents: Benjamin Kingston, a pal (as the nostalgia writers put it) of Ezra and Hem and La Stein. The brouhaha in the courts when he died; *were* his children legitimate, was there ever a marriage? Anyway, the courts made a settlement, cut them in as heirs. Never heard from any of them. The Lord giveth and the Lord taketh away. The speeding velocity of time does its bit. The banker who lived in England didn't ever come back; something about those Insull utility scandals, was quoted in *Newsweek* as to how he spent his time. "If you're going to do nothing, do it better than anyone else." Cynical or ironic?

Well, the rails were still there and the trains ran over them.

The traffic was thinner—they were in the better suburbs—and the landscape more interesting as he looked up from the newspaper. There was a strength in autumn—it brought out a deep responsive chord in him—the trees beginning to shed, the fields fallow and the new housing, unfortunately, creeping out over the hill and stream. Serviced by monolithic science-fiction-looking shopping centers. Great masses of colored lights and Cal-

402

der facades—huge parking lots full of Detroit's trash, drug-store sophistication.

The judge decided: please, *no* negative emotions. It would be good to have those two cocktails and see the family faces and friends around the table, reflected in the Chippendale (copy) mirrors he and Emily had found in London three years ago, the year the Human Rights Congress was such a colossal fiasco.

He needed a rest after this long, long railroad hassle. Palm Springs' sun would soak the fatigue and legal debris out of him. He had once gone from Palm Springs, with some old crock of a lawyer whose deposition he needed in some public land case—Waldo something—gone with him up to Kingston House. A desolate sun-punished place, desert winds they called Santa Anas, blowing. The place in need of paint and masonry repairs—and with a mania for an asymmetrical lack of architectural beauty. A three-story collection of outmoded grandeur still impressive by size and boldness alone. The old crock said it was now a historic moment. Inside (Waldo had a whole ring of keys) the doors had settled, oak floors warped, so it was hard to open them. Lumps of furniture were covered in linen shrouds, musty-smelling, and the floorboards creaked. There must be termites burrowing all through the place. You could see by wall markings where paintings had once been, and there were mouse nests and their dung in what had been the den of the original founder of the W. G.P. & G., Enoch Bancroft Kingston. He is mentioned in Lucas Webb's *The World of J. Pierpont Morgan,* as being involved in some reorganization of railroad systems in the 1890s.

The old crock Waldo had recited some rigamarole of Kingston history while he hunted for a survey map of the original rail-line in a wall safe. I needed that as evidence in a public land case—a rail-line that went through what is now Robert Kennedy Pass in the national park of the same name. It had once been Kingston Pass, Waldo insisted—but it was abandoned when a tunnel was put through forty miles to the south, shortening the route and lowering the grade.

The judge had meant to ask the old crock about a Jasper or Jackson de Leon, but the desert wind was getting worse. The house was gloomy with its tattered curtains drawn, and it was getting dark. It would be no pleasure driving down the winding road and then into the mass rush-hour crazy driving of the freeway. The old crock had yelled, "Headed for perdition!" in the speeding traffic.

The Lincoln was going up the bluestone drive to the judge's house, and Judge Deleon felt chilled. He should have asked Harold to turn on the car heater even this early in the fall, but he prided himself as he grew older and gained weight, in trying to live as hearty a life, as rugged as he could, considering his sedentary occupation. His family had been free-rolling pioneer stock, the independent followers of Boone into Kentucky he had always imagined, and with their herds and slaves, in their covered wagons, come across a continent to hew and build, to cultivate and to more or less prosper. He felt a vicarious participation in a past he knew very little about. The Deleons had survived, not decayed and gone down like the Kingstons, not becoming decadent, dispersed, neurotic. No expatriates or self-pity, so creatively unproductive, impotent—all that endeavor of Enoch and Ralston Kingston become so trivial.

The bright yellow lights of his house greeted the judge as he walked across the porch to the front door with its genuine Pennsylvania Dutch fanlight and the rewired nineteenth century coach lamps.

He felt elated at the prospects of the dinner, but knew he was weary and it would be good to get away for the vacation. In other times—more extravagant, irrelevant eras—he would have taken his father's private railroad car, the *Foxhall*, ridden in luxury across the nation. But the *Foxhall* was laid up in storage in some obsolete freight siding. The marble bathtub was cracked, the last time he visited it, the stained-glass windows knocked out by black street gangs, an owl nesting in one of the light fixtures.

He remembered how much better Enoch Kingston had ordered things. In the Webb book, there was a mention that in his will Kingston had left orders that on his death, his private car, the *Eagle*, was to be taken out into the open country beyond Kingston Junction and burned.

As Waldo remembered it, and quoted from the will, the wording was:

> I see no sense in disgracing the car in its old age by having it turned into a relic. Rather like a well-loved horse or dog, one offers it an honorable death. I desire it to be taken out in open country, it not be stripped, combustible material added, and it be set on fire, that will burn to ash all that can be consumed. The rest to be scattered. . . .

The judge shook his head. How fine it was that they had no sense of the responsibility to public reaction in those extravagant days.

THE BIG BESTSELLERS
ARE AVON BOOKS!

☐ **The Kingston Fortune**
    Stephen Longstreet   25585 $1.95

☐ **All God's Dangers: The Life of Nate Shaw**
    Theodore Rosengarten   25619 $2.25

☐ **The Bermuda Triangle** Charles Berlitz   25254 $1.95

☐ **The Art Colony** Leland Cooley   25056 $1.95

☐ **Aftermath** Ladislas Farago   25387 $1.95

☐ **Lionors** Barbara Ferry Johnson   24679 $1.75

☐ **Dark Fires** Rosemary Rogers   23523 $1.95

☐ **Creative Aggression** Dr. George R. Bach
    and Dr. Herb Goldberg   24612 $1.95

☐ **Aton** Irving Greenfield   24844 $1.75

☐ **Chief!** Albert A. Seedman and
    Peter Hellman   24307 $1.95

☐ **The Eiger Sanction** Trevanian   15404 $1.75

☐ **Endgame** Harvey Ardman   24299 $1.75

☐ **Alive: The Story of the Andes Survivors**
    Piers Paul Read   21535 $1.95

☐ **Teacher and Child** Dr. Haim G. Ginott 24414 $1.75

☐ **Watership Down** Richard Adams   19810 $2.25

☐ **Devil's Desire** Laurie McBain   23226 $1.75

☐ **Working** Studs Terkel   22566 $2.25

☐ **Jane** Dee Wells   21519 $1.75

☐ **Theophilus North** Thornton Wilder   19059 $1.75

Available at better bookstores everywhere, or order direct from the publisher.

AVON BOOKS Mail Order Dept., 250 West 55th St., New York, N.Y. 10019

Please send me the books checked above. I enclose $_____ (please include 25¢ per copy for mailing). Please use check or money order—sorry, no cash or COD's. Allow three weeks for delivery.

Mr/Mrs/Miss_____

Address_____

City_____ State/Zip_____

                                    BB 10-75

WINNER OF THE NATIONAL BOOK AWARD

"THE LIFE HISTORY OF A
REMARKABLE HUMAN BEING . . .
EXTRAORDINARILY RICH AND COMPELLING."
The Washington Post

THE LIFE OF NATE SHAW

As Told to Theodore Rosengarten

In one of the most extraordinary autobiographies of our time, a black Alabama sharecropper pours out his story. ALL GOD'S DANGERS is Nate Shaw's eighty-eight year saga of courage, integrity, and unquenchable pride—a document of living history told by a fierce, salty, stubborn storyteller who has forgotten nothing.

"NATE SHAW IS A PRIMARY SOURCE . . . the very fiber of our nation's history. One does not read this book—one listens to it, and nods in agreement, or laughs, or frowns, as one does in conversation . . . Nate Shaw strides directly off the page and into our consciousness, a living presence, talking, shouting, sorrowing, laughing, exulting, speaking poetry, speaking history, thinking and feeling—and he makes us hear him."
The New York Times

AGD 10-75

FIRST TIME IN PAPERBACK   25254/$1.95/

Half a Million Hardcovers in Print

Over Eight Months on
The New York Times
Bestseller List

Charles Berlitz

The Bermuda Triangle

THE
NATIONWIDE
#**1**
BESTSELLER!

The Bermuda Triangle book
that will continue to astound the world
long after the others have "disappeared!"

COMPLETE WITH PHOTOS, MAPS, CHARTS, AND DRAWINGS
BT 9-75